Richmond upon Thames Libraries

Renew online at www.richmond.gov.uk/libraries

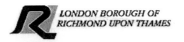
LONDON BOROUGH OF
RICHMOND UPON THAMES

Also by Ezekiel Boone by Gollancz:

The Hatching

SKITTER

EZEKIEL BOONE

This edition first published in Great Britain in 2017
by Gollancz

First published in Great Britain in 2017
by Gollancz
an imprint of the Orion Publishing Group Ltd
Carmelite House, 50 Victoria Embankment
London EC4Y 0DZ

An Hachette UK Company

1 3 5 7 9 10 8 6 4 2

A CIP catalogue record for this book
is available from the British Library.

ISBN 978 1 473 21521 4

Printed in Great Britain by Clays Ltd, St Ives plc

www.ezekielboone.com
www.gollancz.co.uk

For the Rhéaume family

PROLOGUE

Lander, Wyoming

I t was a big freaking spider. That was the only reason he screamed. He wasn't afraid of spiders. Really. But the thing had been the size of a quarter. Right on his cheek. He'd been backpacking solo for fifteen days, and he hadn't been scared once. Until his last day out, today, when he woke up with a scary, hairy, ugly spider on his cheek. Well, that wasn't entirely true. Fifteen days alone in the Wind River Range in Wyoming, not seeing another living soul the entire time? Fifteen days of scrambling across scree fields, traversing open ridges, even doing a little free solo rock climbing despite what he'd promised his dad? He'd have to be a complete moron not to feel a little twinge of concern here and there. And Winthrop Wentworth Jr.—nineteen, the son of privilege—was not a complete moron.

Win had been on the road nonstop for ten months. Biking through Europe, surfing in Maui, scuba diving in Bonaire, skiing in the Alps, partying in Thailand. His father owned a hedge fund and a significant stake in three different sports teams and family vacations had tended toward butlers and private jets and water that you could drink without worrying about dysentery. But Win's dad had earned his money the hard way and liked the idea of his son taking a gap year before he started Yale. He wanted Win to have the year off that he was never able to take as a young man. So Win had a pair of credit cards with no spending limits and instructions to check in every week. He had started off right after high school graduation with five of his private school buddies, biking across Italy and then driving through the old Eastern Bloc countries. Every week or two a couple of friends would take off and a couple more would join on. That lasted through mid-August, when all his friends had headed home to get ready for college. Since then, it had just been Win. He didn't mind. He never had a problem making friends along the way.

It wasn't that Win was a particularly good-looking kid. He was tall, which was good, but kind of scrawny, which wasn't. But he was confident, he spoke French, Italian, and a smattering of Chinese, and he was genuinely interested in other people. And he was rich. Smacking down a black American Express Centurion Card or his gold-colored but just as heavy-sounding JPMorgan Chase Palladium Visa to buy a round or three, to hire a boat for the day for the seven other backpackers he'd just met in Phuket, or to buy a new suit and pay extra to have it tailored while he waited so he could take a woman twice his age to dinner at a very small, very exclusive restaurant in Paris, meant that he made friends wherever he went. It also meant he got laid a lot. Not a bad way to spend a year between high school and college.

But by the middle of the following April, all this adventure had started to drag at him a little. Despite his father's seemingly inexhaustible supply of money, Win had always been a hard worker. He'd actually earned the As he'd gotten in high school. He wasn't the most talented player on the basketball team, but he ran until he puked and was the first man off the bench. So he called his dad from a hotel in Switzerland and said he was pretty much ready to wrap things up. He was going to come home and intern at the hedge fund until he started school in the fall. But first, he wanted to take a solo backpacking trip in the Wind River Range. Fifteen days of just him and his pack, a little something to clear his head.

And it had worked. As he hiked, he could feel the residues of booze and pot clearing out through his pores. By the third day, he felt fresh and sharp again, and by the fifth day, he was climbing some easy lines. His dad had made him promise not to rock climb solo, but Win didn't think it was much of a risk. Fifty-, sixty-foot climbs with ledges and handholds like ladder rungs. Just enough to get his heart rate up a little.

On the last day, he woke up at the same time as the sun. That was the devil's bargain of sleeping in a tent. He laid still for a moment with his eyes closed, hoping for a little more sleep, taking a few deep breaths, and that's when he felt the tickling sensation. He opened his eyes and it loomed. He couldn't help himself. He let out a scream and swatted the spider off his cheek. It moved quickly, scuttling away from him, into the corner of the tent. Win grabbed one of his hiking boots and smashed the living shit out of the spider.

Even now, with ten miles of trail behind him and maybe five more minutes to the trailhead and his truck, Win gave an involuntary shudder at the thought. He really wanted to believe he wasn't afraid of spiders. But this one had been so close. On his face. *Blech*.

Win had originally considered chartering a jet so he could fly in close to Lander, but in the end it had actually been easier to fly to Denver, even with the almost six-hour drive. All he'd had to do ahead of time was call the American Express concierge service. As a Black Card member, he'd arranged to have somebody meet him at the gate and take him right to a Toyota Land Cruiser, Win's age of nineteen be damned. When he got to the trailhead and his rental truck, Win dropped his pack to the ground. It was a hell of a lot lighter after fifteen days on the trail. He'd eaten all his food, for one, and for another, he was simply used to the weight. Still, it felt good to get it off his back. He fished the key out of the inside flap pocket and opened the trunk. He pulled out his cell phone and turned it on. While he was waiting for it to power up, he rooted through his other gear to see if he had any good snacks. He was starving. He struck out on the snacks, and he struck out on the cell phone: his battery had held its charge, but there was no signal up where he was parked. He sighed, threw his phone back into his bag, and then lifted his backpack into the trunk. Screw it.

Barely an hour later, just past two in the afternoon, he cruised into downtown Lander, Wyoming. The idea of calling it a down-town was a bit of a joke. The population was maybe six, seven thousand people. But the place did have something he really wanted: hamburgers and onion rings. He passed the Lander Bar and Gannet Grill, looking for a parking spot, and found one a block away. It was one of those rites of passage if you backpacked in the Wind River Range. Come back to town and stuff yourself full of fried food at the bar and grill. Maybe, after, he'd even get an ice cream. He half thought of grabbing a hotel room, but he liked the idea of hitting Denver tonight better, taking a suite at the Four Seasons and calling up a redheaded girl he'd met in Thai-land who had been taking off part of her junior year of college. He could put down a couple thousand calories, hit the road by three, be out of the shower by ten, and be getting laid by midnight. That sounded a lot better than staying at some paper thin-walled motel in Lander.

He got out of the truck and paused for a second. He knew he should dig his phone out of his pack now that he could get a signal, but he decided it could wait. His dad didn't actually expect him off the trail for a couple more days. He could call him from the road. He'd call the redhead, too. And get the concierge at the Four Seasons to book his room, make sure there was champagne for her if she wanted—he liked how clear he felt right now, and was done with booze for a while—plus some fresh fruit, and a box of condoms tucked away in the bedside drawer. If the redhead wasn't feeling as frisky as she'd been in Thailand, that was okay, too. She was smart and funny, and it wouldn't be bad just to cuddle up on the bed and watch a cheesy movie.

He started for the bar but then stopped. What the heck? The store across the street was a fire-gutted shell. The sign was blackened and he could just make out the letters: THE GOOD PLACE. HUNTING. FISHING. CAMPING. GUNS. He'd bought most of his gear there before he'd headed out on the trail. Barely fifteen days earlier it had been a thriving outfitter store, but now it was empty. A ruin. No boards on the windows, no tape around it to keep people away. He looked up and down the street and saw it wasn't just The Good Place.

He hadn't been paying attention as he'd driven in, too focused on the idea of a good old American gut-busting burger, but Lander looked messed up. He knew The Good Place hadn't been like that when he'd hit the trail, but he couldn't remember if the rest of the town had been so similarly beat down. It was hard for him to imagine that Lander had a thriving business community, but still, this was weird. Empty storefronts were one thing, but these places were actively destroyed. A few stores down from where he'd parked, a pickup truck was lodged halfway through the front wall of a liquor store. It was a mess. Really, all of Lander seemed like

a disaster zone. It looked like a college town after they'd won—
or lost—some sort of championship. White kids rioting. But this
wasn't a college town, so maybe . . .

He let out a chuckle. Maybe the zombie apocalypse had finally
arrived while he was out in the wild. He *had* been gone just a hair
past two weeks. Long enough. He'd been in the mountains all
alone with no cell phone and no way to check in with the modern
world. Who knew what could have happened, but zombies would
be awesome. Still, it was pretty quiet out where he was standing.
A few blocks down he saw a pickup truck move slowly through
an intersection, but he was the only person on the street. The
smell of smoke hung heavy in the air. Melted plastic and charred
wood. He tried to remember the last time he'd seen the vapor
trail of an airplane overhead, and he realized that he wasn't sure
if he'd seen a plane above him even once while he was hiking.
September 11, 2001, wasn't part of his memory, but he'd heard
his dad talk about how weird it had been to see a sky clear of air
traffic. He glanced up. Blue sky with a few clouds. Another stunning day in Wyoming.

Ah, whatever. It was too beautiful out to worry. Zombie
apocalypse or not, he needed some bar food after fifteen days of
freeze-dried chili mac and trail mix. He was ready for a basketful
of fat and salt.

He hit the lock button on his key and walked to the bar and
grill. Whatever qualms he had disappeared as he got to the door.
He could smell something grilling and the familiar odor of a deep
fryer. Oh man. A cheeseburger and onion rings, chicken wings
drowning in hot sauce served with a side of blue cheese for dipping. A couple of cold Cokes so full of ice it would make his
teeth hurt even to take a sip. There was music playing and the
bar sounded like it was hopping. It didn't occur to him that a bar

probably shouldn't be that busy at two o'clock on a weekday until he was already through the door.

The talk died as he entered, and Win stopped. It took a second for his eyes to adjust to the dim light of the bar. When they did, he realized that an extremely large, extremely fat man with long gray hair and a beard that ended mid-chest was pointing a shotgun at him. Whatever impulse Win had to make a little quip died a quick death with the sound of the shotgun being racked. That sound. Was there a scarier sound on earth than a shotgun being pumped?

"Where did you come from?" the fat man asked.

Win hesitated. Had he walked into the middle of a robbery? But wouldn't the guy with the shotgun have locked the door or something? Or robbed a bank instead?

While Win was thinking, the fat man took a couple of steps forward and bopped Win on the side of his face with the shotgun. It didn't feel like a bop. It felt like maybe his cheekbone was broken, but Win thought of it as a bop, because that's what it would have looked like in a movie. He pressed his hand to his cheek and felt a tear in his skin. Slick and sticky blood. He couldn't stop himself from thinking that he'd just been bopped in the same spot he'd seen that damn spider perching when he woke up.

"Jesus frickin' Christ. What the hell?" Win had taken a shot like that, once, his sophomore year playing basketball, but it had been an errant elbow that left him with a broken nose and a black eye. It was clearly an accident. Hustle and vigor and athletic competition and all that, but even though the plastic surgeon had fixed his nose just fine, Winthrop Wentworth Sr. had been livid. Win's dad had gone so far as to have his hedge fund take a controlling interest in the bank where the kid's dad worked just so he could fire the poor guy. "Nobody," Win's dad liked to say, "messes with the Wentworths. Somebody hits you, you hit them back so hard they don't get up. You get in that habit, people stop hitting you."

Win's dad said all sorts of shit like that, but then again, Win's dad had grown up in Brooklyn back when Brooklyn didn't have hipsters or neighborhoods with twelve-million-dollar brownstones. He'd gotten in plenty of fights as a kid, and maybe one or two as an adult. There was a story that might have just been a legend, or might have been true, of his dad sealing his first billion-dollar deal by putting another man's head through the passenger window of a car. That wasn't Win, though. So he just stood there with his hand on his cheek.

The man had backed off, but the shotgun was pointed right at the middle of Win's body. He said, "I'll ask it again, and maybe you want to answer this time. Where'd you come from?"

"Whoa, whoa," Win said. "Wind River Range. I was backpacking. I got back to the trailhead maybe an hour ago."

He wanted to sound brave, but he knew he didn't. He didn't *feel* brave either. Having a shotgun pointed at him sucked away whatever courage he might have had.

"How long were you out?"

"Fifteen days." Win risked a quick glance around the room. Nobody was moving to help him. If anything, he thought he saw a couple of other guns in evidence. "I just came in here to get a burger and a soda before I start my drive to Denver."

"You were out backpacking for fifteen days?"

"Solo. Hit the trailhead an hour ago. I've been dreaming about a big hamburger and some onion rings." Win probed a little bit at his cheek. He winced. He could feel something sharp under the skin. Was it his cheekbone? Had this guy broken his cheekbone? So much for Denver and getting laid. He'd be headed straight to the hospital. Stitches at the least, maybe minor surgery.

"Look, I'm sorry for whatever I stepped into here, but if you can just—"

"Spiders?"

"What?" Win's hand was still on his cheek, but he couldn't stop himself from grimacing. That spider that he'd squished on the floor of the tent.

The man pulled the shotgun tight against his shoulder. Win didn't like the way the man's finger stayed on the trigger or how he'd started to squint down the barrel. "I said, did you see any spiders?"

"Spiders?"

"Are you deaf?" the man said. "Do you want another tap on the face? Did you see any spiders when you were out there?"

"Yeah. One. There was a spider on my cheek when I woke up this morning. Right where you smashed me with your—"

But Win never got to say the word *shotgun*.

It had gone off before he'd had a chance to finish his sentence.

National Institutes of Health, Bethesda, Maryland

The goat did not want to go through the door. The poor thing was terrified, bleating and bucking and pissing on the floor of the lab. It was all the two soldiers could do to get the goat into the NIH Clinical Center's biocontainment unit's air lock. Professor Melanie Guyer could sympathize. She'd spent her entire career studying spiders, was a standout in her field, but she'd never seen spiders like these. In her opinion, people were scared of spiders for no good reason. Or, rather, that *had* been her opinion. She'd changed her mind. She'd seen what these spiders could do to rats. Jesus. The whole world had seen what they could do to *people*.

It had been a week since Los Angeles. Longer since she'd had a real sleep. What was it? Ten days since she'd gotten an egg sac overnighted from Peru to her lab at American University? FedEx, she thought, had never shipped a more dangerous package.

Ten thousand years. That's how old the egg sac had been. It had been dug up near the Nazca Lines—great line drawings etched in the high desert of Peru—by a PhD student in archaeology who was friends with one of Melanie's graduate students, Julie Yoo. The egg sac had been buried near the drawing of a spider. The rest of the Nazca line drawings, birds and animals and geometric designs, were maybe two thousand years old. But not the spider drawing. The spider was different. Older. Much older. According to Julie's friend, the box and other items they dug up near the spider were ten thousand years old.

Maybe the crackpots weren't so far off in their theories about Nazca. How was it that an ancient civilization could have constructed such beautiful and precise images? On one level, the *how* was simple: rocks removed so that the white earth underneath became lines in the red dirt. The plateaus were protected from the weather so that the Nazca Lines could survive for thousands of years. Two thousand years. Or ten thousand years. Old enough that the question of *how* was also unsolvable, because they weren't really drawings in a traditional sense. At ground level, they were simple lines and shapes. No meaning. But from above, they came so alive you could feel the beating pulse of these people praying to ancient gods. They didn't have airplanes then, they couldn't fly, so how had they designed them? Who knew? Melanie thought. Archaeologists had agreed that the simplest answer was that somebody had simply done a good job of planning. The Nazca had made the designs, staked out lines, and removed the stones. The egg sac had been found buried in a wooden box along with some of the stakes that the Nazca had used.

Careful measurements and good engineering. Human ingenuity. Math. Science. That's what she believed in. At least that's what she used to believe in. Now? She was beginning to be open to the idea that the Nazca Lines could have been made some other way, and for some other purpose, too.

She used to think that the ancient Nazca designs were a sort of prayer. She'd prayed to them herself, once, years ago. Back when she and Manny were still a couple, back when doctors had told her that having a baby would require an act of God. Not that seeing the Nazca Lines or breathing a fervent prayer as her plane circled above them had done any good. She and Manny had split up, and she was left with her lab and her spiders. But that was the thing. Maybe the older drawing, the drawing of the spider, was there as something different from the other lines. Not a prayer.

Maybe the spider was a warning.

Ten thousand years was a long time in human history. A blink of the eye in the history of the earth, but beyond the scope of human records. It was a span of time in which meaning was lost.

Maybe if they'd been able to understand the warning, her world wouldn't have gone to hell.

Melanie rubbed her eyes. So tired, but she didn't have time to sleep. She didn't want to sleep. She was afraid of falling asleep. She knew what she'd see if she fell asleep: Bark, her graduate student and former lover, cut open on the operating table, his body shot through with silk and egg sacs. Patrick hovering over the surgeon and the nurses, taking photos with the lab's camera. Melanie standing on the other side of the glass. Julie Yoo running down the hall toward her, too late with the information. And then, so quick: the spiders hatching from inside Bark's body.

Melanie rubbed her eyes harder. She didn't want to picture it. The blood and the gore were bad, but worse were the spiders themselves. A black wave. A single thing made of a thousand individual organisms.

She'd never been afraid of spiders or bugs of any kind. Not once in her whole life had she been grossed out. When other kids or adults shrank away from creepy crawlies, Melanie leaned in, fascinated. What made them work?

But these were different.

She reached out for her coffee and then stopped herself. Her hand was shaking. She was jittery. Too much caffeine. Not enough sleep. Too many nerves. What had it been? Ten days? Eleven? Twelve since she'd gotten the egg sac? Time was elastic.

The goat screamed again. That was the only way to describe it. Not a bleat, but a scream. It kicked out and caught one of the soldiers in the thigh, but the man just swore and wrapped his arms tighter around the goat. The pair—Melanie had stopped bothering to try to learn their names a few days ago—finally forced the goat through the door of the air lock and then jumped out, closing the door behind them. The poor goat stood in the air lock, forlorn. Forsaken. It had stopped bleating and stood there, shivering.

The soldiers stopped for a moment, catching their breaths. They looked out of place in the pristine lab, their combat uniforms a stark contrast to the lab coats and jeans and T-shirts worn by Melanie and the other scientists, who came in and out with such frequency that Melanie finally had to order armed guards to secure the entire floor.

Armed guards. That was her new reality. Armed guards, a re-purposed hospital room for a bedroom so that she could be closer to her research, and spiders that could strip a goat to its bones in less than a minute.

The first soldier went through the airlock protocol, going down the list one by one. Once he was done, the second soldier double-checked each step himself. Then they turned to look at Melanie. Everybody was looking at Melanie. It felt like everything was on her.

Two weeks ago, her biggest worry had been how to break off her ridiculous relationship with Bark. But now, suddenly, she had an entire floor of the National Institutes of Health to command. She could order armed guards to make sure that she and Julie Yoo and the three other authorized scientists were not disturbed. Between her ex-husband, Manny, and his boss, the president of the United States, whatever she wanted just seemed to happen.

When she said she needed her equipment, overnight, presto

chango, her entire setup at American University was duplicated at the NIH. Duplicated. There was even a Grinnell College mug on the desk, almost exactly like the one on her desk at American, but without the tiny chip on the rim. Actually, her equipment wasn't duplicated: it was improved and added to. There was new lab equipment she didn't know how to use even if she'd wanted to. And if she went anywhere outside the lab, she was trailed by five Secret Service agents. Not that she'd done more than go outside once or twice to stand in the sunlight and marvel at the hundreds of soldiers ringing the National Institutes of Health. She was, according to Manny and President Stephanie Pilgrim, the most important woman in the world right now. There were other scientists working on the question of how to deal with these spiders, of course, but Manny and Steph trusted her. They were counting on her. She was, in their eyes, the only hope for the human race.

No pressure.

What she needed right now was to figure out what in God's name these spiders were, because they sure as hell weren't like any others she'd ever seen. When the egg sac had come to her office from Peru, she'd been excited to see it begin hatching. For a few hours it seemed like she'd been on the verge of a big discovery, the nearly two dozen spiders in the insectarium arousing an intense curiosity. They didn't act like spiders, at least not as she knew them, and they were *hungry*. Then she'd come to understand that the spiders weren't only in her lab, and that there were certainly more than two dozen of them. Much more. Hundreds of thousands of them. Millions. Outbreaks in China, India, Europe, Africa, South America. And in the United States. How many people were dead already?

She couldn't think about it. Not now. Right now she needed to focus on these spiders, because she'd been tasked with figuring out how to stop them.

"Okay," she said. "Julie, we shooting?"

Julie Yoo gave the thumbs-up. She stood over a bank of computer monitors, supervising the three techs who were running six Phantom Cameras, capable of shooting ten thousand frames per second. Whatever happened to the goat, it was going to be recorded in excruciating detail so Melanie could play it back at a speed that made a bullet look slow.

A small crowd gathered by the glass. There'd been large crowds before Melanie had ordered the lab cleared of all nonessential personnel. Now there was only Dr. Will Dichtel, Dr. Michael Haaf, Dr. Laura Nieder, and a dozen or so graduate students and lab assistants. Dichtel was a chemist who'd carved out a specialization in entomological toxicology. He'd made himself a small fortune synthesizing a modified version of the brown recluse spider's venom that was now used in making microchips. Haaf was from MIT, an arachnid specialist, like her, and Nieder was there because she worked for the Pentagon trying to figure out how to adapt insect swarm behavior for the battlefield.

Melanie went to the air lock and went through the same checklist as the two soldiers had. You couldn't be too careful. She knew what was coming. She looked back at Julie, who gave her the thumbs-up again, and then at the scientists crowding the glass. Her hand hovered over the keypad.

The goat was staring at her.

The poor thing was shaking so badly.

Melanie hit the button that opened the inner door of the air lock.

And they came to feed.

The Staples Center,
Greater Los Angeles
Quarantine Zone, California

What was the old joke? Join the army so you can travel to foreign places, meet new people, and then blow them up? He'd joined the army because, well, what else was there? He was smart enough to go to college, but he hadn't taken high school seriously, and even if he had, money was a problem. Maybe Detroit was an appealing place for artists and hipsters who could buy houses for pennies on the dollar, but Quincy's dad had been insistent that he get out. Quincy's dad was old enough to remember a time when Detroit had good jobs for union men, but not old enough to have had one of those jobs himself, so the week after Quincy graduated high school, his dad drove him down to the recruiting center.

Quincy hadn't been opposed to the idea of joining the army, and he didn't have any better plans, so by the time his friends were starting classes at community college, he was through basic training. And now, standing inside the Staples Center, he was closing in on a decade in the army. He looked around at the egg sacs stacked up on the seats and in the aisles, and realized he wasn't sure he'd get to celebrate a full ten years in uniform.

The worst of it was knowing that before his squad had gotten the assignment, there'd been an argument about it. Somebody had used their political capital to make sure that the job of burning down the Staples Center and the roughly infinite number of spiders inside went to the army instead of to the navy or the Marines or the air force. There was always a political squabble before any mission, and if he screwed this up, there'd be a political squabble afterward to deflect blame. Not that he cared, because if he did indeed screw up, he suspected that he'd be sort of dead. He wasn't really worried about making any mistakes of his own per se. It was more that something might go wrong while they wired the stadium. Like, you know, one of these egg sacs opening up and a torrent of spiders devouring him or laying eggs inside his body so that at some undetermined future date he'd suddenly split open so that spiders could go ahead and eat some other people.

Absent the spiders, the job wasn't particularly complicated. They didn't want to blow the building so much as implode it. The idea was to get a real blaze going and then, once it was so hot that there was no chance of anything surviving, collapse the Staples Center in on itself in order to keep the blaze contained. The embers would continue to smolder and burn for days or even weeks beneath the twisted steel and concrete of what had once been a basketball stadium. Like the coals in a good charcoal grill. No spiders would be crawling out of that inferno.

First, however, he had to finish laying the charges and get the hell out without being eaten.

The egg sacs were clustered on the stadium seats, with the greatest infestations in the nosebleeds, where the lights did not seem to carry as clearly. The sacs were white and misshapen, running the gamut from rounded, volleyball-sized orbs to football-shaped ovals to lumpy packages that could have been anything. They were almost chalky. Quincy had accidently brushed against one while running a wire around a corner, and it had been cold and surprisingly substantial. It had left a dusty white mark on his sleeve that he'd been able to brush off. It was easier to avoid touching the egg sacs lower down, near the courtside seats where Quincy always saw celebrities pretending to actually care about basketball. There were still egg sacs down there, but there were fewer of them, more scattered. On the hardwood court itself, the sacs were littered in piles and small groups. You could still see the Los Angeles Lakers logo in the center of the court, and if somebody had given Quincy a basketball—and he was feeling suicidal—he could have dribbled, with some difficulty, from one end of the floor to the other.

He finished wiring in the charge and wiped the sweat off his forehead. He looked up to do one more check that he'd wired the last one, and with profound relief, left the building.

Outside, in the bright California sunshine, Quincy felt almost giddy. Somebody handed him a beer, and he carried it back to the tent that had been erected as a temporary command center. There were a bunch of cameras set up. He'd heard that the big boys in Washington were going to be watching live.

Demolition work wasn't like what you saw in the cartoons. There wasn't a box with a handle and plunger, and no countdown over loudspeakers. Just a button to press. Best estimates were that the heat would peak at close to two thousand degrees. Glass and metal would melt, concrete would buckle and twist. The Staples Center was going to turn into a spider hibachi. No, Quincy thought, there was nothing to worry about.

Nothing to worry about if you didn't count the more than four hundred and ninety other sites around Los Angeles where there'd been confirmed reports of egg sac infestations. Lucky him. He was going to get to travel around Los Angeles burning them up, too.

At least none of the infestations were as bad as the Staples Center, but Quincy had heard rumors that not all the egg sacs were the same. If the ones in the Staples Center were dusty and cold, that wasn't true for all the infestations. He'd heard at least one other soldier claiming that the sacs were sticky and warm, that you could actually *hear* spiders moving inside, who knows how many, just waiting to come out. And another soldier told him that he'd seen an egg sac that was absolutely huge. Big enough for a person to fit inside.

Forget the people who might have been infested—Quincy had seen all the videos—the egg sacs alone were terrifying. Thousands of those little time bombs all over the city. Each one of those thousands of bombs holding thousands of spiders, all ready to explode.

Tick, tick, tick.

University of Southern California, Greater Los Angeles Quarantine Zone, California

It seemed as though half the city was on fire. The orange flames from the Staples Center flickered through the night. From the air it would have been beautiful. Lights among the darkness of power outages and disaster. But by the next day, clouds of smoke and soot clung to the sky. It was clear that no help was coming. It had been a solid week since Los Angeles had turned into somebody's nightmare, and the sound of gunshots was not uncommon.

Two men dragged an old woman across the concrete of the stadium tunnel like she was a piece of luggage.

The Prophet Bobby Higgs was not pleased.

"How many times do we have to tell you morons," he said to the pair, "that we don't care if somebody is talking shit about us. It doesn't help our cause if you behave like jackbooted thugs." He glanced at the men's feet. Huh. They *were* wearing jackboots. Or something close enough. He wasn't sure what jackboots were, but both men were wearing the kind of steel-toed construction footwear that he thought of when he thought of jackboots and neo-Nazis.

The larger of the two men grunted and let go of the woman's jacket. Her body shifted and her arm fell to the ground with a thunk. Though which of the men, exactly, was the larger was a difficult distinction for Bobby to make. They were standing in the tunnel underneath the University of Southern California's football stadium, and both men looked like they could have played on the defensive line, either at USC or on an NFL team. Giants. Six foot six or seven and easily three hundred pounds each. But right now he thought Gill, the one who'd dropped the old lady, was the bigger of the two. Or maybe it was just that Gill looked a little meaner than Kevin. Not that Kevin was particularly gentle, but Gill had just enough intelligence to be creative in his cruelties. "She was talking about trying to get to the fence."

"Of course she was talking about trying to get to the fence. The army blew up the Staples Center yesterday, and they've been going around town burning down buildings and houses and doing everything but helping people," Bobby said. He stepped over and grabbed the woman's hair, pulling her head up so he could see her face. Her eyes were closed. She was late sixties, maybe seventies. Not in the plastic, Hollywood fashion of old ladies determined to buy their way out of aging, but in the midwestern, unashamed way of wrinkles and gray hair. She looked like a grandmother.

"She's terrified. There was a brief window when the quarantine broke and you could actually get out of here, but since the army got its shit together and started actually enforcing the quarantine, every single person who didn't make it out is kicking themselves. Us included. Nobody wants to be here. We all want out. So yeah, she's hungry and scared and believes the pathetic lies that the federal government is telling us." Bobby stood up and wiped his hands on his suit pants. He shook his head and stepped back. "She thinks that if she gets to the fence she'll find a friendly soldier who will believe that a kind old lady like her could never harbor eggs. She's been a good little citizen her whole life. Why wouldn't they help her? How can a lady like her possibly believe that her government is going to forsake her?"

Kevin shifted a little on his size fourteen feet then looked at Gill. He seemed to notice, for the first time, that Gill had let go of the woman, so he let go too. The woman was completely unconscious, unable to break her fall. She hit the concrete with a solidness that was slightly disconcerting. Maybe she was dead? No. She was breathing. Just knocked out. Getting clubbed by one of those fellow's fists could do that to a person, Bobby thought. He sighed. Either way, they needed to get rid of her.

Gill stared at Bobby blankly, and then, after what seemed like an eternity, realized that Bobby's answer had been to a different question than the one he wanted to ask. "What should we do with her, boss?"

Bobby wanted to smack the oaf. He could hear the buzz at the end of the tunnel. This must be what it was like to be a professional athlete before a game or a rock star before a show. They were all out there, waiting for him. He checked his watch again. Five more minutes. He'd scheduled his address for five thirty this afternoon, but by eight in the morning there was already a crowd building in USC's football stadium. His men had gone through the quarantine zone with loudspeakers and flyers. Instead of bobblehead dolls or foam fingers, the first ten thousand people into the stadium were promised food and water and the chance to hear the Prophet Bobby Higgs tell them exactly how the federal government was conspiring to make them martyrs. By noon, there were already more than three thousand people in the stadium. He should have been getting ready to bound onto the makeshift stage, not dealing with these two idiots. But these two idiots were part of the reason why he had a crowd, why he had food and water to give away. His army was the reason why people were willing to listen to his words. His words meant a lot more with muscle behind them.

"What do you think you should do?"

Gill looked at Kevin and Kevin looked at Gill. The two men were clearly stumped by the question.

Bobby sighed. "Make her disappear. Beating up grandmothers isn't exactly going to win the hearts and minds of the good people of Los Angeles." Sure, if they'd brought him a young man it might serve a purpose to string him up from a light pole and hang a LOOTER sign on the body, but an old lady like this? Bad optics. Bobby shook his head. It was time to play the stern father. "And please, stop beating people to death just because they have the temerity to either criticize me or look to the federal government for help. The whole point is to appear as if we are benevolent."

The two men continued to look confused.

"For God's sake," Bobby said. "Your job is to hand out food, keep the peace, and tell the people that the government has left them to die and that the Prophet Bobby Higgs will keep them safe. Understand?" Both men nodded. "And stop beating up old ladies. If you need further clarification, talk to Macer."

Gill seemed to brighten up. "That's it. Macer. Macer said to bring them to him if we find a bit one. She's got it. The mark we're supposed to look for." He reached down with one of his shoebox-sized hands and pulled back the collar of the old woman's shirt. There. Bobby could see it. The bloody slit where a spider had gone in.

She was infested.

He had to resist the urge to scream. There were too many of his men around, and while they were loyal to him, it didn't serve his purposes to look like he was scared. But these unbelievable idiots. Bringing her to him like this?

"And what else did Macer say about that? He said if you find somebody with a bite mark, put her into the box. Quick now. Into the cube."

The two men nodded and then picked up the old lady and dragged her toward the end of the tunnel. Bobby shuddered. The old lady wasn't just somebody threatening to leave the quarantine zone, somebody afraid of the danger. She *was* the danger.

"Good timing, Bobby," a man's voice said. "You know what they say. Show, don't tell. I was beginning to think we were going to have to rely on your charm alone. But hell, putting her out in front of the crowd will do the trick. Show them what this infestation really means."

Bobby turned and scowled at Macer Dickson, who was walking toward him from the field. Macer wasn't as big as Gill and Kevin, but he was scarier. Solid, like he was carved from a tree. And smart. Nothing like the army of men they had working for them. Bobby knew that if he ordered it, his other men would kill Macer. He could do it. He could order Macer hung up from a light pole, just another traitor killed for collaborating with the federal government. Or he could shoot Macer himself. He let his hand drift to the butt of the Desert Eagle .45 he kept strapped to his hip. *Boom*. Right in the face. How smart would Macer be with a bullet right through his grill?

That was the problem, though. Macer was plenty smart. From the time the spiders keeled over until Bobby was, in essence, the acting king of what was left of Los Angeles? Barely four days. And every passing day made Macer's stranglehold even tighter. Macer was the reason why he was now the Prophet Bobby Higgs when, up until the spiders came, he'd just been another grifter working West Hollywood and paying Macer for the privilege.

Macer was one of those men you knew existed in the cracks of Los Angeles, even if you weren't actually acquainted with him. A finger in every till and pocket. A hundred men on the payroll. Running drugs from Mexico, guns from Europe, and girls from Thailand. Bobby had never met the man, but he'd worked on Macer's turf. Bobby had a sweet gig, renting himself out to rich, lonely, married housewives. Getting into the bedroom was never the hard part. Bobby could turn on the charm like flicking a light switch. What was important was that after he took them into the bedroom, he could get the women to pull out their purses and pay him for the privilege. Sure, he'd had to give one of Macer's men a clean twenty percent, but that was the cost of doing business. Bobby had never really put much thought into Macer himself. Why would he? Macer was just a whisper. And then the spiders came and Macer scuttled out from wherever he'd been working the strings. Power abhors a vacuum or some such, and Macer was a damn Shop-Vac.

It was slick, really. Almost like Macer knew it was coming. The minute that President Pilgrim—Bobby couldn't believe he'd voted for her—had ordered the quarantine, Los Angeles had gone into gridlock. In the first hours after the infestation, there'd been thousands of people who'd gotten out, broken through the quarantine lines, but since then, the army or the navy or the Marines or maybe all of them had rolled out tanks and armored Humvees and fenced the crap out of the entire place. There was a rumor that fifty miles out of the city, toward Nevada, there was a checkpoint you could go through where soldiers swept you to make sure you were clean of bugs and then you were free to get the hell out of California. But there was also a rumor that instead of sweeping you for bugs, the soldiers just shot you in the head, threw your body in a Dumpster, and then set the Dumpster on fire once it was full.

So for all intents and purposes, Los Angeles was an island. Lockdown city. It was terrifying what the federal government could do. They couldn't figure out how to make a simple tax return, but they could turn Los Angeles into a prison. And that prison looked as good as a death sentence. There were egg sacs scattered across the city. Everybody knew that meant the spiders were coming back, but the government seemed to expect them to believe that no, actually, the spiders were gone, never to return. Did the government really think people would just roll over? Well, yeah, probably. That's what most people were doing. But not Macer. Macer had a plan.

If Macer had been a simple thug, Bobby didn't think the plan would have worked. Cops were still cops, and even though he'd seen plenty of evidence to contradict this opinion, Bobby thought Americans were basically good hearted. They came together in times of crisis. If Macer had sent his men out looting, nothing would have come of it. But Macer was organized, and it was like he was counting on man's better nature, too. He sent his men out to grocery stores and warehouse clubs, to Target and Walmart and Home Depot. Anywhere he knew people would rush in the aftermath of the disaster. He had his men keep the peace. They organized orderly lines and distributed food and water. They made sure everybody got a fair amount. If people fought, they shut it down. Whenever they came across a good-sized man they deputized him, and they all helped to spread the word: the Prophet Bobby Higgs was going to take care of them.

Macer was the brains and Bobby had become the voice of Los Angeles's new reality.

And that was another thing that scared Bobby about Macer.

He'd never even met the man until all this shit had gone down, and yet, when they did meet, Macer was already sure of Bobby's role, already knew that Bobby could pull it off. Like Macer had been scouting all along for somebody to play the role of a prophet on the off chance that the apocalypse hit Los Angeles.

"Take your hand off your gun," Macer said. "We both know you aren't going to shoot me."

Macer wasn't even looking at Bobby. He was looking twenty feet toward the bright wedge of sunlight that opened up into the stadium. A handful of Bobby's personal guards stood at the entrance, but it was just him and Macer in the tunnel, alone. Time to talk.

"You getting cold feet?" Macer asked.

Bobby considered. He wasn't scared. Not exactly. "I guess it just doesn't seem right."

Macer shrugged. "None of this is right. The government sealing up Los Angeles and saying, 'Good luck.' Does that seem right?"

"She's just an old lady."

"Not anymore. She's infected. If you do your part and get the crowd revved up, then we can use her as an example. She'll be the thing that gets us out of here. There's thousands of people out there, waiting for you. Every one of them is ready to break. We show them what's trapped in here with them, and they'll believe anything you tell them. You want to get out of the quarantine zone? You listen to me."

Bobby was quiet for a moment. He could hear the crowd noise increasing. It was almost time for him to go out and address them. "What if the government isn't lying? What if the government is telling the truth and it's over?"

Macer actually laughed. "Are you kidding? Do you buy that for even a second?" He waited for Bobby to shake his head and when Bobby did, he stepped close and clapped him on the shoulder. "Okay then. We've got a real audience. I asked Lita to give a rough count, and she puts it at close to forty thousand. Forty thousand! That's a lot of people who are waiting to hear you speak. Now go work your magic."

Bobby nodded. He rolled his shoulders and walked to the end of the tunnel. He had to bet that Macer had it nailed. It *was* a sort of magic, he knew, his ability to move a crowd like this. He'd never gotten a real break as an actor, and grifting had been the natural backup plan. He wasn't the best con artist—the best he'd seen was a blond girl who was maybe seventeen and who could leave you broke inside a week and thanking her for the privilege—but he'd been good enough. He'd found his niche, separating bored Hollywood housewives from their household allowance. At least he thought he'd found his niche until Macer told him it was time to become the Prophet Bobby Higgs.

He'd seen it coming. The spiders. That's what Macer's men told anyone who'd listen, that the Prophet Bobby Higgs had warned the government that the spiders were coming. The Prophet Bobby Higgs had tried to save them.

But did the government listen? Of course not.

And why didn't the government listen? Because the government didn't care about the common men and women of Los Angeles.

And could we trust the government now that they said it was over? Could we trust them to keep us safe?

Absolutely not.

And who, Macer's men asked, could we trust?

The Prophet Bobby Higgs.

He'd tried to save them before, Macer's men told every person who came to them for food or shelter, but nobody would listen. Shouldn't you listen to the Prophet Bobby Higgs now?

He stepped close enough to the edge of the tunnel to let his eyes adjust to the light, and then he bounded out. Macer's little army had made a gauntlet for him. Beefy men, like Gill and Kevin, forging a tunnel through thousands of pilgrims. More than thousands. As Bobby climbed the stairs to the stage, he could see that the field was full of people, and the bowl of the stadium too. As he appeared on the stage, forty thousand voices became one, chanting his name, chanting Bobby, Bobby, Bobby.

He stepped to the podium and held up his arms. The chanting turned into a swell of cheering, but then the crowd slowly quieted. There was no sound as loud or as lovely to Bobby's ears as the silence of forty thousand pilgrims.

"Brothers and sisters," he said. His voice boomed across the stadium. That was another thing about Macer. He thought of everything. It wasn't just the free food and water and the promise of an answer to draw the crowds. It was the stage and the pageantry. It was generators to run the sound system. It was the cameraman and the image on the giant video screen. Bobby stole a glance at himself. He looked good.

"Brothers and sisters," he said again. "You're here because you know the truth. The government tells you not to worry. The government wants you to believe that the quarantine is designed to keep us safe. President Stephanie Pilgrim—"

He had to stop for a moment as boos and hisses rolled across the stadium. It was hard for him to hide a grin. There were the spiders, sure, and they were scarier than anything anybody could have imagined, but Pilgrim felt personal. The spiders were monsters, but Pilgrim had betrayed them. He held up his hands and the crowd stilled.

"President Stephanie Pilgrim wants you to trust her. The spiders are gone, she says. Nothing to fear. But do we believe her?" He gave the responding chorus of "No!" time to die out and then paused for an extra second so he could lower his voice. They had to hush completely to hear him, the softness an added intimacy. "Of course not. If there was nothing to fear, do you think the US Army would have burned the Staples Center? Do you think there would be a smear of smoke blotting the sky? If there was nothing to fear, do you think, right now, there'd be tanks and military vehicles racing around the streets of Los Angeles, our streets, right here, inside the quarantine zone, looking for infestations and burning the spiders out? Do you know what they're saying in the rest of the country? They're saying, 'It's just Los Angeles. It could have been worse.' "

He glanced over to the glass cube on the other side of the stage. Empty except for the old lady. This was the part he was afraid of. That old lady. What if they were wrong? What if she was just another person who was scared and terrified? No. She had the mark. She'd been infested. She wasn't an old lady anymore. She was going to be their example. She was going to be what convinced this crowd that they needed to do whatever Bobby told them, that they needed to do whatever it took to get out. Because if they were scared before, they were going to be terrified after this.

He hoped. Because God help him if they were wrong about this. About what he was about to do to this old lady.

Macer better be right.

"The federal government is basically saying, 'Hey, so lots of you have died, what's a few more?' Two million more? Three million more? Is there anybody here who didn't lose somebody you loved to the invasion?" He let his voice get louder. "And is that enough *sacrifice* for the federal government? Are they going to come in and save the day?" The question hung in the wind, his voice echoing. "Save the day? Hell no. President Stephanie Pilgrim has gone on television and said if we try to get out of Los Angeles, try to get past the quarantine, we'll be shot on sight. If you want to save your wife, your children, if you want to save yourself, the federal government doesn't care. There are enough soldiers to blow up the Staples Center, to look for these beasts, but not enough soldiers to help us? We've been good citizens our whole lives. Paid our taxes. Abided by the law. Shouldn't the army be here to help us?

"But what help is the federal government offering? The federal government tells us that if we try to get past the fence we'll get a bullet in the head and our bodies shoved into incinerators. Oh, there's nothing to fear, isn't that right, President Pilgrim? She's got troops burning down basketball stadiums and is offering us the promise of a quick death if we try to leave Los Angeles. Does that sound like President Pilgrim really believes we're safe locked up in here, in the quarantine zone? Does that sound like the government is keeping us safe or does that sound like the government is keeping us locked up? Does that sound like the federal government really believes this is over? Think about it. Break the quarantine, and we'll be shot." He paused. "Our *bodies will be incinerated*."

He stood up straight and looked directly into the camera. "An incinerator? It's not enough to shoot us? They're going to burn our bodies. Now why would they do that? Why would the federal government tell us we should shelter in place and then threaten to shoot us and burn our bodies if we try to flee? Why do they feel the need to burn down the Staples Center, to burn down houses and office buildings? That doesn't sound like we're so safe to me."

He leaned into the microphone and got quiet again. He could

feel the crowd leaning in too. He had them. "Now, brothers and sisters, I've got to ask you to do something difficult. I've got to ask you to watch this. Because this is the truth. This is what the federal government is afraid of."

He motioned to the cube. A man—not somebody Bobby recognized—climbed up the ladder against the back of the cube. It was actually some sort of plastic or thick Plexiglas, not glass, but what mattered was that it was a clear cube. Macer's men had drilled hundreds of tiny holes in its ceiling and on all the sides. The cameraman moved in, and Bobby glanced up at the giant video screen where he could see the old lady in high definition. Mercifully, she was still in an unconscious heap. He watched the man on the ladder lift a five-gallon gas can and start to pour.

It wasn't gasoline. Macer had said they couldn't be sure gasoline would catch properly. No. This was lighter fluid.

The liquid pooled for a second on the roof and then started to seep through the hundreds of drilled holes, like pasta water through a colander.

"I know this is hard," he said into the microphone. "But the federal government is telling you it's safe here. The federal government is saying, 'Trust us, Los Angeles is fine now.' "

The man on the stepladder handed the empty gas can down to another guard and reached into his pocket. He pulled out a lighter.

"Los Angeles is not safe, brothers and sisters. The spiders are not gone. This—*this* is what the federal government has locked us in with. This is what they are trying to burn in secret. I truly regret that I have to do this, but I need you to see the truth. I need you to see what is hidden in the fire. President Pilgrim says not to be afraid, but I am telling you, you cannot trust her. You need to trust me when I say, *Be afraid. Be terrified.*"

It was almost beautiful. The yellow spark of the lighter setting off a blue stream of flame. The fire leaped off the roof of the cube and funneled down to where the woman was still lying unconscious.

Bobby realized he was holding his breath. He could hear screaming, sobbing, gasps, but even with those noises, it felt as if the entire stadium was holding its breath with him. One second. Two. Just enough time for Bobby to wonder if maybe Macer was wrong. He could feel that the entire stadium was getting ready to turn against him. Things were horrible. A week ago, the city had been converted into a set from some terrifying movie. Men, women, and children eaten alive by spiders. Fires and looting and the fear of the unknown. It was too much to comprehend. But this in front of them, this was something else. It was just some poor old lady in a cage. The audience didn't know what he knew. They didn't know she was infested. They didn't know what was inside her. If it didn't happen soon, the crowd would turn against him. It was one thing to hang young men for looting, to make an example of them. That was keeping the peace.

Three seconds. Four seconds. And then it happened. The old woman's body started to shake and she split open. He knew it was wrong, but it made Bobby think of a hot dog on a grill, the way she opened up. And almost instantly, the spiders poured out.

He was still holding his breath, but the stadium wasn't. People were screaming. Yelling. Cursing. It was the sound of anger. Of terror.

On the video screen, the cameraman caught the spiders spilling out of the woman's body, zoomed in on their legs scrambling against the sides of the cube. The fire caught them, burning their bodies as they scrambled to get away. But even as they burned, some of them tried to feed on what was left of the old lady.

He looked out at the crowd in front of him. People were screaming and shaking their arms in anger and fear. On the field, near him, a young Latina, maybe twenty-five and holding a baby, was crying. The woman was huddling against a companion, but she watched the burning cube.

Bobby looked over at Macer, still standing at the lip of the tunnel. Macer nodded. It was time.

"This is what's waiting for us," Bobby roared. "So I ask you, do you trust the federal government to keep you safe? Do you want to stay in the quarantine zone?"

The noise of the crowd lifted him and carried him away. He could see it now. He and Macer would get out. They'd run a convoy of sacrificial lambs at the fence, draw the US military into a single spot, and then direct the bulk of their army to a different spot. He could see it now, could see soldiers and their tanks and guns trying to stop them and failing. How could you stop a river from flowing?

Oh, the Prophet Bobby Higgs could see it, all right.

Macer had found them a way out.

They had their army.

Rio de Janeiro Infection Zone, Brazil

It was like watching dominos fall. Not the click and clack of tiles on the table when he played dominos with his friends over a few beers on a Sunday night, but the dominos a child sets up in a line. One goes down and then the next and the next. There was a connection to be made.

Across the world people described it as a sudden occurrence: the bugs just died. There was more coming, however. He knew it. He was sure of it. He'd seen the live footage on the news: people sweeping the spiders out of the streets like so many dead leaves. Then a gust of wind and he'd seen, right there on the thirty-inch television in his apartment, how the top layer of the pile of spiders had caught the air, lifting and shifting. They looked so light. Insubstantial. How could anybody believe the horror they'd caused? That a swarm of them could move through a city like a summer storm, catching everybody in front of them in an unavoidable shower of blood and despair? How could you think these hollow things were a danger? They were only shells with legs, brittle and black, the dregs of a child's nightmare. And like a child's nightmare, ludicrous in the bright light of day.

It was the same throughout the world. Helsinki and Delhi, Los Angeles and Seoul, the Italian Alps, and the terrible, terrifying, flame-filled zone in China. One minute the spiders had been an unstoppable force, a thousand million avatars of death, worse even than the nuclear weapons the Chinese had unleashed, worse than anything he could have imagined, worse than anything that had ever been imagined, and the next minute they dropped to the ground, empty and dead, as if they were consumed from within.

The hand of God. Prayers answered. That was what the religious said. The spiders simply used themselves up in a frenzy of destruction, an unsustainable rate of growth and burn of energy. That's what the scientists said. What both groups agreed on was that the spiders were gone.

But that made no sense to him at all. He'd seen the way the spiders had spread through the city and then, at the same time, like a flower folding in on itself, had reversed course. They'd done that before they started dying off. The newscasters and the analysts discounted it. The spiders' reversal was an afterthought, if even that. Most of them were so focused on the seemingly spontaneous die out that they didn't seem to even notice that the spiders had begun a retreat. Or, if they thought and talked about it all, they said it was just a blessing. How much worse would it have been had the spiders continued to push forward and out in the last hours of their invasion instead of shrinking back toward the center of the outbreak? Were there not enough dead? He'd tried to bring up the question to his superiors, but they told him to shut up and just do his job as a police officer, to let the army and the scientists worry about the spiders. It was not a thing to concern himself with.

He double-checked his gear: a hazardous material suit he'd borrowed from a friend who worked in a lab; a heavy Maglite flashlight that doubled nicely as a club; and his cell phone to use for pictures and video. It didn't feel like enough, somehow, but he couldn't think of what else he needed to bring with him. He'd worn his uniform and used his police identification to get past the cordon, carrying the gear in a small duffel bag.

He'd been shocked at how easy it was to slip past the army guards and the other police officers. All he had to do was leave his bag open so the hazmat suit was showing, wave his badge, and assume the air of somebody who was supposed to be able to go into the infection zone, and no questions were asked. In he went. He supposed it was because he was sneaking *in* to an area that people wanted to flee from. Who in their right mind would sneak into the epicenter of such terror? Who in their right mind wanted to go into the middle of this mad labyrinth?

If it was a labyrinth, did that make him the hero or was he the Minotaur, half man, half beast? It was a maze he'd gotten himself into. Nobody would listen to him, nobody would believe him when he said there had to be more to the way the spiders moved, that they had acted as if they were coordinated. Individually they might be nothing more than eight-legged emissaries from the depths of hell, but together, they were like an army. Invaders. Colonizers. Scouring the earth.

He had no choice. If they wouldn't listen to him, he had to show them. Past the roadblocks and the guards, past the burned-out shells of buildings and cars, into the heart of Rio de Janeiro. He looked at his watch. Two in the morning. He had until five to get in and out. Every television station and radio station repeated it, every cop car with a loudspeaker blared it, every surface that could be stapled with fliers screamed it in bold letters: five was when the bombs would fall.

The center of the city was infested with egg sacs in building after building. Too many to count. Rio was a lost cause. The entire area was going to be blasted to hell, a radius of seven kilometers sacrificed to the spiders even though all the egg sacs had been found within less than a thousand meters of one another, a tight circle of promised doom. The army was going to take that seven-kilometer radius and turn it into nothing but smoke and ashes. No spiders could survive that. No egg sacs would remain. Conventional weapons only: the beaches would remain, no nuclear weapons to turn the sand into glass. But there would be fire and burning. Five in the morning. Not a minute before, the radio and television and fliers and speakers all said, but not a minute later either. If you are in the blast area, you will not be spared.

He walked more quickly.

He passed two buildings at the outer perimeter that had been marked with spray paint to indicate infestations. That wasn't where he needed to go. He needed to see. Needed to prove he was right, prove that there was something to the way the spiders attacked that was worse than anybody had imagined. He needed to take pictures and shoot video and have evidence so that the authorities could not ignore him anymore. If they just burned everything down without understanding, they would never be saved. It was so much more complicated than the authorities thought! If only they would believe him without him having to resort to this. But they wouldn't believe him without the video. With the video? They'd have to. And then he'd be a hero. He wouldn't just be some dumb cop told to do his job and stay out of the way. He'd be the kind of person they made movies about.

That's what he was thinking as he hustled up the block toward the glass-fronted office building. His flashlight beam bobbed in front of him. He'd combed through the news reports and the Internet rumors, watched all the television reporting he could find, and in the end, he knew that *this* is where it had started in

Rio de Janeiro. This building was ground zero. When they made the movie version of this, the hero—he imagined somebody like Bruce Willis as Bruce Willis had been when he was a younger man, when he'd filmed the first *Die Hard*—would have to work harder to get past the cordon, would maybe even have to fight his way into the middle of the infestation in order to serve as humanity's last hope, but in real life, it was easy. The entire core of the city was deserted. A ghost town. Just him and a few million spiders waiting to be hatched.

He better be right, he thought.

He stopped for a minute outside the building to catch his breath. It was a bank. The windows had posters featuring bright, young, single people, happy families, sun-kissed couples in love. All that happiness with a simple loan. In the street, where he stood, however, there were grimmer signs. A car turned over and blackened by fire. Human-shaped lumps of clothing he was afraid to shine his light on. He reached out and pulled on the door. It was locked. The door was locked. Had somebody really stopped to lock the door to the bank amid all the chaos or was it just on a timer? Not that it mattered. He lifted the flashlight, flipped it around in his hand, and struck the glass in front of him with the heavy metal butt.

Instantly he was covered in flashing white light, a wailing piercing through the night. The strobe alarm made him blink heavily, and he had to resist the urge to cover his ears. An alarm. It was a bank after all. He should have been expecting it. He looked around, almost expecting security guards to come rushing at him, but the streets stayed deserted. The siren was playing to an audience of one. He stepped into the building, walking gingerly on the broken glass. It crunched under his boots with every step. Then he stopped. Shit. He'd forgotten to put on the hazmat suit. Better safe than sorry, he thought, which was funny, all things considered. He worked the ungainly plastic coveralls on over his clothes. It didn't seem like much protection once he had the hazmat gear on. It was basically a yellow rain suit with full helmet and glass face mask with a built-in respirator. When he pulled the mask over his face, though, it covered him; every centimeter of exposed skin underneath the suit. The mask seemed to amplify his breathing; he could hear each breath, in and out.

The lobby of the bank was dotted with egg sacs. Softballs and footballs filled with spiders waiting to hatch. He was surprised at how little fear he felt. The egg sacs were foreign but unthreatening. There were more than he had expected, but he knew the real concentration was elsewhere in the building. He might only be a police officer, but he'd had access to the reports and he knew he had to head down into the basement. He walked through the lobby and past the chairs in the waiting area, around the counters and to the metal door that took him to the basement. His flashlight cut a path through the maze for him. The egg sacs were everywhere. Worse, there were bodies all over the floor. Not even bodies. Skeletons. He tried to keep his eyes on the sacs, to see what lay before him, but it was hard with the strobe lights of the alarm. It turned the bank into a scene from an eerie, stuttering movie. It was with a sigh of relief that he pushed through the metal door, and he sped up, rushing to get down to the basement, to get this all over with.

He should have moved more slowly.

He should have looked down.

As he pushed through the door to the basement, he heard a snapping sound and then he stumbled. He was already falling down the stairs by the time he realized that what he'd tripped on had been a body. The snapping had been a bone breaking under-

foot, and he was falling because his boot had snagged on the empty
fabric that had once surrounded a human being.

The strobe lights of the alarm were working here, too, in the
stairwell, and the process of falling was disjointed. He was stumbling. He was reaching for the handrail with his free hand. The
flashlight was in his hand and then it wasn't. He was, for one
brief, blessed, blinking moment of time, safe in the bright light
that came from the same box that shrieked at him, and then, in
the darkness that came between the strobes, he could feel himself
flying. Falling.

When he woke, the alarm was still blaring, the strobe light still
flashing.

How long?

How long had he been unconscious?

He turned his head. The motion made him want to throw up.
Gingerly, he touched the back of his head with his right hand.
He couldn't feel anything but rubber. Of course. The hazmat suit.
The respirator. His left arm was pinned under his body, and when
he moved it to look at his watch, a wave of pain shot through him.
My god. He'd broken his leg. There was no question of that. Just
that slight movement, that twist to pull his arm free from under
him had shifted his leg and been enough to make him nearly black
out again. He used his right hand to peel off his left glove, and
then held his wrist up in front of his face, but he couldn't see the
numbers. There was a great jagged crack across the faceplate that
made it impossible to see. He wrenched the helmet off and looked
at his watch again. No. It was impossible.

He'd been unconscious for almost three hours.

It was five to five in the morning.

Five minutes until the bombs came down.

He looked up, realizing that the door at the bottom of the

stairwell where he lay was propped open by a body that had once belonged to a woman. He reached for his flashlight before he remembered that he'd lost it, that he'd dropped it when he fell down the stairs. But there was light in the basement. The strobe of the alarm, of course, white and hateful, like the beating heart of an alien, but something else too. He could almost see it.

He tried pushing himself forward, but there was something wet and grinding in his leg. The wave of pain that shot through him almost made him faint. He didn't have to look to know that a bone was sticking out, but he needed to see all the same. He immediately wished he hadn't: he could see the ripped, bloody hole in his suit where his jagged thighbone had poked through. At least he couldn't see the flesh. Still, it made him feel sick, and he had to look away.

The siren continued its pulsing wail, but in the space between, he thought he heard something. A brushing. A skittering. And then, with horror, he realized that his head was bleeding too. He could feel blood trickling through his hair, down his neck. He reached for the helmet to seal the suit up again, but he couldn't find it. Could the spiders smell the blood from his leg? From his head? Were they in the basement, looking for a meal? Had they hatched or were they still safely in their egg sacs? Were they already inside him?

Three minutes to five. The second hand of his watch looked even choppier than normal in the strobe. There wasn't much time. He knew he was right. He knew there was a reason for him to be here. The hero wasn't going to die in vain. If he couldn't be Bruce Willis in *Die Hard*, he could be Bruce Willis in *Armageddon*, staying on that asteroid to save the human race, a worthwhile sacrifice. They'd build a statue to honor him. The whole world would know his name.

He reached out to the door frame and pulled himself along the floor, scraping across the hard concrete. The blood dripping from his leg looked black in the flashes of the strobe. Ahead of him, he could finally see it. Glowing. He looked at his watch again. Two minutes. There were black spots dancing across his vision. His head ached where he'd smashed it on the stairs. He couldn't pass out. He was Bruce Willis. He was the hero. There was still time to save the world. His leg hurt so much. His head hurt. The siren. If only the siren would be quiet, the strobe stopping the incessant punishment of light. How hard had he hit his head? The black spots moved through his field of vision, and he thought he saw flashes of red as well. Five spots. Ten. Dozens. He closed his eyes for a moment. No. No. Be Bruce Willis. Focus. He could see the glowing in front of him. All he had to do was take a video and upload it. Then they'd see.

He reached for his phone where it lay on the concrete, but he never closed his hands around it.

It felt like he'd been shot. The sensation was so strong and painful that any thoughts of his broken leg disappeared. The bombs? No, it couldn't be the bombs, not yet. He was still alive, even if the pain made him wish he wasn't. There was at least another minute before the bombs fell. He tried to look at his watch and he realized he couldn't move. Not a muscle.

No! Again. It was as if there was some sadist standing above him with a burning iron rod, piercing his body. He'd never imagined a pain like this. And it was made worse by the way his body was frozen. He couldn't grimace, couldn't curl up to defend himself, couldn't even cry out in pain. Whatever thoughts he'd had of being the hero disappeared. All he could think of was the pain.

It didn't last long, though. Five o'clock came, and with it the bombs and fire.

Minneapolis, Minnesota

That's what nobody told you about joining the agency. There were moments of abject terror, sure. Agent Mike Rich had had plenty of those in the last two weeks. Going into Henderson's crashed plane and seeing a spider crawling out of the billionaire's face? Scary. Taking said spider to Washington, DC, and bumping into the president and her chief of staff? Scary. Okay, maybe meeting Melanie Guyer, hot, brilliant scientist who was all legs and a great smile, wasn't so scary, but Melanie did specialize in spiders, so then again, sort of scary. And then all the shit that went down in India, China, and Los Angeles, and realizing it was absolutely, positively connected to that same spider that he'd trapped under a cut glass tumbler in the wreckage of the billionaire's plane and carried to Washington? Scary. Having to drive his daughter and pregnant ex-wife and her husband out to a cottage in the woods because he thought there was a better than even chance that they were screwed? Scary.

But this was worse.

That's what they never told you. The moments were scary, but you didn't have time to really think. It was between the moments, when you *did* have time and you had to make the big decisions, that was truly the most terrifying. Reaction was always easier than action.

"What do we do, Mike?"

Agent Rosario leaned toward Mike. She kept her voice down, and his partner, Leshaun, leaned in with her. The three agents were huddled at the back of the garage, near the egg sacs. They'd cleared everybody else out.

If you didn't count the man-eating-spider egg sacs, Mike thought, the adjoining home was kind of nice. Typical suburban brick house. A mile from where Henderson's plane had crashed after the tech tycoon and his pilots had been eaten by spiders. The house was on a quiet street off another quiet street that led to a slightly busier street, and it was painted a jaunty buttercup yellow with blue shutters. Well maintained, with a neat lawn and mulched flower beds. One of the flower beds already showed the first promise of tulips. Inside the garage, everything was clean and organized. The owner kept the concrete swept, with sporting equipment hung from pegs on the side wall, and the back wall lined with the kind of stainless steel cabinets you could buy at a home improvement store and install yourself. Really, aside from the presence of the eggs, it was the kind of home Mike wouldn't mind having for himself. His condo was fine, but a real yard would have been terrific, a place for him to play catch with Annie or to kick around a soccer ball. This place was probably in his price range, too. If he'd been here for an open house—and there were no spiders—he'd be calling his bank to see if he could prequalify.

Unfortunately, there *were* spiders. Or the promise of spiders. Maybe ten, twelve egg sacs. Each one the size of a basketball, knitted together and tucked against the dark corner of the garage. He could understand why the owner hadn't noticed them until today. Without the portable klieg lights burning through the shadows, they'd be nothing more than a shape lurking in the corner of your eye.

Except for the fact that, in the last hour, the shapes had started to make noises. A sort of buzzing rattle.

And now, his partner and Rosario wanted to know what Mike thought they should do. He looked past them, out toward the driveway. There was a clump of cops milling around, a fire truck, an ambulance, and several members of the Minnesota National Guard in full uniform and carrying rifles. He had to squint a bit. The spotlights were unforgiving.

"What do you mean, what do we do?" he said, walking a few steps over to the side. He turned off the blinding klieg lights. Better. The overhead fluorescents were on, but the garage felt normal. Small and clean and comfortable. It was almost possible, for a few seconds, to forget about the giant packet of doom in the corner. Almost.

"Pretty obvious question," Rosario said. "What do we do about these egg sacs? They're what we've been looking for, and now we've found them. So?"

"Why are you asking me?"

Leshaun raised his eyebrows. "Because it's humming and vibrating and scaring the living shit out of me. And because you already caught one of them. Like it or not, Mike, that makes you the expert."

It was all Mike could do to stop himself from laughing in panic. If he was what passed for an expert, they were well and truly screwed. His experience with these spiders could be classified as limited, at best. Basically, he'd grabbed a highball glass off the floor of a jet and tipped it over a spider. And that meant he was going to have to answer this question? So what if the spider came out of the wreckage of a plane crash, limping and damaged and *still* going after his flesh like some unstoppable machine? So what if he didn't happen to notice that a few other spiders must have made their way out of Henderson's plane, skittered three or more blocks away, and started laying eggs? Whoops! There goes the neighborhood! Before all this happened, the only thing he knew about spiders was that they creeped him out. But absolutely none of that mattered. Nope. He was the expert now. Jesus.

"What did you do with the other egg sacs you found at the warehouse?" Rosario said.

He shook his head. "I just did what Melanie told me. She asked me if they were warm or not. When I said they weren't, she had me call some scientists at the U. The scientists came out and put them in these bug aquariums."

"Insectariums," Leshaun said.

"Whatever," Mike said. "Point is, I didn't do anything."

Leshaun glanced at the sacs. "So why'd she ask if they were warm?"

"Beats me."

"So the ones at the warehouse weren't warm?"

"No," Mike said. He shook his head for emphasis. "I already said that. They were cool, if anything." He stopped for a second and then walked to the corner. He held out his hand and then hesitated. He really didn't want to touch them. "Which seemed to reassure her, though, so I guess warm is bad?"

Rosario and Leshaun both just stared at him. Waiting.

"Seriously?" he said.

Rosario shook her head. "I'm not touching them, and come on, you're right there."

"Leshaun?"

"Hey, man, I'm still recovering from a gunshot wound. Be my guest."

"Fuck both of you," he said. He meant it, too.

It gave him the heebie-jeebies to raise his arm again, to reach out and touch the egg sacs, but there you go.

They were warm. Like bread cooling from the oven. And though they looked chalky, they were slightly tacky. They felt like the pebbled leather on a basketball.

There was a protocol they were supposed to follow. Sort of. It wasn't much of a protocol, really. In the week since Mike had come across the first colony of egg sacs in the warehouse a few blocks from the plane crash, it seemed like the agency had called in every cop, firefighter, EMT, security guard, crossing guard, Boy Scout, and Girl Scout in the greater Minneapolis area. If you could walk and follow anything resembling an order, you were thrown into the hunt. Everybody got a glossy photo of the sacs and strict instructions: Call it in. Set up a perimeter and make sure nobody touched the egg sacs. That's it. Call it in and then wait. The big-wigs in Washington were still trying to figure out the protocol for dealing with them.

With all the people out looking, they'd still only found five sites in Minneapolis: the original trio of egg sacs in the warehouse, a single egg sac in a tree on the edge of the school grounds where the plane had crashed, two sacs underneath a panel van parked in the back of an office supply company, nine in a long-shuttered restaurant, and the dozen or so here, in the garage of this cute house. At first, they'd searched the old-fashioned way, fanning out and looking here and there. They'd run it like a missing persons case, gridding out the area around the crash site and moving in a larger and larger circumference, systematically checking each part of the grid. But after the second and third finds things had gone to the dogs. Literally. Dogs went totally batshit crazy when they came near the egg sacs. And it didn't have to be trained K9 units or bomb sniffers or anything fancy. The egg sacs under the chassis of the panel van were discovered by some college student taking her Chihuahua for a walk. Her dog just lost his mind, barking and growling and spoiling for a fight, as if his seven pounds was going to fare well against these spiders.

So they'd used dogs, and the dogs had found these other infestation sites, and then they'd . . . waited.

That's it. Get agents on-site and sit tight. It seemed crazy to him. These things were lethal, and they were supposed to just wait? But what did he know? He was no expert.

The problem was that sitting and waiting might be an acceptable course of action at all the other locations, where the egg sacs were chalky and dull and cold and exactly like the ones in the warehouse, but these were warm and they were *humming*. There was no way that seemed like a good thing. Maybe he would have been willing to believe it was going to be okay if Melanie Guyer was standing next to him and smiling and promising it was going to be okay.

But she wasn't.

He didn't have any reassurances. What he had was his partner Leshaun, Agent Rosario, and a couple dozen guys with badges and uniforms standing around with their thumbs up their asses. And he had a group of egg sacs that were warm and vibrating and making noise.

So he had a choice. He could wait and watch, knowing that there was something seriously wrong here, or he could act. But if he acted, what the hell was he supposed to do?

He thought about the first spider he saw. He'd been visiting Leshaun in the hospital when he'd gotten the call from the director of the agency that the jet of one of the richest men in the world, tech billionaire Bill Henderson, of Henderson Tech, had crashed just a few blocks away. The twisted wreckage had been gruesome, but Mike figured it was just some billionaire's luck gone to crap. Until he had seen the spider eat its way out of Henderson's face. There was something undeniably scary about that, made worse by the way the damaged spider had kept coming toward him, dragging two useless legs but still relentless. He'd had a bad cut on his hand, and as it bled, drip, drip, dripping onto the floor, it was like the blood was a siren call for the little monster. He remembered that with stunning clarity. And God, the sound of walking through that plane? He would hear that in his nightmares for the rest of his life, the crunching, popcorn crackle of the burned-out spiders underfoot.

No. Wait. He had something there. Fire.

"We burn them out," he said.

Maybe he *was* the expert.

He certainly felt that way for the next forty-five minutes. They didn't have anything approximating a flamethrower, though some chucklehead cop suggested using the homeowner's Weber grill. Fortunately, one of the firefighters on the scene ran the training sessions for the department. He was, to an almost concerning extent, skilled at setting fires. Mike had the cops set up a cordon and evacuate everybody within a one-block radius, and then directed the additional fire trucks called to the scene to wet down the surrounding houses. This cute little house was going to be a sacrificial victim. There wasn't much he could do about that. But he was pretty sure that burning down the entire neighborhood seemed like overkill. Probably. Maybe not.

"I think we're good," the fireman said. "I've got it set to go really fast and hot. There's plenty of airflow, so it's going to be an absolute inferno. There shouldn't be time for anything to get out. Probably."

"That 'probably' you added at the end there was incredibly reassuring."

"Sorry. Let me take one last check," the fireman said.

After a few minutes, the fireman gave him the signal. Ready to go. But Mike wasn't sure. He motioned for him to wait.

Screw it.

He pulled out his cell phone and called her.

The phone rang three, four times, and just as he was expecting the click through to voice mail, Melanie picked up.

"Not a good time, Mike."

"I'm not calling to ask you out to dinner," he said, and he was gratified to hear the small snort of a laugh. "We've got some egg sacs here I'm worried about."

"What is that? Third site? Fourth?"

"Fifth."

"Look, I'm sorry, Mike, but I'm kind of dying here." There was a sound in the background that Mike couldn't quite make out. Some sort of buzzing noise. "I'm not getting a lot of sleep and people are counting on me, and I'd love to chat, but I can't. Just keep doing what you guys have been doing. Keep an eye on them and let us know if anything changes."

"Uh, yeah. That's the thing." He moved across the grass and up toward the porch where he had some privacy. There were two white painted rocking chairs on the porch, and Mike sat in one. "These ones are warm and sort of vibrating."

Mike held the phone to his ear. The background noise was still there, but nothing from Melanie. "Hello? Melanie?"

Her voice came at last. "Vibrating?"

"You know. Like if you have music up loud and you put your hands against the speakers, you can feel the thump, thump, thump. So, anyway, I know we're supposed to just watch and stuff, but

I've got to be honest, this is kind of stressing me out." He saw the fireman come out of the garage and start shooing the other men and women in uniforms back. The fireman looked at Mike, clearly impatient, but Mike held up his hand to tell him to keep waiting.

"Shit. Shit, shit, shit," Melanie said.

"Yeah, I was afraid you were going to have that kind of reaction." He paused for a second. "To be clear, we're both on the same page here, right? These things are getting ready to hatch?"

"What about the other sites in Minneapolis?"

He shook his head and then remembered he was on the phone. "Nothing. Cold and chalky."

"And you've still only got five sites in Minneapolis? And they're all relatively small infestations? Nothing more than a few sacs at each one? A couple dozen at most?"

"Yeah. Wait. What aren't you telling me?"

He listened to the background noise through the phone, wondering what Melanie was doing, wondering how much worse it was out there.

A lot worse, evidently.

She hesitated but told him. He was pretty sure, as he listened to her tell him about the infestations in Los Angeles, the reports out of Korea and India, out of England and Japan, that she was supposed to be keeping the news to herself, but it was clear she was overwhelmed. The gist of it was that they were lucky in Minneapolis. A few egg sacs here, a few egg sacs there? In the scheme of things, a smattering of egg sacs that weren't hatching wasn't something to worry about.

"Mike," Melanie said. Her tone was serious. "That's the problem. We are on the same page. I'd like to say it's not a big deal. It wouldn't be, if you only had a couple of sites with a couple of egg sacs, because compared to everywhere else that's almost nothing.

But that assumes the egg sacs are cold. What you're telling me is that you've got a few egg sacs that are ready to hatch. You're going to have to take care of them. Now. You can't wait."

"I was really, really hoping you weren't going to say that, but okay. I'll take care of it. Just hold on a second."

"No. You don't understand. You don't have a second. Now. *Right now.*"

"You got it," he said. "Literally, right now."

He lowered the phone and caught the eye of the fireman again. He gave the thumbs-up and then waited until the first flames began to shoot out of the garage.

It was pretty in a strange sort of way. He stood up from the rocking chair and got as close as he could. The heat pushed him back, but he described to Melanie what he had done and what he could see through the flames: the egg sacs flaring up and then melting, a few black balls opening and skittering toward the garage door before sinking into the blaze. Soon, the entire cavity of the garage was like a blast furnace, and it was only a few minutes more before the house itself was captured by fire.

"Well," he said, "at least we've got that going for us."

"What?" Melanie said.

"The bastards aren't fire resistant."

"You better double-check the other sites around town, to make sure none of the sacs are getting warm," Melanie said. "If one of those things hatches . . ."

"I know. Already on it." He thought he should hang up, but he didn't. He knew she was busy, that she had more important things to do than talk to him, but it was reassuring to just hold the phone against his ear and breath in and out with her.

"Mike," she said. Her voice was quiet. Thoughtful. "What's your kid's name again?"

"Annie. She's at her mom's right now. Or maybe on her way to soccer." He laughed. "Things aren't exactly normal, but even spiders taking over the world isn't a good enough excuse for her soccer coach. Two practices a week plus games, spiders be damned. She's only nine. Can't wait to see what her schedule is going to look like once she's in high school."

"Can you get her out of the city?"

"Pardon?" Mike turned his back to the burning house and walked farther away.

"Can you get Annie out of the city?"

"Her stepdad has a cottage up on Soot Lake. It's two hours north of the city. Pretty remote. I sent them up there last week when shit went to hell. But I brought them back after the spiders started dying out. I just figured—"

He spun around, looking at the house enveloped by flames. It was so obvious. It wasn't just this one infestation. It didn't matter that the other sacs they'd found in Minneapolis showed no signs of hatching as of yet. How could he have thought it was just this one house? They could look all they wanted, and maybe they'd find every egg sac in Minneapolis. And maybe they'd be lucky, and the egg sacs would all be dusty and cold, waiting for some later time. But they'd never find *all* the egg sacs. Or if they found all the egg sacs in Minneapolis, they would miss some in Los Angeles. And if not Los Angeles, then somewhere else. They'd already spread past the point of containment. There were more. Of course there were.

There was a reason why Melanie was telling him to get Annie out of the city.

They were out of time.

The White House

For once, Manny wasn't worried about the polls. Mostly, that was because they hadn't bothered taking numbers since the cargo ship had hit Los Angeles and dumped a million of those vicious sons of bitches on American soil. What was he going to learn from a poll? That Americans don't like being eaten by spiders? Yeah. That was useful information. He could manage a campaign with information like that: Steph, make sure you come out strong against spiders. You, as a candidate, and we, as a political party, are very anti-spider. Posters and lawn signs showing the black silhouette of a spider in a circle with a big red bar through it. Crowds chanting, "No more spiders, no more spiders." Oh, it was a winning strategy. The only thing that could make it better was having whatever yahoo the other guys picked as their candidate come out as pro-spider. Against a pro-spider candidate, Steph could win hands down.

He shook his head and then took a sip from his Diet Coke. He was getting loopy. It was too much to take in. There were men and women in military uniforms zipping in and out of the Situation Room, aides scurrying with folders and cups of coffee, cabinet members and analysts and pretty much everybody who could fit. In the corner, Ben Broussard, the chairman of the Joint Chiefs of

Staff, was huddled up with the secretary of defense, Billy Cannon, and enough starred generals to make a constellation. And across the table, the national security advisor, Alex Harris, was conferring with a couple of CIA analysts. To Manny's right President Stephanie Pilgrim was listening to two senior analysts explain the fallout from China. Literal fallout, since China had nuked half its territory into oblivion.

Manny took another sip of his soda. At least he'd been able to get some sleep. Not a lot, but he really didn't need much. It was funny how little he needed to get by. He was, let's face it, kind of schlumpy. When he and Melanie had been married they'd gotten a few weird looks. She, six foot and athletic, stunning in a gown or just jeans and a T-shirt, and he looking disheveled even in a tuxedo. But if he wasn't a chiseled specimen like some of the military men and women circulating in and out of the Situation Room, he could at least outwork them. That's what Manny Walchuck did. He outworked you. He was a grinder. He sat up straighter and looked at the video screen. The burning of the Staples Center was running on a loop.

He'd seen it dozens of times, but it was still hard to watch. The ruins of the stadium clear in glorious sunlight. That's California for you, Manny thought. California didn't care that spiders had come to eat the human race. California—Los Angeles in particular—was sunshine and eighty degrees. Not what you'd expect to see in the Situation Room. Eight different times since Steph had been sworn in, they'd come down to watch a military operation of one sort or another. A missile strike. A team of commandos going into a compound. But those videos all had the same thing in common: the grainy green-tinged hue of night vision, dark shadows, and flashes of light. To watch this, the Staples Center illuminated by daylight, was unsettling.

There had been an argument over leaving the stadium alone for a few days. The idea was to try to catalogue it and count the egg sacs, but Manny had overruled them all. They had tanks on the streets of Los Angeles and a city in ruins. Best guess? Two million dead. Three? They didn't know. There'd never been anything like it. And a stadium full of egg sacs that people wanted to study.

No way, Manny had said. Burn the whole thing down. So they did. Cordite or thermite or some kind of -ite or other. The air force had suggested bombing the building, but there was concern that the spiders might ride the wave of an explosion. Air currents. So it came down to a good old-fashioned burning. Whatever engineer had been in charge had rigged it so that the blaze moved from the outer shell inward, driving any loose spiders toward the middle. According to the briefing, the temperature in there had been in the thousands. Hot enough that the air itself could have caught fire.

Nothing could have survived it.

Which would have been wildly reassuring if Melanie hadn't been so damn right about there being tons of other places where the spiders laid eggs. If it was as simple as burning down the Staples Center, he'd be taking a nap right now, but it wasn't. The egg sacs were everywhere around Los Angeles. They had a nice little visual of it too: a map dotted with infestation sites. The whole of Los Angeles was ringed with them. Some were small—fifty, sixty egg sacs—and some were of similar scale to the Staples Center. Which he maybe could have lived with, except that he knew there was no way they'd found all of them. Not with the city in ruins, not with so many people dead and such . . .

Ah. Jesus. There was a part of Manny that wanted to stand up, say, "Well, to hell with it," and just pack it in. Go take a suite at the Ritz and order room service and watch pay-per-view until the end came.

But he couldn't do it. He wasn't a quitter. So he'd have to settle for watching the video of the Staples Center burn and die. He liked seeing the building buckle and fold in on itself. It was as close as he was going to get to some sort of reassurance.

Plus, he'd always been a Celtics guy.

He felt a tap on his elbow and looked up to see Steph.

"A word," she said.

They left the room together and walked a few paces down the hall. They weren't exactly alone—the president was never really alone in the White House—but there was a cordon of privacy, and she kept her voice low.

"I need you to keep Broussard on a leash for me," she said. "He and the other brass are starting to play their favorite tune—that I can't possibly understand the military implications."

Manny sighed. The chairman of the Joint Chiefs of Staff, Ben Broussard, was a dick even at the best of times. Not that this was the best of times. He'd been agitating for more military latitude. If the Chinese were dropping nukes, he said, shouldn't the United States be ready to do the same? The guy was a heartbeat away from turning into Dr. Strangelove.

"I'll talk to him," Manny said, though he knew it wouldn't help. Broussard wasn't a fan of his. Wasn't a fan of Steph either. Broussard had been one of Manny's blind spots. Something he'd realized too late. He'd known Steph for so long, worked with Steph for so long, that he often forgot that there were men who couldn't stomach the idea of a woman being in charge. Sure, when everything was hunky dory, it wasn't a problem. With the Russians just cartoon villains from Reagan-era movies, and the Chinese an economic threat more than an ongoing military worry, men like Ben

Broussard were willing to let Steph play at being the president. Because that's how they thought of it: as a thing they let her do. Like she was some cute little girl playing dress up. Steph had taken his advice on getting Broussard confirmed, and it had been a mistake. The bigger mistake, though, was when they'd decided to let Broussard stay in the post once they finally understood what kind of man he was. The problem was that it was too late to do anything about it. Now that it mattered, now that there was something real and vital and terrifying to face, now that Broussard thought it was time for men like him to be in charge, it was too late to replace him. Instead, Manny would have to work around him.

"I'll talk to Billy too," he said. Billy Cannon. The secretary of defense. Maybe it was just a difference in confidence. Cannon was a military lifer, decorated and carrying a scar from combat. Smart enough to play politics and sure enough of himself not to give a shit about politics when things really mattered. Cannon recognized the truth, which was that Steph was a hell of a president.

"You're doing it, aren't you?" Steph said. She nodded at some Marines saluting her as they walked past. "Moving the pieces on that little chessboard in your head?"

Manny shrugged. "I can tell Broussard that you want to hear his contingency plan for evacuating the West Coast and sealing off everything east of the Mississippi. It's bullshit, because there's no way to actually make that happen, but I can direct him toward Cannon. Cannon will play ball, and that will buy you a couple of days of having Broussard out of your hair."

Steph nodded and then turned through the doorway that led into the Oval Office. She called to her secretary to say that she didn't want them to be disturbed, and then led Manny through the Oval Office into her smaller, more intimate private office.

As soon as the door was closed, she pulled him close, kissed him, and said, "We've got maybe twenty minutes, tops. Make it good."

He shouldn't have been surprised, but he was. He and Steph had slept together on and off for most of the time they'd known each other. On, mostly, in college, and in between her boyfriends and his girlfriends, and then totally off while he was married to Melanie. Mostly back on for the past couple of years. The First Hubby, George, was a nice enough guy, but that was all he had going for him. She'd never really been in love with George. Maybe in a different world Steph would have divorced him and found somebody else, but that wasn't the world she lived in. The voting public wasn't ready for a male president to get divorced, let alone a woman. As it was, her political opponents did their best to paint Steph as some sort of bitch-whore. She had to walk such a fine line. So it was an arrangement that worked well for both her and Manny. They both had high sex drives, even if their political engines revved at an even higher frequency. Steph wasn't going to find anybody else as discreet as him, and as chief of staff he didn't really have a lot of time to date. It was a convenient arrangement. They could never quite figure out how to be a couple—it just wasn't in them, Manny suspected—but they were perfect as fuck buddies. He laughed at the thought. Such an undignified term. Fuck buddies. Could you really be fuck buddies with the president of the United States? Not that it would be the first time such unseemly things had gone on in and around the Oval Office.

She leaned in to kiss him again and he pulled back slightly. "Really? Now?"

"For God's sake, Manny, if you're trying to slut-shame me, we're going to have some issues."

"No, I just . . . It just sort of seems like we're in the middle of—"

"Manny Walchuck, if you give me a lecture on what we're in the middle of, I'm going to have you taken out in front of the White House and shot by a firing squad. Please do not try to tell me what is appropriate and inappropriate." She leaned in to him again and this time he let her kiss him lightly on the lips. "How long have you known me? What's the one thing that always relaxes me? Well, we've been working nonstop for more than ten days, and I need a break. But I'm not going to get a break, so this is what I want. I might be the president of the United States, but I'm also Stephanie Pilgrim. I suppose I could go swim some laps or get on the treadmill or even watch an episode of some stupid television show, but that's not what I need right now." She reached out and ran her fingers up the back of his neck and into his hair.

"Sorry. It's just that there are probably some calls . . ."

"Manny, I am asking you, as my friend, to do this for me. I need to blow off a little steam, and this seems both quicker and healthier than scarfing down a pint of ice cream while I watch an episode of a reality show. So, this can go one of two ways. You are my oldest friend, my long-term lover, and one of the few people I trust completely. You can either make love to me right now because, in our own weird way, we love each other, or you can do it because I will order you to in my capacity as the president of the United States. What's it going to be?"

Manny grinned. "A powerful woman is a sexy thing."

"In that case," Stephanie said, "as the president of the United States I am issuing an executive order. You, Manny Walchuck, are hereby ordered to make love to me."

"Yes, ma'am," Manny said.

"And make it good."

The perks of office.

Càidh Island, Loch Ròg, Isle of Lewis, Outer Hebrides

Aonghas watched Thuy cut through the water.

He couldn't believe she could stand to swim. He was perched on a rock, wearing a thick Irish wool sweater and he was still cold. It was the kind of hand-knit sweater tourists paid a fortune for when they went to visit the Aran Islands. There were cheaper versions that came from China or Cambodia or wherever it was that people imported factory-made clothing from, but the authentic items were still hand-knit. Sometimes by old ladies, sometimes by men who needed a way to make money when the seas were too rough for fishing. He'd been told a number of times that every village had its own distinctive pattern, so that when you pulled a body out of the water—ears and eyes and cheeks nibbled to the bone by the fish—you could at least tell where the person had come from. The good sweaters, and this was a good sweater, were so tight knit the spray of water off the ocean beaded up on the wool instead of soaking through. But it wasn't enough to keep him warm, and he didn't understand how she could be in the water.

She said it made her feel alive, vibrant. She'd been a swimmer her whole life. She was tall, particularly for somebody of Vietnamese descent, and even though she hadn't swum competitively since she missed qualifying for the Olympics by barely one-tenth of a second, she still liked to get in the water every day that she could. Even here, on Càidh Island. Every morning since they'd been stranded here, she'd put on her suit, pulled on a swim cap and goggles, and slipped into the water. She was never in very long. Five minutes, maybe ten. Today was closer to ten.

She pulled herself onto the rocks, teeth chattering and skin tinged blue. Aonghas stepped forward and wrapped the thick cotton bath sheet around her. He rubbed her shoulders and kissed her. She tasted like salt. Her lips were ice cubes against his.

"Better?" he said.

"Better."

It had been their little ritual for the past week. It felt like some sort of promise between them.

She pulled the towel tighter around herself and held out her hand so he could slide the engagement ring back on. She was afraid it might fall off her finger and drop into the depths as she swam. He worked it over her knuckle and pushed it home. He liked the way the ring looked on her hand.

From behind them, his grandfather's voice boomed. "You've got yourself a crazy one, Aonghas," Padruig said. "I like it. A woman as crazy as you."

That was part of the ritual, too. Thuy swam, Aonghas asked her if she felt better, Thuy said yes, and then Padruig told them they were crazy.

Ritual was all they had. It was almost seven in the morning, which meant that Padruig would have breakfast on the table accompanied by a pot of steaming coffee. They'd sit and eat—granola and homemade yogurt with fruit out of the deep freezer and still holding a bit of ice, some sort of scone, savory or sweet depending on his grandfather's mood, and orange juice made from frozen concentrate—and listen to BBC Radio nan Gàidheal. After breakfast, he'd do the dishes while Padruig and Thuy played a few rounds of Scrabble. It drove the old man crazy that Aonghas's fiancée beat him every time, but still they played. Midmorning, he and Padruig would take care of any maintenance that needed doing. In the afternoon they would read or take naps, and then, after dinner, the three of them drank sherry and played cards. If it weren't for what was waiting for them outside their little fortress, where Càidh Island stopped and the rest of the world began, it might have felt like vacation.

That reality was there, though. In deference to it, Padruig allowed Thuy to keep her cell phone turned on. Insisted on it, actually. It had never even occurred to Aonghas to try to bring a cell phone to the island. His grandfather's well-documented tendency to look at any piece of technology as though it were something malodorous aside, the fact that Thuy could even get a signal out here was quite the surprise. He barely got service in his town house in Stornoway.

When they'd first landed on Càidh Island, before the world had gone to shit, she'd had enough of a signal to get at least one e-mail through. But now, despite her phone showing between one and two bars of service, nothing came through. The cell phone might as well have been a night-light for all the good it did. She couldn't access the Internet, no social media, no news from her parents or her brother. Even though news reports on the radio were that communication systems were overloaded worldwide, each day without hearing from her family made Thuy's jaw clench a little tighter. The BBC said that Edinburgh had been spared from spiders, but there'd been panic and looting, the panic resulting in at least a couple hundred people dead from fires and accidents.

Both men had tried to comfort her, to point out how unlikely it was that her family had been caught up in the nonsense that came from the fear, but it didn't help. Part of her anxiety, Aonghas realized, was that she was worried that her parents were worried about her. Which made sense to him. They'd seen a man explode with spiders at the Stornoway airport, and it was only luck that had let them get out of there. Thuy's parents would have heard that the flights were grounded, would have spent the past week agonizing over whether or not their daughter was in Stornoway when it happened, maybe even mourning her death.

Thuy smiled at Padruig and gave him a peck on the cheek before walking past him and toward the castle. If it was a miracle they were still alive, it was perhaps a greater miracle that his grandfather had given him and Thuy his blessing to get married. If anything, Aonghas suspected his grandfather might actually like Thuy more than he liked his own grandson. He went to follow her, but his grandfather took his arm.

"A word," Padruig said. "I've been thinking about your question."

Aonghas looked at the old man, confused. "What question?"

"What you said when you came back to the island."

Aonghas shook his head. "It's a bit of a blur, I'm afraid. I just remember being scared and relieved. Scared at what we'd seen and what was happening, and relieved that you're such a crazy coot that we've got our own private island."

"Well, yes. But the question is important. You asked me why are they all coming to the surface at the same time. You don't remember that?" Padruig waited until Aonghas shook his head again. "Why. That's what you said. Not *how* is it that these spiders are suddenly appearing all over the world at the same time, but *why*."

"So?"

"I wonder if I might just have an answer for that."

First Forward Checkpoint, Greater Los Angeles Quarantine Zone, California

The fencing zigzagged back and forth creating a chute to funnel people. It stretched for miles. Farther than Lance Corporal Kim Bock could see. The line moved at a decent pace. Hundreds of people an hour. But it might as well not have been moving at all for how little it seemed to matter. The crowd never got smaller.

Mothers and fathers and sons and daughters. Men in rags and men in suits. Families with suitcases and kids with their school backpacks hurriedly stuffed full of whatever they could grab. Refugees. Tens of thousands of American refugees.

And the worst thing was that she knew the mass of humanity before her was only a fraction of what there had been. These were the people who were left. These were the people who'd survived.

Kim's platoon had been told there were ongoing army operations within the quarantine zone to find sites where there might be infestations. "Infestations," Honky Joe told them, after talking with his father, some sort of hotshot on Capitol Hill, not an actual politician, but one better, one of those guys who gave the

politicians the information, was military code for there being a
whole ton of egg sacs full of baby spiders just waiting to hatch
scattered throughout Los Angeles. Not to mention the very people walking in front of Kim and her squad, who themselves might
be full of spiders. According to the latest reports, the spiders had
spread to a distance of five miles from central Los Angeles before
the creepy little monsters had started dropping dead. No, actually,
that wasn't quite accurate. Near as the military could tell, the spiders had gone out nearly seven miles before starting to pull back
and stopping at five miles, some sort of an arachnid retreat, and
then dropping dead.

"Like putting up fortifications," Private First Class Elroy Trot-
ter said. He cradled his M16 and looked out over the line of refugees sidling toward them.

Her team had been working the fence since 0400 and it was late
morning. They were on duty until 1600 hours. Not bad, actually.
The first couple of days they'd pulled shifts of eighteen, twenty
hours at a time.

In some ways, the setup reminded Kim of security lines at an
airport. Like passengers lining up to get through body scanners.
Not a perfect metaphor, since they didn't have body scanners, but
good enough. Though body scanners would be nice.

"Fortifications? How's that?" Kim asked.

Her platoon was close to the chokepoint. The fencing narrowed and narrowed until the refugees couldn't help but go single
file. At the end was a sort of holding pen you had to pass through,
and here it really *was* like the indignity of going through an American airport. But worse. At an airport, you had to take off your shoes
and pull out your laptop, but here nothing was allowed through.
Not a bag, not a purse, not a phone, not a wallet. Not a stitch of
clothing.

On one hand, it seemed like overkill, but on the other hand, as Private Honky Joe had pointed out, since they weren't actually sure where on earth these spiders had come from, how could they be sure the spiders couldn't hide their eggs in suitcases or in the hem of a pair of pants? Like bedbugs, only a little more blood-thirsty. Not that clothes or suitcases were their main worry, of course. The main worry was that one of these people was a walking time bomb, that some man or woman would just be moping along in line, dumping their clothes meekly, and waiting their turn when—*blam!*—they'd open up and it would be spider city.

Elroy motioned an old black dude forward into the holding pen. The man seemed skeptical. In the holding pen, people were ordered to strip down and throw all their possessions into Dumpsters. Each time a Dumpster was filled—which was as fast as they could shuffle people forward—it was replaced and hauled a couple of miles away, its contents added to the burn site. The smoke was a plume that fell over everything.

"You know, fortifications. Like castles and stuff. Think old-school war, not the modern urban tactical warfare bullshit we're trained in," Elroy said.

"Yeah, our training has been really helpful now that we're battling an alien invasion." Private Duran Edwards had spent the first couple of hours on his first shift ogling any decent-looking woman who stripped down, but he'd gotten bored with it. They weren't really people anymore. Just widgets on an assembly line.

The thought of people being treated like widgets made Kim wince a little bit. It was a little too close to her idea of what the Nazis sorting Jews at concentration camps must have looked like. Which, when you added in the discomfort of stripping down completely and throwing away whatever small piece of your life you had managed to salvage while fleeing from an apocalyptic invasion of flesh-eating spiders, helped to explain why the line of refugees moved in fits and spurts. Most of the men, women, and children looked exhausted, their eyes glazed over in tiredness or even just in resignation. But not all of them, and there was a lot of shouting. The thing that made her feel better was that she'd seen what happened once the refugees made it through the sorting. Lines and lines of buses waiting to shuttle them onward. Bottles of water and military rations stacked in neat rows, blankets and basic clothing for people to grab. For all the bellyaching she and her squadmates were doing, the US military had stepped up. It was one hell of a feat of organization to have things running as smoothly as they were. She didn't know exactly where the buses were headed—she'd heard Reno, and she'd heard Las Vegas—but wherever it was, it was away from the nightmare of Los Angeles, away from the bodies of the dead and the buildings stuffed full of egg sacs.

"They aren't aliens, Duran. Jesus." Private Goons shook his head.

Kim considered Goons for a second, and then looked at the rest of her squad and at the guys in Private Sue Chirp's fire team, which was working alongside them. With their helmets and body armor, mirrored sunglasses and rifles and bulging pockets, she thought, it was the Marines who looked like aliens.

"Like the government would admit it if they were aliens," Duran muttered. He'd been muttering a lot.

"What do you guys know about World War One?" Elroy stared around at the group, but nobody offered a response. One of the refugees, a sunburned man in his forties, overheard the question and looked like he wanted to respond, but the line moved again, and he shuffled past. Even Honky Joe was quiet. Honky Joe knew about everything and was almost never quiet. It meant that whatever Elroy was talking about was something Honky Joe had already figured out and decided was important.

"In certain parts of Europe, the Allies and the Axis fought—"

"Axis was World War Two," Sue Chirp said.

"Whatever. Point is, the Allies and the Germans dug in and fought back and forth over the same ground. Sometimes for months and years. And what they'd do is dig trenches and put up barbed wire and there'd be this no-man's-land in between. You could cross it, sure, but it was almost certain suicide. They'd see you coming and mow you down with machine guns."

"And," Goons said, "the point is?"

"The point," Honky Joe said, pushing off the chain-link fence and handing a bottle of water to a little girl who couldn't have been more than four or five, "is that the spiders didn't retreat from a radius of seven miles to five miles. I'm not even sure they'd understand the concept of a retreat, but even if they did, why would they? It's not like the government was handing the bugs their asses back to them. As we figured out pretty quickly, bullets aren't the most effective deterrent for these suckers."

"So why'd they fall back to five miles before they died out?" Goons asked. "If it wasn't a retreat, what was it?"

Honky Joe looked at Elroy and waited. That was one of the things Kim liked about Honky Joe. He'd probably figured it out days ago, but he wouldn't steal the moment from Elroy. Elroy waited until all of them were looking at him. The truth was that the job was boring. Hand out water bottles and energy bars as needed, keep the line moving. Farther back, where the crowds were thicker, as the fencing started to narrow, there'd been some real unrest, and up ahead, where the sorting happened, there was occasionally the burst of gunfire, but right where they were was quiet. It was good to have something to talk about.

"It's a defensive shift," he said. "They're setting up to play defense. They clear out a perimeter and secure it, just like the Allies and the Axis"—he waved at Sue—"Germans did. So you can see your enemies coming while you take a breather. It's a no-man's-land. Literally."

Kim pushed her helmet back a little and wiped at her forehead. It was hot out there. "How would that work against fighter jets and mortars and stuff like that?" she asked. "And why set up a defense in the first place? They were winning."

Elroy paused. They all paused. And then Elroy shrugged. They stayed quiet for a few beats. Not talking didn't mean it was quiet where they were—tens of thousands of refugees and military men and women packed into a couple of square miles, the hum of machines and generators and the floating sound of boom boxes and dogs barking meant that it was never quiet—but the pause felt like something solid. After a couple of seconds Kim found that she was looking to Honky Joe again. They were all looking to Honky Joe.

He shook his head. "You can't think of it that way. Duran might as well be right. We should treat this like an alien invasion. There's no point trying to think of what they are doing as having a real-world strategic correlation to anything we might do. We don't even know if it makes sense to think of the spiders as a 'they,' like an army that has a command structure. Each spider might just be doing its own thing, and we're putting our own meanings on it, seeing patterns where there aren't any."

Private Hamitt Frank—Mitts—had been quiet for all of this. In fact, he hadn't talked much the last few days, but he spoke now. "You believe that? You really believe there isn't a pattern?"

Honky Joe considered. "No." He shook his head. "No. I don't believe it. There's a pattern, but we haven't figured it out. I do know this, however: there's no point in thinking of these creepy little bugs as a conventional foe." Right in front of him, a young man, a kid, really, pushed an older woman in the back. "Hey, watch it, asshole," Honky Joe said. The kid looked like he wanted to say something back, but he was smart enough to realize that he'd gained the attention of a dozen men and women kitted out in full military gear. He moved on.

Honky Joe shook his head. "We're asking people to put up with too much here," he said, and then he looked at Kim. "When you ask what good is their defensive perimeter against modern weapons, you're assuming that these spiders are *thinking* about modern weapons. Whatever these spiders are, they've never had any contact with modern humans."

"How are you so sure of that?" Kim said.

Mitts laughed. "Don't you think it would have made the news if they'd come out before? They aren't exactly subtle little buggies, are they?"

"But the point is," Honky Joe said, "them falling back had nothing to do with what we were doing in response to them. When do you retreat? You do it for two reasons. The first is because you're losing, and it's the only way to survive."

"Well, given that they weren't exactly losing, we can probably rule that one out," Elroy said.

There was a small laugh. Kim smiled too. Black humor came with any job like theirs. Firemen and cops, soldiers and ambulance drivers. They all had the ability to laugh at the worst things you could imagine. There wasn't another way to get through it all.

"You're right," Honky Joe said. "It's hard to argue that we had the bugs on the run. So what's the other reason to fall back?" He wasn't really asking, but he paused for effect anyway. "Strategic decision. Either to fortify a defensive position or to build strength for the next offensive thrust."

"So which is it?" Kim asked.

Honky Joe shrugged. "Maybe both. I mean, a defensive position would be the argument when you consider that there are supposed to be, at this point, hundreds of different places where they've laid egg sacs throughout Los Angeles. Pull back and protect your resources. Except that they pulled back and then they all seemed to die out, just leaving their egg sacs behind. So are those the resources? The egg sacs? Are they prepping to go on offense? Maybe. You could argue they are simply waiting to move forward. If you think about how quickly they spread just using humans as a breeding ground and establishing themselves on the ground? Well, the next time they start marching it's going to make the first attack look like a friendly noogie. Not that any of it matters."

"What do you mean?"

Honky Joe let out a mean-sounding laugh. "What's the point? We're here enforcing a quarantine that already failed." He didn't have to say it. He didn't have to remind them about what had happened on Highway 10 after Los Angeles had fallen, the way they'd had to cut and run in the face of the spiders swarming toward them, the panic of cars and drivers and gunfire and explosions. "We can keep all these poor folk bottled up as much as we want, screen them until kingdom come, but the genie's already out of the bottle. Somewhere out there, people who've fled from Los Angeles are carrying spiders. Or if they're not, it doesn't matter anyway. Those spiders dropped dead, but they laid a bunch of eggs, right? Which means they're coming back. We're guarding an empty hen house."

Kim wanted him to be wrong, but she knew he wasn't. Still, she couldn't help herself. "So why are we here? If, as you say, there's no point to this, then, well, what's the point?"

Honky Joe shrugged. "The military does what the military does. America doesn't always win, but we never lose. What else is there to do but make it look like we know what we're doing?"

"So we just follow orders?" Kim asked. "Keep it orderly? Pretend we know what we're doing?"

For her, it was a series of questions, but everybody around her took what she said as statements. Follow orders. Keep it orderly. Pretend they knew what they were doing.

None of them talked for a little while after that. At least not to each other. Here and there one of them would exchange a few words with a refugee. Hand out a bottle of water or some rations, or simply encourage people to keep moving forward. After twenty minutes or so, Kim took a break, slipping through the gate and out of the funnel chute. She stopped in a portable latrine and then went to sit in her Joint Light Tactical Vehicle. She turned the engine on and let the air-conditioning blast over her. She tried checking her phone but there was no signal. The circuits were still overloaded.

She noticed Sue next to her, climbing on top of her Hummer—they had a patchwork of old and new vehicles—and staring toward the sorting area. Kim got out and joined Sue on the roof of the Hummer.

They could hear the dogs barking. Baying. Howling.

The sorting was a simple process. Enter the holding area and strip down. What the refugees didn't realize was that the reason they had to go naked was more complicated than it seemed. Sure, there might be spiders hiding in your backpack or nested in the hood of your sweatshirt, but that's not what they were really worried about.

Once naked, each refugee was stopped and given a quick physical exam by a Marine. Maybe twenty years ago it would have been a problem, but this was the new military, and there were enough female Marines so that the inspections were sex segregated. No marks on your body? No problem. You went through the secondary screening—past the dogs—and on to freedom. But if you had cuts or scrapes or other sores that couldn't obviously be explained, you were in for a more thorough examination. Those refugees were taken off to the side, to a secondary holding area. It was quick, actually, since not that many people needed the extra screening, and if you were part of a family, you could wait for your mom or uncle or daughter or whomever to finish their screening before being led out—also past the dogs—to the buses and the supplies.

They'd had a few false alarms. Some idiot had made a joke about swallowing some spiders, and that had almost gotten him shot. The same kind of guy who thought it was funny to make a joke about carrying a bomb or smuggling coke while going through security at the airport. The physical exams hadn't turned up anyone who was infested.

But the dogs had.

Every hour or two the dogs would go crazy.

Yesterday, they'd been stationed by the final screening area, where the dogs worked. A pregnant woman had gone through the gate. She was a beautiful woman. Even Kim could appreciate that. Part of it was because she seemed so unafraid and so proud of herself. Most people tried to cover themselves with their hands and hunched over and rounded their shoulders, consciously or unconsciously trying to hide their nakedness. But not this woman. She was of Japanese or Korean descent—Kim wasn't good at telling the difference—and pretty far along. Seven or eight months pregnant. Her hair fell to her mid-back, and her breasts were swollen and ready for the baby that was coming.

When she stepped through the gate, the dogs went berserk.

There were between five and ten military dogs working in the final screening area at any one time, people walking through tight aisles of fencing, separated from the dogs by chain-link and little else. Elsewhere, farther up the line, Kim had heard that handlers were trying to move through the mobs of people waiting to get into the funneled area, to prescreen when they could, but here it was much cleaner: one refugee, one dog, one second. Usually. But not now.

The dogs were barking and snarling. One of the dogs lunged and pulled her handler to his knee. Kim could see flecks of spittle coming out of the dogs' mouths as they howled and barked and strained at the pregnant woman. The handlers were outside the fence, thank god, because otherwise Kim wasn't sure they would have been able to keep the dogs off the woman.

The reaction was frighteningly quick. A team of four men in biohazard suits—they could have been women, really, for all that Kim could make out under the orange rubber suits—swept into the enclosure, grabbed the woman, and hustled her to a waiting van.

Outside the enclosure, a young man had made it through one of the parallel screening areas. Nobody needed to tell Kim he was the woman's husband or boyfriend. He screamed and ran after her, banging against the back of the van until a Marine Kim didn't recognize took mercy and smashed the man in the back of the head with the butt of her M16.

The unconscious man was scooped up onto a litter and taken to the first aid tent.

The van with the pregnant woman in it drove away. It didn't come back.

From where she stood on the roof of the Hummer with Sue, Kim didn't have a clear view of the final screening area. Which was fine with her.

Hearing the dogs was bad enough.

She could hear the barking.

She could hear the wailing of another human being having someone they loved torn away from them.

The CNN Center, Atlanta, Georgia

Teddie Popkins woke with a start. She'd fallen asleep with her head on her keyboard. How long had she been out? She could feel the imprint of the keys on her face. A little roadmap of her napping habits. Thankfully, her computer was off. One time, at Oberlin, she'd fallen asleep in the middle of writing a paper, and she'd woken up with nearly five hundred pages of gibberish, the side effect of having her cheek pressed against the keyboard. Another time, she'd fallen asleep while holding a soda and spilled it on her laptop. She'd needed to get her dad to buy her a new one.

But no harm, no foul this time. She'd probably only been sleeping for ten minutes. It had been a terrifying week—no, ten days? Two weeks?—what with the spiders in Los Angeles and Delhi and the nuclear explosion in China and the general sense that things were totally out of control, but it had also been good in some ways. For one thing, she'd gotten a promotion. The word *associate* had been stripped away from her title of associate producer. And for another thing, while the horror was pretty horrible in a horrible sort of way, it was also a generic sort of horrible. From where she was, it was a bit like watching a movie. She didn't know anybody personally in Los Angeles or South Africa or China or Russia or anywhere else the spiders had invaded. It was all at a remove. Maybe if the spiders had come to Atlanta or erupted in Manhattan and eaten her dad, William Hughton Van Clief Pop-kins III—the name alone would have been a mouthful—and his new wife, Bitsy, a former yoga instructor, it would feel more real. As it stood, however, she discovered that she had a skill that some of the other producers lacked: she could put aside whatever fears she might have—though she really *was* strangely settled—and work her ass off.

Her boss, Don, had told her to go home and get some sleep, but she wanted to see the tape roll.

It had taken her close to a week to get the piece ready to go, but she was excited about it. Nobody had believed her, even Don, who was unreasonably supportive of her other work, but once she'd done the editing and showed them the reel, they all saw what she was talking about: the spiders hunted as a pack. They had a strategy.

She looked at the monitors that showed the live set and then glanced at her watch. Any second.

She smelled Don before she heard him. He'd started smoking again sometime in the past week.

"You ready?" he said.

"Polishing up my trophy case for the eventual Oscar."

He laughed and then stopped. "You're joking, right?" She nod-ded. "Okay, good. Sometimes I can't tell with you kids. You actu-ally had me worried for a second that you thought you could win an Oscar for news reporting."

"How about a raise?"

He shook his head. "You just got a promotion that came with a substantial raise, Teddie. Besides," he said, turning to look at the monitor, "let's see if we survive this thing. If we're all still alive in a month, sure. Whatever. You can have another raise."

"I still kind of think we should go with the other thing—"

Don shook his head. "No. The counting is enough. I'd like to think that despite everything, by which I mean working for a cable news network, I still have some journalistic integrity. We can't run something that's a complete hunch."

She was quiet, and he gave her a reassuring smile. He was a good guy and a good boss. "You think we'll all still be alive in a month?" she asked.

"I hope not," Don said. "Do you know how hard it's going to be for me to justify boosting your salary again so soon?"

"It's got to be over, don't you think? There hasn't been a report of a new brood hatching since Los Angeles went quiet."

"It's not a brood. Wrong word."

"Tell that to the anchors," she said.

"Yeah." He leaned against the corner of her desk to watch the monitors play the loop she'd made. "I'll get right on that. Here we go."

Desperation, California

F red groaned and threw his cards on the table. "I'm out," he said. "I give up. I cannot play one more game of Uno with you. It's torture. I thought this game was basically supposed to be pure luck. If it was poker, I'd at least understand how you keep winning, because you cheat when we play poker," he said, pointing at Gordo. "Oh, don't look so surprised, mister. I've seen you trying to sneak a look in the mirror so you can see what cards Amy's got."

Amy gave Gordo a hard look, and he offered up an embarrassed grin. All teeth. "If it makes you feel any better, baby," he said to his wife, "you're still up about nine hundred million dollars."

They'd taken to gambling in increments of a million dollars at a time. There hadn't really been a discussion of how they'd settle up when they got out of Fred and Shotgun's shelter; even at pennies on the dollar it was a lot of money. That is, if there was anything approximating money in the new world now that the shit had hit the fan. The good news, Gordo figured, was that all three men were in the hole to Amy, and he and Amy had a communal approach to money.

"I don't actively try to look at your cards," he said. "But sometimes you kind of . . ." He trailed off. It was clear from Amy's face that he wasn't helping himself.

Fred let out a huffy sigh. "Well, I've had my suspicions with Uno, but as far as I can tell, you aren't cheating. So why do I keep losing?" Fred stopped and held up his hand to his husband. Shotgun was standing nearby, his hands clasped behind his back, not part of the game but still opening his mouth to answer Fred. "Rhetorical question," Fred snapped. "But I'm done. I'm going to go get on the exercise bike."

Fred pushed his chair back and left the kitchen, followed quickly by Amy, who shot Gordo another dirty look.

"A little too much together time, huh?" Shotgun said.

Gordo laughed. "You could say that. I was a bit farty last night"— they'd had enchiladas for dinner, and the beans hadn't been cooked enough—"and she threatened to send me out as spider bait."

"I've been thinking about that," Shotgun said.

"About sending me out as spider bait?"

"No. About our dilemma."

"Which is . . . what, exactly?"

"Boredom," Shotgun said. "I'm afraid I did too good a job here." He waved his hand to indicate the kitchen, but Gordo knew that he meant the entire shelter. He also knew, immediately, that Shotgun was right.

Oh, there was plenty they *could* do. A catalogue of thousands of movies to watch, thousands of books to read. A fully stocked workshop. An exercise room with a spin bike and treadmill and free weights. There was even a squash court that Gordo hadn't known about. A squash court! But the only person who didn't seem to be bothered by being locked up in here was Claymore, who was, technically, not a person, but rather a chocolate lab.

Gordo reached down and gave Claymore's ear a scratch. The dog had four humans paying attention to him and digs big enough for him to run around like a maniac when it suited him. Shotgun had rigged up a tennis ball launcher and then trained Claymore to drop the ball into the hopper. The *whoomp* of the launcher flinging a ball down a hallway was always followed by the scrambling sound of Claymore's claws on the polished cement floor. No, Claymore was a happy dog. Fed and petted and exercised. What more was there?

For the four people, plenty. There had to be a sense of purpose. But they were just killing time. That was the heart of the matter. If Shotgun had started with a smaller budget or had been less thorough, it would have been better for them all. But Shotgun was a self-made man, rich as hell and analytical. An autodidactic engineer who'd built whatever he couldn't buy. The whole shelter—and to call it a shelter seemed silly, given the immensity of the space—was self-maintaining. Lights dimmed and turned on and off depending on who was in the room, the HVAC system kept the temperature at a comfortable seventy-two degrees during the day, and dropped it five degrees when they were sleeping. There were even sleek, disc-like automatic vacuums that scurried around the shelter sucking up dirt and dog hair. They barely had to worry about cleaning.

So the problem was that even though there were all sorts of things they *could* do, there really wasn't anything that they *had* to do.

"We're just sort of waiting," Gordo said.

Shotgun nodded. "Not a condition that the human race is well suited for. Hence *Waiting for Godot*."

"Never seen it."

Shotgun looked chagrined for a moment. An odd expression on such a tall, thin man. "Me neither. But you know what I mean. There's an absurdity. I don't know if you've noticed, but we've all been drinking. A lot. Fred, particularly, always seems to have a drink in his hand. I'm worried."

Gordo reached out and pulled all the Uno cards into a pile, carefully stacking them and sliding them back into the box. "And?"

"What do you mean, *and*?"

Gordo glanced up, trying not to smile. "And," he said, "I've known you long enough to know that you wouldn't be raising this topic if you didn't already have an idea how to solve it."

"Perhaps." His hands were still clasped behind his back. "I might just have a task for us to take on," Shotgun said. "At least for you and me. And maybe, eventually, Fred and Amy will get interested. An idea how we might keep ourselves busy."

"Just an idea?" Gordo asked. "Because I can't help but notice that your hands are clasped behind your back."

"You're an observant man."

"Well?"

A smile bloomed over his face. He put his hands in front of him and placed a small, metal cylinder on the table.

The metal was shiny and polished in some places, but still bore the rough, milled marks that told Gordo that Shotgun had fabricated the piece in the shelter's machine shop. The cylinder looked like a valve for a hose, the sort of thing you'd use to spray down kids with water on a hot summer afternoon. It was heftier, though, with a series of step filters and several drilled ports for airflow.

It took him a minute, but then he looked back at Shotgun to find him positively beaming.

"You know what it is?" Shotgun said.

"I do."

"And you know what it's for?"

"Self-defense," Gordo said. "I mean, seriously? What's cooler than a homemade flamethrower?"

Chicago, Illinois

It felt like he had eaten glass or something. Good lord, his stomach hurt. He couldn't stand it. Food poisoning. Had to be. The chicken at lunch must not have been cooked properly all the way through. That was it.

He rolled over on the rough cot. It wasn't comfortable, but he wasn't about to complain. He'd gotten out of Los Angeles by the skin of his teeth, and getting out was all that mattered. The entire high school gym was full of people like him. It was night, and the lights were off, but the gym was alive with the sound of a thousand refugees. It was better with the lights off. He didn't have to see the glassy stares of women who'd lost their children, of men looking for their wives, of children looking for anybody. And with the lights off, he could clutch at his stomach without having to hide it. It might be a simple case of food poisoning, but he didn't want to call attention to himself.

He'd seen what happened to people who garnered attention. When he'd gone through the final screening, right in front of him, a pregnant Korean lady had been yanked out of the screening area. The dogs had started barking and howling, and in less than thirty seconds a squad of hazmat-suited goons had scooped the lady up and put her in a van. Her husband had been in the adjacent screening area, and he'd started screaming and kicking and fighting with the guards until he'd been knocked out.

Start to finish, thirty seconds.

So when he went through the screening without causing a single whimper from the dogs, he mouthed a silent prayer.

Oh. Jesus. He curled in tighter on himself. It hurt so bad. He needed to see a doctor. Needed something. But he wasn't a dummy. Somebody had asked about the pregnant woman, and one of the soldiers said she was getting an extra screening, that she and her husband would be back in an hour or so. There were buses leaving all the time, to take the refugees on to Reno and from there to Denver, the soldier said, and the pregnant lady and her husband would just be on a later bus. No big deal, right?

Wrong. He wasn't stupid. The soldiers had everybody throw their clothes and possessions into Dumpsters, and the Dumpsters were then dragged away to a burn site. The soot and smoke hung greasy against the sky. The van with the pregnant lady had gone in the same direction. No way she was coming back.

The bus took him to an additional screening area in Reno, and once he'd passed through that, to the refugee center in Denver. First chance he'd gotten, he'd taken another bus on to Omaha, and then from Omaha to Chicago. Just as he figured, he didn't see the pregnant woman or her husband again, but he saw faces that looked familiar, a woman who had been lined up behind him, two men who looked like they were brothers.

Chicago turned out to be the end of the road as far as free buses and shelters went. So he was stuck in Chicago, and at least for now, stuck in this shelter, clutching at his stomach and trying not to groan. What else was he supposed to do? Where else could he go?

The wave of nausea shot through him again, and he could feel the shit gurgling in his intestines. It was like somebody had a hand inside him, twisting his gut.

He tried stretching out on his back, but that didn't give him any relief. The gymnasium was hot, and he was sweating. Why was it this hot in May?

National Institutes of Health, Bethesda, Maryland

Sergeant Faril, a large, muscular woman who'd been assigned as Melanie's personal bodyguard, woke her up by gently shaking her shoulder. Melanie didn't really think she needed a bodyguard—the NIH building was surrounded by military—but Manny and Steph had insisted. There were reports of riots across the country, the very clear beginnings of societal breakdowns. Sure, there were other scientists working on the spiders, but in the USA, she was the lead, and that meant she was suddenly a very important person. The kind of person who rated special protection. It was all very odd and seemed unnecessary, but it was also convenient, since Melanie had forgotten to set her alarm.

"Sorry, Dr. Guyer. It's time. You told me to make sure you were up by 0610."

Melanie groaned and threw her arm over her eyes. "I'm hitting the snooze button."

"For how long, ma'am?"

"Five minutes, okay?"

Melanie didn't know if she actually fell back to sleep or not, but when Sergeant Faril shook her arm again, at six fifteen on the dot, she knew she didn't have any more time to waste. She jumped in the shower and told Faril to call out the countdown in fifteen-second increments so she wouldn't linger. Two minutes of hot spray. Her bedroom was a repurposed hospital room, one floor down from where her lab had been set up, and though it had all the usual hospital charm, which meant none, it did have good water pressure. When Sergeant Faril told her that two minutes were up, Melanie was feeling vaguely human again. She'd twisted her hair up to keep it dry, so it took her barely a minute to dry off and slide on a clean—cleanish, really—pair of jeans and a T-shirt. Three minutes from getting into the shower to completely dressed? Not bad.

Sergeant Faril was by the window, staring out at the parking lot. "The president is here, ma'am."

Melanie nodded. No time to brush her teeth. She took a quick slug of mouthwash, spit it in the sink, wiped her face, unplugged the charger from her tablet, and headed out of the room. Julie Yoo was waiting outside the door with a coffee.

"Cream and sweetener," Julie said.

"I like it black."

Julie's smile dropped and she looked like a kicked puppy. "Sorry, I thought—"

"I'm kidding, Julie. Cream and sweetener is perfect. Just trying to keep things light." Melanie counted as they went down the hall and took the stairs: eleven uniformed and armed soldiers on this floor alone. Seriously? Why was it she needed Faril to watch over her?

"I'm a little nervous," Julie said, trotting beside her.

Fair enough, Melanie thought, as they came out the institute's front door. It looked like half a battalion was in the parking lot. Or something. She didn't actually know how big a battalion was. But there were a couple of tanks and a helicopter and at least two hundred men and women in camo milling around with M16s. Not to mention blue-suited Secret Service agents and a couple of limousines parked near a white canopy tent that stretched from the limos to a black rectangular trailer, so that the president could exit her ride without having to suffer any direct exposure to a sniper. Of all the possibilities, Melanie thought, the Secret Service was still worried about somebody with a rifle?

"Here?" she said to one of the young soldiers tasked with guarding the entrance. She couldn't get over how young they all looked. The body armor and machine guns made them look pumped up, bigger than they were, but underneath it all, they were baby-faced men and women, the same age as the undergraduates she'd been lecturing to barely two weeks earlier.

The soldiers parted so that she and Julie could go up the steps and into the trailer. Inside, the president and Manny and two uniformed men she didn't recognize were already seated at a long, thin conference table, chatting with doctors Dichtel, Haaf, and Nieder. It gave Melanie a little surge of irritation that the other scientists were there before her.

"Nice digs," she said. "Is it a double-wide?"

Steph nodded hello, and Manny stood up to peck her on the cheek. Steph looked tired, Melanie thought. No surprise.

"It's not elegant, but it works," Manny said. "We're shielded in here."

"Shielded? From what?"

He shrugged. "I don't know, actually. Conventional weapons and minor explosives, but more importantly, against listening devices, wireless equipment, and stuff like that. It's a black box. Literally, but also in the sense that it's a portable, secure area. One of the Secret Service's toys."

"Who, exactly, is going to be listening in?"

"Used to be the Russians, then the Chinese, but who knows."

"Seems like overkill," Melanie said.

Steph sighed. It wasn't loud, but Steph *was* the president, and it was enough to signal everybody to look at her. "Melanie," Steph said, "the black box is something the CIA and the NSA designed so I could meet with people without worrying about being overheard. It's designed specifically for important meetings outside the White House or other secure installations. But you know what? I've never actually been in here. Do you know why I've never actually been in this black box?"

Melanie shook her head, even though she knew Stephanie wasn't really waiting for a response.

"I've never been in this black box before because, as the president of the United States, I don't go to people for important briefings. They come to me. If I *do* go somewhere, it's the Capitol Building or an embassy or somewhere other than a parking lot in front of the National Institutes of Health. But here I am. I'm the leader of the most powerful country in the world, in the middle of a crisis, unlike any other crisis that has ever occurred in the history of humankind, wondering if the millions of people dead in Los Angeles and the tens of millions dead around the world is the worst of it or only just the beginning. I'm here because I need to know if what you said is true: Are these spiders getting ready to hatch again? I'm a busy woman, Melanie. But I'm here. I came to you. And why did I do that? Why did the most powerful woman in the world agree to come to you? Because right now you're the person who knows the most about these spiders, which means I might be the most powerful woman in the world, but you're the most *important* woman in the world. So when you called Manny and said you've figured some things out, and that no, this is not over, and this is, in fact, probably just the beginning, and you need to talk to me, the result is that I come to you. But it doesn't mean I don't have other things going on, Melanie, so as fascinating as this black box is, and as potentially unnecessary as this black box is, it's not what I'm interested in right now. You said you needed to talk. So talk."

Melanie talked.

Spiders, she began, are some of the oldest-known living things on earth. They've been evolving for more than four hundred million years. At that moment, there were upward of forty-two thousand known species around the world, and it was clear that these spiders, Swarm X, as she'd taken to calling them, were a distinct species. Nobody had ever seen anything like these spiders before.

"No shit," Manny said.

Melanie shook her head. "But we knew about them."

"That's impossible." This came from the man wearing a dress uniform decked out in medals. "How could we know about them? This was a total surprise."

Melanie stopped pacing and sat down. "We've been looking at this too simply. We need to think laterally here. Of course, if we'd known explicitly about this species, we would have tried to prepare. Spiders that can reproduce rapidly, that use humans as carriers for their eggs, that can strip a man to the bone in less than fifteen seconds, and hatch by the millions? Yeah, I'm guessing the government *might* have planned for that if we'd known ahead of time this was coming. Don't you guys have a contingency plan for an extraterrestrial invasion, for God's sake?"

"Seven," Manny said.

"What?"

"Seven, actually," he said. "Seven different contingency plans for extraterrestrial invasions, depending on what kind of aliens and how they announce themselves and, oh, whatever. It doesn't matter. Keep going."

"Okay, uh, I was joking about the alien thing, but the point is, the gentleman . . ." She pointed to the uniformed man who had spoken.

"Colonel Choi."

"Colonel Choi is right. If we'd known about these spiders in the way that he meant, we'd have tried to prepare for them. What I'm saying is that we knew about them without knowing about them. We knew they existed but only somewhere deep in our caveman brains. Think about it. Why are so many people afraid of spiders? There's a decent number of poisonous spiders, but the chances of a human dying from a spider bite are remote. More people are killed by cows than by spiders in the US every year. The daddy longlegs? Toxic as hell, but a daddy longlegs can't even bite a human.

"The reality is that the chances of a human getting killed or even harmed by a spider are so low that the meaningful number of poisonous spiders might as well be zero. And yet, most people are scared shitless of them. I think there's a reason for that. You see something creepy crawling out of the corner of your eye, and it's not your cell phone–talking, sushi-ordering, Internet-using brain responding. It's that little nugget of gray that is an evolutionary holdover from when we thought banging two rocks together was a scientific accomplishment. That's the part of your brain that's screaming."

She took a sip of her coffee and looked around the room. Julie had heard it already, and she'd talked most of it out with the other three scientists while working in the lab, but this was new to Manny and Steph and the two uniforms. "Near as we can tell, the Swarm X spiders have been a distinct species for at least two hundred million years."

"And in all that time," Colonel Choi said, "humans have never come across them?"

Melanie shook her head. "I don't think that's the case. Remember that what seems like a long time to us, one hundred years, five hundred years, one thousand years, is like the blink of an eye from an evolutionary perspective. It's quite possible humans have come across these spiders before, maybe a bunch of times. But it happened before there were records. Either the entire population of the region was wiped out without a trace, or whatever people were left had no way to create a warning we'd understand. If there'd been an outbreak like this in the last fifty, hundred, two hundred years, of course we'd have known about it. Even in the last thousand or two thousand years, say. But we need to take the longer view. We've got a different idea of history from Mother Earth. When I say these things evolved a long time ago, in a different world from what we have now, I mean a long, long time ago."

"But they wouldn't stop evolving," Choi persisted.

"Not entirely true. I'm not an evolutionary biologist"—she held her hand up to keep Choi quiet—"but even if you were going to make the argument that everything is still evolving, change can happen really slowly or really quickly. But the thing is, some species *do* stop evolving in any meaningful sense. Think about sharks. They're a prehistoric animal. On an academic level, yes, they are still evolving, but on a practical level, not so much. They've evolved as much as they need to."

Manny looked confused. "What do you mean, as much as they need to?"

One of the scientists, Laura Nieder, spoke up. She had the name and voice of a lifelong Brooklyn Jew, but her parents were both Cambodian, and she had, apparently, been born and raised in a small town in Georgia, before going to Princeton and then getting scooped up by the military. "Dr. Nieder. I'm with the Pentagon. I specialize in the weaponization of animal behaviors. What

Dr. Guyer means is that there's no point in sharks evolving any more than they already have. Pop culture aside, sharks don't really attack humans all that often, but there's a reason we're afraid of them. In the world that sharks inhabit, they are, in essence, the perfect killing machines. Any evolutionary changes would, at this point, probably be disadvantageous for them."

"This is where I come in," Will Dichtel said. "Dr. Dichtel. Harvard." Dichtel was a large man. Solid and blond, the kind of Norwegian farm stock that grows out in South Dakota and Nebraska. He'd mentioned more than once to Melanie that he'd come from the sort of family that would not be impressed that he was giving the president a briefing. He'd tell them the next time he went home for a visit, and they might nod and tell him that was good, but the talk would almost certainly turn to the weather and seeds and crop cycles. He was a smart guy, and had done some extraordinary work, and Melanie wondered how much of it had to do with showing his family that there was a life outside the prairie. "I do entomological toxicology," Dichtel said. "Basically, I study insect and arachnoid venom."

The president rubbed a hand over her face. "Are you kidding? These things are poisonous too?"

"Not exactly." Dichtel touched the keyboard in front of him and the monitors sprung to life, playing a series of images. A woman covered in spiders. A close-up of a brown recluse, visibly different from the Swarm X kind. A fly encased in a web. The remains of a human body, a trail of Swarm X spiders moving away. And more.

"There's two things going on here. First, the breeding spiders secrete an anesthetic as they are biting, so when you see one of them open up the skin like this"—the image froze on a spider partway through a slit on the back of a lab rat—"the victim doesn't even feel it. Zip, they're inside the host. The anesthetic has antibacterial properties and seems to foster extremely quick healing. By the time the anesthetic has worn off, the entrance wound has almost completely knitted itself up. The host is none the wiser. It's just a scab. It's really fascinating. Can you imagine what it would mean to be able to synthesize an anesthetic that also fostered increased healing?" Dichtel looked around the room, clearly expecting the others to be as excited as he was. It made Melanie smile. Scientists. Always losing sight of the big picture.

Dichtel cleared his throat. "Second, spiders don't chew. At least not in the way we fundamentally understand chewing. The classic image is an insect caught in a web, right? So there's basically two different ways spiders eat. They vomit digestive fluids onto their prey, chew up the flesh with their chelicerae, and then suck the liquefied meat and fluid into their mouths. Or, more rarely, they bite their prey and then inject their digestive fluid, so they can eat their prey from the inside out."

"That's disgusting," Manny said. He was grimacing, his eyes narrowed on the monitors. Melanie recognized the expression. It was how he watched scary scenes in movies.

Dichtel continued. "These spiders are a sort of hybrid. Their digestive fluids are incredibly powerful. Normally it takes some time for spiders, but with these, there's almost no waiting period. If you watch slowly"—he touched his keypad and the monitor showed a close-up, slow-motion video of spiders on the back of a goat—"you can see that the flesh is almost sloughing off as they eat it. They are, quite literally, dissolving their prey as they are chewing it."

It was a disturbing image, but Melanie had seen the footage over and over, in real time and on video, so she'd forgotten how disturbing it was until she heard retching. She turned to see the other uniformed man vomiting into a wastebasket. An aide whom she hadn't noticed standing in the corner stepped forward and took the wastebasket away.

Manny had his hands partially covering his eyes now. He didn't even seem to realize it. "Holy crap. So one of those things can just sort of melt you down and eat you?"

"No," Melanie said, standing back up. "That's the bright side of things, I guess. It takes a bunch of them. The Swarm X spiders—"

"A ridiculous term," Dr. Haaf said. "A group of spiders is a cluster or a clutter, not a swarm."

Melanie smiled. She liked Haaf, even if he did find it necessary to mention that he was at MIT about once an hour. Still, the man had no appetite for loose language.

"You're correct, Dr. Haaf," Melanie said, "but for our purposes, it will serve. As I was saying, the Swarm X spiders rely on overwhelming their prey. In theory, there's no real limit to the size of prey they could hunt. If they can take down humans as quickly as they do, there's nothing to say that if there was enough of them they couldn't go after something bigger. Which brings us back to the question of evolution."

Melanie looked around the room. Haaf and Nieder nodded at her, though Dichtel still seemed a little skeptical. Julie just shrugged. It made sense to the scientists, even if it sounded crazy.

"Remember how I said that these spiders have been around for at least two hundred million years? Well, that means they existed during the same time dinosaurs walked the earth."

She stopped. After a few seconds Manny spoke. "Wait. Let me get this right. Are you saying that these things . . . You're saying they hunted dinosaurs?"

"I admit, when you say it out loud it sounds kind of crazy."

"But? Maybe not so crazy?" Manny said. "Because I'm hearing a 'but' in your voice."

"Yeah. We think they may have evolved to hunt dinosaurs. That would explain a lot of their adaptations."

Julie Yoo spoke up. She'd been quiet, but she'd been the one to come up with the theory in the first place. As much as they wanted to argue against her, the other scientists hadn't been able to poke holes in it. "We think the Swarm X spiders may have been responsible for the extinction of the dinosaurs."

"Pardon me?" President Pilgrim looked aghast. "Dinosaurs? Are you shitting me?"

Colonel Choi leaned back in his chair. "Wasn't it a comet or something?"

"In theory, an asteroid," Julie said. "And this is just a theory, too. But it actually makes sense. The spiders wouldn't have had to kill all the dinosaurs. Just enough so they died out on their own."

"So how come there isn't any fossil record of these spiders?" Colonel Choi asked.

Melanie looked at him. Huh. Not as stupid as she thought. Maybe he *was* here for a reason. "Good question."

"And?"

"And, that's it. Good question. It's actually a really good question, and I'll add it to the list of questions, because right now we have a thousand questions for every answer we may have come up with. The short answer is probably, we don't know. Maybe there is a fossil record, but we just didn't understand it."

"Melanie," Steph said, "can you cut to the chase here? What do you know?"

"Did you see the thing on CNN last night?"

Steph and Manny and the two uniformed men looked blankly at Melanie.

"They ran a story that analyzed the footage of people being attacked in Delhi, Los Angeles, Japan, anywhere there were cameras.

I want, no, I *need* to talk to whoever figured it out"—Manny took a note—"because they found the pattern. It looked like the spiders ate everything in their path, right? But they didn't. It was just the utter fucking chaos. One in five."

"One in five what?" Steph asked.

"One in five people survived."

Choi addressed the man next to him. "So we can expect civilian survival rates of twenty percent. We've been modeling ten percent, right?"

"No, you don't understand," Melanie said. "These spiders have been around for two hundred million years, and we are sure that leaving one out of five isn't new behavior."

"So why," Manny asked, "are they doing it? Clearly they could just eat everything in their path. What's the point of leaving one out of five people alone?"

Melanie felt sick. She and Julie and the scientists had talked about this, and it all made sense, but they'd discussed it in the way that scientists can in the lab, divorced from the reality of the consequences. It was another thing to say it aloud. The spiders cared about only two things: feeding and breeding. Those one in five people were kept alive to either carry eggs or be the next wave's lunch.

"I might be off on the numbers. You have to understand, they're not leaving one in five people *alone*," Melanie said. "One in five people *survived*, which isn't the same thing."

"What are you talking about, Mel?"

"What I'm talking about, Manny, is that the spiders were like some sort of giant tidal wave, washing over everything in their path. A tsunami. And at first look we think, how could anybody survive that? And then we realize some people did survive. Five percent, ten percent, twenty percent, we think that's the only number that matters, but it isn't. This isn't about surviving the first wave. It's never been about surviving the first wave. Right now, it looks like they are leaving one in five people *alive*. Not *alone*. Alive and alone aren't the same thing."

She touched her tablet to display a picture of the inside of the Staples Center, the familiar chalky-white egg sacs under the artificial lights of the stadium.

"That's taken care of," Choi said. "Burned out."

"So there's this site and how many other sites in Los Angeles, so far?"

Choi leaned back to grab a tablet from his aide. "We're up to five hundred and seventeen confirmed infestation sites, but the Staples Center was the largest. We've been burning the rest of them as quickly as we can. Last count, we've already taken care of one hundred and eighty. Nearly thirty-five percent so far. Some of the smaller sites have just a dozen sacs or so. We're trying to figure out if we can just clean those up with flamethrowers."

Melanie shook her head. "Reprioritize."

"Pardon me?"

"Reprioritize. It's not about the size of the infestation. It's about the egg sacs themselves. If they're active, those need to be taken care of immediately."

"Active? What do you mean?"

"Sticky or warm. Some of them look more classically like what you'd think of as cobwebs. If they feel sticky or warm to the touch, and particularly if they're making a sort of rattling or buzzing noise. Those are the immediate threat. I think we can expect those to be hatching soon."

"How soon?" Choi asked.

"Maybe right this second, maybe in a couple of days. But take care of those first. The other egg sacs, the ones that are hard and almost dusty, that are chalk-white instead of the slightly creamy tinge of the fresh-looking ones, those can be taken care of *after* the fresh ones."

Choi turned to his aide, nodded, and the aide booked it out of the room.

"But it doesn't matter," Melanie said. "Not really. The trouble is you can burn out all the infestation sites you find, but no matter how much you scour Los Angeles, you'll never get them all, because some egg sacs are mobile."

Manny leaned forward. "What do you mean *mobile*? You're talking about the spiders breeding inside people? We know that. You were the one who suggested doing visual screenings, looking for entry points, any sign that people had been cut open by a spider. The checkpoints outside Los Angeles are all using visual screenings, and we've had really good luck with dogs, too. We're catching them. The checkpoints flag anybody who is infested."

Melanie shook her head. "What are your numbers? How many people are you pulling out?"

"I don't have the exact number in front of me, but it's low. Nowhere near as bad as we were afraid of. Maybe one out of every five thousand refugees. The dogs have been a godsend. They lose their shit when somebody who's infested comes through."

Manny stopped talking and stared at Melanie.

She just shook her head.

"Oh shit," he said. He suddenly looked miserable. "How off are we?"

"Best guess?" Melanie said. "Ten percent infection rates."

"As in ten percent of the people who made it through the attacks in Los Angles are carrying egg sacs inside their bodies?"

"The functional number is going to be less," Melanie said, "because there are going to be a lot of survivors who had no contact with the spiders whatsoever, people who were outside the swarm zones. But, essentially, yes. Of the people who had direct, physical contact and who made it out alive? Ten percent. One in ten of those people passing through the checkpoints, best guess, are carrying spider eggs inside them."

Manny said, "And we've been letting them through?"

The room was quiet for a few beats.

Then Steph said, "They're out there, then. It's too late. Containment isn't an option." She turned to Melanie and asked the question Melanie had been waiting for.

"How long do we have?"

"At best?" Melanie said. "My guess is that they all hatch at once. That's what happened with the first wave. Again, it's like cicadas. There's some sort of mechanism that controls when they emerge, and I think it's probably a good bet that the second wave, when it hatches, is going to come in one giant swell. So, best-case scenario, maybe another week. But keep in mind, and I know I keep saying this: we're working with really incomplete information. I'm basing that best-case scenario on what I know about the first swarm, and we really don't know enough. I think there is a very small chance it could be longer, and an infinitesimally small chance that they never hatch at all. But I think best-case scenario, which is really a guess, is a week."

Steph stared at her. "A week, at best. Okay. And, at worst?"

"At worst? At worst, it's already too late. They're ready to hatch, maybe even hatching as we speak."

Melanie could hear Steph, Manny, and the military people suck in their breaths. Which made this part even less pleasant.

"I don't think that's the really bad news, though," Melanie said.

She touched her tablet again and sent a photo to the monitors. She knew that, at first glance, it looked like any other egg sac, oval and pointed at one end. At second glance, however, it was clear that the scale was off. The photo wasn't particularly high quality and the lighting was bad. But it was *not* the same as the others. The egg sac was huge, at least three or four times larger than the others, and even with the dim lighting and the grainy quality of the photo, it looked almost gelatinous.

"This is from Delhi," she said. "I haven't seen the pictures yet, but supposedly the Koreans have found something similar. Or maybe even bigger."

She paused and looked around the room. "I think it's safe to say that whenever this next group of spiders hatches, we're in for something different."

Stephanie stood up, leaning in so she could get a closer look at the monitor. "Different how, exactly, Melanie?"

"I don't know," Melanie said. "But it's hard to imagine that it's going to turn out to be good news."

Hanalei Bay, Kauai, Hawaii

Florence turned off the television and looked out the front window. She could see her nephews on the beach already, digging in the sand. They were shockingly obedient boys, six and nine, wearing baseball caps to keep the sun off their faces, wearing rash guards to keep the sun off their plastic-smooth arms and backs. She'd get some more coffee and go join them. Such a simple pleasure, digging holes in the sand and waiting for the waves to come and wash them away. The smell of the saltwater mist drifted through the screens, and the gentle swell of the waves was a soundtrack to the morning. The boys still hadn't adjusted to the time change, so they were up at what might have been an unbearably early hour for other people, but both Florence and her sister had always been early risers. And it was a peaceful start to the day, particularly on a morning like this, when the waves weren't coming in with enough vigor to draw out the surfers yet. The ocean was unusually gentle in front of the rental house today. There was nothing to see but her nephews, the water, and the wisps of cotton-candy clouds that seemed like they were hanging in the sky just to make the view even more beautiful. Florence honestly couldn't remember the last time she'd been so happy.

She spent a lot of time complaining to her friends about her shitty luck, how life wasn't fair. She was thirty-seven and athletic. Good-looking. At least a seven or eight on a scale of one to ten, with long legs and bright blue eyes. And while she wouldn't have described herself as rich to somebody else, that was only because she thought it sounded tacky. She'd been very successful. Maybe she wasn't private-jet rich, but she was rent-a-house-on-the-beach-so-she-and-her-sister's-family-could-take-a-vacation-in-Hawaii-and-have-all-of-them-fly-first-class-without-putting-much-thought-into-it rich. Which was, when all was said and done, rich. She owned a marketing firm. She'd started the company a decade ago, and for the first two years it had been just her, and then, for two more years, she had a few employees and could call herself boutique, but boutique had gone by the wayside a while ago. She'd just hired her sixty-third employee. Good-looking and rich and *fun*, she thought. If she preferred the theater and chamber music, she was also more than willing to head to the Cineplex to watch a superhero movie or to a bar to hear a band that didn't understand the concept of sonic moderation. She'd do karaoke and go bowling, she'd hike and bike and kayak, and she could fake a passing interest in most major sports. Florence was smart and funny and if she wasn't up for absolutely everything in bed, she was at least reasonably interested in sex. So why was it that with all these things in her favor, she didn't have a husband, didn't have kids? She should have been a catch. She loved her nephews, but those should have been her kids out there playing on the beach. It wasn't fair.

The part of her that still remembered the women's studies classes she took at college hated it when she thought like that. She had all these other things to keep her happy. A good career, good friends, a loving extended family. Why did she yearn for a husband

and kids? Still, all her good friends, all of them, to a one, were married now and starting families. They had a toddler holding their hands, sleeping babies against their breasts, matchbox houses with neatly clipped yards and husbands gone slightly to paunch. The unfairness of it all made Florence want to cry. She knew women who were truly happy in their childlessness—partnered and single women alike—but she wasn't one of them. Her deep dark secret was that she just wasn't happy in her singlehood no matter how much she should have been as a modern feminist. She'd always, *always*, been that girl fantasizing about a wedding and kids.

So when she went out with her friends, even though she knew they'd heard it all before and were tired of it, she would end up complaining about how it wasn't fair, that she didn't understand why she'd never been able to meet the right guy. She wasn't jealous of her sister, but she was confused. How was it that her sister, Lynn, who'd never worked a day in her life, who was nowhere near as pretty as Florence, had managed to snag a guy like Grant while she was still in her early twenties, and then, like it was no big deal, pop out two little boys?

Her friends always went through the motions. It's hard, they'd say. Guys are jerks. She'd done all the right things, they agreed, and she deserved a good guy who'd make her happy and help her churn out a couple of munchkins before she hit forty. They'd sympathize and empathize, and after a little while they'd start encouraging her. You're so pretty, they'd say. You're rich. Luck, they'd say, is a fickle thing, and you're due for something to go your way in the guy department. Thirty-seven is young. It's not too late.

But, Florence thought, as she looked out over the beach, it was probably too late now. The timing might be just a little bit off to meet a guy and start a family.

What with the spiders and everything.

For once, however, she wasn't cursing her luck. Sure. No husband, no kids. But it could be a lot worse. She could have been
eaten by spiders. Right now, being an aunt seemed plenty good
enough. And there hadn't been a single confirmed outbreak on any
of the Hawaiian Islands, which seemed like a miracle. And given
that they were on Kauai, one of the smaller islands, looking out at
Hanalei Bay, which was literally almost the end of the road that
went most of the way around the island, she figured there probably wasn't a better place they could be. At first, of course, they'd
all been annoyed when they'd packed up and gone to the airport
and gotten there only to find that President Pilgrim had ordered
the airlines to stop flying anywhere, but it had seemed like pretty
great luck in short order. It made her feel unsettled that the owners
of the rental house, who lived in Los Angeles, hadn't responded to
her e-mails or attempts to phone, but Florence was able to set that
unease aside. Nobody else had shown up to claim the rental house,
and she was happy to pay for the extra time they were staying. At
times, Lynn and Grant were anxious about getting back to Seattle,
but they'd mostly settled into the rhythm of their semipermanent
vacation. It helped, of course, that while the rest of the world was
freaking out, Florence had kept them busy. They'd gone hiking
and taken surfing lessons. The boys were getting pretty confident
on their scaled-down rental boards. They'd chartered a fishing
boat one of the days, and she and Lynn went grocery shopping
on a regular basis. That, actually, was becoming a concern. The
shelves of the grocery store were starting to look almost bereft,
and last time they'd gone there'd been a police officer there, limit-
ing what people could by, but they'd stocked up when things had
first gone to hell. Florence couldn't believe that this crisis would
last more than a few more weeks. They might run out of gourmet
coffee and frozen chicken fingers for the boys, but they weren't,

by any stretch of Florence's imagination, going to go hungry. Yes, for sure, Grant and Lynn spent a few hours every day watching the news on television or checking their phones, and yes, Lynn had burst into tears a couple of times, but mostly it had been fun. For the boys, it was an adventure with the added bonus that they got to miss even more school than originally planned, and whatever limitations their parents and Florence had originally put on them had been stripped away. Just yesterday, Florence had taken them into Lihue and bought the biggest television they could find to put in their bedroom in the vacation house, so they could watch cartoons while the adults were watching the news. Today, Florence had promised to buy them their very own surfboards. They'd gotten good enough—and the trip was now long enough—that rentals seemed kind of silly. As long as credit card terminals kept working, they were in good shape.

Florence rubbed some suntan lotion on her legs and arms, grabbed the wide-brimmed straw hat that she thought of as her "Julia Roberts hat," and headed out the door to join the boys on the beach. Maybe she'd let them bury her in the sand.

Hanalei Bay wasn't the worst place in the world to be right now.

Shinjin Prefecture, Japan

The worst place in the world to be right now, Koji thought, was here. He was wearing what the other scientists were calling, aspirationally, an "isolation suit." Isolation, as in Koji isolated inside, spiders, hopefully, isolated outside. But it felt pretty flimsy. It wouldn't stop a knife, let alone these things. He'd seen the video of the three men who'd tried going in without an "isolation suit." That had not been a success. He was not thrilled to be the fourth man in, "isolation suit" or not.

He could have been on vacation, instead. In Hawaii. He was *supposed* to be on vacation, in fact. His wife had booked the tickets months ago and arranged to rent a condo a ten-minute walk from the beach. If she had planned their vacation to start only a couple of days earlier, he might have been on the beach at this very minute, the sand warm beneath his toes. But no. Instead, he was tiptoeing through an old Buddhist temple full of egg sacs.

Somewhere out in the sticks. A prefecture he'd barely heard of. A rural village so small it didn't have a name. Or rather, its name was a bastardization of the closest village to it, which was named after a local river, so that the name of this particular village meant, literally, "up the hill from that other village that was named after a river." It was ridiculous. Half the team was still working out of the university, but the other half had been flown here. Helicopters and soldiers and a weird display of military tribalism that made him very uncomfortable.

The temple itself had been cordoned off, with fencing and yellow tape, and was under guard. All completely useless in the event that these egg sacs hatched. Which was why he was inside the temple. To make sure none of these sacs were going to hatch.

Whee.

Koji pointed the flashlight to his left. He knew the team was recording everything. There were omnidirectional cameras on his helmet, rigged so that the scientists back in the other village—the one named after the local river from which this pissy, tiny village took its own name—could see whatever he saw and then some. Thermal and radiation cameras too. But they still needed some idiot to walk in and do the recording.

Couldn't that idiot be a robot? No, they'd decided. Too much risk of it accidently causing damage, which might lead to the egg sacs hatching. Couldn't that idiot be a soldier? No, because a soldier wouldn't know what to look for.

No. That idiot had to be Koji. And it was his own damn fault. He'd been the one who'd argued so vociferously that a robot was a bad idea, and that a soldier was a bad idea too. He was the one who'd argued the loudest that it needed to be a scientist in here, that *only* a scientist would know what to look for. Not really thinking through what that actually meant. So, of course, when it came time for a scientist to volunteer, everybody looked at him. There was no choice but for him to say he'd be the one to do it. Westerners thought the Japanese were about honor and saving face and all that sort of crap. Every time Koji hung out with English scientists he'd try to disabuse them of the notion. Maybe for older generations, like his father and his grandfather it was that way, but it's different now. They're modern. But when all the other scientists looked at him, Koji was too embarrassed to do anything other than volunteer.

And now that he was in the temple? Now that he was shining his beam of light on the egg sacs, stepping carefully, oh so carefully? Now that he'd won his own argument and was actually the set of scientific eyes inside the temple? Well, now he had no idea what he was looking for. Or, rather, he had only the tiniest bit of an idea. He'd seen the photo from India of the oversized, distended egg sac with the disturbingly gelatinous sheen, and he'd read the reports from Korea. The measurements they sent seemed suspiciously like they were missing a decimal point.

The sound of the respirator was a little disturbing. Like Darth Vader. The idea of a breathing apparatus seemed silly before he went in—this wasn't Mars! This wasn't a mile beneath the surface of the ocean! He could breathe just fine!—but now he was glad for the helmet's glass faceplate. He knew that the thick rubber of the suit couldn't possibly be a match for these monsters, but it was, in the tiniest possible way, a little bit reassuring to have this small barrier between him and the room. The problem was that the suit was hot. He'd been in it for less than five minutes, and already he could feel himself sweating, rivulets of salt and liquid sliding down from his temples, behind his ears and gathering in the small of his back. He was so hot inside the suit and the connected helmet that the glass faceplate was fogging over. If it got much worse, he didn't think he'd be able to see through the faceplate at all. Which was fabulous. Exactly what he wanted: to be walking blind in the middle of this monster-movie set.

It was already hard enough to see inside the temple. Some genius had cut the power in case the electrical frequencies, the hum of the wires running through the temple, might accelerate the growth of the spiders or perhaps enrage them. There wasn't any real evidence of this, but there was no real reason not to cut the power, so somebody somewhere had flipped a breaker, and that left Koji wandering through the dark temple relying on a flashlight to see. Of course, nobody had thought to point out that Koji himself would be wired for sight and sound, so if the spiders reacted poorly to electronics . . .

The main room was larger than he'd expected. He'd seen the drawings and measurements and looked at the early video footage and photographs from the first people who had tried going into the building—and the way those videos ended was always disturbing—but now, with dust motes flitting nervously in the miserly streams of light that gleamed in thinly through the clerestory windows, Koji understood that the relative size of the building didn't matter. It didn't matter if the size of the main room was comparable to a football stadium or a basketball court or a tennis court, or that, in truth, it wasn't even big enough to accurately be compared to any sporting venue. What mattered was that it was big enough so that if he shone his flashlight in one direction, great swaths of the room around him were still in shadow and darkness. What mattered was that the room was large enough so that he couldn't see everything around him. Couldn't they have just put in some more windows whenever it was they'd updated the temple for power and water?

He looked down at the thick sausage fingers of his glove and squeezed a little tighter around the handle of the flashlight. He couldn't really feel the metal tube, which was unsettling. It had never occurred to him how much holding something required tactile feedback from your body. Your skin telling you, yes, we are touching this metal, and your muscles and nerves telling your brain, yes, we are squeezing this hard enough. Probably squeezing harder than necessary, he thought, but with the gloves on, better squeezing too hard than accidently dropping the flashlight. He didn't like the idea of scrambling around on the ground chasing after it.

The fog on his face mask was about a third of the way down now, low enough to start getting in the way of what he could see. He tried to wipe at the glass with his free hand. His stupid, meat-thick gloved fingers squeaked uselessly across the glass. Of course. It was fogging up from the inside. The issue wasn't the room, but rather the temperature difference between inside the suit and out. All he had to do was take off his helmet and wipe the glass from the inside.

He chuckled. Not a problem! Why wouldn't he take his helmet off while inching his way through a room full of egg sacs containing hundreds of thousands of murderous spiders? Why would it matter that it took two different technicians to get him securely into his suit? Why, sure, he'd just pop that helmet off and wipe the visor clean!

"Koji, did you say something?"

Even with the headset and a throat mike and the cameras all wired with microphones, they'd agreed to try not to communicate unless absolutely necessary. The same argument that had necessitated cutting the power to the building could be made for radio communications: Who knew what might wake the sleeping beasts? They were going to stay quiet if they could.

"No," he whispered. "Now shut up." Assholes. Sitting in their comfortable, air-conditioned command center down the hill, across the river, in the slightly less provincial village. Oh, Koji, you're so brave, we're so proud of you, but no, we don't really want to volunteer in your place. He wished his wife were in the command center so that she could see what he was doing. She often made passive-aggressive comments at parties about how boring Koji's job was, about how nobody wanted to listen to the work stories of an entomologist. Well, how boring was his job now?

He wanted to vomit. Ugh. That would be unpleasant inside this hot suit. He swallowed hard.

He took another step and then swept the flashlight from one side of his body all the way to the other, covering an arc of one hundred and twenty degrees or so. A wide cone of what lay before him. He tilted the flashlight up. With the fog on his mask, he had to lean his head back to see the egg sacs laced into the rafters above him. They were such foreign-looking things and yet familiar at the same time. Loose cobweb strands hung down, drifting lazily in the air. He couldn't feel it inside his suit, but there must have been a slight breeze moving through the temple. He looked back down. There didn't seem to be a pattern to the way the egg sacs were deposited. They were globbed in the rafters, sewn against the walls, and stacked on the wooden floor. In places, the sacs were piled so high they almost reached the ones in the rafters yet much of the floor was clear. He had to be careful where he stepped, and the path wasn't straight—Koji found himself breathing hard inside the suit as he sometimes had to take four steps sideways and three steps back to move one step forward—but it was possible for him to pick his way to the far side of the room. That's what he and the other scientists were interested in. The far side of the room. Because there, behind stacks of egg sacs that were easily as tall as he was, there was something giving off a light of its own.

What had he been thinking, arguing against a robot with a camera, or even using one of those fiber optic cable cameras that detectives used in every television show? It looked so easy in the movies, didn't it? Cops could slide a cable underneath a door or through an air vent and have perfect clarity. Why couldn't they have done that here, snaking one through the piles of egg sacs? Or a little toy helicopter! Couldn't they have just flown one of those in, watched from relative safety? But they couldn't. Not according to Koji. Oh, no, Koji had to open his big mouth and blah, blah, blah, and now Koji found himself trying to work his way through this deadly maze.

The isolation suit was a weird mix of high and low tech. The specialists had actually finished off the whole procedure of getting him into the suit by wrapping duct tape around the seams where his gloves and boots met the suit. But then, also, inside the glass visor, low and on the right, a digital heads-up display projected how long he'd been in the suit, how much air he had left, and another number that nobody had bothered to explain to him. What mattered was that he had plenty of air. He turned his head left and took a sip from the rubber straw. The water was already lukewarm and slightly brackish. But he was seriously sweating now and even a little out of breath. That's probably why the faceplate was fogging so badly. Maybe if he could get his breath under control?

As he was thinking this, he brushed past a pyramid of egg sacs and heard a loud, crystalline crunching sound. He froze in horror.

"Koji?"

"Shut the fuck up, okay?" he hissed. Who knew if the spiders could hear or if they reacted to radio waves or microwaves or electrical pulses or anything other than the presence of human flesh? Also, who gave a shit? Having them yammering in his ear wasn't something he needed at that second.

He pointed the flashlight at the ground. There. Under his boot. He hadn't even felt it. If he hadn't heard the sole of his boot grinding the web of the egg sac, the glass-snapping sound of spiders being broken under his foot, he might not have noticed. But under the glare of the flashlight, it was obvious that he'd stepped on an egg sac. There was larval goo leaking out the edges, and he saw dozens, perhaps hundreds of pieces of black thread—legs—poking out. Oh. Oh. No. Was one of those black threads moving?

He waited. And waited. He silently counted to one hundred. Nothing.

"Koji?"

"Stepped on an egg sac," he whispered.

"Be careful."

"Go fuck yourself."

"There's no need for that language."

"Are you the one in this fucking suit?" he hissed. "I hope spiders come out of your rectum, asshole."

The radio went quiet for a moment. And then, gently, the voice said, "Keep going, please."

It made him feel better to think of the horrible things he wanted to keep saying in response, but he stayed quiet and moved forward. Step, by step, by step, each one closer to the glowing corner. It wasn't a bright light. It was more like the moon through thin clouds on a summer night. Silvery and filtered and almost soothing.

And then he cleared the last pile of egg sacs.

He swallowed the scream before it could come out as anything other than a weak bark. Because of the cameras mounted on his helmet, the scientists monitoring back in the village had the same view he did. Thankfully, they stayed quiet.

Apparently, the Koreans had not, in fact, misplaced a decimal in their measurements.

In front of him, the glowing light came from a singular, giant egg sac. It was the size of a pickup truck. Ten men could easily have fit inside the silk cocoon. It was pulsing, almost like it was breathing, and now that he was closer Koji could see that the light pulsed too. He couldn't see what was inside the egg sac, but that wasn't what terrified him. What made him want to scream, what made him want to vomit inside his isolation suit, was what was *outside* the sac: spiders. Thousands of them. Some of them were black, and some were red-striped spiders, but all of them were skittering up and around the giant egg sac, crawling on the normal-sized sacs arrayed in piles and columns and hanging from the ceiling above. The rest of the room had been quiet, a cemetery made of egg sacs instead of tombstones, but here, in the corner, surrounding this giant pulsing embryo, there was life.

He stayed as still as he could, knowing that the scientists back in the village could see all of it. They could hear it too, because Koji realized the quiet of the temple was an illusion. The sound had been dulled by the rubber suit and the helmet, but it was there. A soft, skittering drag of eight legs across spider silk, eight legs moving over the wooden floorboards, eight legs crawling into the rafters above him.

Above him.

He tried to look up, but his visor was so fogged now that there was only one small, coin-sized area of clear glass near his chin. He couldn't see what was above him.

"Koji," the radio said. "Koji, get closer. We need to see what's in the egg sac."

The spiders moved around and past him. He had to keep his head tilted back to look through the unfogged circle. He saw a spider crawling up the leg of his suit. He didn't move. He just breathed in and out, watching the spider—and another, and another—moving over the orange rubber. He kept waiting for something to happen. For the spiders to swarm over him. For one of the spiders to start tearing through the rubber. For the small, clear circle of glass to fog over like the rest of his visor. Miraculously, none of these things happened.

"Koji," the radio said again. "Move forward."

Somehow, despite himself, Koji did.

Forward Checkpoint, Greater Los Angeles Quarantine Zone, California

The army wasn't entirely stupid.

Sure, this wasn't the same kind of operation that Lance Corporal Kim Bock and her squad had trained for, but they had scout teams and surveillance in place. They had a good fifteen minutes' warning after the first part of the convoy—minivans and sedans, pickup trucks and SUVs—blew through the outer cordon to be ready for them.

Kim's entire platoon had been sacked out one second, and the next, they were awakened under orders to scramble, the sound of blaring sirens getting their attention. There weren't that many places the convoy of civilians could come through, so by the time the first car came into range, a blue Ford Focus, every goddamned Marine from a mile around had their safeties off and was ready to fire.

It was a bloodbath.

Hundreds of civilian vehicles trying to rush the fence, tires spinning, and then turning to fire and melted rubber as Kim and the Marines around her lit them up, dancing the vehicles off the road like tin cans. M16s and .50 cals and at least one Abrams tank getting in on the action. Despite how many cars were rushing the line, it was no contest. The Marines had pulled in every available unit and outnumbered the civilians. Maybe if they'd only been using rifles, a few cars would have slipped through, but they were firing heavy guns, the kind of weapons that could put bullets through engine blocks, leave cars looking mangled.

When the firing stopped, the tip of the .50 cal on the JLTV was glowing red.

She realized she was crying. This wasn't what she'd signed up for.

"It ain't right," Mitts said, speaking for all of them.

"What the hell were they thinking?" Elroy said. "Why now? There aren't any spiders chasing them."

Kim wiped her eyes. She noticed that Honky Joe was staring out at the burning wrecks of cars and trucks, looking grim. Teams of medics and other squads were already moving out, looking for survivors, but Honky Joe was just staring. "What?" she asked.

"Look at the cars."

"I don't want to look," she said. But she did anyway. "What is it you want me to see?"

"They've all got one driver—and only one driver—in each car. No passengers," Honky Joe said. "They knew we were going to light them up. This wasn't a real attempt to get through the fence. These people weren't desperate. This wasn't a move of last resort. This was deliberate. Somebody thought this up. They came here ready to sacrifice themselves. This was a suicide mission. A distraction."

He shook his head. "We got played."

Highway 10, California

"**W**ell, that was easier than I thought it would be," Macer said, staring out the window at the passing scenery.

He was sitting next to Bobby in the back of a black Audi A7. Up front, driving, Lita had the car humming along at close to one hundred miles per hour. It was a smooth ride. When Macer had told him the plan, Bobby had figured they'd be in a pickup truck or something suitably semi-militaristic, the sort of vehicle you could easily imagine in a postapocalyptic road movie, but Macer had preferred a certain level of luxury. "It's not like the owner will miss it," he'd said.

Fair enough. In the ashes of the spider invasion of Los Angeles, there had been so many vehicles just abandoned that there really was no reason to settle for anything less than leather seats. Plus, Macer had said, "If it comes to that, would you rather be in something designed to haul boxes or in a vehicle designed to haul ass?"

The plan had worked so well that Bobby could barely believe it. Supposedly, if you were willing to strip naked and subject yourself to inspection—and possible immolation—you could pass through a government checkpoint and leave the quarantine zone, but that seemed more like a myth than a real option. No, to get out required ingenuity, which Macer had in spades. It was simple, really: have a couple hundred volunteers run a feint at the main choke-point, wait for other troops to be called in as reinforcements, and then drive like hell through one of the more minor checkpoints.

It had been forty minutes since they'd gone through the fence, and Bobby kept expecting to hear a helicopter gunship overhead, kept bracing himself for the car to explode into a ball of flame. But Macer seemed relaxed, just looking out the window. They zipped past several burned-out hulls of cars. Lita was really cruising. Oh well, Bobby thought, a speeding ticket wasn't at the top of his list of worries.

Bobby had been skeptical of Macer's plan, but he'd admitted that he didn't have a better idea of how to get out of the quarantine zone. After their little pep rally, it had been surprisingly easy to find a few hundred volunteers willing to drive their cars and trucks, in unison, directly at the main chokepoint set up by the army. All Macer—or, rather, the Prophet Bobby Higgs—had to do was promise that the family of every volunteer would get guaranteed safe passage in the main caravan. There were a lot of crying husbands and wives and children, but it turned out Bobby was right to have faith in humanity: people were surprisingly willing to sacrifice themselves so that their loved ones could live.

And when those hundreds of volunteers attacked the checkpoint, it happened just as Macer predicted: the army overreacted, pulling their troops away from the secondary roads. Bobby and Macer and the rest of their followers had been able to breeze right past. Sure, there'd been a few casualties—the pilgrims in Macer's convoy who took the point had to face the skeleton crew of Marines left to man the barricade—but the rest of them were through the fence and on the open road fast enough that it was oddly anti-climactic. The hardest part, honestly, was the first ten minutes past the fence, once they'd broken through but all the vehicles were still clustered together, thousands of cars full of US citizens fleeing the government.

Bobby knew he should feel bad about sacrificing so many people, but in the scheme of things, it was such a small number. What did it matter that a few hundred more sheep were fed to the wolves when millions had already died? It was certainly worth it if it meant he was no longer trapped in Los Angeles, just waiting for the spiders to return. That was worth any cost. And besides, he'd done something truly noble. He *had* rescued thousands of trapped people. The drivers who had sacrificed themselves for the diversion had done so willingly. They were heroes. *He* was a hero. He was the reason why the long line of cars behind them was able to drive away from Los Angeles, from those horrifying spiders. He'd delivered his flock to safety, he thought.

And then he felt the car start to slow. Lita pulled to the side of the road and stopped.

"What are you doing?" he asked.

"Get out, Bobby," Macer said.

Bobby turned to give Macer a harsh word, but then noticed that Macer was pointing what looked like a gun at him. Small, black, sinister, and very much shaped like a gun. Ergo, it was, actually, a gun.

"What the hell, Macer?"

"I'm not going to ask again, Bobby," Macer said. "Out of the car."

So Bobby got out of the car and stood on the side of the road. Macer waved the gun at him, motioning for him to back up, so he took a few more steps back. Two cars and an SUV barreled past, probably moving close to a hundred miles an hour themselves. Macer reached out with his free hand to close the door, and Bobby couldn't help himself. "But why, Macer? Why?" He could hear how whiny his voice sounded.

For a moment, Bobby thought Macer was going to just close the door and have Lita drive away without giving him an answer, but then Macer rolled the window down. He was still pointing the gun at Bobby.

"Why? Did you really believe I was interested in some sort of religious revolution, Bobby? Did you really think I wanted anything other than to get out of Los Angeles?" Macer looked at him, then laughed. "My god. You really started thinking of yourself as some sort of savior, didn't you? You bought into it."

Macer closed the window and Lita hit the gas, but Bobby thought he could still hear the acid of Macer's laughter even after the car was out of sight.

He stood on the side of Highway 10. The sun felt like a hammer after the comfort of riding in the Audi, and he was suddenly very thirsty. There had been a cooler full of ice and water and soda inside the car. He looked down the highway. A black sedan blew past him, trailing a cloud of dust that made him cough, followed by a pickup and a couple more cars.

But then a minivan stopped for him. He watched it slow down and then back up to where he was standing. The passenger-side window slid down.

The driver, a woman in her late thirties, leaned toward him, talking over her passenger, another woman about the same age. They didn't look like they were related, but Bobby spied a couple of kids in the backseat.

"What are *you* doing out here? I said to Celia, 'My god, that's the Prophet Bobby Higgs,' and she said 'No way,' and I said 'Yeah, it is,' and then we passed you and it was you, so I stopped."

Bobby looked ahead, wondering how much of a head start

Macer and Lita had on him. The asphalt shimmered in the heat and sun. A red convertible sped past them. The two women in the minivan were staring at him.

"And I thank you for stopping," Bobby said.

It was almost reflexive. The way his voice changed. He slipped into the cadence of the Prophet. His voice was calm, warm.

"But what are you doing on the side of the road?" the woman driving the minivan said again.

Bobby reached through the window, taking the hand of the passenger and reaching out for the hand of the driver. "Why," he said, "I was waiting for you."

The passenger got in back with the kids, and Bobby sat up front. He told the women he needed quiet to commune with God. They hushed the children and Bobby closed his eyes.

He knew there was a limit to how far Macer could run. Macer didn't need him anymore? Macer thought he could just leave Bobby behind?

Well, Bobby thought, he'd see about that. Even without Macer, he could be the Prophet Bobby Higgs. He didn't need Macer. He could rebuild his army on his own. He'd gather his flock to his side and then he would lead them . . . Where? He didn't know, but it would come to him. He would lead them forward, and sooner or later, he'd catch up to Macer, and then Macer would pay.

Sixpence Bar, Atlanta, Georgia

I t had never occurred to Teddie before to question why the place was called the Sixpence Bar. It was not British in any way. The beer selection skewed heavily toward Budweiser and other watery brews that would have horrified true Brits, and the menu didn't make a nod to fish and chips or anything else that seemed like it belonged in a British pub. It was, unquestionably, a bar though. Not a very nice bar. In fact, it was kind of a dump, but it was also tucked into an alley around the corner from the CNN plaza head-quarters, and seemed like a good place to get well and truly drunk. So, sure, it earned the word *bar*, but *sixpence*? No. She couldn't figure that one out. It was a mystery.

It was also a mystery as to why her boss, Don, was now plop-ping himself on a stool next to her. He would have had to leave their building, cross the plaza, skip the dozen or so restaurants and bars that most people from the mother ship frequented after work, and ducked down the alley that held the Sixpence Bar.

"I'll have what she's having," he said to the bartender.

"Triple shot of tequila?"

Don hesitated. "God, no." He looked at Teddie. "Jesus, honey. Uh," he said, looking back at the bartender, "I'll have a Pimm's Cup."

"Does this look like that kind of a bar?"

Teddie looked around the Sixpence at the same time that Don looked around him. God. It really was a shithole. There was a television behind the bar playing a baseball game—seriously? A baseball game? Was Major League Baseball just going to pretend that things were normal? Apparently, yes—and a row of dark wooden booths stretching back toward a hallway that contained what she assumed would be the bathrooms. Not that she had any intention of going to the bathroom in here, at least not until she checked to make sure her tetanus shot was up to date. The whole place was dimly lit, not in the mood lighting way that dimly lit could be in certain places, but in the way that a bar can become dimly lit when the bartender doesn't bother changing the lightbulbs that burn out.

Wow, Teddie thought. She really could have picked a better place.

"Fine," Don said. "Beer. In a bottle, please."

Teddie looked at her glass. It didn't look very clean. "How did you find me?"

"Well," Don said, "the last thing you said to me was that you were going to find the nearest bar and get sloshed."

"Technically, this isn't the nearest bar. It's not even close to the nearest bar."

"I know. This is the seventh place I looked."

"Sorry. Why didn't you just call me?"

"Is your cell phone on?"

She looked at her phone, which was sitting on the bar. It was not on. "Sorry."

"You already said that."

The bartender brought over a bottle of light beer and made a great show of taking the cap off. He looked at Teddie and lifted the bottle of tequila.

"Yes, please," she said.

"Nope," Don said, reaching out and covering her glass. "She's good for right now."

The bartender shrugged and turned away. This was not a man who seemed overly invested in his job. She looked at Don with a pout. "You seemed to hear me just fine back at the office when I said I was going to get sloshed."

"Well, about that. I can understand why you feel the need to get drunk, but this might not be the best time." He took a sip of his beer and made a face. "Blech. I'd forgotten how much I dislike piss water. Before I came in, when I saw the name, I was hopeful that there'd be a nice selection of English and European beers."

Teddie perked up. "I know, right? With the name? You'd think they'd at least—"

"Teddie." Don cut her off. "People have been looking for you."

"Why? What people?"

"Let's just say that your piece on the way the spiders move through crowds has garnered some interest." He took her elbow and got off his stool. "Here," he said, handing her a bag. "Your laptop. You're going to need this."

She took the computer bag and slung it over her shoulder. She wasn't drunk, exactly, but she'd had a single shot of tequila before ordering the triple shot, so she wasn't exactly undrunk either. That changed once they went out the door and walked out of the alley into the sun-dappled street.

There were two military helicopters, bug-eyed with chain guns hanging from the body, in the open square, plus a dozen or so police cars, and a mix of cops and uniformed soldiers. They were all looking in her direction. Waiting for her.

She suddenly felt very, very sober.

Minneapolis, Minnesota

There wasn't enough coffee in the world to make this feel like anything other than six in the morning after a night without sleep. Agent Mike Rich looked at himself again in the bathroom mirror and then waved his hands under the motion-sensing faucet so he could splash some more water on his face. It didn't help that the institutional fluorescents made even a healthy guy look like a zombie coming out of a microwave, but he already looked like crud even without the lousy lighting. It was a bad sign when people could walk up to him and Leshaun, look at them, and tell Mike that *he* was the one who looked like he could use some rest. Leshaun had taken a bullet two weeks ago, for goodness' sake. Admittedly, it wasn't that bad of a wound as far as gunshot wounds went, but under normal circumstances Leshaun would still have been on medical leave for at least another week or two.

These weren't normal circumstances, though. If they were, Mike might have gotten some sleep instead of driving through the night to make sure his daughter, his pregnant ex-wife, and her new husband, Rich Dawson, were all safe and tucked away in Dawson's cottage in the woods. Again.

Safe. Mike pulled some paper towel from the dispenser and

dried his face. Were they really safe? Was there such a thing any-more? The newspapers and television reporters kept swinging back and forth between hysteria and optimism, but Mike was seeing the information closer to the source, and even the best reading of it was scary. The truth was, they'd gotten off lightly in the United States. Los Angeles was a tragedy, but compared to China or even Delhi, it was nothing. He couldn't believe how few people were giving the president credit for her quick decision to shut down air traffic. How much worse would things have been if people were jetting all over the country with those little beasts laying eggs in-side their bodies?

He came out of the office bathroom, grabbed a stale donut from the table in the hall, and went into the conference room. It was packed. Six in the morning and the bureau chief had called every single field agent in Minneapolis into the office. They should have been out there doing the same thing they'd been doing since the first egg sacs had been found, which was looking for more, but instead they were crowded into the conference room waiting for new orders.

Leshaun had saved him a spot. As Mike sat down, he put one hand on the back of Mike's chair and passed over a takeout cup of coffee with his other hand. "How'd it go?"

"Not bad," Mike said. "Annie cried a little bit, but I think she was okay. I told her that when all this was over I'd get her a puppy."

"Whoa. A puppy? Bringing out the big guns."

"Yeah, well, I'm saving the pony for when I need to really im-press her." Despite himself, Mike grinned. He'd been partnered with Leshaun for a long time now, and they were a good match. Leshaun always knew when to push him to be serious and when it was time to lighten things up. And right now, Mike needed that. He'd thought the first time he'd driven with Dawson and Fannie and his daughter up to Soot Lake, the night Los Angeles turned into another ring of hell, had been the worst night of his life. He'd been wrong. He'd felt so good motoring across the lake in a borrowed—okay, temporarily stolen—fishing boat to bring them back home to Minneapolis, and when Melanie had told him to get his daughter back *out* of Minneapolis again, he'd felt sick. The first time, he'd thought of the evacuation as a precaution. A "just in case." But this was different. He could hear it in Melanie's voice. She was worried. This time, when he'd said good-bye to Annie and his ex-wife, Fanny, he'd been struggling a little bit not to cry, and kept going back to hug his daughter just one more time. He was okay with a firm handshake from Dawson.

The bureau director came into the room and they all quieted down. Jake Stigler hadn't gotten his job by being the sharpest tool in the shed. He was more like one of those multitools with the pliers that a certain kind of guy likes to keep in a little nylon holster on their belts: good at most things, great at nothing. That was Stigler. He was profoundly, totally, competent. Nothing more, nothing less, and even though Mike had worked with plenty of cops and agents who could barely get over the bar of basic competence, he still wished they had a better boss. Stigler was good at following orders and filling out paperwork, at running the standard operations and investigations, but he wasn't much of a lateral thinker. All the biggest wins for the Minneapolis bureau since Stigler had taken the job had come from an agent doing something that he or she hadn't cleared with the boss first.

Right now, standing at the front of the room, Stigler looked uncomfortable. Mike glanced at Leshaun, who gave him a "heck if I know" kind of look. Mike took a sip of his coffee. It was only warm, not hot, but he and Leshaun had been partners for long enough that Leshaun had doctored it up just right for him: a cannonball splash of skim milk and two packets of natural artificial sweetener. One of Annie's teachers had told her that artificial sweeteners caused cancer, so she'd made him switch to the natural kind of fake sugar back in the fall. Whatever the heck "natural" artificial sweetener was supposed to be. Probably dandelions ground into paste by hippies in Vermont, Mike thought. It still had that slightly funky, bitter taste the sweeteners in the yellow or pink or blue packets that he'd been using for years had, natural or not. Leshaun was a blended coffee drink with extra chocolate syrup kind of guy, which always made Mike feel both virtuous in his use of skim milk and natural artificial sweetener and at the same time completely annoyed that Leshaun hadn't ballooned up into a pile of cream and sugar.

Stigler cleared his throat. "As of this evening, we're ceasing all operations in Minneapolis. Not just us. Every single federal agent is being pulled out. We're on a military transport plane headed to the East Coast in twelve hours. Plane leaves at six p.m. sharp."

Mike choked on his coffee.

The room erupted into a clamor of agents trying to ask Stigler questions, agents talking to other agents, agents pulling out their cell phones.

"Hey!" Stigler's voice was loud, cutting through the chaos and stilling the room. Mike wasn't sure he'd ever heard Stigler yell before. It was surprisingly impressive. "Phones down! Put your goddamned phones down." Mike saw a couple of agents guiltily lowering their cells. "The original orders were to confiscate your cell phones and keep you sequestered until four o'clock and then march you directly from here to the airport. There was a lot of pushback on that"—more yelling as Stigler held up his hand— "including from me. The pullout now includes family, which is why you are being notified now. Twelve hours. Next of kin only.

Spouses, kids. I can't promise you there will be room for parents. The plane is leaving at six o'clock. On. The. Dot. With or without you." He wheeled and pointed at a younger agent in the corner, who was trying and failing to surreptitiously type on her phone. "Put your goddamn cell phone away. Now."

"What the hell, Chief?" This from Beth Gomper. She was originally from New York City and resented being posted in Minneapolis.

"What do you think, Beth? Didn't you hear what I said?" He looked out over the room, and Mike could see that Stigler looked exhausted. He wondered how long Stigler had known about the evac order. Did he know the night before, even as Mike was driving Annie up to the lake?

"Look, the truth is that we are working with seriously incomplete information here," Stigler said. "But what we know is that people are coming east from Los Angeles. Too many of them to stop now. I think the army is still trying; they've got roadblocks and fences up, but there's no point. Thousands of cars broke through. Too many to track. Too many to stop now that they are all spread out. Washington didn't say how many they think might be infected, but it's clear it isn't going to be contained to California. At this point, they're hoping we can just keep it to the western states and make sure it doesn't reach the Midwest."

Stigler rubbed the back of his neck and sighed. "Every single fed is getting lifted out of here. Do you have any idea how big a deal that is? Washington is afraid that when the news gets out that we're abandoning everything west of the Mississippi it's going to create a panic. They want to keep this as quiet as possible for as long as possible. So find your spouses, find your kids, and keep it quiet."

"Do you really think it's going to stay quiet?"

Mike didn't see who asked the question, but he thought by the voice it might have been Finkelbaum. She was older, near retirement age. Divorced. Childless.

"For your sake," Stigler said, "I hope so. For all our sakes. There will be riots if it leaks. It's going to be crazy enough at the airport without the news spreading. This is the kind of thing that can create a panic. If you want to get out of here without having to wade through a riot, I'd suggest keeping this as quiet as possible while you go about the business of evacuating your family. The plane takes off at six o'clock, but the sooner you are at the airport and on board, the better."

There was a chorus of voices again, but this time Stigler just held up a hand and let the voices come at him. Mike looked to Leshaun, who mouthed a single word as a question. Annie?

Mike nodded, but the embarrassing truth was that his first thought hadn't been of his daughter. His first thought had been that if they were shipping every bureau agent to the East Coast, it damn well *should* create a panic, and then he had realized it was worse. What Stigler had said was not just every bureau agent, but every single *federal* agent. Good lord. The government was giving up half the country.

The next ten minutes were a blur of orders. No radio traffic. No phone calls or e-mails or texts. Pick up your kids and spouses and get your asses back in time. Family only. Don't tell your neighbor, don't tell your dentist. Don't tell your kids' teachers or breathe a word of it. The only goal here was to get the feds out without making it seem like they were abandoning the good people of Minneapolis. A tall order, since they were, for all intents and purposes, abandoning the people of Minneapolis. Abandoning everybody west of the Mississippi.

By six thirty in the morning, Mike and Leshaun were out in

their agency car. It was, ironically, a beautiful morning. Unseasonably warm again, the sun turning building glass into a mirrored playground.

"I never thought I'd be glad that my family all lives in the back hollers of Tennessee," Leshaun said. "But I guess that's as far away from everything as you can be and still live on this same goddamned earth. They're probably as safe as anybody can be in all this. It's so backward out there that if the world ends, they won't hear about it for another thirty years." He looked at his cell phone and then slid it back into his pocket. "This won't stay quiet. You know that. It's going to leak before the planes take off. Somebody, somewhere, is going to make a phone call or send an e-mail. Washington was right in their initial idea to sequester us and then march us to the airport. Just don't give us a chance to mess it up."

"Wouldn't have worked," Mike said. "Maybe for agents like you, who don't have family, but you think I would have just left Annie behind?"

"How many people you think we're talking about? All the feds west of the Mississippi? Even if you're not talking support and office staff and locals who happen to work with federal agents? Plus spouses and kids? It's going to get out. No question. And once it does, it's going to explode. Riots. Panic. People looting and shooting each other. Highways and streets are going to be jammed. Doesn't matter that there isn't a place to go. Running seems better than sitting still."

"You know that driving with me to go get them might mean we get caught out," Mike said, "right? There's a really good chance we get to the cottage and by the time we turn around, the roads are blocked up and we can't get to the airport. It's a risk. You sure you still want to come with me to get Annie?"

"Family isn't only blood."

Mike nodded, and they were quiet for a few minutes.

The quiet gave Mike time to think. "This doesn't make sense," he said. "Sure, it was terrifying, but we've only found five sites in Minneapolis with egg sacs, and we haven't even heard a whisper about sacs being found anywhere else other than Los Angeles. And since the spiders dropped dead, there hasn't been a single confirmed attack. So why are they pulling everybody out? I mean, it would make sense out West, in California, Nevada, Oregon, but here, in Minneapolis?"

"You heard what Stigler said: the quarantine line is broken. You think people need any more of a reason than they already have to start panicking again? Two million people dead in Los Angeles? China's going to be glowing nuclear green for the next forty thousand years. It's not going to take much of anything to get people streaming for the exits. Just the news that the quarantine zone has broken down is going to be enough to get people trying to run away."

"No," Mike said. "You're right about civilian panic, for sure. It's a powder keg and there are a lot of matches. I meant about Washington. It doesn't make sense that they'd pull us all east. There's nothing to cause this. Nothing has happened yet. Shouldn't they want us out in the field trying to enforce a secondary quarantine zone? There's going to be a second quarantine line, isn't there? Sure, Stigler said keeping people in LA is a bust, but he also said the new goal is to keep it from spilling out of the West and completely across the country. With all nongovernmental air traffic grounded, it will still take a couple of days for people to get from California to Minnesota. If it was pretty much contained to LA in the first place, there's something we're missing."

"What about your lady scientist out in DC? Can you call her?"

Melanie. Oh, shit. Melanie. Mike had called her to tell her about the pulsing egg sac, and she'd told him to get Annie out of town. And Melanie was talking with the president. Had he caused this? Had she gotten off the phone with him and done the math and realized that it might not be just Minneapolis? Did it mean that the real fear was that there *already* were infestations in other parts of the country? Or that something worse was on its way?

"Oh, man. It's not what's happened," he said. "It's what's *going* to happen. Something's coming. How long?" He looked at Leshaun. "How long until you think word leaks that the government is pulling back and people start panicking?"

"Hours, maybe," Leshaun said. "Maybe less. Hopefully long enough to get us to Annie and back." He started the car, flicked on the cherries, and mashed the gas.

Desperation, California

I t was weird to be above ground again. The beauty of Shotgun's shelter was that it was completely self-contained. Even if they weren't in the middle of a spider apocalypse, there wasn't really any need to go outside. Shotgun was, if anything, overly prepared. To the point where it was boring. Sure, Shotgun's digs had a vibe that was closer to a billionaire's hip, urban loft than to the traditional survivalist's bunker. It was, undeniably, the coolest end of the world hideout Gordo had ever seen. But it was so well thought out they were basically just killing time. There wasn't much to do. Other than invent a homemade flamethrower.

Gordo pulled the trigger and sprayed another great scathing swath of fire into the night.

He was surprised at how loud it was. Something to do with airflow, he supposed.

"Well," he said, letting go of the trigger and watching the last of the gasoline breathe itself into a bright nothingness, "looks like we've got one hell of a homemade flamethrower. I was a little afraid it would be anticlimactic, but nope. Shooting a flamethrower is exactly as cool as I thought it would be. Want to go ahead and post the plans up online so the good people of the world can make their own?"

"Let's do it," Shotgun said.

They shut and sealed the blast doors behind them, trundled through the garage—Gordo stopped to run his finger across the paint of Shotgun's midnight-blue Maserati and to glance in admiration again at the twin-engine, six-seater plane—and into the workshop. They uploaded the plans from Shotgun's laptop to several online maker communities. If you didn't have a 3D printer that could work with metal, or you didn't have access to your own personal machine shop, it wasn't like you could whip up a homemade flamethrower with off-the-shelf parts from your local hardware store, but there'd be at least some people who could put the weapon together. It wasn't a real answer, though: the flamethrower had a limited range. It was good for clearing a small swath around you. It was personal protection, not an actual way to win the war. Still, it was better than nothing, and they both had a sense of satisfaction after they uploaded the plans.

And then they were bored again. Fred and Amy were watching some sort of Swedish art house film and drinking, so Gordo and Shotgun were left to their own devices.

"A bigger flamethrower?" Shotgun suggested.

"It's not exactly the kind of thing that scales up in any sort of useful fashion," Gordo said. "You can turn up the volume and turn up the volume, but at some point, you're going to cook yourself. A flamethrower can only go so big before it's just as harmful to the user."

"Fair enough."

"What we need to come up with is a way to kill spiders from a distance."

"You mean like, I don't know, bombs?"

"Don't be a smart-ass," Gordo said. "The point is to come up with something that the military hasn't already come up with, because all that stuff was designed to fight humans. Not little spiders. Like a ray gun or something. I don't know. I'm just your assistant. You're the engineer with all the patents."

"The spiders aren't so little." Shotgun considered for a minute. "But maybe you're onto something."

"With what?"

"You said you can only turn the volume of the gas flow up so high before you cook yourself, right?" Gordo nodded, and Shotgun continued, "But maybe we could try something where you really turn the volume up."

Gordo was confused. "Like an audio weapon?"

"Subsonic," Shotgun said. "And we turn the volume up as high as it goes. To eleven."

Càidh Island, Loch Ròg, Isle of Lewis, Outer Hebrides

Thuy was talking on her cell phone, standing on the rocks outside the castle, and Padruig looked happy about it. That was odd enough for Aonghas, but odder still was the knowledge that once Thuy hung up, Padruig was planning to make a call of his own.

"Love you too," Thuy said. She lowered her phone and then burst into tears. Aonghas had seen her cry before—after a truly stressful few weeks of medical school, after she found out her aunt had passed away, and even out of joy, after he asked her to marry him—but not like this. She was crying so hard it sounded like a sort of barking, a seal waiting for its supper, a dog afraid of its own shadow. Great tears were billowing out of her eyes, and her shoulders leaped and shook so hard that Aonghas was afraid she might drop her phone. He looked at Padruig, unsure what to do, and his grandfather gave him a look that meant, *How did I raise a boy who is as big an idiot as you? Go hold and comfort your fiancée, you blasted moron!*

So Aonghas held and comforted Thuy until she stopped crying, which was several minutes at least. She leaned into him and seemed

130

to find a real comfort in him, which made him feel like a little bit less of an idiot, even though he didn't understand why she was crying *now*, when she'd finally heard that her parents, her brother, her brother's boyfriend, and even her brother's boyfriend's dog, a German shepherd named Terrance, were all safe. It would have made sense to him if she'd cried before, when she hadn't heard. Or it would have made sense that she was crying if she'd just heard some of them had been, well, eaten. But she'd just gotten good news, right? He looked over Thuy's head at his grandfather, and Padruig gave him a different look, this one saying, *Your job as a husband will be to accept your future wife as the complicated, wonderful woman that she is. Or something like that.*

After a few minutes, Thuy had cried herself out and said she wanted to go inside to make herself a cup of tea and sit on the couch and stare at the ocean through the grand window for a while. She handed Padruig the cell phone and left the two men standing out on the bare rocks, the wind surprisingly gentle, an occasional gust lifting a drifting soft spray of seawater over them.

Padruig held up Thuy's phone, a Henderson Tech 4600 that she'd gotten the weekend before coming to visit Aonghas in Stornoway. "Are you sure they'll be able to send the documents on this thing?"

"I've told you, yes. She can check her e-mail on there. If we've got a cell signal and if the circuits aren't overloaded, it will come through."

Padruig looked skeptical, but evidently he decided to believe his grandson, because he started poking at the phone. It looked like a chicken pecking for corn. Not surprisingly, since he hadn't actually unlocked the home screen, nothing happened. "How in the devil's name do you operate this thing?" Padruig said. "This infernal contraption is cursed."

"It's just a phone, Padruig, not an instrument of Satan."

Padruig harrumphed. "It might as well be. You can trace the decline of modern civilization to these things."

"You said the same thing about television, microwaves, and people no longer dressing up to fly on airplanes. Here, give it to me." Aonghas took the phone and dialed the number on the scrap of paper that Padruig handed to him. It was a London number. There was just silence at first, and Aonghas held his breath, afraid that maybe the cell phone lines were overwhelmed again, that Thuy's call had been a lucky fluke, but then there were a series of sharp, chippy beeps, two long tones, and then the click of a telephone receiver being lifted.

"Who is this and how in the hell did you get my private number?"

Without a word, Aonghas handed the phone to his grandfather.

"This is Padruig Càidh . . . Yes. That Padruig Càidh." He listened for a moment and then cut off the voice on the other end of the line. "I know you're a fan and I know this isn't exactly a good time for you, but I need you to send me something . . . Yes, now . . . No. I don't care if you're in the middle of something."

It went like that for a minute or two, and then finally the voice on the other end acceded to Padruig's demand—as, in Aonghas's experience, everyone acceded to Padruig's demands—and his grandfather handed the phone back to Aonghas.

"He said we'll have the maps within the hour. Every known contact point."

"How is it, exactly, that you have the personal phone number for the director of MI6?"

"How do you think?" Padruig asked. "Harry Thorton. The man's a fan. He's been sending me letters since he was a young man. A few times a year. Ideas on what the next Harry Thorton mystery should be. He keeps asking me to ring him the next time I'm in London so he can take me for a pint and talk about Harry. I killed him once, remember? In *Thirty Strikes a Minute*, he was the character who got thrown off the clock tower."

"You really think you're right about this?"

Padruig looked out over the water. The waves rolled against the island in the same rhythm they had always seemed to come. The ocean, as always, unconcerned with the plight of humankind. "Did I ever tell you what your grandmother said to me on the day we found out your mother was going to have a baby?"

Aonghas was surprised. His grandfather almost never talked about his dead wife. She'd been, by all accounts, an extraordinary woman. She'd put up with Padruig for one thing, but she had also been smart and funny, a good cook, and a modern woman. She had gotten a job to help support her and Padruig when he'd first started writing, and he always said she was the person who'd come up with the idea for the first Harry Thorton mystery. She'd denied it publicly, in interviews, and even privately, to her own daughter, but Padruig insisted it was true. But he didn't usually bring her up out of the blue. More than thirty years dead and gone, and the thought of his late wife still made his grandfather sad.

"I wish she had lived long enough to hold you, or, better yet, for you to have had the chance to get to know her," Padruig said, "but do you know what she said to me? The very night that your parents told us they were having a baby? This was before we found out that your grandmother was already sick." He paused. There was a hitch in his voice, and Aonghas realized his grandfather was crying. "No. That can't have been right. Not we. Not before we found out your grandmother was sick, but rather, before *I* found out your grandmother was sick. I've never put it together before. She must have already sensed it. Must have, somewhere inside her, known what was coming, known she had only a few months to live, even if the doctors hadn't told us that yet."

He snuck a handkerchief from his jacket pocket. The handkerchief was pale yellow linen. Delicate. He turned his back for a moment so that Aonghas wouldn't see him wipe his eyes. He turned toward Aonghas again and cleared his throat. "She said to me, 'You watch over the baby.' That's what she said. Like she knew that the crash was coming for your parents. Like she already knew she wouldn't be there for you either."

"How come this is the first time I'm hearing this?"

Padruig gave a sort of choking laugh and then folded the handkerchief up and put it back in his pocket. "The lass hasn't told you, has she?"

Aonghas felt disoriented. Light. He wouldn't have been surprised if he had suddenly grown wings and lifted from the rock of the island, gliding out over the water. His grandfather wasn't making sense.

"The lass? You mean Thuy?"

Padruig smiled, and it was a real smile. Something happy and genuine and real, and for a moment, even though he didn't understand what his grandfather was talking about, it made Aonghas feel even lighter. Hopeful.

Padruig looked up at the castle, and Aonghas followed his grandfather's gaze. Thuy stood inside, near the window, holding a cup of tea and looking back at them. She was smiling, too, and lifted her hand in a gentle wave.

Both men waved back.

"Told me what?"

Padruig clapped his hand on Aonghas's shoulder. "Why, that she's pregnant, of course. Why do you think she agreed to marry you? It certainly wasn't for your looks, you great galloping fool."

The White House

Manny could see it coming a mile away. Steph had her tells. First she'd start tapping her thumb against the edge of the table. Next, she'd fidget with one of her earrings. At some point, she'd pick up her drink and hold on to it with both hands as if she was acutely aware that her fidgeting fingers were a sign that she was losing her temper. She was good at keeping her feelings in check. She had to be. Women who became too obviously angry got dismissed as too emotional to be good leaders. With the chairman of the Joint Chiefs of Staff and his assorted brass not so subtly indicating that they thought her unwillingness to start dropping nukes was because she couldn't overcome her emotions—in other words, because she was a woman—for Steph to get obviously angry was not the right play.

Losing her temper may not be the right play, but it would have been cathartic for her. It would have made Steph feel better, and Manny would have gotten a kick out of watching her lean on Ben Broussard and his crew of military advisors. President Pilgrim had learned how to come down like an avalanche when she needed to. You don't get elected president of the United States, particularly when you're a woman, without developing sharp elbows and the willingness to throw them. Manny remembered, years ago, when Steph was still Governor Pilgrim, how she had to deal with the state's director of highways. He was a holdover from the old regime and a different era, a good ol' boy who liked to hunt and got a kick out of calling his dogs "bitches" in front of Stephanie as often as he thought he could get away with it.

He didn't.

Steph was a politician, which meant she kept score.

The man had, at one point, gone behind Steph's back on a funding issue, and when she caught him, he had the gall to tell her he did it because he didn't think she understood the numbers. Women and their difficulty with logic, and all. It had been a work of art the way she'd destroyed him. Manny had always thought of anger as a thing with heat, but maybe thinking of her like an avalanche really was the best metaphor, because she was ice cold. The man had left her office sputtering and red-faced and he'd resigned his office in disgrace.

No, an angry Steph was not a Steph he wanted to deal with. But if angry Steph was directed at Broussard, well, Manny could live with that.

"You've already ordered the pullback of federal assets from all stations west of the Mississippi, and that's a good start," Broussard was saying. He'd been saying it was a good start for nearly five minutes, but what he wasn't saying—what he was merely implying in a surprisingly passive-aggressive way for a military man—was that President Pilgrim had otherwise screwed the pooch. Pulling out federal assets was the right move, Broussard said, but there were so many other things she could have done, if only she'd listened to Broussard earlier. The military men around Broussard—and they were all men—nodded solemnly. Broussard was right, they all were saying, Steph *could* have done more. The military was right, as always, and the president had made a mistake by not swallowing their advice whole. Steph could have done more, and they wanted her to learn from her mistake: this was Steph's chance to make up for her earlier inaction. There was only one possible thing she should do, in their minds.

Steph put down her drink and stood up. "Gentlemen, I'm not sure how much clearer I can be. Even if we didn't still have military teams conducting operations in the greater Los Angeles area, I wouldn't authorize nuclear strikes. Not now. You've been telling me to make nuclear strikes along the western seaboard for the past five days. Los Angeles and San Francisco and Seattle and everything in between. And then east, you say, all the way from the Canadian border where Montana and South Dakota meet, south to Denver and Albuquerque and down to the Mexican border, and oh, by the way, maybe we shouldn't worry so much about those borders, and maybe we should keep using our nukes until we run out of things to nuke. The answer to everything is not a nuclear strike." Broussard opened his mouth, but Stephanie held up her hand. "Ben, I'm still speaking, and if you interrupt me, if you say a single word, I'll have Special Agent Riggs and his fellow Secret Service members handcuff you, gag you, and shove you in a closet somewhere in the East Wing."

Manny stole a glance at Tommy Riggs. Most of the agents were athletic looking, but scaled at a normal human size. They didn't stand out in a crowd. Special Agent Riggs looked average enough when he was standing by himself, in a conference room or on a lawn or somewhere else where it was hard to get a sense of proportion, but here, in a room with other people, he looked like a man who'd been run through a photocopier at one hundred fifty percent. He had to be almost seven feet tall, and Manny couldn't even guess at how much Special Agent Riggs weighed, but he'd bet good money almost every pound was pure muscle. When Special Agent Riggs got into one of the president's armored limousines, a vehicle that had more in common with a tank than a car, it sank a little bit on its springs. Or at least it felt that way. Everybody looking at Special Agent Riggs right now was probably thinking the same thing, which was that he could rip Ben Broussard in half without even trying. And Riggs, despite working for the Secret Service, which was supposed to be politically neutral, wasn't very good at hiding the fact that he thought President Pilgrim was the greatest thing to happen to the United States of America since the election of Lincoln. Given that Riggs was black and originally from Georgia, being in second place to President Lincoln was nothing shabby. Manny had no doubt that Special Agent Riggs would take a bullet for Steph, but he wasn't sure if a bullet could even hurt him.

Special Agent Riggs didn't move, but he did smile. Just a little bit.

"I've been listening to you, Ben. To all of you," Steph said, looking around at the assembled military men, "but you haven't been listening to me, and you haven't been listening to the scientists. The Chinese panicked and they are going to pay for it. When they dropped their first nuclear weapon they thought the outbreak was limited to Xinjiang Province and that they could contain it. But you have to think they were wrong and they didn't contain the outbreak. We haven't gotten any good intelligence out of China since they lit up half their country, but it seems self-evident that they wouldn't have wreaked such devastation on their own country if the outbreak had been contained.

"If we had a similar situation, if we were simply talking Los Angeles, God help me, I'd do it. If I'd thought there was even a slim chance that sacrificing Los Angeles, or even all of California, would save the country, I would have ordered a nuclear strike days ago. But the truth is, gentlemen, if there ever was a hope of containing the outbreak to Los Angeles, that hope was gone almost from the beginning. You tell me, were you really prepared to launch a nuclear attack against our own citizens, on our own soil, when the *Mathias Maersk* crashed into the port? Because that was the minute it would maybe have worked. That afternoon, that evening. If we'd gone nuclear at that point, I do believe there's a chance we could have contained the spiders. But after that? It was already too late. What's that phrase? Closing the barn door after the horses are already gone? Now you idiots want to blow the barn to oblivion while I'm trying to corral the horses. You're masking all of this in military terms and jargon, talking about yield and overflow and collateral damage and incurred civilian costs, but let's be honest. Your 'plan' would turn the western seaboard into a nuclear wasteland."

Stephanie looked around the room. She was still angry, but she also looked sad and tired. Manny thought she looked like she was burdened with the weight of the world. "No. If we start using our nuclear arsenal, there's no going back. What will the cost of that be? Isn't there a point where we have to ask, can we really save America if we've destroyed it? Give me a break, Ben, I'm not stupid. I understand what's at stake. I'm not saying this as some sort of empty rhetoric, and I don't care if it sounds cheesy. There's a truth here. We're talking about saving America. Saving the world. And I know there's a truth in what you're saying, too. There might be a point when nuclear weapons are the only real option. If we're looking at another outbreak—if these spiders start some inexorable march across the continent—then I'll authorize nuclear weapons. If we reach the point where the only way to save the country is to sacrifice it, then I'll let you be as gung ho as you want. But we aren't there yet. Not yet. And I don't believe that's where we need to go. You've all read the brief on Professor Guyer's theory. If she's right, it's too late to worry about trying to contain Los Angeles. But that does not mean it is too late to try to halt the spread. This is simply not the time to use nuclear weapons. Not yet."

Steph shook her head and echoed herself. "Not yet." She picked up her drink and took a sip.

Ben straightened up in his chair, glanced at Agent Riggs, and then spoke. "Madam President—"

"Goddammit, Ben."

He lifted his hands off the table in a gesture of supplication. Steph sighed and let him speak.

"Okay," he said.

"Okay?"

"Okay. I hear you. No nuclear weapons. But there's something else we can do. It's drastic, but it does not include nuclear weapons. You're not going to like it either, but if you want to avoid going nuclear, this will make sense. Just give me a minute here. Look, I know that you don't like me."

Manny shifted in his chair, glancing around the room. He could see the surprise on the faces of the soldiers, the cabinet members, even on the normally stony faces of the agents and aides in the room.

"And frankly, to be honest, I probably deserve that." Ben stood up. He was speaking to the president, but he let his gaze fall on everyone in the room. "I'm not necessarily a likable guy. I'm saying this because I want to make sure you understand what I'm suggesting we do here. I want you to really listen to what I have to say. I want to make sure that if you reject this plan, you aren't making the decision because of me, personally. I get that you don't like me. I push too hard, and I know you don't think I give you the respect that you deserve as the president of the United States and my commander in chief. And I know you think that a part of that, heck, maybe most of that, comes from you being a woman. I know you think that if you were a man I'd treat you differently. I don't think that's true, but then again, it might be. When all this is over, we can talk about that, and I'll try not to be such an asshole. Because if you are right, that I'd treat you differently if you were a man, well, then I owe you an apology. I'll say it now. I'm sorry. And I am sorry. I'm not saying that because of some sort of political sensibility or even out of any sort of personal shame that I might be sexist or that I might not be a particularly likable person. I'm saying it, saying I'm sorry, right here, right now, because I think my job is to give you military advice, and I think you're not listening to it because of personal reasons."

From Manny's viewpoint, Steph looked like she was literally taken aback. She rocked back an inch on her heels. "*I'm* not listening for *personal* reasons?"

"Hear me out. And when I'm done, if you want my resignation, I'll give it to you."

The room was pin-drop quiet. At any other time—say, when spiders weren't eating American citizens and threatening the total destruction of humanity, when he wasn't a part of a debate over dropping nuclear bombs on US soil—Manny would have enjoyed the show. Every single person in the room was looking back and forth between Ben and Steph. Steph's hesitation couldn't have been more than a second, one tiny, individual tick on a watch, but it felt like it could have contained a universe unfolding, big bang to black hole in the space between Ben asking and Steph nodding at him to carry on. When she nodded, Manny heard what sounded suspiciously like a roomful of people letting out their breath.

"You're right," Ben said. "You're right that it's too late for Los

Angeles. And you're right that even if you had ordered a nuclear strike on Los Angeles, it probably would have come too late to contain these things. But that doesn't mean there isn't something we can do, and I'm not talking about nuclear strikes anymore. I still think there was a time when nuclear weapons would have been a way to address some of these problems, but we're past that. I hear you. *We*," he said, gesturing to the military men around him, "hear you. No nuclear weapons. So let's look at the reality of where we are now. We're trying to burn the egg sacs littered around Los Angeles at hundreds of sites, but according to Dr. Guyer, we've got tens of thousands of civilians who have escaped from the quarantine zone who might be carrying spiders inside them. So what's the reality? The reality is that we are thinking about an unconventional thing in a conventional way. Or, maybe, we've always understood that we needed to think unconventionally, but we've been thinking the wrong *kind* of unconventional. We tried treating this spider invasion like a flu pandemic, like a biological agent spreading through infection, and I think that's the right direction, but we didn't go far enough. We can't treat it like *a* biological weapon. We have to treat it like *the* biological weapon."

Alexandra Harris, the grandmotherly national security advisor, didn't hesitate. "You're talking about the Spanish Protocol?"

"What the fuck is the Spanish Protocol?" Manny asked.

"You know how it is, Manny," Alex said. "We've got contingency plans for everything. Land wars in Europe. Terrorist attacks in New York or Chicago or Houston. Gas in the subways. Natural disasters. Mudslides. Meteor strikes. Hurricanes. Alien invasions. We plan and plan and plan. We've even got a Red Dawn contingency."

"Red Dawn? Like the movie?"

"Like the movie. If the Russians or the Chinese or whomever

invade the Midwest, we've already got a response plan in place. Everything."

"Everything," Steph said dryly, "but not, evidently, a contingency plan for spiders."

"Not for spiders," Alex agreed, "but I think Ben's right. We can use the Spanish Protocol as a way to try to salvage things."

Steph looked like she was getting angry again, but before she could speak, Manny jumped in. "Let's just save ourselves some trouble here. Can somebody please answer my earlier question? What the fuck is the Spanish Protocol?"

Alex took a deep breath. "The Spanish Protocol. It's named after the Spanish flu outbreak near the end of the First World War. Roughly twenty million people died worldwide."

"I don't think we can compare this to a flu outbreak anymore," Manny said.

"Neither do I," Alex said. "That's Ben's point. It might be named after Spanish influenza as some sort of an homage to the idea of a pandemic, but the Spanish Protocol came from the CIA in the 1970s. At least, that's where it had its roots. Height of the Cold War. The worry was the Soviet Union trying to wipe the entire country off the map. The idea was to come up with a plan that would guarantee the survival of at least some Americans, even if that meant other Americans would die. They wanted to guarantee that, whatever happened, enough Americans survived to keep the communists from inheriting the earth. The CIA wasn't thinking of a flu pandemic."

Manny felt that familiar sinking feeling, like his heart was dropping down into his gut. He'd been feeling it all too often since this all started. Was there ever going to come a point where he got some good news? He didn't even want to ask, but he couldn't help himself. "What were the CIA analysts worried about, then?"

"*The* flu pandemic. Or *the* bioweapon," Ben said. "A concept, not a specific thing. We didn't know what the Soviets had, but we knew what *we* had, and it scared the shit out of us. Infection rates that made the Spanish flu look like the common cold. A wildfire running across the country, passed from sneeze to sneeze, cough to cough. The original response plans were set up for the kind of research being done in the 1970s, but the agency has updated it every few years for the last forty plus years. They've made adjustments to account for advances in research, updating for what the Iraqis and the Iranians were up to, for the Russians and the breakaway former Soviet states, for the Chinese and the North Koreans, for terrorists and for do-it-yourselfer home garage scientists. Today's model accounts for a doomsday scenario, the release of something with one hundred percent infection rates and mortality rates above eighty percent. I'm talking biomechanically engineered viruses that pass from person to person and leave you bleeding from the eyeballs. Things that don't even exist yet and are just science fiction, like nano-weapons. The Spanish Protocol is there in the event that one of these nightmares comes to life on American soil. It's supposed to be a last-ditch way of stopping the spread of something that is inherently unstoppable."

"Why haven't I heard of this before?" Steph asked. Her voice was so hard it could cut glass, and Manny, not for the first time, was glad that she'd been the horse he backed. In normal times, it would have been enough for his candidate to simply have been elected, but the honest truth, swear to God and on his mother's grave, was that Manny could not imagine a living person more suited to the pressure than Steph. There wasn't anybody better able to step up and take control in a moment like this. She had the weight of the world on her shoulders, but she could bear it.

"Because it was the kind of crackpot idea that there was no point briefing you on," Alex said. "We've got terrorists driving school buses full of explosives into government buildings and bringing automatic weapons onto subways. And one of the problems with planning for everything is that there's too much to worry about. The CIA and the NSA regularly hire novelists and screenwriters to brainstorm ideas for how America might be attacked. Most of it is crazy Hollywood stuff. Your job, as the president, is to lead the country, and our job, as cabinet members and agency directors, is to make sure you know about the things that are likely to be problems, not every single thing that could possibly happen in our wild speculations. There were already enough concerns that we knew were real. What would you have said if we'd come to you two years ago and told you we wanted to brief you on a crackpot contingency plan on the off chance some Russian scientist still living out the Cold War crop-dusted New York City with an engineered strain of the bubonic plague? When all this started, we were in the middle of running a simulation of war with the Chinese, and you thought *that* was a waste of time. I think a month ago, most people would have bet on war with the Chinese over an invasion of spiders as the greater threat to the country."

"If the Spanish Protocol is such a crackpot idea," Manny said, "why is it you knew exactly what Ben is talking about?"

"Madam President," Ben said, stepping in. "The Pentagon has all sorts of plans in place in the event that aliens come from outer space. And in the event of an alien invasion, we would have taken those plans out and briefed you and awaited your orders, but given that ET has yet to phone home, we're waiting on that. We pay people to imagine the worst, and some of our analysts have very active imaginations. We run numbers on everything, and there are a lot of plans that just get filed in the proverbial drawer because they seem so outlandish. And the Spanish Protocol seemed like one of those plans, the thing you'd keep buried away. But we've run out of normal ideas and plans, and I suggested this to Alex a few days ago. We're coming to the Spanish Protocol because there aren't any other options left."

He motioned to his aide, a thirtysomething black soldier who had kept so still that Manny hadn't even noticed him. The aide touched some keys on his laptop, and the monitors sprang to life. It was, Manny could not help but note, a PowerPoint presentation. That was the military for you, he thought. They could put a missile through a window from a thousand miles away, but they still gave presentations like it was 1997.

It turned out that the premise of the Spanish Protocol was surprisingly simple: fracture the country into as many separate pieces as possible in an attempt to create at least a few islands of safety. It meant turning the United States of America into the Balkanized States of America.

The science behind the protocol was designed for bioengineered weapons not flesh-eating spiders, but it was uncanny how much it made sense. Viruses need something to carry them. A host. And in the same way that viruses travel inside human bodies, so do these spiders. An infected person who is completely isolated from other people is no longer a danger. Even though this virus—the spiders—doesn't pass through handshakes and coughing and kissing like a normal virus, it still requires a certain physical proximity. In other words, the idea of trying to quarantine Los Angeles had been the right impulse. They just hadn't gone far enough.

There were a lot of details. The presentation took almost an hour. Manny felt sick thinking about what it meant on the ground. California. Nevada. Colorado. Washington, Idaho, and Oregon completely written off. Everything west of Nebraska used as the primary containment areas. Once that was done, the second and ultimate dividing line, if it worked, would be the Mississippi. At the same time as they were shattering the western half of the country into thousands of pieces, making it as difficult to travel as possible, they'd start working on the second stage: breaking apart the rest of the country. Manny was terrified about how reasonable it seemed. Worse was how quickly Ben thought the military could achieve this objective.

During the Civil War, brother had fought against brother, a line running between North and South, but the country had held. The country had, in the end, stayed whole. A more perfect union. But here was Ben proposing that the military could, over the space of forty-eight hours, with the help of millions of tons of ordnance— no nuclear weapons used, at least not yet—finally split the country in half. Not North and South, but East and West.

And then, as soon as this deep fissure was carved down the middle of the country, the military would move on to secondary targets. Illinois and Ohio, the highways through Tennessee and Kentucky. From Maine all the way to Florida, a highway that Manny had driven on in high school. Highways and overpasses, on-ramps and off-ramps. Rail lines. County highways and big-city bypasses. All bombed into irretrievable ruins. Civilian air traffic shot down on sight, and anybody attempting to travel from one zone to another on foot or by bicycle or by any other means subject to lethal force.

If they made it impossible for people to travel, by extension, the spiders couldn't keep spreading.

The plan itself also took into account a situation like the one they were facing now: a failed quarantine. The plan wasn't designed simply to throw up some yellow police tape and pretend that a simple line would stop anything, but rather to interrupt the opportunities for movement, to break the country into as many pieces as possible so that if the spread of spiders—because with what Melanie was claiming, the spiders *were* coming back—could not be stopped, it could at least be slowed. It was a chance to buy time, the hope that a crumbled infrastructure would mean localized pockets of spiders eating themselves into extinction, rather than a constant spread. That was what the Spanish Protocol counted on: the virus burning itself out. For the spiders, it was the same idea: no new hosts.

"What you're talking about is like having the entire country commit suicide. We're going to be bombing ourselves back to the Stone Age. Each highway interchange, each bridge, each tunnel. My god, the years it would take to rebuild! And the people who will die from this action? You're asking me to kill tens of millions of Americans," Steph said. "We'd be abandoning America. We'd be carving up the country into splinters. And what about the people already in infection zones? Should I just abandon them to their fates?"

"No," Ben said. "I'm not asking you to *abandon* them. I'm asking you to *sacrifice* them. There's a difference."

The Spanish Protocol didn't call for bombing Los Angeles or turning the Southwest into a sea of nuclear glass. It didn't call for military strikes on defenseless civilians. What it called for was something both harder and cleaner, which was to cut off parts of the country in order to save the rest. Creating a sort of no-man's-land buffer zone, cracking the map into a million pieces so that the spiders in the high rises of Chicago couldn't spill into the hills and hollers of Arkansas or vice versa. Ben wasn't proposing killing people for no reason. Ben was proposing cutting them off and letting them die, turning America into a feudal state, the map a jigsaw puzzle of citizens left to fend for themselves.

Was there a difference? Manny wondered. If the military deliberately destroyed highways and bridges and tunnels, was it any different from killing the people in infected areas directly? No military strikes on people or cities. Instead, it would be military strikes on the infrastructure that allowed those people to move from city to city. Interstate 29, running through Fargo and Sioux City to Kansas City. Highway 55, running from Chicago through Memphis. Every place where Interstates 94 and 90 and 80 and 70 ran trucks and cars like blood through an artery. Highways were the heart of America, and what Ben was proposing was heart surgery. No. That wasn't right. Not heart surgery. The Spanish Protocol called for cutting out the entire beating heart of America and throwing it on a fire.

"What if we get the best-case scenario?" Steph asked. "What if Melanie is wrong, and we aren't about to have another outbreak, and these spiders don't come back? What if that's what happens, and I've ordered *this*? What then?" She looked at Manny. "Even if Melanie is right, you're asking me to give up on more than a hundred million Americans, to leave them on their own when they are counting on us most. And that's *if* we can contain the outbreak to the western half of the country. If not, the next step is to break up the entire country. I'll have as good as said to each and every American citizen, there's nothing the federal government can do for you. We're leaving you to die, so good luck."

Manny stood and reached out to hold Steph's hand. He realized it was a surprisingly tender and private act to do in such a public place, but he didn't care. He could see how much this was weighing on her, and he had a sudden stunning sense of clarity.

"Ben's right," he said, a catch in his throat. He gave himself a second to gather himself, then said, "I'm sorry, Steph. But he's right. I know it sounds cold, but we've got to do it, and the truth is, they haven't gone far enough. We can't stop at the Mississippi. We can't just cut the country in half and hope it works. We've got to break the country into a million pieces. It's the only way to save it. Think about the real reason the federal highway system was built. It wasn't so you could order something from Seattle and get it cheaply to New York City in a week's time. We built the interstates for war. The United States built these roads because we wanted a way to move tanks and missiles and troops to wherever they might be needed throughout the country, from coast to coast. Realistically, the whole point of the highway system is to move people across the country as quickly as possible. Right now, that's the last thing we need. Can you imagine these spiders hatching in Chicago? New York City? Boston? Washington, DC? With the highway system intact, there's no possible way to stop it. We've already seen that we can't effectively block every road and inter-section just using cops and soldiers. Can you imagine these things in every city in America?

"Doing it this way is like radical surgery. We've got an infection, and we've got to amputate. You cut off the leg to save the body. We're always playing the game of what if. We're always rolling the dice on best case and worst case, but the worst case here? We've seen it already. We've seen it in Delhi and Rio de Janeiro. We're *lucky* that so far we've only lost Los Angeles. Steph," he said, his voice so much gentler than his words, "we can't wait and take the chance of the worst-case scenario. The Spanish Protocol sounds drastic, but the reason we're talking about it is because we've seen the worst case play out. The worst case is China."

He stopped and took a big breath. "We might end up having to use nuclear weapons, Steph. That's the honest truth. But if you want to avoid lighting up the map and radiating the whole world, at least for now, you have to try the surgery first."

Steph took her other hand and clasped it over his, so that his hand was between both of hers. She looked so sad it almost killed

Manny, and in that moment, he realized that maybe he did love her in whatever weird way it was that he could love her, and he wished they were alone so that he could just take her in his arms. But they weren't alone, and she didn't need that from him—she was strong enough to stand there and make the hard decisions without anyone holding her up—and maybe that was what he loved most about her.

"That's a hell of a leg to be cutting off, Manny," she said, but she was already talking to the room, already changing from Steph, his best friend and on-again off-again and mostly on-again lover, the sad, hurting woman who he wanted to shelter, back into what she'd been born to be: President Stephanie Pilgrim, commander in chief. "Do it," she said to Ben. "Order the strikes. Order the strikes starting immediately. All of them. Highways and bridges. Anywhere you can stop the people who might be carrying these spiders into the rest of America. Maybe we're too late, but we have to try. I'll do everything I can to prevent using nuclear weapons, and if that means sacrificing America to save America . . . I don't see any other options. Do it, Ben."

The room was silent.

She looked down at the table, and when she looked up again, Manny could see that her eyes were wet. "I'm ordering the Spanish Protocol," she said. "I'm throwing America on the mercy of God. And God help us all."

National Institutes of Health, Bethesda, Maryland

Melanie started the Japanese video again. It was just her, Dichtel, Nieder, Haaf, and Julie Yoo in the conference room. She'd shooed out Sergeant Faril and all the other minders and guards and lab assistants and various other people who were in and out of the corridors of the National Institutes of Health. There were plenty of people who seemed pissed about the way she'd simply taken over an entire floor of the building. Two floors, maybe? Maybe more: the soldiers, guards, and ancillary staff had to go somewhere, and they had probably taken over additional space in the building, but that wasn't her problem. There were only four biocontainment units of this level in the whole damned country. There was one at Emory University Hospital in Atlanta, one at the University of Nebraska Medical Center, one in Missoula, Montana, and one here. Given that she was based out of American University in DC, the NIH building in Bethesda was a no-brainer. So tough cookies to the people who were feeling put out. She had things to do. Like figure out what the heck she was actually seeing.

The video was edited down to just a couple of minutes, with

subtitles translating the limited commentary and data on the screen. None of the information meant a lot on its own: temperature and humidity didn't do much for Melanie. The man in the hazmat suit and the scientists overseeing everything from back in the lab occasionally spoke—or swore—and their dialogue showed up as white characters spelling out the translation on the screen.

"Is that translation accurate?" Melanie asked, looking at Julie Yoo.

"You know I'm not Japanese, right?" Julie said.

If Melanie weren't so tired, she would have kicked herself. Embarrassing.

"Don't look at me," Laura Nieder said. "I'm Cambodian, but via the state of Georgia and then New Jersey. I'm reasonably fluent in Spanish, and I can swear in Italian, but I don't know a lick of Japanese."

"Actually," Dr. Mike Haaf said, "I can speak some Japanese. Huge fan of anime." Melanie stared at him, and Haaf stammered a little. "Yeah, near as I can tell, it's an accurate translation."

They watched the camera mounted on the man's helmet edge closer and closer, through the dim room littered with egg sacs, around the pillar of white nuggets blocking the view, until the giant, pulsing, glowing cocoon was all that filled the screen. The silk was translucent, the light radiating outward, like a flashlight through skin. Black dots skittered across the surface of the cocoon—because that's what it looked like, more than an egg sac—offering a sense of scale for what they were looking at. They'd all seen the spiders, and they knew that if they looked like dimes on the surface of the silk pod, the cocoon had to be huge. The size of a king-size bed or a car, big enough to be terrifying. Big enough that they'd watched the video three times already, not believing what they saw.

The light inside the cocoon was pulsing. It wasn't obvious, not off and on like Morse code or a lighthouse on the rocks sending a message, but more subtle. The way the glow came just a little brighter, just a little dimmer, like listening to a lover's soft breathing in the night, only not nearly as comforting, because this light was ominous, filled with the promise of something they didn't understand.

"Whoever the Japanese fellow operating the camera is, he's a champ," Dichtel said. "Walking through a collection of egg sacs would be bad enough, but it's got to be terrifying when there are hatched spiders already swarming."

"Why aren't they eating him, though?" Haaf said.

"Smell?" Nieder leaned closer. "The suit blocks the smell?"

"Holy shit!" Melanie jumped forward and hit the pause button. "Did you see that?"

The other scientists in the room most definitely had not seen what she had seen. It took several minutes of Melanie scrolling backward and trying to freeze the image at the right moment, and then having to call in a tech to help figure out how to enhance the fragment, slow it down, and then zoom in closer, before they all sat back and watched the short clip taken from the video stream in an infinite loop in front of them. It reminded Melanie of the way, when she was still pursuing her doctorate and needed to take a break from the lab, she'd go online and look for things that could make her laugh, the way she'd watch a .gif of a dog failing to jump off a couch successfully, or one of some guy accidently punching himself in the balls, three or four or five seconds of hilarity in an endless repeat on her computer screen. But this wasn't funny. All the other scientists could see what she'd seen, and none of them were laughing.

"Jesus. They're emptying themselves into it? They're feeding it, aren't they?" Nieder said.

"That's what it looks like."

They watched the loop run over and over again, the spider lining itself up and then reaching out to—reaching through—the shell of the silk cocoon, and then only seconds later, tumbling off with an odd lightness and grace, looking like a leaf drifting from a tree on a still autumn morning.

Melanie glanced over at Julie and saw that her graduate student was looking at her tablet instead of the monitor. "Julie?"

Julie looked up and shook her head. "Just zipping through the unedited feed, but there doesn't look like there's anything else in there that we missed."

"Okay," Haaf said. "Can we agree that we really need to know exactly what is inside the giant egg sac that these spiders seem to be emptying themselves into? That if these other spiders have gorged themselves on everything in their way and are now disgorging themselves into an egg sac that appears to be about the size of a truck, we need to find out what is going to hatch? And why it's glowing?"

"There wasn't one of these at the Staples Center site, was there? In Los Angeles?" Dichtel asked.

Melanie stood up and crossed over to the window. They were at the front of the building, and she could see the glint of glass and metal in the parking lot, but instead of it coming from Fords and Chevys and Hondas and other cars, there were tanks and military vehicles and a helicopter that looked as menacing as any bug she'd ever studied. "Seems like something the army would have noticed, that we would have noticed," Melanie said. "The Staples Center was just the standard egg sacs we've come to know and love."

"So what the heck is this?"

It took nearly an hour to get through to the Japanese lab. Regardless of the help Melanie was afforded, they were routed to the wrong lab at first, and even when they did get through to the command center, it seemed like it took forever to get someone on the phone who had the authority to talk to them, and from there, it took longer still to find scientists who had the authority to talk to them *and* who actually had some answers. And once they had the videoconference running with a small group of scientists who had the authority and the knowledge to talk with Melanie and her scientists—their Japanese counterparts—the conversation itself was an awkward first date of pauses and hesitations, delays caused by translators and conversation by committee. Like most first dates, it was profoundly unfulfilling.

The Japanese, afraid of what was coming, had burned the entire temple to the ground. They seemed quite proud of the way they'd done it, a mix of explosives and something approximating napalm. They wanted to make sure that anything with eight legs had flames stuck to their legs like glue.

The second the conversation ended and the image of the Japanese scientists turned into an empty blue screen—they'd been using some sort of encrypted military videoconferencing program on a beefy military laptop in an even beefier military protective case—Melanie picked up the laptop, screamed "Motherfuckers!" at the top of her lungs, and threw it against the wall. It was not a satisfying experience. The laptop bounced to the floor, apparently unharmed, leaving a small dent in the drywall.

"Cowards," she said, still seething, but no longer throwing computers. "How could they just burn it down without finding out what the hell it meant?"

"I'm sure they thought the risk was—"

"Screw them," Melanie said. She spun away from the table and walked back over to the windows. She didn't care that she had cut off Dichtel, and she didn't care that the Japanese scientists and their government thought they had been protecting themselves. "We needed to know what was in there." She leaned her head against the cool glass and looked out. It was kind of a lousy view, but it was what she had.

She nearly jumped out of her skin at the loud boom that rattled the windows.

The other scientists scrambled to their feet and came over just in time to see two more jets streak overhead so fast they were gone in the blink of an eye, followed closely by two more window-rattling twin booms that left no doubt what the first sound had been.

Melanie looked behind her. All the scientists but Haaf had run to the window to look for the jets breaking the sound barrier overhead. Haaf, however, was still sitting at the table, staring at the blank wall across from him. She recognized that look. She'd had it on her own face plenty of times.

"Dr. Haaf?"

He kept staring at the wall, but his lips were moving.

"Dr. Haaf? Mike?" Melanie tried again.

"In the background of the conversation," Haaf said, turning to Melanie. "It was some chatter separate from the main conversation. I couldn't catch all of it." He looked embarrassed again. "Remember that I learned most of my Japanese so I could watch untranslated anime, so take this with a grain of salt. But I'm pretty sure that's what one of the researchers was saying. 'Off switch.' "

All the other scientists had turned from the window as well, the jets forgotten. Everything forgotten except for Haaf. He stood up, halfway embarrassed and halfway lost in concentration. "Maybe I've got the translation wrong. It's not an exact translation, I don't think, but the one guy in the background, the fellow who they said had been in the suit. The guy who was actually in there with them, wearing the hazmat suit and filming, right? That's what he was trying to say. He was muttering and angry and talking to the woman next to him."

"What?" Melanie said.

"I could swear he was saying something about an off switch."

Shinjin Prefecture, Japan

"Because it's just a theory," Koji said to his assistant. "And nobody other than you thinks there's anything to it. What was I supposed to do? Shout over the others?" He shook his head. "They wouldn't have listened to me even if I had."

Soot Lake, Minnesota

The roads had been murder. Even using the sirens on their agency car and Leshaun driving like he thought he was the second coming of Steve McQueen, it still took them until almost noon to get to the parking area by the boat ramp at Soot Lake. The good news, Mike thought, was that the traffic was all people leaving the city. No. *Leaving* wasn't the right word. *Fleeing*. How much worse was it going to get when word got out that the government was pulling back resources? Pulling back resources. Yeesh. That was a euphemism if there ever was one. The government wasn't pulling back resources, it was orchestrating a full-on retreat in advance of the coming doom.

He looked at his watch again. The clock was ticking, but it didn't matter how bad the roads got outside Minneapolis, he thought, as long as he was safely on that government plane with his daughter—and ex-wife and her new husband—by six o'clock, as long as they were flying east, away from this ridiculous nightmare.

Leshaun called him over. His partner had found a small, dinged-up fishing boat with a pull-cord twenty horsepower engine. It wasn't fancy, but the lightweight aluminum shell would barrel across the water fast enough, and, equally important, it didn't require a key.

He stepped into the front of the boat. He could never remember if the front was the stern or aft or the gunwale or some such other nautical bullshit. Why did boat people have to make stuff so complicated? What was wrong with front and back, left and right? He untied the rope from the stainless steel ring on the dock and Leshaun cranked the throttle.

It was loud going and the lake was choppy. There was enough of a wind to put up two- and three-foot waves, and the aluminum boat could have been an old-fashioned wooden roller coaster for all the comfort it offered. The engine buzzed and all Mike could think about was the sound of insects. Yes, he knew that spiders were technically arachnids, but really? Were there really people that pedantic that they were going to split hairs on that right now? He'd call them bugs if he felt like it. He held on to the seat with one hand and the side of the boat with the other. Even though the air was warm, the spray off the water was freezing, which made sense for a Minnesota lake in May. At least the boat was making time. Pacing the shore like a race car.

"There," he yelled back to Leshaun, pointing out the cove where Dawson's cottage lay nestled against the shore. Leshaun turned the tiller and the boat skipped even more, taking the waves broadside.

The dock was empty. No Annie standing out there and waiting for him this time, as she had been when he'd come to pick her up just a few days ago.

At another time, he would have appreciated the cottage. It wasn't opulent, but it wasn't one of those shoebox cabins that were held together with spit and rags. Dawson might not have been a showy guy, but he made good money and he liked nice things. Cedar shakes and wide, mullioned glass, a multilevel deck designed so that you couldn't quite figure out where the deck itself ended and the dock began, and a broad swath of low-growth native plantings that left a little picnic area on the south side of the house. Because Dawson was the kind of humongous asshole who married your ex-wife but was actually a pretty great guy who made you feel terrible about all your own bad decisions and whatever ill you'd wished on him, he'd offered to let Mike borrow the cottage on more than one occasion.

Leshaun tucked the boat gently against the dock on the other side from Dawson's boat. Mike hopped out, leaving Leshaun to tie off their stolen fishing skiff. He ran up the steps fast enough that he could feel his jacket flapping.

The shotgun blast almost took his head off.

Holy fuckity fuck. His ears. He patted himself down. There were a few buckshot holes in the edge of his jacket, but he didn't think he'd been hit. You know, he thought, remembering the shoot-out with the meth-dealing Aryan who'd put a bullet in Leshaun, he'd been having people fire guns at him way too regularly in the past couple of weeks. Fortunately, as Leshaun came bounding up the steps, his service revolver in his hand, Dawson had already dropped the shotgun to the deck.

"Oh my god. Are you okay?"

Mike turned to Leshaun and motioned for him to holster his gun, but Leshaun had already lowered his weapon and was pulling back his coat to tuck it away. Mike looked back at Dawson, digging into his ringing ear with his pinky. "What the hell, Rich, why on earth did you try to shoot me?"

"I didn't. I mean, I did, but only because you told me to. And I wasn't trying to shoot *you*, not really. But you told me that if anybody showed up I had to put a hole in them, that I needed to keep everybody away from Fanny and Annie, even if that meant killing them."

Mike glanced over Dawson's shoulder and saw his ex-wife staring at him from inside the cottage door. She looked frightened.

"I assumed you'd look to see who it was first," Mike said. "Thank goodness you aren't a great shot." He and Leshaun finished walking to the door. "Where's Annie?"

"She's got headphones on," Fanny said. She reached out and took Dawson's arm. Mike realized Dawson was shaking. "She's watching a movie on her tablet and she borrowed Rich's good headphones. They're noise canceling."

"They must work pretty well if a shotgun wasn't enough to get her attention," Leshaun said. He leaned in to kiss Fanny on the cheek and then shook Dawson's hand.

"We were watching the bombings," Dawson said. "On television." He pointed to a small satellite dish bolted to the side of the cottage. "I didn't hear the boat until the last minute, and then you were running up the stairs and I just . . ." He gulped. "Sorry."

Mike took a deep breath. He could relax. He was okay. His jacket had a little extra ventilation, but he was okay. All they had to do was get back to Minneapolis in time. "We've got to go. Right now. We need to be—" He stopped talking. He'd been about to tell Rich and Fanny that they needed to leave right now, that very second, to get in the boat and then into the agency car, to ride buckled up in the back of their sedan while the cherries ran and Leshaun mashed the peddle to the ground, so that they could blaze into the airport and load up on a military transport plane before things went to hell in the Midwest, but now he paused. "Bombings? What bombings?"

Dawson looked at him queerly. "You don't know? Why are you here? I figured that's why you came."

"No. We've been ordered to pull out. The whole agency. And not just us. Every federal government asset that can get out. Not just from Minneapolis. Everywhere west of the Mississippi. We've got to be at the airport by six to get on a plane, but we can bring family with us." He realized Fanny was staring at him like he was crazy. "What?"

"You really don't know?"

He didn't. So they took him inside and sat him down in front of the television, where he watched scattered video captured by shaky cell phones: highways exploding, jets streaking through the sky, bridges collapsing. The news anchor trying to keep her voice steady as she described the destruction of roads and tunnels, the military and police trying to turn the country into an impassable patchwork quilt. The station replayed the president's brief speech which included her order for all citizens, wherever they were, to hold in place, and a clear and frank statement that the military *would* be destroying transportation hot points, regardless of whether citizens were still using those hot points or not, and that the military *would* use lethal force to prevent people from traveling. In other words, the president had said, "In plain English, stay the hell off the roads. Stay home."

Mike sat there, watching the television and understanding that whatever the plans had been to get federal agents like him east with their families, those plans had been canceled.

As he was watching, his cell phone buzzed. A text from the bureau chief to every single agent under his command: *Due to rapidly deteriorating conditions, our timeline has been accelerated. Wheels up in one hour.*

Mike felt sick. There was no way he'd get back to the airport in time. He was too late to get them out.

Oslo, Norway

They'd found the yellow-tinged barn stuffed full of egg sacs like a sausage ready to burst. The farm was out on the fringe of the city. A lonely outpost left over from the days when Oslo was more of a notion than a reality, from when the only thing around was farms, fields, and trees. Had the spiders hatched back then, they would have moved more slowly: horses and chickens and cows and other livestock would have outnumbered humans ten to one. Back then, traveling twenty miles in a single day seemed ambitious. The spiders would have had to march along at their own pace. No jets or cars or trains or boats, fewer ways to spread their relentless hunger. But by the time the spiders came, almost all the farms had given way to houses, office buildings, and shopping centers. This barn, the one crammed with egg sacs, was a mere relic from an earlier time. The farm itself was only a third of the acreage it had been in 1950. It had been a working farm until the mid-2000s, but the farmer was too old now. The fields had been fallow for years, and the barn was no longer a working concern. The farmer was in his early nineties, and his only son, a man himself in his midsixties, kept expecting his phone calls to go unanswered. The son had an agreement already in place with a developer: the moment the farmer died the bulldozers would roll. A comfortable retirement for the son and modern town houses on an urban green for the developer. That was the plan.

There had only been one outbreak in Norway, originating twenty miles away. An engineer who'd come home from a trip to China, feverish and scared, talking nonsense one day and then bringing destruction the next, his body opening up like Pandora's box. The Norwegians reacted quickly. They had benefited from unaccountable good fortune. Some countries, like India and China and Brazil, were the unfortunate inheritors of sleeping broods of spiders who had been waiting thousands of years to hatch. Norway was only a secondary site, lucky enough to have seen the reports out of China, to see the footage from India, from Rio de Janeiro and Los Angeles. The moment the traveler's body erupted, Norway ordered burn zones and pullbacks. There were quick decisions by the military. Lives were lost—thousands, tens of thousands, perhaps as many as a hundred thousand; they were still counting the dead and missing—but it could have been much worse. That's what everybody was saying. They'd been lucky in Norway. And luckier still: they'd found the infestation site in the barn so easily.

The barn hadn't been painted in perhaps forty years. The wood was worn down by the winters and the wind and the sun. It listed strangely to one side and had done so since a bad storm in the 1980s. Back when it was a working farm, the farmer had spent many nights listening to the wind and worrying that the building would fall in on itself, killing the two dozen cows that were housed inside. It had been a large barn at one time. Not by the industrial-farming standards of today, but large enough that if there had still been two dozen cows and the attendant bales of hay, there would still have been plenty of space for the rusted-out farm equipment that the farmer kept thinking he might try to sell as antiques.

It was all too late for that, of course.

The Norwegians congratulated themselves on how quickly they'd found the infestation and stomped it out. They decided, based on the American reports of the Staples Center in Los Angeles, that there'd be a singular breeding ground, and if they could find it and contain it before the spiders spread fully, they would be protected. They had found the barn almost as soon as the spiders started dropping dead. Not that it had been particularly difficult. You could see the white egg sacs straining through the cracks in the boards from the road. They were squeezing out of every opening; the barn itself packed so tightly that there was no way inside. The Norwegians did not even bother doing an accounting.

How many egg sacs were inside?

Who cared?

Burn them all!

A demolitions expert rigged it so that everything burned inward, a controlled and rolling flame from which there was no hope of egress, and the barn and everything inside was sacrificed in the name of prudence. No scientific study necessary. It was a great conflagration. Those who had not already evacuated or who had already returned could see the glow of the fire from a distance of twenty kilometers. Those who were closer, the demolitions expert and the firemen who had volunteered, the soldiers who had been assigned to cordon off the area, and the television reporters who had insisted they be allowed inside to witness it, all said that the sound of the egg sacs burning was terrifying in its own right. The egg sacs in the barn, too many to count, had been chalky, white, cold and calcified, inorganic looking so that it was hard to imagine that they contained anything alive. And as the fire burned around them, the egg sacs shattered and popped, the heat twisting them open with violent cracks, each explosion sounding like a gunshot.

When the fire burned itself out, the soldiers combed the embers to make sure there was nothing left. And nothing was left of the barn.

But it wasn't only the barn.

The Norwegians had failed, unaccountably, unforgivably, to search the high school auditorium, only three kilometers away from the barn. It was in an area that had been particularly overrun with spiders, and perhaps this oversight had to do with the simple fact that the Norwegians had thought they'd found the main infestation. After all, the Americans, the Japanese, and the Indians were all reporting that they found egg sacs concentrated in large, dark buildings. In the panic and the confusion and sheer overwhelming terror, they found the barn and thought they'd found the solution: here are the spiders you need to destroy. Could they be faulted for not continuing to look? Could they be faulted for not understanding that the barn contained one type of egg sac—the hard, almost petrified versions designed to last through floods and wind, snow and rain, to sleep for thousands of years until the next time the rhythm of the years called the spiders out to feed—and the high school auditorium contained another? If only they'd found those other egg sacs, they'd have seen immediately that there was a difference. The softness of the webbing, the heat of the egg sacs, speaking to a very different timeline. And in the back, the pulsing glow of the largest of the sacs, large enough that perhaps six or eight of the old farmer's cows could have nestled inside, would have made it clear to every person that something new and horrible was coming.

But the Norwegians hadn't found these other egg sacs. And in the dark, quiet loneliness of the high school auditorium, underneath stage lights that remained unlit, nestled among the rigid, worn-down seats in the audience, and woven against the walls and throughout the theater rigging, the sacs grew warmer, the pulsing glow at the back of the auditorium grew brighter.

The Interstate 80 High Times Truck Stop and Family Fun Zone Restaurant and Gas Station Taco Bell Pizza Hut Starbucks KFC Burrito Barn 42 Flavors Ice Cream Extravaganza Coast-to-Coast Emporium, Nebraska

Well, shit. Babcock Jones lit another cigarette. A little warning would have been nice before the government blew the holy hell out of the highway. Technically, President Pilgrim did say the government was going to be dropping bombs, but he didn't think she really *meant* it. He just about crapped his pants from surprise at the first explosion.

He came up the hill—it wasn't much of a hill—here because it was the closest thing to peaceful he could find so close to the interstate. His business was on one of the most traveled stretches of Interstate 80, so a little bit of quiet was an important thing. Also, as long as he walked up the grassy rise, five or six hundred yards away from the Interstate 80 High Times Truck Stop and Family Fun Zone Restaurant and Gas Station Taco Bell Pizza Hut Starbucks KFC Burrito Barn 42 Flavors Ice Cream Extravaganza Coast-to-

Coast Emporium, Mags let him have a smoke, figuring that the exercise might counterbalance the ill effects of the cigarette. She'd quit back in 1992 just like it was nothing. She woke up one day and said, "Think I'm not going to smoke anymore," and *bam!* Two packs a day down to none. He'd tried to quit, too, but he couldn't, and Mags had declared that the only way he could have a cigarette was if he hauled his sorry ass up the rise. So he obeyed.

That woman scared him. Forty-six years they'd been married, and she still scared the ever-loving pixie dust out of him. Which was probably a good thing. They'd gotten married right out of high school, and left to his own devices, Babcock Jones would have just kept pumping gas and been happy with a couple of beers on Friday night and a baseball game on the radio. But Mags had insisted he make something of himself, and the very first lesson he'd learned in his marriage was to do what Mags told him to. So they took out a loan that scared him almost as much as Mags scared him, and they bought the gas station. Then the gas station had become a gas station and a restaurant, and then it had become a gas station and a restaurant and a truck stop, and now, forty-six years into their marriage, Babcock Jones could walk up the sloping rise of grass, pull out a cigarette, and see something resembling an empire. The Interstate 80 High Times Truck Stop and Family Fun Zone Restaurant and Gas Station Taco Bell Pizza Hut Starbucks KFC Burrito Barn 42 Flavors Ice Cream Extravaganza Coast-to-Coast Emporium was like a city unto itself. He had billboards two hundred miles out in either direction, and there wasn't an American worth his salt who didn't stop for a fill-up and the chance to see a good old-fashioned midwestern spectacle of a truck stop.

And now, he figured, those drivers weren't going to have much of a choice but to stop. Sure, he was going to lose out on traffic in one direction, but there'd be a hell of a backup in the other. Still, a warning from Uncle Sam would have been nice. Some sort of a howdy-do, we're going to be blowing your highway up Mr. Babcock Jones, so be ready for some loud noises. He took another puff of his cigarette and realized his hand was shaking.

When Babcock Jones wasn't listening to his beloved bumbling Chicago Cubs on the radio—it hadn't been the same since Ron Santos died, but he'd been listening all his life—he relaxed by watching war movies and documentaries on his television. It was a state-of-the-art seventy-inch set he'd had special ordered and installed with surround sound, and he'd even paid for somebody to come out and adjust the contrast and all that shit. Until a few minutes ago, he would have argued for all he was worth that what he could see on his television set was better than what you'd see in real life. More colors, he liked to say. But that had been before the missile. Or maybe it was a bomb. He wasn't really sure. What he was sure of was that it had happened fast and it had been loud.

Who'd have thought he'd ever see something like that, live in the flesh, right out here in Hicksville, Nebraska?

He was standing at the top of the rise when it happened, trying to get his breath back from the walk and enjoy his cigarette at the same time. It was a gradual slope of grass, but he was a little heavier than he wanted to be. If he was being honest with himself, a *lot* heavier. Back when it had just been the Interstate 80 High Times Truck Stop and Family Fun Zone Restaurant and Gas Station, Babcock had kept his weight under control. He'd always been a stocky fellow. Mags complained about his smoking, but not about his belly. More of him to love, she always said, though sometimes he worried he might have a heart attack and die on top of her, and she'd be trapped underneath him and end up dying herself in a manner so embarrassing that it was probably a good thing they'd both be dead or Mags would have ended up killing him. But she said she loved him no matter what shape his body was in, and there was a lot of him to love right now. It started when they'd added the Taco Bell, and it had gotten worse with each additional temple of fried gastronomy. He liked to start his day with a breakfast burrito from the Burrito Barn and one of those chocolate caramel Frappuccinos at Starbucks. Then, after he did his rounds in the truck garage, he'd stop for a small personal pizza at Pizza Hut, and then maybe grab a milk shake from 42 Flavors Ice Cream Extravaganza to tide him over until it was time for lunch, which was always a family meal complete with fries and a large Coke from the KFC. For dinner, Mags usually made him eat a salad. He'd just taken the first few heaving puffs of the cigarette and had turned from looking at his little empire to the west and to the way Interstate 80 stretched off eastward into the distance, connecting the country and running through his backyard, when the overpass half a mile down exploded.

A bomb, a missile, he didn't know which, but it had blown the shit out of the overpass. The overpass *and* Interstate 80 running in either direction for a good hundred yards. He actually saw the jet coming back for the second pass before it unloaded. Whatever blacktopped highway had been in good working order after the first hit was taken care of by the second pass with the kind of hot vengeance that reminded him of how Mags could be when she thought he wasn't listening to her. The third run extended the damage even closer to where Babcock stood on the grassy rise, and for a moment he wondered if his insurance would cover him if the government blew up the Interstate 80 High Times Truck Stop and Family Fun Zone Restaurant and Gas Station Taco Bell Pizza Hut Starbucks KFC Burrito Barn 42 Flavors Ice Cream Extravaganza Coast-to-Coast Emporium. Probably not. That probably fell under the act of war provision, he thought, but that thought was quickly replaced by the idea that maybe it would be a good idea for him to move before the jet came back for a fourth run. There was no fourth run, however. Whoever had been flying the jet seemed to think that they'd done a good enough job. Babcock guessed that the pilot was right. A plume of smoke was resting against the horizon. Nobody was going anywhere without a pair of hiking boots. A few idiots might try cutting through the soft farm dirt that lined the roads, but that wasn't going to work out so well. They'd get stuck axle deep and have to wait for one of Babcock's tow trucks to come and haul them out. He turned and looked to the west. The traffic was already stacking up. Babcock smiled. The Interstate 80 High Times Truck Stop and Family Fun Zone Restaurant and Gas Station Taco Bell Pizza Hut Starbucks KFC Burrito Barn 42 Flavors Ice Cream Extravaganza Coast-to-Coast Emporium was going to see a downtick in business from truckers blowing across America, but they were about to see a serious uptick in truckers and families who were no longer going anywhere.

Thirty miles west of Babcock's truck stop, Macer Dickson sat in the back of his Audi feeling a little guilty about dropping Bobby Higgs off on the side of the road. But only a little guilty. Jesus Christ. The Prophet Bobby Higgs. The guy really thought he was special. What a dickbag. But he'd served his purpose. There'd been a few panicked hours when Macer thought he was going to be trapped in the hell that had become Los Angeles, but recognizing what he could do with Bobby had been a stroke of genius. That idiot could work a crowd. The hilarious thing was that he'd actually started to believe all of it. Believed that Macer was helping him to build an army, believed that there was a higher purpose to what they were doing. The only thing Macer was interested in building was a human shield. He wanted out of Los Angeles, whatever it took.

Oh, but to hear Bobby at the end? He thought he really was some sort of savior. As if Macer had ever intended to use Bobby as anything other than a tool for the greatest jailbreak in modern history. Macer wasn't a particularly bad guy. Sure, he sold drugs and girls and controlled a good chunk of the criminal traffic in Los Angeles, but he really wasn't any worse than he needed to be. That didn't mean he was a saint, though, and it hadn't taken him very long to figure out that this was one of those situations that called for putting Macer Dickson first. So screw Bobby, and screw the people who crammed into USC's stadium thinking that the Prophet Bobby Higgs could deliver them to safety. The truth was that he *had* delivered a number of them to safety, but they weren't his problem. What mattered was that Macer Dickson was free and clear, headed away from Los Angeles. He was going to have a new, safe beginning, and he wasn't going to feel guilty about leaving Bobby behind.

It had been smooth sailing since he'd kicked Bobby out of the car. Lita was a hell of a driver. She seemed to operate on coffee and gummy bears, and they hadn't once been pulled over for speeding. Which was good, because there were more than a few guns in the car and the trunk was mostly full of cash. Once he got to Chicago, the cash would go a long way toward helping him set up a new operation, and if not, well, that's what the guns were for. One of the reasons he'd been so successful in Los Angeles was because the only thing heavier than Lita's lead foot was her trigger finger. Macer was not a particularly bad guy, but Lita had a mean streak a mile wide. Things were good. And they were about to get so much better. He'd been seeing the billboards for the truck stop about once every ten miles for nearly two hundred miles, and while he normally wasn't one for that sort of American circus of bullshit, he'd gotten seriously interested in the idea of getting some KFC.

The way Lita kept the gas pedal tight to the floor, they'd be there right quick, fifteen, twenty minutes to go thirty miles. Gas for the car, gummy bears and coffee for Lita, and a bucket of KFC and some Red Bull for him. A ten-minute stop, max, and on they'd go. The open roads of America were in front of him, clear highways ahead.

A quick stop and then nothing in their way, nothing to stop Macer's flight from Los Angeles.

Chicago beckoned, he thought.

"Hey, Macer," Lita said from the front, "do you see that smoke up ahead?"

Macer leaned forward to look out the windshield. "Fire of some sort? Probably nothing to worry about. We'll make a quick stop for gas and food and keep going. There's going to be a flood of people headed east, and we need to make sure we stay ahead of the circus."

Càidh Island, Loch Ròg, Isle of Lewis, Outer Hebrides

Padruig had gone down into the cellar and come back with a world map that Aonghas remembered from his childhood. It had hung in the library until he'd gone off to university and Padruig had decided to have the castle redecorated. The map was the same as those that used to hang in classrooms across the United Kingdom, and, in some of the smaller, poorer schools, probably still did. Every man and woman Aonghas's age had learned geography in their early school years, and every man and woman Aonghas's age had secretly yearned as children to be picked by the teacher as the student allowed to take the long stick with the metal question mark at the end and hook the handle of the map, unrolling it from its spool and then fidgeting with it until you felt it catch securely open. On the rare occasions that Aonghas had brought childhood friends with him to Càidh Island, they'd all been amazed at the presence of the map in his grandfather's library. He hadn't thought of the map in years, however, hadn't even realized that his grandfather had held on to it, but there was a certain nostalgia to unrolling it across the table in the dining room.

Thuy glanced at the pages of notes the two men had made and held up the black marker. "Just draw right on it?"

She'd made the usual jokes about a doctor's handwriting when she volunteered to be the one to mark the map. Aonghas had laughed, but had also pointed out that his fiancée was not actually a doctor, as she had not technically graduated from medical school yet, and Thuy had said "close enough," and then Aonghas had pointed out that even had she graduated, she still had several years as a resident at the Stornoway hospital ahead of her before she'd be practicing as a doctor on her own, and in response, Thuy, quietly, so that Padruig couldn't hear, had pointed out that Aonghas might want to think about what else he pointed out if he wanted to have sex with her that night when they went to bed, or maybe earlier, say after lunch, if things went particularly in Aonghas's favor.

Aonghas had stopped pointing things out.

"Right on the map," Padruig said. "Let's mark it up. It's been moldering in my cellar for years. I'd forgotten it was down there, but sometimes it's a good thing to be forgetful. Forgetting you have something and then remembering it is a little bit like having a genie grant you a wish. We needed a map for our work, and poof, a map!"

Thuy beamed at the old man, and Aonghas couldn't stop himself from feeling a mild bit of jealousy. The two of them had turned into thickened porridge. He still couldn't believe that his grandfather had known his fiancée was pregnant before he did, but Thuy swore up and down she hadn't meant to tell Padruig. She'd just bumped into him a few moments after taking the pregnancy test and couldn't help herself. But why, Aonghas asked, did she have one of those pregnancy tests with her in the first place? Thuy gave him the crooked little grin he liked so much and admitted that she'd had her suspicions that a recent and somewhat comical mishap with a condom might be worth checking on. She'd ducked into the druggist's in Stornoway the day she was supposed to fly out, when she'd said she was just running out to grab them a couple of coffees. She'd bought the pregnancy test but hadn't had the nerve to take it. With all the time to think—too much time to think—on Càidh Island, she had finally decided it was better to just tear open the plastic wrapper and let out a wee little stream and have an answer one way or another.

"And you told my grandfather first," Aonghas had harrumphed. Thuy had smiled again and kissed him. He tried to sulk for a few more minutes, but he couldn't help himself: even with everything that was going on in the world, it made him wildly happy. She made him wildly happy. Beside which, they'd been alone in their bedroom at the time, and what with hugging each other in celebration, and hugging leading to kissing each other, and kissing leading to . . . Well, he got over his feelings of annoyance quite quickly.

His little tweak of jealous about Thuy and his grandfather's relationship also passed quickly. He realized that instead of any jealousy, he should be feeling complete relief. Seeing the two of them get along, he couldn't believe he'd ever been nervous about introducing Thuy to Padruig.

"What did we decide?" Thuy asked. "How are we weighting Olso?"

"Secondary," both Aonghas and Padruig said at the same time. Some of the reported outbreaks had been easy to agree on. Locations that seemed to have spontaneous spider infestations were labeled primary, while secondary outbreaks were locations that had likely been swarmed after spiders were brought in by an infected traveler. There was also the question of timing. Primary locations seemed to happen earlier, almost concurrently, while secondary locations were a function of migration and the spread of newly hatched spiders. Xinjiang Province was a primary. Los Angeles was a secondary. Delhi was a primary. Stornoway, where Aonghas had seen the Indian fellow unzip himself into a storm of spiders, was a secondary. Some of the reported outbreaks had been more difficult to categorize. They'd argued over London and Frankfurt for hours, with Aonghas sure the cities were primary outbreak sites and Padruig convinced they were secondary.

"Even if we mislabel a few outbreaks as secondary swarms, I don't think that will make a huge difference," Padruig said. "We might not be able to pinpoint the exact start of this, but we can come close."

Thuy nodded. Aonghas and Padruig double-checked the list as she used the marker to draw large circles around Xinjiang Province, around Delhi, around Rio de Janeiro. Part of Aonghas felt incredibly comforted by the exercise. In many ways, this process was similar to how he and Padruig had broken down new Harry Thorton mysteries when Aonghas had first taken over the franchise. They'd argue about an idea for hours and hours and when they came to some sort of consensus, they'd pull out the thick roll of butcher's paper that Padruig kept for that very purpose and diagram the novel's plot ahead of time. Who killed whom with what and where? The timeline for characters both major and minor, floor plans and murder weapons, and the location of escape routes. Every bit of the novel deconstructed before it had even been constructed. And then, at some point, Padruig would take the whole thing, roll it up, throw it into the fire, and tell Aonghas it was time to just write the damn story and forget about all the other nonsense.

The spiders really were just another mystery to solve, Aonghas thought, and having Thuy there with them felt so natural that he had to remind himself that she hadn't always been. How could he have had a life before he met her? How could he have been so stupid as to wait to ask her to marry him? Or, he thought, chagrined, to wait so that his grandfather accidently told her Aonghas had a ring and planned to propose so that she could accept the offer of marriage before he even had the chance to ask? Really, Aonghas thought, smiling at Thuy's thin fingers as they carefully marked the map, his grandfather could be a bit of an ass at times.

When Thuy finished marking the map, they all stood back to look at what they'd wrought.

"Huh," Thuy said. "Peru?"

"So it appears," Padruig said. "May I borrow your mobile phone again, dear? I have a call to make."

Desperation, California

"**Y**ou're calling it the Spinal Tap?" Amy said. "Are you guys literally the dorkiest people alive?"

Gordo tried not to purse his lips, but he couldn't help himself. "It uses sound, and we even fabricated it so that it goes up to eleven, and . . . Oh, never mind."

Amy and Fred had finished their movie and come down to the workshop to see if they could persuade Gordo and Shotgun to play Catan as a drinking game. Every time you rolled a seven you had to do a shot, she'd said. Which sounded both fun and like a good way to get alcohol poisoning. But when Gordo had explained what they were doing instead—trying to devise a way to kill spiders from a distance using something other than the conventional weaponry of explosives and projectiles that did a fine job of tearing apart human flesh but seemed to have failed miserably so far on spiders—Amy and Fred had come up with a new and different drinking game that, as far as Gordo could tell, mostly involved making fun of him and Shotgun for being nerds.

Amy was pretty well blasted, but in the fun sort of way that she got. He'd had a girlfriend once, in his senior year of high school, who turned into the nastiest version of herself when she was drinking. He'd been fortunate that they'd been in high school, where his girlfriend's drinking had been limited to illicit house parties. Sometimes, when Gordo wanted to feel good about his life choices, he'd go online and read her blog: according to her infrequent updates, she'd turned into a drunk in college, entered rehab for alcohol right after graduation, moved to Florida, gotten married and immediately pregnant at twenty-three, had five kids in seven years, and then reinvented herself as something called a "psychic energy home consultant." He remembered that one time, right before they'd broken up, she'd tried sneaking into his bedroom after she'd gone to a party with some friends. She'd been so drunk that she'd actually snuck into Gordo's parents' room, waking his parents, of course, and then proceeding to tell them, in great detail, that she didn't like having sex with Gordo very much because even though his penis wasn't all *that* small, he didn't seem to know what to do with it other than pretend it was a jackhammer. Gordo sighed. Thankfully, his wife was nothing like that. As a drunk, Amy was plenty charming. She got giggly and sweet, and, most of the time, even friskier than she already was.

"To the Spinal Tap!" Fred shouted. He lifted his Kir Royale— of course Shotgun had stocked the shelter with cases and cases of champagne and cassis liqueur—and clinked his glass against Amy's. The two of them knocked back their drinks and got up to go to the kitchen for a refill.

Shotgun shook his head at his husband's back and then looked at Gordo. "The only thing that would make it better is if we could actually run the Spinal Tap using music from the movie *This Is Spinal Tap* instead of running a simple, single, subsonic tone."

"Speaking of movies, you know, if this was a movie, this is when the eccentric scientists would try to get through to the White House but be dismissed as some sort of cranks," Gordo said, "and then we'd have to spend the next few scenes in an elaborate plot to sneak through security so we could talk to the president."

"First of all," Shotgun said, "I think we're more engineers than scientists. Or, at least, I'm an engineer. I don't know what the hell to call you. Running programs to take advantage of inefficiencies on the financial market doesn't really make you anything other than an opportunist."

"It's arbitrage," Gordo said.

Shotgun shrugged. "So you're an arbitrageur?"

"That's not a word."

"Actually, I think it is a word, but given that you wrote the program that you use to find the inefficiencies, I think we'll say that's good enough and lump you in with me. Let's just say we're both engineers."

"Fine. Engineers. Much better. So we have a spider-killing machine that we've named the Spinal Tap, in homage to a fake documentary, and even though we haven't actually tested our spider-killing machine, and we don't really know if our spider-killing machine works, the *engineers* are going to have to come up with an elaborate scheme to sneak into the White House to get the attention of the president," Gordo said.

"Or I can just call a guy I know," Shotgun said.

"You're going to call a guy?"

"I'm going to call a guy."

"Oh. Well. That seems significantly easier than my plan. Who are you going to call?"

"Robert Gibbons."

"Robert Gibbons?" Gordo said. "As in the director of the CIA?"

Shotgun hesitated and then nodded. "Classified and all that stuff, but I'm not sure how much they are going to care about that anymore. I've done some work for Gibbons. Technical consulting, mostly. A few design things. He's loaned me out to the Pentagon once or twice."

Gordo stared at Shotgun. If he'd been pressed, he would have said that Shotgun was his best friend. Sure, he talked to his brother on the phone once a month or so, and there were a couple of buddies from college and some other guys he'd known when he'd lived in New York, but since he and Amy had moved out to Desperation, he'd spent more time with Shotgun than with anybody other than his wife. "I've got to say, I never really figured you as the type to do military work."

"Because I'm gay?"

"Well, duh. That's part of it. But more so because Fred's such a pinko peacenik."

"I love that man to death," Shotgun said. "Best thing that ever happened to me was persuading Fred to marry me. So, sure, on some level it makes sense that I might not want to do military work. I'm not even convinced I really believe in war. There's the concept of a just war, or a good war, and you could argue we've had a couple of those, but mostly war seems like a swampland of immorality. And yes, a generation or two ago I might not have been able to get security clearance because being a fag"—Gordo winced—"made me a risk. In a lot of ways it's complicated. But on another level it was a simple decision for me: I was overruled by my own curiosity. When I've done engineering work for the CIA or the Pentagon, it's because they've called me in to solve a problem they'd already taken a swing at. It's not that I necessarily like doing military work, but they pay me a boatload of money and the problems are usually too interesting for me to say no to."

"Like what?"

"Classified."

Gordo grinned. "Piss off."

"Seriously. Classified. But I can give you a hint. Remember that thing when all the GPS satellites went down for a week last summer? That was me."

They both laughed, and then Shotgun hesitated again, and Gordo figured that maybe Shotgun was worried about having disclosed classified information, even if what he'd said had been not much of anything. Though the fact that Shotgun evidently had the phone number of the director of the CIA was a little scary. But that wasn't what was on Shotgun's mind.

"Can I ask you a question and get an honest answer?" he asked.

"Of course."

"Is this what you expected?"

"What?"

Shotgun shrugged. "I don't know. All of this. We've both been planning for the day when the shit hits the fan. And we're not the only ones. I mean, forget the Internet, and forget the religious doomsday preppers. We're smart guys, and I think not *too* crazy."

"We were right about all of this," Gordo said. "I mean, not about spiders, but about the end of the world as we know it. I think that makes us not crazy at all. We were right."

"That's the thing. I'm starting to feel like maybe we weren't right. I mean, I did everything I could think of. And I thought of everything. Planned for everything." There was the sound of glass breaking in the kitchen, and Shotgun winced. "As in, it doesn't matter if that was Fred dropping his glass or Fred dropping an entire bottle. We're stocked with everything and then more of everything, and then redundancies of the redundancies. This was one of my prime preoccupations for years. But since the Chinese dropped their first nuke and then the spiders came out and we've been holing up here, underground, I've got to admit it: I'm bored."

Shotgun looked suddenly relieved. "There. I've said it. Hiding out in the shelter is boring. Oh, man, it's so boring."

"Yeah, but—"

"Tell me, Gordo, when have you felt most alive since we locked ourselves down here? Those first few hours, sure, when there was adrenaline and fear, but since then? Because I can think of two things that have felt exciting for me, and I bet it's the same two things for you."

Gordo knew Shotgun was right. "Making the flamethrower nozzle and then designing the Spinal Tap." He winced. "Okay. Amy's right. That name has to go. Nobody is ever going to take it seriously if we call it the Spinal Tap. But so what if it's boring? We're safe down here, right? Wasn't that the whole point of getting ourselves ready? Otherwise, why build shelters and stock up and move out here? I mean, why else would you move to Desperation if not because you were getting ready for the end of the world? Certainly not for the shopping."

Shotgun was already shaking his head. "But that's not it, is it? It wasn't ever about being safe. It was about the great adventure. I never thought the point of survival was to figure out how to kill time. That's what it feels like, right? It hasn't even been a month and I'm already losing my mind. It's got to be worse for Fred and Amy because literally all they can do is kill time. No wonder they've been drinking nonstop. What else is there to do? No, I think what I liked about getting ready, about preparing this shelter, was that it was another sort of problem solving. It was a way to keep my mind busy between projects. An analytical kind of checklist making. It was sort of a game, and, to be completely honest, it was another way of showing how smart I am. I could see there was a looming disaster, and even if I didn't predict that it would be an onslaught of spiders, I did accurately predict the end of the world. But now that we're actually living it, despite all my thinking and planning, it's not what I thought it would be," he said. "I don't want to hide down here and then peek my head out in a few years to see how the rest of the world has fared. It's just not very interesting. I think maybe I expected surviving the end of the world was going to be some sort of great adventure, but it's not. It's boring. Boring, boring, boring. And, honestly, I worry about Fred. Do you really think he's cut out for just holing up in this hole in the ground?"

"Okay."

"Okay, what?"

"Okay," Gordo said. "I agree. I'm bored too, and while I think it was a great decision for Amy and I to ride this out with you and Fred, you're right. There's a limit to how many games of cards we can play, how many movies we can watch. My fantasy about surviving the end of the world was never about sitting in the bunker. It was about what came after. But before we worry about having some sort of great adventure, let's call your friend at the CIA and see what happens when we tell him about whatever the hell we're going to call this spider-killing thing now that we aren't going to call it the Spinal Tap."

"How about the Spider Stereo?"

"Not better," Gordo said. "Just make the call."

USS *Christopher Martin Graham,* Gulf of Mexico

The pilot had just enough time to take a piss, pound an energy drink, and eat a granola bar before his crew told him it was time to head out on another mission. He gave the thumbs-up, climbed into the cockpit, secured his helmet, and fired her up, ready to fly his dragon across the sky so he could drop more fire on America's roads and highways.

The King Royal Hotel, Chicago, Illinois

Perry Pozloski, the assistant night manager for the King Royal Hotel, one of Chicago's most expensive, ritziest, and oldest hotels, couldn't believe he was feeling wistful for the winter. The winter in Chicago could be something shrill and mean, a lot like his ex-wife. The difference was that when Chicago opened herself up to you, she came alive.

Pozloski was born and raised on the South Side. White Sox all the way. Chicago all the way. He was the Bears even when they tried to go all offense, the Bulls with or without Jordan, the Blackhawks in triple overtime. He took a week in the summer to go fishing in Wisconsin, and a week in the winter to drink beer in Jamaica with his high school buddies, but it had never once occurred to him that he might live somewhere else. His ex-wife had been from Pittsburgh originally, and Pozloski thought that her heritage might have been part of the problem with their marriage. She was a Steelers' fan, for Christ's sake.

He sighed and put the thought of his ex-wife out of his mind. He got wistful, occasionally, when he remembered what she looked like in her underwear, or, even better, out of her underwear, but the truth was, he had been a lot happier since she'd left him. A year ago, he'd run into Jenny Growolski, who'd been his high school sweetheart—they used to joke that if they got married she'd be Jenny Growolski-Pozloski—and it turned out she was coming off a divorce of her own and had moved back to the neighborhood. They started dating a few days after they ran into each other and Pozloski figured that if things kept going the way they were, he and Jenny might end up married after all. Maybe his ex-wife had ruined his twenties, but he was only thirty-two. He and Jenny were plenty young enough to start a family. They'd been talking about it, in fact. In a general sort of way. No specifics. Not without a rock on her finger, Jenny had said. No. Not a rock. That was one of the things he liked—okay, loved—about Jenny. His ex-wife had insisted on a rock, even though, at the time, he'd only been the night porter at the King Royal Hotel, pulling in minimum wage plus tips, with tips being a joke on the graveyard shift. He'd used a credit card to pay for his ex-wife's engagement ring, and he supposed that had been one of the things that presaged the end, right there at the beginning, because their money problems had been something else, and it was no real coincidence that his ex-wife had really started cheating on him just after he'd declared bankruptcy. That happened about the same time he realized that going from a single credit card to more than a dozen wasn't something they could recover from. But that wasn't what Jenny was talking about when she asked for a ring. In fact, she'd insisted that she didn't want an expensive ring.

"I had a rock, a big old diamond ring, when I was married and living in New York, and that didn't stop me from getting divorced and moving back home, Perry. If I get married again," she'd said, looking at him in that way that made even Perry Pozloski know that she didn't really mean the "if," and that she'd say yes if he asked her, "I don't need a fancy ring. But I need a ring. I'm not having kids unless there's a real commitment there, but a real commitment doesn't need to cost a lot of money. I'd be happy enough with sterling silver."

So if Pozloski didn't miss his ex-wife, he did, sure as heck, at that moment, miss the Chicago winter. Not how the cold could be just a pure hate at times. Not the way the wind came across the plains like a great chomping jaw of ice and pain. Tourists at the King Royal Hotel, in their cashmere coats and cars that had been warmed by waiting drivers, liked to tell you that Chicago was called the Windy City because of the politics, but Pozloski knew the truth. Pozloski knew the way the wind could scrape through the alleys and down the Magnificent Mile, the way you might drink an extra beer so you could put off leaving the bar and facing the demon blowing down the collar of your jacket and tightening your spine so much that you'd wake the next morning with muscle spasms.

He didn't miss *that* part of winter, but he missed the way it made the King Royal feel: it was a grand, old building, and in the middle of winter the radiator heat made it warm and cozy. Not like now. Now, even though they were having a short re-spite from the unseasonably warm weather, the King Royal Hotel didn't feel cozy. It felt stuffed to the gills. And the guests, the business travelers and couples and families who could afford to pay for the kind of personalized service that the King Royal Hotel was famous for—people who wanted the gilt and history of a Chi-cago landmark that also featured six-hundred-thread-count sheets and concierges who'd been trained to forget that the word *no* existed—had turned into vicious beasts. Not all of them. Some of them were still gracious and warm, in the way rich people could be when they were conscious of being rich and thought it was their job to make you not feel bad about the fact that they were rich and you weren't and, oh, if it isn't too much trouble, can we have some more ice and lemon wedges and I need housekeeping to do a better job in the bathroom and can you please do something about the noise of sirens coming through the windows of my eighth-story room? But many of them had dropped the thin veneer of civility, and the King Royal Hotel was as full as full could be. A mix of businessmen acting like spreadsheets still mattered in a world of flesh-eating spiders, travelers on late spring breaks who had checked in but who could never leave, and yes, men and women and families who were refugees, people who'd fled their homes out of fear and who had the means to tide themselves over in a place like the King Royal Hotel.

The man in the Royal Suite was one of those. A refugee with a platinum card. Mr. Kosgrove was from Las Vegas. The night Los Angeles had fallen, he'd left Vegas in his cherry-red Ferrari without a single suitcase, driving straight through to Chicago and flipping his keys to the valet like he was the kind of guy who wasn't worried about his bazillion-dollar car getting scratched up by a parking monkey. As the assistant night manager, Perry Pozloski had gotten used to dealing with Mr. Kosgrove's . . . one might call them eccentricities. A pair of thin blond women who might as well have been twins exiting through the lobby in thick, matching, white King Royal Hotel robes at three in the morning. He had to charge $450 to Mr. Kosgrove's bill for those robes. A frantic phone call one night from the kitchen asking Pozloski what they should do about Mr. Kosgrove's order for eleven steamed lobsters and an ice bucket full of melted lemon butter. The request that any furnishings trimmed with pink be removed from the Royal Suite immediately. Actually, the last and most recent of Kosgrove's eccentricities had been the easiest to deal with, necessitating the removal only of an ottoman, two throw pillows, a chair in the second bedroom, which had remained unoccupied except for a few shopping bags, and a painting hanging in the master bedroom over which there was quite a bit of a heated argument about whether or not the landscape, as depicted by the artist, contained pink or was, as one housekeeper argued, merely "dawn-tinted." To be safe, Pozloski had taken the painting down.

Which was why he was down here, in the subbasement of the King Royal Hotel, looking for a different painting, something suitable to hang up in Mr. Kosgrove's room. If any of the rooms in the hotel had been empty, Pozloski could simply have swapped the painting out, and he could easily have found a piece of art in one of the hallways or the lobby or the dining room that he could have traded for the landscape painting, but truth be told, he didn't mind the excuse to disappear for a little while. The subbasement was dark and dingy and cobwebby and Halloween movie horror show creepy, but it was also a really good place to smoke some pot. He could kill two birds with one stone: find a new piece of art to replace the maybe-just-a-little-bit-of-pink painting from Mr. Kosgrove's room, and, at the same time, he could get high as all heck. He deserved the chance to relax a bit. He did.

Pozloski had mostly stopped smoking pot at home. Jenny didn't disapprove of him getting high, exactly, but she didn't seem to approve of it either, and, well, sometimes a man is in love. Getting high at work was a different matter, however. Technically, he could have been fired for smoking pot while he was working. The employee manual for the hotel was unambiguous: no drugs or booze, legal or otherwise, while you're on duty. And maybe at a different time it wouldn't have just been a technicality, and Pozloski might have actually been fired for smoking pot on duty, but since he'd gotten the joints from the manager, he didn't think his position as assistant manager was in too much jeopardy. He supposed he could have just eaten some pot-laced candy or chocolate like a lot of the women on staff did, or used a vape like most of the guys did, but for him, smoking pot was as much about the *ritual* of smoking pot as it was the getting high. Call him old-fashioned, but he liked joints. Liked the paper and the crinkling sound that came with pulling a hit into his lungs. Liked the glow and the smell of the lighter. He liked standing around and drawing the joint down to a nub. But being the assistant manager and smoking pot meant, however, that he couldn't just step out onto the loading dock. He had to try, at least a little bit, to be discreet. Normally, it would have been enough to go into the laundry room and stand near the vent, but with the painting from the Royal Suite to replace, the subbasement made sense.

The elevator went only as far as the basement, so he had to carry the painting from Mr. Kosgrove's suite down a flight of crumbly concrete steps. The bulb was an old pull-chain, clear-glass filament that swung overhead, and the glow pooled at the bottom of the stairs so that the space beyond was a dark pit. There was just enough light to see the cord dangling from the next pull-chain light. A cobweb brushed against his face as he stepped forward and turned the light on. He wiped the sticky silk off his face, rolling it between his fingers and flicking it to the side. What with all that had been happening, a web should have freaked him out, but he'd never been scared of creepy crawlies.

The subbasement didn't run the whole length of the hotel, but it was still very large. If the ceiling was higher and all the decades of detritus were cleared out, the staff could play basketball down here. Pozloski raised his hand and made a shooting motion. "Swish," he said. He couldn't have told you why he never imagined himself as Chicago Bulls legend Michael Jordan. It was always Steve

Kerr, awkward white boy shooter. That was whom Pozloski liked to pretend to be whenever he played basketball. To most people, Kerr was probably better known now as a coach than he was as a player, but when Pozloski was a little kid, he remembered Kerr as a boss on the court. Ice cold. Not that Pozloski could shoot in real life, but in his imagination? He tracked the flight of his invisible basketball, over the two couches stacked one on the other, past the cemetery of broken lamps from the 1970s, past the dust-shrouded pile of indeterminate items, and through the net that was hidden somewhere in the dark. *Swoosh!* Game! Buzzer beater! Subbasement champion of the world! And why, he wondered, as he pulled one of the joints from the inside breast pocket of his uniform's blazer, was it called a subbasement? Didn't that just mean under basement? Wasn't that, you know, a basement?

He took another look at the painting from Mr. Kosgrove's suite and then leaned it against a dresser that was pushed hard against the wall. Next to the dresser, he saw a haphazard pile of Regency chairs. He carefully lifted one of the chairs off, centered it under the lightbulb, and plopped himself on it. He'd get a little dusty, but he could brush that off. The joint was between his lips, the plastic lighter in his hand, and the two things together made him very happy.

He sat for a while, smoking the joint and wondering what manner of treasures might be buried down here among the trash. He didn't come down to the subbasement very often, maybe once or twice a year. The last time he'd been down here, he'd found forty or fifty paintings neatly shelved and covered with a drop cloth near the back of the room. One of those, he was sure, would be free of pink for Mr. Kosgrove. But what else was down here? It was like some crazy aunt's basement, full of junk that should have been tossed—chairs with only three legs, lamps with no plugs, old rotary phones from the 1950s—mixed with furniture that could maybe fetch a pretty penny at an antique sale. If Pozloski had been the larcenous type, or, he was willing to admit, less lazy, he might have made some money.

He finished the joint, dropping the unsmoked nub on the floor in front of him and rubbing it with the sole of his shoe until it disintegrated into wisps of paper. Then he pushed himself up out of the chair. Whew. He was surprised at how stoned he felt. He used to be a once a day guy, but with that little look Jenny gave him any time he said he was going to get high, it had become more like once a week, once every other week. Damn. The joints the manager had given him must have had some seriously strong pot in them. Feeling good even if he was down here for the most ridiculous of reasons: Mr. Kosgrove was clearly insane. Who demands that everything pink be removed from a hotel room? But Mr. Kosgrove seemed to have very healthy credit limits on his plastic and carried a roll of $50 bills for tipping. And for $50, Pozloski was more than happy to wander around in the cobwebbed darkness of the subbasement looking for a different painting for Mr. Kosgrove's room.

He started heading back toward where he'd remembered seeing the old paintings, but when he pulled the cord on the next light, nothing happened.

"Chicken biscuits," Pozloski said. Jenny wasn't a fan of swearing either, so he'd worked hard to get out of the habit. His go-to phrase, "chicken biscuits," was, he had to admit, a deeply satisfying substitute epithet. Just listen to the way it sounded: "chicken biscuits." It had its own sort of rhythm that could hang with any curse word on the market. "Chicken biscuits," he said again. Oh, man. Chicken biscuits. He could go for some chicken biscuits.

Okay. Yeah. He was pretty high.

He pulled the blue plastic lighter back out of his pocket and rolled the flint. He held it up in front of him, the flame true and bright, a beacon of warmth. He took a step. There were little motes of dust floating everywhere, and Pozloski decided he'd talk to the general manager about getting the subbasement cleaned out. It had to be a fire hazard. He took another step forward, and then another, and then he stopped, because he was starting to feel uneasy. The farther he got away from the last working light, the less impressive the lighter's flame seemed. Three steps ago it had seemed like a torch, like it could light up the whole night, but now it seemed sort of pitiful. And hot. Really hot. Chicken biscuits! His thumb. He let the flame die and shoved his thumb into his mouth. Ouch. Good thing he was high. He gave the plastic lighter a minute to cool down, standing in the darkness. The lights behind him served as waypoints of a sort, but they weren't particularly comforting. Once it was cool enough to give it a try, he flicked the flint of the lighter with his left thumb. It took him three tries, and he thought of that creepy Roald Dahl story he'd read in high school, where the dude's wife was missing her fingers or something because they'd been betting fingers on who could light a lighter a certain number of times in a row, and then he realized he was giggling. He was giggling, and there was a weird echo down here, so his giggling sounded an awful lot like somebody moaning.

Wait. He held the lighter as far forward as he could without actually moving. What was . . .

Oh. Chicken biscuits.

Whatever thought he'd had of replacing Mr. Kosgrove's painting and getting a nice tip in return was wiped away by the sight of the young man lying on the floor in front of him. Pozloski stepped forward and held the lighter over the man's body. Latino and young, younger than Pozloski. Early twenties, and looking like shit. For a second, Pozloski figured the guy for a junkie. It wasn't unheard of for junkies to sneak into the hotel and hole up in nooks and crannies wherever they could, nodding out until somebody stumbled across them and had them thrown out. Their security was pretty good, but it happened a couple of times a year. This guy was sweating and pale and shaking, but he didn't look like a junkie. For one, he was wearing decent clothes. Dirty, but it wasn't the sort of hard-packed dirt you found on the truly down and out. This was the dirty from lying on the floor of the subbasement of the King Royal Hotel kind of dirty, not the dirty of living on the streets kind of dirty. The guy was wearing jeans and a T-shirt, sure, but the shoes were a giveaway. Pozloski never actually bought anything fancy, but he read GQ and *Esquire* and, even completely high, he could recognize an $800 pair of loafers, even on the feet of a sweating, moaning, shivering dude lying on the floor of the subbasement of the King Royal Hotel and illuminated only by the hot, hot flame of a lighter. Hot, hot!

Chicken biscuits.

He swapped thumbs, sticking his left one into his mouth now, giving the lighter a few seconds to calm down.

It was not a good few seconds.

Pozloski figured the man must not have been moaning before. He would have heard him. But now? Now that the man was moaning, it was like he couldn't stop. A long, low groan of pain and despair. The sound reminded him of his fishing vacations up in Wisconsin, the way the screen doors would screech on their hinges in the mornings, but this screen door didn't seem like it would ever close, and as soon as the lighter had cooled down long enough for him to light it again, he rolled the flint with his sore right thumb.

Dude did not look particularly terrific.

"You can't be down here," Pozloski said. His voice sounded

both too loud and too soft at the same time. The words came out of his mouth almost like he was yelling, but the subbasement swallowed them whole, muffling everything. He tried again. "Do you need help?"

"Oh, oh, oh," the man said, convulsing, and then arching his back with a spasm as he dug his heels into the floor.

"Okay," Pozloski said. He felt like he had cotton wadded up behind his eyes and cobwebs in his mouth. He really should have smoked only half the joint. That was some really strong pot. "Are you hiding from someone? You really shouldn't be down here."

"Please," the man said. Begged, really. "Please. Oh, please. They're in me." And then he screamed.

That didn't seem good.

Pozloski was high, but he wasn't a moron, and he knew he should run. He knew he should race for the stairs, should get the heck out of the subbasement, get the heck out of the King Royal Hotel altogether. He knew he should steal the keys to Mr. Kosgrove's cherry-red Ferrari and make the car scream rubber all the way to his apartment, calling Jenny while he drove so she'd be waiting for him on the sidewalk, and together they'd take that cherry-red Ferrari as far north as they could get, so that by the time dawn hit they'd be well into Wisconsin, blowing past the fishing cottage he and his buddies rented, leaving Chicago and this moaning man a distant memory in the car's mirror. That's what he should have done.

But he couldn't. Even if the army wasn't out there blowing up highways like chicken biscuits, even if travel was a real possibility, Pozloski couldn't make himself move.

The heels of the man's $800 loafers were scraping against the floor, twitching and dancing, but Pozloski's $60 shoes were rooted in place.

It wasn't anything like the videos he'd seen of Los Angeles

and India, nothing like the grainy footage on the Internet, where people had popped open like hot dogs on grills that were cranked too high. There was no explosion of spiders, no sudden moment where Pozloski was enveloped by black death. It happened slowly. So much more slowly than Pozloski had expected.

First, the man stopped twitching. His eyes rolled back and his moaning turned into a rough rattle that then turned into nothing. It wasn't hard to figure out that the guy had given up the ghost. Underneath the guy's T-shirt, Pozloski could see a gentle rolling movement, like a tennis ball inching its way from the man's stomach, up his chest, across from one side to the other, and then back down again. And then, where the T-shirt had lifted up so Pozloski could see the soft flesh of the guy's belly, a bulge turned into a line turned into a thin release of blood that turned into . . .

Chicken biscuits. He jammed his right thumb back into his mouth. It was going to be a hell of a burn, he thought. His thumb was going to be blistered for days.

The darkness was terrifying, of course, but also a sort of relief. Toward the entrance, the light of the pull-chain bulbs was a clear pathway out, but where he was standing, the darkness felt absolute. But the darkness was almost preferable to seeing whatever it was that was going to come out of that guy's belly. Pozloski had a pretty good idea of what he was about to see, but he also knew that actually seeing it would make it real. If he left the lighter unlit, if he simply kept his right thumb in his mouth, the lighter dark in his left hand, he could pretend there was nothing to see. Pretend that the soft skittering sounds that were now all around him were unrelated to anything he'd seen on the news, were unrelated to the reason why Mr. Kosgrove had been camping out in the Royal Suite in a fearful retreat from Las Vegas, unrelated to what was a certain death awaiting him.

Chicken biscuits.

He flicked the rolling flint. And, of course, it didn't catch. Left thumb. There was just a quick spark, enough for him to imagine something moving, and then pure darkness. Flick. Spark. Movement. Darkness. Flick. Spark. Movement. Darkness. And again, he was thinking of that stupid story about the man who gambled on getting a lighter to catch, the man's wife fingerless, the way he'd had nightmares for a week of his high school life after reading that story. It was enough to make him giggle *again*.

Oh, for goodness' sake. He really wished he hadn't smoked that joint.

This time, the flame caught.

It was anticlimactic. Pozloski had assumed that once the lighter flared and caught, he'd enjoy a second of light, the spiders would attack him, and then he'd be dead. The end. But nothing of the sort happened. The spiders seemed wholly uninterested in him.

They were big. Bigger than he'd expected. Heavy looking. On television and in the photos he'd seen online, they'd been all black, but these ones had a red stripe bisecting their backs. Twenty or thirty of them were moving over the body of the dead man. He should have been disgusted, should have been puking at the sight of the man laid open, but it wasn't gory. There was a shellac of white silk holding everything in, a bloodless human fillet.

As far as he could tell, there was no urgency in the way the spiders were skittering around. There was no pattern to the little buggers' movement either. If he had been pressed to describe their movement, he would have come up with a single word: aimless.

Chicken biscuits!

He shook his hand and the blue plastic lighter slipped out of his fingers and bounced off his knee. He heard it hit the floor and bounce away from him. He jammed both thumbs together into his mouth. He'd thought about buying a Zippo once, but he'd never been a *smoker* smoker, just a pot smoker, and having a Zippo, no matter how solid and cool he thought they looked, seemed weirdly ambitious. Like he was making smoking pot a priority or something. But right now he would have been pretty darn pleased to have a solid lighter that he could hold without burning the bejeebers out of his thumbs. Or, you know, a flashlight. Actually, a flashlight would have been better than a lighter.

He considered his situation for a minute. The thing to do, really, was to phone the authorities.

Oh, for flippity-flap's sake. His phone. Jenny was right. He *really* needed to quit smoking pot. He pulled his phone out, unlocked the screen, and used the glow as a light.

The spiders were still uninterested in him. They were crawling over the body and across the floor, but slowly. Like they were waiting for something to happen. One of them moved off the man's $800 loafer and drifted across the floor in front of Pozloski. Tentatively, hesitantly, almost experimentally, Pozloski lifted his foot in the air. The spider was truly pretty big. Sporting equipment comparisons went through his mind in a quick arc, from Ping-Pong balls to pool balls before settling on softballs. He and Jenny were in a slow pitch league, and aside from the color and, well, the fact that it had eight legs dripping off the sides of its creepy, hairy body, the spider on the floor in front of him would have done an admirable job of substituting for the bright yellow softballs they used in the league.

He brought his foot down. He had to press a *lot* harder than he expected.

He heard a potato chip crackle and a gushing yogurt sound. It was really, really gross. He was careful to make sure he ground the sole of his shoe into the mush of the spider, finishing the job.

Huh. He'd sort of thought he might get swarmed, but the other spiders didn't react at all. They completely ignored him. He scraped his shoe clean against the floor, holding up his phone so that the electronic glow showed him the other spiders still skittering over the dead body.

Okay. He really needed to call this in. He flipped the phone around so he could dial the front desk. Or maybe 911? Or . . . the army? Who was he supposed to call?

No signal. Not a single bar. Figured. There wasn't even Wi-Fi down here. His phone was useless. How was it that he could stumble across scary monster spiders hatching from a man's body while he was at work but his crummy cell phone provider couldn't ensure proper service?

Pozloski carefully backed away from the dead body and the spiders, using his phone as a flashlight until he had once again reached the island of light from the first pull-chain bulb.

He stopped and looked back at the subbasement. He stood quietly, holding his breath, listening. He could hear the skitter of the spiders moving lazily around the room.

And then, at last, he didn't feel quite as high. And now that he wasn't quite so high, he realized that a logical reaction might be to run like hell up the stairs.

And after he thought about that for a few seconds, he decided that running like hell truly was the right decision. So he ran.

Desperation, California

There was nothing like the president saying, essentially, every man for himself to inspire confidence in the military. Kim had seen at least a dozen fistfights between Marines since the president had enacted the Spanish Protocol. Not that Kim knew it was called the Spanish Protocol, and even if she had, she wouldn't have cared. To her mind, it was the "good flipping luck out there" protocol. Or the "you should have listened to your parents and gone to college and become a lawyer" protocol. She didn't know how many Marines had been assigned to this part of the fence, but they'd been ordered to stay in position and keep screening refugees even *after* the fake-out that had seen thousands and thousands of them streaming out of the quarantine zone several miles to the south. And then, once the president decided that everybody was screwed and there wasn't any point doing the screenings, they'd gotten all sorts of insane orders. One platoon had been sent west, right into the heart of Los Angeles, another had been sent—so Kim had heard—to Vancouver. The entirely wrong country, for fuck's sake! And her platoon had even screwier orders. They'd already been ordered back to the first temporary internment camp, the one that had been overrun by spiders when Los Angeles fell, when their orders had been changed: Staff Sergeant Rodriguez told them they were expected to pick up a shotgun and get it to Washington, DC.

Must be a hell of a shotgun, Kim thought. A shotgun wasn't necessarily the weapon she'd choose in a fight against a whole screaming horde of spiders.

They'd been debating it in the Joint Light Tactical Vehicle ever since they had gotten the revised orders. It was a rough and shitty trip from the quarantine zone to Desperation, California, and not one they could have made in a conventional vehicle. There were some stretches of highway where they could run true on for thirty or forty miles, but then there were other stretches where the asphalt was just an idea. Craters and smoke. Overpasses turned to rubble. More than once they'd come across cars that were overturned, tractor-trailers burning, civilians sitting in traffic jams like somebody was going to magically repair the road in front of them. But nothing could stop Marines, no sir. The convoy was a mix of ten Hummers and JLTVs, for a platoon total of thirty-two Marines in all, and they took roads when they could, and where the roads were destroyed, they bounced across fields and rocks, hard-packed dirt and sand. It would have been profoundly easier if the air force had started bombing the crap out of the highways *after* Kim's platoon had made it to Desperation. Under normal circumstances it would have taken maybe four hours to get from where they'd been to Desperation, but with the federal highway system now resembling Kabul more than the America that Kim had grown up knowing, the trip had taken them close to sixteen hours. And that was with Staff Sergeant Rodriguez pushing the pace.

For the last hour of the ride, they'd been arguing over what the best weapon would be when they had to fight the spiders.

When, not if, Kim thought.

"I still say a nuke is the way to go," Duran said.

"And I still say the point of this is to figure out what weapon is going to let you survive and thrive and be a Marine. What's the point of a weapon that leaves you a piece of charred toast," Elroy said. "We're talking a personally usable weapon. No nukes."

"A shotgun still doesn't make any sense," Mitts said. "Sure, close quarters, urban combat against a conventional foe? Load it up with buckshot and it turns anybody in front of you into a window. It's like aiming at a barn. Impossible to miss, but only if you're shooting at a barn. By which I mean a person, not a couple zillion hungry spiders."

Kim tried to tune them out. The roads here in Desperation itself weren't great, but they weren't bombed out, either. Once they made it off the highway and onto the side roads, there didn't seem to be any imminent risk of a fighter jet unloading on them. So far, the air force had seen fit to warn their platoon before making runs. A nicety they didn't seem to be offering civilians. Since the roads in Desperation didn't seem to go anywhere other than into and just past Desperation, and since Desperation, California, wasn't anything but an old mining town stocked with hippies and survivalists, Kim guessed that the air force wasn't going to bother. Operation bomb the crap out of everything and leave people to fend for themselves and screw you, Marines, good luck out there from all of us in Washington, DC, did not, at this time, seem to include the bombing of the dusty road that petered out just a few miles past Desperation, California. Though maybe it should, Kim thought. The town, if you wanted to call it a town, could do with a good bombing. They passed a rusty trailer and Kim saw a pretty young woman about her age wearing a tie-dyed T-shirt and jeans standing beside a dour-faced boyfriend. They passed a bar, and then another bar, and then another, before rolling past a gas station cum hardware store cum grocery store called Jimmer's Dollar Spot.

"Think we'll get to stop there on the way back?" Elroy asked, pointing out the window as they passed another small building with a sign reading LUANNE'S PIZZA & BEER. The sign was peeling, but not too badly. A woman was out on the porch, arms crossed, watching them roll by.

"Wouldn't count on it," Mitts said. "We only got assigned this mission because we were the closest squad in the area, but there's some sort of rush job going on." He mimicked Staff Sergeant Rodriguez's barking voice: "High. Est. Pri. Or. I. Ty."

Elroy grunted. "This sucks. I could go for some pizza. And if it's a rush job, why didn't they just send birds?"

Kim shot Elroy a grin. "You're asking like everything the military does makes sense even in the best of times. Rodriguez says highest priority, but maybe it's not highest priority for the pilots or whoever decides where the birds go. Or, maybe all the planes and helicopters are busy blowing crap up. Who knows? It's not like things are exactly normal out there."

Elroy shook his head, looking as sad as if his dog died. "Cold beer. Did you see the sign? Pizza *and* beer."

It was another ten minutes of driving before the convoy pulled up in front of the house.

Lance Corporal Kim Bock couldn't help but think that it was weird as all get out to be parked in front of what looked like a house that came from the year 1922. It was a cute house, but weird location. Put it in a nice, developed suburb with wide streets and fully grown trees rather than plopped smack dab in the middle of the desert, and it was the sort of home Kim could have imagined herself living in someday, with a husband and kids, once she left the Marines and started what her parents liked to call her "real" life. Not that a "real" life seemed particularly likely right now, given the state of the world. All things considered, Kim thought the odds were high she'd spend the rest of her days living out some sort of *Mad Max* postapocalyptic fantasy. Or, you know, she'd get eaten by spiders.

The Marines unloaded from their vehicles, stretching, shielding their eyes from the glare of the sun, bullshitting, drinking water, a few people lighting cigarettes. Kim offered Sue a piece of gum. Staff Sergeant Rodriguez motioned for Kim and Sue to come over, so they did, M16s slung over their shoulders. They followed Rodriguez up the front porch steps of the blue house. Kim didn't know enough about architecture to be able to say what kind of house it was, but it looked like it could belong in some kind of old-fashioned magazine. White shutters, mullioned windows, a door painted somewhere on the spectrum between pink and red. Planting boxes all across the porch with neatly tended yellow and blue blossoms. There was an irrigation system, thin black tubes snaking down the porch pillars and watering the flowers. The porch itself spread across the front of the house, deep enough for a swing, rocking chairs, a chaise lounge, cocktail tables. If she squinted just right, Kim could imagine a young family sitting out there, the father and mother sipping cocktails while little Dick and Jane sat on the floor of the porch, playing Snakes and Ladders. Staff Sergeant Rodriguez, however, seemed completely unaware of the absurdity of the situation. He wasn't known for his sense of humor. He strode right to the door and hammered four hard, authoritative knocks.

There was the loud, happy barking of a dog. She could see it jumping up and trying to look through the glass. A black lab? No. Chocolate. After five or ten barks, the dog disappeared down the hallway and then, a few seconds after that, Kim could see a man approaching.

When the door opened, Kim wondered if she should squint just a little harder.

"Mint julep?" the man offered. He was beautifully dressed. Even Kim could appreciate his sartorial style. Sockless feet in buckskin loafers, sand-colored linen pants that were somehow un-wrinkled, a powder-blue shirt that seemed to float just above his body and fit him the way clothes, Kim suddenly understood, were supposed to fit.

And he was holding a silver tray with a sweating pitcher and a half dozen glasses.

"I'm Fred," he said. "We've got plenty more inside. We mixed up a whole tub of it. The mint is fresh, too. I've got a lovely lit-tle hydroponic setup downstairs. There's more than enough to go around, so don't be shy. You boys"—he looked at Sue and Kim and winked—"got here sooner than we expected, but don't worry, the canapés are almost ready."

A tall, thin man wearing a Chicago Cubs cap materialized be-hind Fred. His thick, dark hair had hints of gray, and he was wear-ing sneakers, khakis with cargo pockets, and a black T-shirt. Quite a contrast to Fred.

"I see you've met my husband," he said. "I'm Shotgun."

It took Kim a beat to understand. The shotgun wasn't a thing. The shotgun was a person.

Two more people popped into the hallway behind Fred and Shotgun. A man and a woman, both white, both in their early thirties. The man had his fingers hooked through the collar of the chocolate lab, and he stood next to the woman like they were a couple. The woman had a tray of her own, made of some sort of light-colored wood, maybe bamboo, though it was hard to tell from a distance, and covered in what looked like . . . yes. The canapés promised by Fred.

"Olive tapenade on toast," the woman said. She stepped forward, slipping past Shotgun and holding out the tray.

Kim glanced at Rodriguez. He was normally stone faced, but he looked absolutely confused. She could see that his orders were at war with the basic social conventions of acting like a guest, but then he reached out, took a glass off Fred's silver tray, and poured himself a mint julep. The ice leaped out of the pitcher, clinking into the glass in a muddle of mint and booze and sugar water. He hesitated and then handed the glass to Sue, who passed it on to Kim.

She took a sip. Her parents were wine drinkers. She was more of a beer gal. She'd never had a mint julep before.

Huh. Not bad. Strong, though.

Staff Sergeant Rodriguez poured another for Sue and was pouring one for himself, so Kim went ahead and took a canapé from the woman's tray.

"How many of you are there?" the woman asked. "We've got some puff pastries in the oven, and Fred has made an absolutely incredible pulled pork for tacos later. I know it's not technically May fifth, but it's close enough for a Cinco de Mayo party. But we want to make sure we have enough for everybody. Shotgun said it would be a platoon, but neither he nor Gordo," she nodded behind her at the other man, and Kim noticed a tasteful ring on her finger, "could tell me exactly what that meant. Evidently, according to Wikipedia, you Marines can be rather flexible in the way you account for your numbers."

"There are thirty-two of us, ma'am," Rodriguez said. "But we have our own rations and—"

"Nonsense," Fred said. "The secret to the pulled pork is to give it a salt and sugar rub the night before. You have to give it a quick rinse before popping it in the oven so it's not too salty, but then you roast it at a low temperature for hours and hours and hours. And then, this is the real trick: you finish it at a high heat for just a couple of minutes. We'll have plenty. I made three shoulders, which doesn't sound like much, but is actually quite a lot of pork, particularly when you pair it with tortillas and rice and salad and salsa. Oh. Fuck-a-nuts. Unless you have vegetarians. Do you have any vegetarians? I don't really have a vegetarian option, though I could probably whip something up. It would be a shame, though. The pork is to die for. Oh, and there's flan, too. I'm not a fan of flan myself, there's just something about the texture, but I couldn't think of another desert that would go with the Mexican theme."

Kim took another sip of her mint julep to hide her smile. Rodriguez was completely unsettled. He was a good guy and a good staff sergeant, about as likable in that role as any man could be. But she was sure that while his orders probably contained contingencies for civilian unrest or even what to do if they encountered a swarm of spiders, he did not have any guidance for what to do if they encountered a Cinco de Mayo party.

"Uh, no vegetarians in the platoon, sir," Rodriguez said. "But we are under orders to get you and your weapon to Washington, DC, immediately."

Shotgun stepped out onto the porch, joining his husband, Gordo, Amy, Kim, Sue, and Rodriguez. He looked around at the mix of Hummers and JLTVs. "Seems like a long drive."

"We won't be driving, sir. We're supposed to hold position and keep you secure until the birds arrive."

Fred held the tray in one hand and lifted the pitcher, offering it to Kim. She looked at her glass. It had somehow become empty without her noticing. She held it out for him to refill.

"What, exactly, do you mean by birds?" Fred said.

"Sorry, sir," Rodriguez said. "Helicopters. From here to Las

Vegas. Closest place we could land a plane with the capacity to fly you directly to Washington. I'm actually a little surprised we didn't show up to find you'd already left. The Pentagon has put getting you to DC as an extremely high priority."

Fred raised an eyebrow. "If you fellows are in such a hurry, why didn't you just fly here in the first place?"

Kim felt Elroy slide up behind her and nudge her in the back, and she was gratified when Rodriguez's answer was similar to hers.

"I don't know, sir. Perhaps they were all in use. The military does a lot of things extremely well, but not everything makes sense to the people who are on the ground. Just following orders," Rodriguez said, "which were to drive here and make sure Mr. Shotgun gets on that helicopter."

Shotgun looked pained. "I've got my own plane. I could have just—"

"No, sir. Civilian aircraft are being shot down on sight. The president's shutdown of air traffic still stands. There have been quite a few civilians who have disregarded the restriction, and it's ended poorly for them. I'm afraid that if you try to fly yourself you will almost certainly catch rocket."

"Yes, well, I didn't think they were actually enforcing the no-fly order with lethal force."

Kim took a sip of her mint julep. It was still yummy. "I don't know what information you've been able to get," she said. "But it's pretty bad out there."

Shotgun took off his Cubs hat and ran his fingers through his hair. "Okay," he said. "Helicopter it is. How long does my husband have to get packed?"

"Sir?"

Shotgun put his hat back on. "Do you really think I'm just going to jaunt off to Washington and leave my husband behind?

And Gordo has helped me with the weapon design, so he and his wife are coming too. All four of us. Plus the dog."

Rodriguez looked pained. "I'll have to confirm that we can do that, sir."

"Just make it happen. Otherwise, you aren't getting me on a helicopter and you aren't getting the ST11."

"Sir?"

Fred sighed and rolled his eyes. "The ST11. The weapon, silly pants." He handed the tray of mint juleps to Shotgun. "Appetizer time is over. If that helicopter is showing up anytime soon, we need to start eating. Amy and I will finish making dinner for the troops, and then *I'm* going to go pack a bag."

He and Amy were gone in an instant, leaving Kim, Sue, Elroy, and Rodriguez standing there with Shotgun and the other man.

"Your husband," Kim said, somewhat cautiously, "is . . . something else."

Shotgun sighed, put the tray down on one of the side tables, and poured himself a mint julep. "He's from San Francisco. He's not particularly familiar with the idea of restraint. It's part of his charm. But seriously," he said, taking a sip of his drink, "I hope we've got an hour or two before the helicopters show up, because his pulled-pork tacos really are extraordinary. I wouldn't miss them for the world."

Soot Lake, Minnesota

Leshaun was supposed to be on watch from midnight to six a.m., but Mike had woken up sometime close to four and gone out to spell him.

The cottage wasn't perfectly situated—he and Leshaun had taken an hour or so to check out the perimeter—but it could have been a lot worse. The woods behind the island were thick and twisted, with no roads for miles and miles. There was a reason why the only approach was by boat. Yes, there was a single, narrow path weaving through the trees and up to the cottage if you wanted to hike in, but if intruders took that path, it was going to be like fish in a barrel. Otherwise it had to be a water approach. An island would have been better, of course, particularly one with high ground. Anything where they could have had unrestricted views and advance warning of bad guys attempting to approach. And a full team of agents, with sniper rifles and night vision gear. That would all have been nice, but Mike figured, while he was wishing for that, he should have wished instead that there weren't any spiders in the first place. Of course, it actually wasn't spiders that he or Leshaun were worried about.

Twice already boats had come buzzing in toward the dock, and twice Mike and Leshaun had drawn their weapons and held position. The driver of the first boat, a grizzled-looking old black dude with a short white beard, had nodded, waved, and put the boat into a wide turn before motoring on down Soot Lake. The other boat, containing three younger men, all tattooed and shirtless, had come in much closer. One of the men was holding a hunting rifle, and Mike and Leshaun had stood there, Glock 22s raised, as clear a "no trespassing" sign as you could ever hope to post. Still, the driver of the boat idled there, maybe twenty yards off the end of the dock, staring at them. At least the guy with the hunting rifle was smart enough to keep it cradled in his arms. Mike knew that the boat didn't idle there for as long a time as it felt, but it was a stare down, no question. Which was the whole reason he and Leshaun were out there, guns drawn: the sort of men who were willing to have a stare down when you were holding weapons on them were the sort of men you generally didn't want as cottage guests during a military emergency.

A military emergency. That was a totally inadequate term, Mike thought, but it wasn't like he had a better one. The apocalypse? No, the spiderpocalypse! He snorted. Okay. That was sort of funny.

He was sitting on an Adirondack chair on the lawn, a spreading view of the point and the dock and the water before him. The first hint of dawn whispered over the lake, and it was warm enough that he was comfortable without the light jacket he'd borrowed from his ex-wife's husband. The sky was a mix of stars and scattered clouds. The clouds, pinned against the night sky, were like smoke from a campfire, and Mike thought the name Soot Lake seemed suddenly appropriate. He heard the call of a loon and then, a minute or so later, the lonely splash of a fish. It was terribly peaceful here. Maybe when all this was over, he'd take Dawson up on his offer to loan him the cottage. Would that be so weird, to be friendly with your ex-wife and her new husband? Honestly, the more time he spent with Dawson, the more he liked the man. It would be good for Annie, he thought, to see the adults in her life working hard to like each other, and it would be good for her to see him and Dawson getting along.

Like she was summoned by the thought, Annie stepped out from the front door of the cottage. She was wearing shorts and a sweatshirt. He was pleased to notice that the sweatshirt was the one he'd given her for Christmas, a zip-up hoodie with the agency's acronym emblazoned on the back. It was too big for her, but it was thick and warm and she'd grow into it. Though, if he thought about it, it was sort of odd that the agency would have sweatshirts at all. But it had, online, what amounted to a gift shop that agents could order from: sweatshirts and T-shirts and baseball caps, pens and coffee mugs and even Frisbees, all bearing the agency letters or seal.

She leaned against the door frame, lifting one foot to rub the back of her other calf. She scanned right to left until she saw him, sitting on his chair. She stretched and rubbed her eyes, then padded down the steps and across the grass toward him. The moon and stars were silver rivers of light against the breaking dawn, and Annie positively glowed. For a moment he couldn't believe how big she was, how she didn't look like a little kid anymore, and then, in the shifting light, she looked young again.

"Hey, beautiful," he said. "Sorry. I keep forgetting. I know you're too old for me to call you beautiful all the time."

She shrugged. "It's okay."

"Couldn't sleep?"

"No. Can I sit on your lap?"

"Of course."

She settled on his lap and leaned against him. She pulled her hood up and then brought her knees to her chest and tucked her sweatshirt over her legs so that only her feet were sticking out. He grabbed the strings of her hood and pulled them tight so that it scrunched around her face. She giggled and stuck her tongue out at him and then he used his hands to peel the hood loose again.

They sat like that, just the two of them, staying quiet for five or ten minutes as the sun slowly started to breathe light into the sky. The clouds took on depth, and the first oranges and reds painted themselves onto the world. The water was still ink-black, flat and featureless in the calm of morning. Mike could feel Annie's gentle weight against him, her soft breathing counting out the morning for him. Just when he thought his daughter had fallen asleep, he felt her shift.

"Did you see any last night?" She was whispering. Or trying to whisper. She was eight—no, nine now, Mike realized, cringing at the mistake—and wasn't very good at whispering. It didn't matter, though. They wouldn't hear her inside the cottage.

"Any what?"

"Any bad guys."

"Oh," he said.

"That's why you're out here, isn't it? To keep the bad guys away?"

"No bad guys. It's been quiet. Uncle Leshaun was out here most of the night. I took over around four. What time was it when you came out of the house?"

"Maybe five thirty?" She was quiet for a minute then said, "I know. I know about bad guys. I know about the spiders. And I know the president said nobody could travel anymore."

"What else do you know?"

"I'm not a baby," she said.

She wasn't angry. It was just a declaration. The statement of a little girl who was old enough to know that she didn't really understand all that was going on. She might not be a baby anymore, but she was *his* baby. She'd always be that, no matter how old she got. She was sitting on his lap, curled up under her sweatshirt, leaning against him. There was no feeling more comforting to him than holding his daughter. He pulled her tight against him and let his chin rest on top of her head.

"I know," he said. He was surprised to hear the slight hitch in his voice. "You're a big girl. I'm proud of you. You know that?" He felt her nod. He felt her breathing in and out, but the rhythm was off. Was she trying not to cry? She shifted her weight.

"It's okay to be scared," he said. "This is scary."

"What did they want?"

"Who?"

"Those men on the boat," she said.

"You saw that? I thought you were reading."

"I heard the motor."

"I don't know what they wanted," he said. "I think a lot of people are really scared right now. Not every person makes good choices, and sometimes, when people are scared, there are people who try to take advantage of that fear."

"Bad guys."

"Bad guys," Mike said. He liked how simple it was for her. Bad guys and good guys. In her book, he was a good guy, and he liked that too. "Leshaun and your mom and stepdad and I are all here. We're all going to work together to keep you safe. No bad guys. Okay?"

"What about the spiders? You'll keep me safe from the spiders?"

He should have expected the question, but for some reason he hadn't. It took him by surprise, and he felt poleaxed. He wanted to

reassure her, to tell her everything was going to be just fine. Bad
guys or spiders, the bogeyman in whatever form, he'd keep it all
away from her. He was her dad and she was his beautiful Annie,
and there was nothing on earth that would get through him to her.
But he knew it wasn't true. He'd known it in his bones from the
minute he'd held her, slippery and crying in the hospital. He'd
never felt a fear like that before. She was wrapped in the hospital blanket, mewling with her eyes closed and covered in some
sort of gel that the nurse had swabbed on her eyelids. She'd been
so unbelievably tiny. Weightless, almost. Fanny was smiling and
drained, sweat still spotting her hairline, and he'd looked down at
his daughter and felt fear like he'd never felt before.

The other guys at the agency—and some of the women, too—
joked about what they'd do when their daughters were ready to
date. Cleaning their guns in front of the boyfriends, showing up at
prom with a SWAT team, or just, you know, killing the first couple of boys your daughter brought home. It was a version of the
same fear, Mike knew. Worry over the understanding that there
would come a time when their children moved beyond their orbit,
when their little girls became young women and went out into
the world, a place where they could no longer be protected. But
Mike had always wondered what the hell they were thinking. Did
they honestly believe they could protect their children before that?
Sons or daughters, did they truly believe they could keep the world
at bay even a little bit? Because even in those first moments in the
hospital he'd understood how much of the rest of his life was out
of his control. This little thing in his arms, this tiny package of feet
and hands and mouth and ears and nose was so fragile. No matter
what he did, there'd always be something out there to be scared of,
and not just when his daughter started to date, but now, standing
in the hospital, holding her as a newborn, and now, at two in the

morning on the day of her second birthday, rushing her to the emergency room with a fever of 104, and now, when she comes home crying from kindergarten because her butterfly didn't hatch, and now, explaining to her that even though he and mommy love Annie very much, they no longer want to be a mommy and daddy together, and now, sitting in this chair in the unseasonable warmth of early May, holding her on his lap, and knowing there was absolutely no truth to the promise, knowing there was no way to keep her absolutely safe.

But that didn't stop him from saying the words.

"We'll keep you safe," he said. "Promise. Okay? I promise. I love you."

"I love you too, Daddy."

The sun poked above the horizon.

The White House

Manny signed the paper and then handed it back to his aide. "And if Congressman Wilford calls again, tell him to go fuck himself."

"Literally tell him to go fuck himself, using that actual language, or do you want me to be polite about it?" Sharon Robinson had been working for Manny long enough to know to ask the question. He'd had aides before who would have taken such a statement as a suggestion and replace his salty language with something more politic, telling the congressman only that Manny was unavailable.

"Literally," Manny said. "I literally want you to tell him to go fuck himself. In fact, I want you to literally tell him to go fuck himself, to unscrew his tiny dick and shove it up his own ass, and then I want you to tell him that I said he is a total shithook."

"Okay," Sharon said. She typed his words into her tablet. "Shithook."

Congressman Wilford truly *was* a shithook, in Manny's eyes. Even at the best of times, Wilford, a fourteen-term congressman, was the sort of pork-ladling asshole who made Manny embarrassed to be in Washington. But this wasn't the best of times, and he'd had the temerity to call four times since Steph had authorized the Spanish Protocol. He wasn't calling because he was worried about the country or the safety of his constituents, but because he wanted to twist Manny's arm over a boondoggle for which he'd been trying to get federal funding for more than a decade. A casino project built and owned by Wilford's brother. According to Congressman Wilford, the time had never been better to build a casino in his district. Why, after all this was over, the country was going to need some good news! As long as you had to rebuild the overpass and the bridge, what better time to put a new exit in, one that, conveniently, would lead directly to this proposed casino?

"Scratch that," he said. "Tell him to literally go fuck himself, and *then* tell him I said he's a swizzle-sticked, dickbag, shithook excuse for a human being and that I hope spiders come out of his toilet and eat their way into his body through his ball sac."

"That seems a bit harsh."

"Fine. Forget the part about the spiders."

Manny took a sip of his Diet Coke. He was, he realized, not in a particularly good mood, which was no surprise given the stress. He looked at Sharon as she typed out his response to the congressman. Sometimes he wondered if she suspected that he and Steph were sleeping together. If she did, she never even hinted at it. That was one of the things that made her such a good aide. She was smart and he never had to second-guess the decisions she made in his stead. In fact, the only fault he'd ever been able to find with her was her inability to come up with creative ways of cussing out people on her own. Not that he usually swore at congressmen and senators. Well, not all the time. Not as much as he wanted to. But maybe a little more than he should. Okay. He had a problem with his temper.

"Anything else?" he asked.

"You've got a meeting with Director Gibbons at two."

"What about?"

"He's got a CIA contractor who claims he might have a weapon that would be effective against the spiders." She shrugged. "Gibbons said it sounds kind of crazy, but it's the same guy they used for Project Dark Cloud."

"And remind me, what was Project Dark Cloud?"

"The thing with the GPS satellites last summer."

"Ah. I liked that. That was pretty slick."

"Gibbons said the contractor is an odd duck, one of those survivalist types, but also brilliant, and it might work, and if so, it's probably scalable. Also, Gibbons said that he heard from his counterpart in MI6, and he's making all kinds of noise about Peru, and you need to talk about that as well."

"Peru?"

"Yep. Sorry, I don't know more. I didn't actually talk to him. His assistant to my assistant, and then my assistant to me, and then me to you. You know how it is. But, evidently, it's important enough that he's insisting on a meeting with you and the president. Two o'clock."

"Okay. Anything else?"

She looked at the clock on her tablet. "You've got fourteen minutes of quiet time until your phone call with the Israelis. Close your eyes or something. You look like shit."

"Thanks, Sharon. I'll remember that the next time you ask for a raise."

She walked out of his office, giving him the middle finger as she closed the door.

Manny decided she had a point. He looked like shit and felt like it. What he wouldn't give for a simple political scandal or trade crisis to deal with. He slipped his shoes off and then lay down on the couch. Fourteen minutes. He took deep breaths in and out, in and out. Years ago, when he and Melanie were in couples counseling, their therapist told him the best way to meditate was to quietly say the word *one* over and over again, and so Manny whispered the word to himself with each breath.

Jesus, he hoped that the director of the CIA's weirdo contractor really could deliver some sort of spider-killing machine. He imagined a giant box emitting heat rays, the spiders melting away. A death cube.

Peru.

What had Sharon said about Peru?

He sat up quickly, then felt a little lightheaded. Hadn't Melanie also mentioned something about Peru?

National Institutes of Health, Bethesda, Maryland

Simple pleasures. Simple pleasures. That had been her mantra since she'd moved her lab into the NIH building. Thirty minutes of running laps around the building—a whole posse of Marines watching her the entire time—or fifteen minutes of watching sports highlights. She knew that other scientists and entomologists around the globe were studying the outbreak, trying to find the answers, but it felt like the weight of the entire world was on her shoulders. Not just Manny and Steph, but, oh, seven billion people all needing her to figure out what was going on with these spiders. There wasn't much time for her to decompress, so she'd tried to make sure she could at least have a few simple pleasures to help her relax. Like lunch. It was weird to have the US military tasked with your personal safety, but the upside was that even her most simple requests were fulfilled with stunning alacrity. She couldn't vouch for the battlefield prowess of the American military, but if the Pentagon ever ran short of money, it could turn itself into a mean take-out delivery service. She'd asked her minders for Thai at noon, and by twelve thirty the conference table was decked out with Pad See Ew, Panang curry, ginger shrimp, Thai fried rice, Rad Nah, and . . .

"Seriously? Who ordered pad Thai with just tofu in it?"

"I like tofu," Julie said. "And we've been eating a lot of meat."

Melanie shook her head, heaped up her plate, and sat down. She wanted to enjoy the food, but the conference table didn't do it. Admittedly, this had not been the most uplifting week or so of Melanie's life, and there was something dispiriting about fluorescent lights and conference tables, particularly when it was an incredible spring day outside, the sort of weather that made her appreciate living in Washington. But inside, the fluorescent lights buzzed and washed everything out.

Julie was shoveling the pad Thai into her mouth as she stared intently at her laptop. She had an idea about predicting swarm points, and she'd been running numbers all morning. They'd argued over whether or not to include the report from Chicago in the data set: there'd been a hatching in the subbasement of a luxury boutique hotel down near the Magnificent Mile, but for some reason, the spiders were not aggressive. According to the reports, the spiders had hatched from a man's body that was found in the bowels of the building, but then they'd only sort of crawled around and scared the shit out of the night manager, who was the one who called it in. Also, the guy was claiming they had red stripes. Red stripes! There weren't any photos, because the Chicago authorities' immediate reaction—which, Melanie thought, was probably reasonable enough, albeit absolutely infuriating—had been to burn the entire building to the ground. Melanie told Julie to include it in the data even if the report seemed sketchy. Julie's idea was better than nothing, and nothing was what they had. She was ready to grasp at any straw. Including, she thought, as she looked out the window and saw the helicopter shoot in low and straight, this young woman.

The helicopter landed in the cleared-out parking lot ringed by military vehicles and a woman climbed out. From her perch, high up in the building, Melanie couldn't tell what the woman looked like. Could barely tell it *was* a woman. And when, five minutes later, Teddie Popkins was finally ushered into the conference room, Melanie was surprised at how young she looked.

"Are you even out of college?" she asked. "What are you, twenty?"

"Well, that's a condescending way to start things off, but I'm twenty-three. I graduated two years ago."

"Sorry. I didn't mean it that way. I'm just exhausted," Melanie said. "Do you know why you're here?" She saw Teddie glancing at the plastic takeout containers. "Go ahead. Help yourself."

"Thanks. I've been on some sort of military transport plane or helicopter for . . . I don't even know. The food left something to be desired." Teddie picked up one of the paper plates and started scooping out rice and curry.

"Sorry about that as well." Melanie sighed. "I said I wanted to talk with you, and somebody decided that meant bringing you to DC instead of, I don't know, getting you on the phone."

"Well, phones have been a little hit-and-miss since the army started bombing everything. We can't reach half our reporters, and the ones who are still trying to do their jobs are almost impossible to reach. Anyway, I'm assuming you brought me here because of the segment I put together?"

"I want to know what you didn't run," Melanie said.

"Pardon me?"

"I know I seem brisk, but I just don't have a lot of time. I'm Dr. Melanie Guyer, and this is one of—this is my colleague, Julie Yoo. We're basically the front line here, trying to figure out what makes these things tick. I saw the segment on CNN, and I want to know what you didn't put on the air. What got left out."

Teddie hesitated, and then she walked over to the side table

and pulled a bottle of water from the tub of ice. "I'm just an associate producer. No. Producer, actually. Newly promoted. Did you
know that I was a Spanish major at Oberlin, for Christ's sake? I
only ended up at CNN as a fluke. Is that in your file?"

"I don't have a file, Teddie," Melanie said. "You're assuming
a level of organization that is impossible in the middle of this in-
sanity. Given that I already said you got flown out here somewhat
by accident, you—" She stopped. She could feel herself getting
impatient. What was it with these kids thinking they were all special snowflakes? This wasn't, not even a little bit, about Teddie.
Melanie took a deep breath. No wonder she preferred working in
a lab with her spiders over teaching undergraduates.

"Okay. So you were a Spanish major. But you figured something out, and the thing is, there's always something more to the
story. What was the thing that was just so crazy that you *didn't* put
it on the air?"

Teddie took a bite of her curry. She looked at Melanie and then
out the window.

Melanie sighed. "Okay. Sorry. I just thought there might be
something. I'll try to have somebody figure out how to get you
home, but it might take a while. Again, sorry about the whole
flying you out here instead of just having a phone conversation
thing."

"They look fake," Teddie said.

"What?"

Julie had looked up from her computer and was staring at Teddie. "Oh my god."

"Right?" Teddie said to Julie.

Melanie shook her head. "I'm sorry, this might be obvious to
the two of you, but it's not to me. Spell it out."

"You know what it's like to watch those early movies that used computer animation? CGI? How it never looked quite right? You'd have actors doing their stuff, and it was all fine, and then there'd be one of the special effects shots and all of a sudden it was just wrong? And it always bothered me, because it was so fake looking even though it looked totally real at the same time? You know?" She looked at Melanie, and Melanie nodded. "So, it used to bother me, but now when you watch movies it's really hard to tell. Like they've figured out how to make stuff not look all fake. Some of the footage—not the shaky stuff, not the cell phone videos or people running, but the good footage shot on tripods from mounted cameras—had that look. The wide-angle stuff caught the spiders from a distance, so you could really see how they moved. When you can see hundreds or thousands of them, the way they move together, it looks fake. You know?"

Melanie suddenly understood. She'd seen it, but it hadn't really registered. By the time she was watching newscasts and video, fake looking or not, there was no question that it was all too real.

"So I slowed the video down and took the still shots, and we ran that, and, I guess, that's what caught your interest and why I'm here. But I couldn't stop thinking about how they just don't look real. They look mechanical or something. And then I remembered this movie I loved as a kid. I can't even remember what it was called, and I know it wasn't much of a hit, but it was about these kids searching for some sort of treasure. At one point they disturb some rocks and these ants start streaming out of the rocks. I mean, I loved this movie. I used to have dreams that I was the girl, that I was finding the treasure. But I remember when they showed that scene, when the ants started streaming out of the rocks, the other people in the theater all sniggered. It was so cheesy looking. Whoever had done the CGI had gotten the details right. I mean, the ants looked like ants, with their shells and legs and antennas and stuff, but the way they moved? I was like maybe seven or eight, and even I could tell they weren't real." Teddie stopped and considered her plate and took another bite of curry-covered rice. "A couple of years ago, I read an article about using CGI for crowd scenes in movies, and in the article they said that one of the ways that special effects has gotten better is that they are able to program in the sort of random movements that happen when you've got thousands of individuals in the same space. *That's* what was missing with the ants. They all moved exactly the same way. No randomness. And it's like that with the spiders. The way they move. There's no chaos to it."

"Like a pattern?"

Sergeant Faril stuck her head into the conference room. "Sorry, Melanie. I know you said you didn't want to be disturbed, but Manny's calling. He said it's urgent."

"Tell him I'll call him back. This is more important."

Faril retreated.

"It sounds crazy, doesn't it?" Teddie shrugged. "I don't know. I don't think there's a pattern in the way they move, but it's sort of like some lazy CGI person just made them as a special effect. Instead of a million spiders, there's just one big spider in a million parts. But think about it. Wasn't the way they all just died off last week kind of crazy? I know that there's some scientist claiming that they, in essence, grew and moved too quickly and burned themselves out, but doesn't that seem like complete bull? . . . Oh. That was you, wasn't it?"

Melanie waggled her hand. "Keep going."

"Yeah. Well, sorry. But it just didn't sit right with me. I mean, I suppose I could buy that they would exhaust themselves from growing so fast and everything, so your theory sort of makes sense. Somebody gets bitten and then, what, five hours later they're opening up and spilling out spiders like a bag of frozen peas? If they are going to hatch that quickly, a super-condensed life cycle where they die that quickly is believable, too. And I can believe the faster they spread and grow, the faster that life cycle is. It makes a sort of intuitive sense."

Melanie was trying not to be defensive, but she couldn't stop herself from correcting Teddie. "At their fastest, it was closer to twelve hours from the spider entering a host to the point of hatching. But we think the gestation period was longer at the start, maybe twenty-four to forty-eight hours. Before Los Angeles, there was a plane crash in Minneapolis; a private jet flying back from Peru, where all signs seemed to indicate that one of the passengers was a host. Our best guess is that it had been at least twenty-four hours since he'd been attacked."

"Wait, so it got shorter?"

"Exactly."

"Like some sort of countdown clock."

Melanie stared at Teddie and then nodded. "Maybe. Where did you go to school, again?"

"Oberlin. But, okay, the thing is with your theory, that they just burned themselves out, that their metabolisms couldn't handle the rapid expansion, how is it that they all just sort of keeled over dead at the exact same time? The theory makes sense in a lot of ways, that they'd have some sort of internal countdown clock that ticked faster the faster they grew and spread, but how is it that this clock happened to go off at the same time? They didn't all hatch at the same time, so why would those internal clocks line up like that? If they came out in waves, wouldn't it make more sense for them to croak in waves too?"

Melanie looked at Julie Yoo. Her graduate student just shrugged. Melanie turned back to Teddie. "We're doing the best we can with limited information. These things aren't exactly easy to study. There's been a lot going on, and it's complicated."

She suddenly felt a hot lump in her throat. God. She had been trying not to think about Bark. And she hadn't been thinking about Patrick at all, which made her feel even worse. But they'd come unbidden to her mind.

It was easy to focus on the problems in front of her and to let what was going on out in the wider world stay in the background. It was too abstract. Who could understand what it meant to say two million were dead, or five million, or ten? Those numbers weren't real to Melanie in the way it had been to watch that spider slip through Bark's skin, the panic of realizing what had happened, of watching through the glass as he lay cut open on the operating table, his body threaded through with egg sacs and silk, her other graduate student, Patrick Mordy in there, assisting the doctor and nurses, Julie Yoo running down the corridor yelling, trying to tell them it was too late, and then . . .

Oh.

She was crying now.

The producer from CNN, Teddie, looked scared, but Julie got up, crouched down beside Melanie, and wrapped her arms around her.

It was just all too much. Too much to have those images running through her head. Too much pressure. She'd made her entire adult life about working in the field and then taking it back to the lab, about data collection and careful experimentation. It took more than seven years from when she'd had her first inkling of what might be going on inside the *Heteropoda venatoria* spider and what the venom might do in a medical setting, back when she was actually a junior in college, until the time she'd published the paper that was her first scientific breakthrough. And that had been working with a spider that wasn't going to kill her. Seven years! And now, the president was coming to her and counting on her to figure out how to stop these spiders and giving her just days to do it?

And now, some blond bimbo—she knew it wasn't fair to think of Teddie that way, but she was angry and sad and terrified and goddammit!—barely out of undergrad with a background in Spanish was telling her something so obvious that not thinking of it herself made her doubt almost everything else she'd come to believe about these spiders.

It took several minutes for Melanie to stop crying and to get control of herself. She stepped out to the washroom to splash water on her face, grateful that she wasn't one of those women who found it necessary to load up on makeup every time they went out in public. Her makeup would have been a mess after that, and besides, who would she have been trying to look pretty for? The spiders? Sergeant Faril?

She came back into the conference room and sat down in front of Teddie and Julie. "Sorry," she said.

Teddie made a face that was as much a grimace as it was a smile. "That's okay. I'm sure you just need a good night's sleep. And I guess my theories are sort of cockamamie. I don't know anything about spiders. Until all this happened, I thought an entomologist and an etymologist were the same thing. But it was pretty clear in the video that the spiders weren't killing everything, and if you looked closely and slowed it down, you could see that the spiders weren't moving about randomly, and, more, that there was a pattern, too, in the people with gashes on them. The other stuff, I know, it sounds really crazy. But you asked me what else I *didn't* include, and that's what I was thinking. The way they move together just isn't right. Individually, it's all creepy and skittering, and at least to me, looks the way spiders should look, but man, as a group? It looks wrong, it really does. It looks like there's something off. I don't know."

Melanie took a deep breath. "Any chance you've got that footage you're talking about with you?"

Teddie unzipped her bag and pulled out her laptop.

Delhi, India

How much worse could it have been? If the spiders hadn't started dropping, if they'd just kept feeding and feeding, laying new eggs at that accelerated pace? How bad could it have been, not just in Delhi, which had a population of around twenty-five million in the greater metropolitan area, but in all India itself? How bad?

For most Indians, that was a question that they were already asking. Even as there were fires still burning throughout the city and beyond, even as the rough counts of the dead and missing were being tallied—six million, eight million, twelve?—that was what people wondered. How much worse could it have been?

But that was the wrong question. What should have been asked, as the soft, sticky egg sacs in cellars and attics, stacked up in the dark corners of a broken city, began to open, and as the larger, truck-sized egg cocoons pulsed with light and started to unravel like the seams of an old shirt, was not how much worse could it have been. The question they should have been asking was how much worse could it get?

Greater Los Angeles
Quarantine Zone, California

On a purely intellectual level, Quincy understood that energy drinks had not always been a thing. There was a time when soldiers were actually given amphetamines to keep them awake— he was pretty sure that was still actually a thing with fighter pilots and Special Forces types—or had to resort to coffee. Not him. Not any of the other men and women assigned to burn crews in Los Angeles either. Red Bull or Monster or anything cold and in a colorful can was the drink of choice. The cold part was a bit tricky, since power was only intermittent throughout the city. Quantity wasn't a real problem, though. There were plenty of convenience stores and bodegas, most of them already semi-looted, but energy drinks weren't a high-demand item. He'd had his partner, Janet Bibsby, pull the Joint Light Tactical Vehicle into the parking lot of a 7-Eleven on their way to the next address they'd been assigned for cleansing. The 7-Eleven was soot damaged and smoking lightly, but it wasn't too bad inside, and he'd been psyched to find that the cooler case was still cold despite the power being out.

He took another sip of his Red Bull. His hands were shaking a bit from all the caffeine and whatever other chemicals were in there. He'd been bagging maybe two hours of sack time on average, and it was a drag. The Staples Center demolition had been sort of terrifying, partially because it was his first time seeing the egg sacs, and partially because there were so many of them. Mostly, since then, it had just become work. *Yes sir, I'll burn that building real good, sir.*

He looked out the window of the JLTV. It was just him and Janet Bibsby on this run. They were down to dealing with smaller infestations, supposedly. Their list of targets consisted of single-family dwellings and small apartment buildings.

"Next left," he said. She didn't have to slow down since she was only doing five or ten miles an hour. The streets were in rough shape. LA looked like a war zone. It *was* a war zone. Smashed cars everywhere. Tons of fires that were plain old arson or accidents, not actually deliberate attempts to destroy spiders. And the bodies. He tried not to look at those.

Absent the destruction, this would have been a nice little street on which to raise a family. Well-maintained lawns and small ranch-style houses, though Quincy had the feeling that a starter home probably cost triple his best guess. You've got to pay for the sunshine, baby.

Janet pulled the JLTV alongside the curb. Even if the address hadn't been marked on the list, it would have been obvious. Spotters had marked it with a big black *X* spray-painted on the house's red garage door. Quincy slammed back the rest of his can of Red Bull, reached back for his gear bag, and got out.

Ahead of him, Janet had pulled out a cigarette and was already puffing away. He didn't let her smoke in the JLTV, and it pissed her off to no end. It might have bothered him if she was hot and he wanted to nail her, but she looked almost uncannily like his younger brother, and he hated the smell of smoke. Cigarette smoke. He already smelled like the regular kind of smoke. They'd been burning shit down for days now. Everything smelled like regular smoke.

He waited for Janet to finish her cigarette, sorting through his gear. Supposedly, troops trained in the use of flamethrowers were going to be coming in the morning. That would be handy for some of the smaller infestations. He'd seen a design for a home-made flamethrower that some dude had put up on the Internet, and they'd even tried to put one together, but they couldn't get it to work. A flamethrower would be pretty great for this gig. Anybody could pull the trigger and bake some spiders. But until the new units showed up, the army was stuck with guys like Quincy. He'd be a lot more comfortable wiring bridges for demolition, or rigging the standard explosives, but he was okay with doing it this way. The trick was to make sure everything was contained. There was a lot of emphasis on the idea of making sure that no spiders or egg sacs were blown clear of the demolition areas. It wouldn't do to have it start raining spiders.

Janet crushed her cigarette out on the driveway and they walked up to the front door. Might as well go in the easy way, Quincy figured.

It had gotten kind of boring. *Routine* wasn't exactly the right word, because there was nothing routine about this, but it had been the same everywhere he'd gone since the Staples Center. Sure, twice it had been nothing at all. The first false alarm was two days ago, an apartment in a six-unit building, and the second time, yesterday, was a preschool. Empty. Both times, he and Janet had swept the buildings from top to bottom, but there was nothing. False alarms. The other places they'd gone to had all been infested, but the infestations were nothing like the Staples Center. There'd be a room or two littered with cold, chalky egg sacs. The most they'd seen, in the basement of an office building that had clearly seen better days, was maybe fifty or sixty football-sized sacs. But it was the same thing at all the sites. Wire it up, burn it down. This was their sixth, no, seventh stop of the day?

The monotony, the tiredness, all that explained why they marched right up to the front door without bothering to look around.

They should have done a recon. Taken a walk around the home, clearing the area. If they had, maybe they'd have noticed the wisps of cobwebs drifting out of the bushes. The black dots skittering over the shed and across the fence posts. Maybe they would have looked through a window and seen the way this house was not gently glutted with egg sacs.

But the routine had gotten to them.

Quincy opened the front door and stepped inside.

At first, he thought he'd been shot.

That was the only thing he could think of. For a moment, he thought this house was another false alarm, and some homeowner had been holed up inside, trying to ride things out the way that people had refused to evacuate from New Orleans when the floods came. He was sure he'd been shot by a homeowner sitting there on his couch, a .45 in his hands, just waiting for some punk to come and try to loot his house. Because that's what it had to have been, a .45. Quincy had never been shot before, but he was sure a 9 mm bullet wouldn't feel like that. There was no way a simple 9 mm was going to hurt that much. Right in the meat of his arm. And then, oh god, the burning, on the side of his neck. And his cheek. He reached with his free hand to feel for the bullet wounds.

He tried to reach with his free hand.

His arm wouldn't move.

And there hadn't been the sound of a gunshot. He would have heard it. From that close, it would have sounded like a cannon.

His arm and his neck and his cheek, oh, please, stop the pain. And why wouldn't his arm move?

It all happened quickly. One or two seconds. By the time he was starting to think that maybe he hadn't been shot, he realized that not only could he not move his arm, but he couldn't move his legs either. He teetered, and then he felt himself falling, like a tree cut down in the forest.

He landed on his side and couldn't move at all. He couldn't even close his eyes. He was paralyzed. He had to watch. Janet Bibsby had fallen next to him, on her side, facing him, and her eyes were frozen open as well. He could see how scared she looked, could see the spiders crawling up and over her.

These weren't the same spiders. The briefing and pictures had emphasized the size and color, and he supposed these were probably close enough to the same size. In the scheme of things, what was the difference between a lemon and a grapefruit? But these had a vivid red stripe. And they weren't eating them to the bone, because he'd seen videos of that. Seen a woman overwhelmed and then disappearing under a carpet of spiders, reduced to nothing in thirty seconds.

Whatever it was that made it so they couldn't move didn't do anything to reduce the pain of the bites. They were burning, stinging, and they hurt so much that Quincy thought that if he could move it wouldn't have mattered. He'd have just curled up into a ball and cried like a baby. He could see the swelling, weeping wounds on Janet's neck and face and on the bare skin of her hand, and he knew that hers felt the same way: like somebody was pouring battery acid inside a hole in your flesh made with a rusty knife.

She was staring at him, like she was pleading with him to do something.

There was nothing he could do.

He saw tears dripping out of her eyes.

There were ten, twenty, fifty spiders moving over her now. She started to look cloudy to him, and for a few seconds he thought there was dust in his eye, but then it was obvious. The spiders were covering her in silk.

He couldn't even close his eyelids. Nothing. He had to just stare at her, to watch. And he could have sworn there was something else in the room, just out of the corner of his eye, something glowing and pulsing. There was a steady brightening and then dimming. But whatever it was, he couldn't get it into focus. All he could see clearly—or maybe this was imagined, if Janet truly could not move a muscle in the same way he could not move a muscle— was the panic, the fear on Janet's face, as she slowly disappeared underneath layers and layers of silk.

Oxford, Mississippi

Even before the government had started bombing highways, Santiago Garcia knew they were stuck at home. His wife had wanted them to get in the van and try to drive south, through Louisiana and Texas, across the border, and to her brother's place in Tanques, on the west coast of Mexico. Even if he'd thought they'd be safer in Mexico, they couldn't do it. There was no way they could make the trip with their daughter, Juliet. There was a reason they didn't take vacations, he said.

But that didn't mean he was complacent. They owned a combination gas station and convenience store a half mile south of the university, and he immediately closed them down. His wife and their son, Oscar, took turns sitting out front with his shotgun and waving off potential customers. Their house, a tan, single-story three bedroom with clapboard vinyl siding, sat on the lot directly behind the convenience store, so he felt comfortable leaving them and running around Oxford, checking items off his list. First, he persuaded their doctor to write him prescriptions for six months of Juliet's medicines. He had to go to three different pharmacies to get everything filled, and he almost maxed out one of the three credit cards they never touched and said they were keeping strictly for emergencies. But this, he thought, was an emergency. The second thing he did was rent a backhoe, parking it in front of the gas station and instructing his son and wife to make sure it was also protected. They already owned a generator, to keep the fridge humming and Juliet's medications cold, so he started taking trip after trip in his pickup to the hardware store and the grocery stores.

Their house, and the convenience store and gas station combo, were back to back on corner lots, with a vacant lot next to the store, and Mrs. Fine's house next to their house. Once he had all his supplies Santiago went and talked to his neighbor. Mrs. Fine was a widow, nearly eighty, and she and her late husband had bought their tiny two-bedroom house almost sixty years ago. But the Garcias had been her neighbors for fifteen—moving in just after her husband passed—and she trusted Santiago. She was scared, and at first she said no, but then she decided Santiago was right. She packed a suitcase, directed Oscar to carry a bin full of pictures and a few other personal items over, and moved into the Garcias' house.

He was surprised at how quickly he was able to take her house down with the backhoe. Still took almost all day and into the night, and it wasn't until the following morning that he was able to start digging.

A university student passed by on his bike and then stopped. He was one of those white boys who liked to dress like they were from a different era, and he watched Santiago work for five or ten minutes before finally calling over.

"Got to ask, man," the kid yelled, "what are you digging?"

Santiago was making slow and steady progress, and he was pleased with himself, so he stopped for a minute, turned in his seat, and smiled. "A moat," he yelled back. "I'm digging a moat."

The college student gave him a thumbs-up, nodded, and then biked away.

Soot Lake, Minnesota

The three tattooed men from the other day came back for a look. They were still shirtless, and they still looked like trouble to Mike. They kept their boat far enough offshore that Mike didn't even bother putting his finger on the trigger of the rifle, and Leshaun didn't move from where he sat in the chair on Dawson's dock, but it bothered Mike to see them again. It was hard to believe they were making an innocent pass.

He was inside the cottage, lying on the bed with the window open, watching them through the scope. Leshaun was a better shot, but with the scope, either of them could bag a headshot from three hundred yards or less. They hadn't seen any tactical advantage in advertising that they had the rifle, though, so they'd decided to split time: one of them outside with a handgun, one of them on call as sniper if backup was needed. Between him and Leshaun, he wanted to hope it wouldn't matter, but just in case, he'd given Fanny the Glock 27 and made her fire off a few shots earlier in the day, to make sure she could still hit the broadside of a barn. Dawson seemed about as comfortable with the Mossberg 12-gauge shotgun as he was going to get. If it truly got to the point where Fanny and Dawson needed to fire their weapons, things would be pretty bad. Still, better safe than sorry.

On this, their second visit, the three young men in the boat stayed a hundred yards or so from the dock for an uncomfortable length of time. Mike wasn't sure if it was the same guy holding the rifle, but through the scope, he could see that the other two had handguns. They finally took off, heading farther down the lake.

Maybe two hours later Mike thought he heard the soft echo of gunshots, but the sounds were so faint he wasn't sure if he had just imagined them.

He went outside to talk with Leshaun. They both agreed: if there had been gunshots, and if they came from those three young men, he and Leshaun had to assume that they'd be back, probably at night.

"That's how I'd do it," Leshaun said. "They've come by twice, and they've seen that we're armed and not interested in company. You know, maybe we made a mistake there, that first time? If we'd waved and been a little friendly, maybe they would have boated away never to return, but by flashing our guns and running them off, we were signaling to them we had something worth protecting."

"Do you really believe that?"

Leshaun laughed. "No. They look like the kind of trash that has been waiting their whole lives for a moment like this, waiting for the opportunity to give into their base impulses. Being friendly would have been a mistake. They would have taken any sign of kindness for weakness. But it was a nice idea, if you believe in the basic goodness of human nature."

Neither of them believed in the basic goodness of human nature. They'd both been agents too long.

After Mike ate lunch, he went back out to the dock to trade off with Leshaun. His partner had been sitting out in the full sun, but Mike pulled the chair into the shade of the boathouse. He'd been there for long enough to be bored by the book he'd brought down when he heard Annie's footsteps.

"Want to swim with me?"

"Not really, but I will." He stripped off his T-shirt so that he was just wearing his shorts, all clothing that he'd borrowed from Dawson. Leshaun was similarly dressed in borrowed clothes, though they were tight on his partner. He unclipped his holster and put it on top of the shirt. "Just don't splash my pistol," he teased, and she actually laughed.

The water was freezing. In deference to his daughter and the financial penalties she imposed on him for swearing, he barely managed to swallow *fu*— before catching himself and saying the word *freezing*. But he thought the curse word plenty. On the dock, it was still hot, remarkably and unseasonably warm, but it didn't matter how warm it was outside. Two hours north of Minneapolis in early May meant that the water was ball-shrinking cold. He was actually worried he might have a heart attack, and he was thrilled when, after a few minutes, Annie wanted to get out.

Fanny called down from the cottage and asked if they wanted a snack, but they both waved her off and lay out on the dock.

Mike had to admit it was sort of nice. He kept glancing across the lake and listening for the mosquito sound of an approaching motor, but he was also just hanging out with his kid.

"It kills me, it does, that you're turning into such a big kid, but it's also wonderful. You're growing like crazy. How about, when all this settles down, we get you a new bike? Your old bike's a little small for you."

"Rich said he'd get me a new bike when the baby's born," she said brightly.

For a beat, Mike thought maybe he'd feel some sort of pain at how easily Annie said it, how pleased she seemed. But it didn't hurt at all. He supposed he truly was happy for his ex-wife. And, god, he thought, remembering how exhausting a newborn was, he was absolutely not envious of the idea of having a baby.

"You excited about it? Having a brother or a sister?"

"I guess," she said. "Dad. Can I ask you a question?"

"Sure."

"Do you and Mommy still love each other? Because you've been super nice to each other the last couple of days. I know that you guys are all worried about the spiders and those men in the boat, but you and Mom haven't fought once."

He sat up and looked at her. She was lying flat on her back on the wooden dock, with her arms and legs spread out. She had her eyes closed, but she didn't look upset. He reached out and squeezed her hand and she squeezed back.

"I'll always love your mom, honey, and Mom will always love me, but we're not *in* love, if that's what you're asking. We're not in love like a mommy and daddy. Mommy's in love with Rich, and I'm happy for her. He's a great guy, and he makes your mom happy. I hope that's okay with you."

"It's okay. I used to want you and Mommy to be together again, but now I don't. I like Rich. And I don't remember what it was like anymore, you know? When you and Mommy were married. You talk about it sometimes, but I don't remember it. I'm sorry."

"You don't have to be sorry."

"But I am sorry," she said. "Not because I want you and Mommy to get married again, but because I'd like to be able to remember what it was like when you were married. It wasn't all bad, was it?"

"Wow," he said. "That's kind of a big-kid question. No. No, it wasn't all bad. Your mom and I got married because we fell in love, and parts of our marriage were wonderful, but we weren't a very good fit. I think if you asked your mom, she'd say the same thing. But I can tell you that even though we couldn't make it work, we had you, and you're the best thing that's ever happened to me."

"Okay," she said. She opened her eyes. "I'm going to go get a lemonade."

"Okay? That's it? I say you're the best thing that's ever happened to me, and you say you're going to go get a lemonade?"

"Sorry," she said. "Would *you* like a lemonade?" She giggled. He reached out to try to poke her in the side, but she scampered up and then skipped away, blowing him a kiss. "I love you, Daddy."

"You too, honey," he said. He watched her walk up to the cottage and shook his head. Where had that kid come from?

His shorts were still damp, but he pulled the T-shirt on anyway and held the holster in his lap. Out of habit, he pulled the Glock out, checked the clip, and confirmed there was one in the chamber.

He'd heard people say they weren't sure if they could shoot somebody, but he didn't understand that. How could you be unsure? How could you pause for even a second? If those three guys came back Mike wouldn't hesitate. He would put them down where they stood.

Damn right there was something worth protecting in that cottage.

Nazca, Peru

Pierre Schmidt kept waiting to be eaten alive. He'd come to Peru as part of a team that had been given permission to work on the Nazca site. It was an incredibly small team, just Dr. Nicholas Botsford and five graduate students: Pierre, Cynthia Downs, JD Killens, Natalie Wiff, and Beatrice Anton. They'd been there working for six months when he'd found the egg sac. Dr. Botsford had agreed to let him send it to Julie Yoo, and when they'd gone to Lima on one of their rare trips away from the field, he'd FedExed it to Washington, DC, using the account number Julie provided.

And then all hell had broken loose.

First China had dropped a nuke on itself, which had, of course, seemed unconnected, and then there'd been the crazy news out of India. Man-eating spiders! Why would Pierre have thought it had any connection to the egg sac? How could it? And then, well, in the midst of everything else, an e-mail from Julie Yoo:

Pierre: It's probably too late, but if it isn't, the egg sac you sent me hatched. We think the spiders it produced must be the same ones that are in India and the other places. Not sure how it's connected, but it must be. And if there are more of those where you are, they will be hatching. Get out of there. Love, Julie.

The "Love, Julie" had been nice. In fact, the "Love, Julie" had been the whole reason he'd made the argument to Dr. Botsford that they should send Julie the egg sac. He had a thing going with Beatrice, but honestly, that was pure convenience. Dr. Botsford was having an affair with Natalie, which was pretty gross given the age difference, but whatever, and Cynthia and JD were engaged, so he and Bea had fallen together out of lack of other options more than any sort of real interest. Honestly, they didn't really even like each other, but their base camp was isolated and at night, once Dr. Botsford and Natalie had gone off to have creepy old professor–young student sex in their tent, and once Cynthia and JD had gone off to have slightly less creepy engaged people sex in their tent, Pierre and Bea were left alone to hang out. At some point a month or two in, they'd started sleeping together more out of boredom and the sense of feeling left out than out of any real attraction. So there was a big part of him that was looking forward to the dig being over—their permit expired in August—and having the chance to start his postgraduate fellowship at—ta-da!—American University, where, conveniently, Julie Yoo, the greatest crush of all the crushes he'd ever had, was finishing her PhD.

He probably wouldn't have recognized the thing in the decayed wooden box as an egg sac if he weren't totally in love with Julie. They'd hooked up in April of their senior year at Cornell. It was just the perfect amount of time for him to want to kill himself for waiting so long to go for it, but not long enough for him to have any real shot at continuing the relationship long distance when they went off to their respective graduate programs. Over the past five years, they'd seen each other here and there, between boyfriends and girlfriends, and every time, Pierre found himself more wrecked afterward. He'd seen her, in fact, the weekend before he headed off to Peru, and he'd thought about e-mailing Dr. Botsford to say he wasn't going, and just staying to be with Julie. But he hadn't. The chance to work on the Nazca site was the sort of opportunity that would make his entire career. No matter how much of the credit Dr. Botsford was going to grab for himself, there'd be enough spillover from analyzing anything they found that it meant Pierre would be able to dance out of his postgraduate fellowship with good academic job offers. So, instead of staying in Washington for Julie, he'd ended up living in a tent and sleeping with Bea because neither of them had anything better to do at night.

But because of Julie, when he unearthed the egg sac, he'd recognized what it was. He couldn't really say that he was a fan of spiders, but he was a fan of Julie, and he was smart enough to know taking an interest in her work would be good for him. Plus, you know, the egg sac had been buried under the spider line, and he'd already been keeping an eye out. Julie said her professor had some sort of crackpot interest in the Nazca spider line, and since Pierre had his own crackpot interest in Julie Yoo, he'd been hoping for something cool. It had actually been pretty extraordinary, because the egg sac had been found buried in a wooden box near some wooden stakes, all of them testing out at around ten thousand years old, which was way older than the rest of the lines. And then, the egg sac. Okay, he hadn't *really* recognized it right away. It was weird. Hard and cold, like a fossil or something. Actually, it would have made sense if it was a fossil, but he'd put it in the FedEx box to Julie . . .

And then. Well. Scary-time.

So, yeah. He'd spent most of the past ten days or so expecting the red dirt of the Nazca plains to explode with spiders. Every night, in his thin nylon tent, after Bea rolled off him, neither one quite happy about the experience, he fell asleep waiting for skittering spiders to envelop them.

But nope. Nothing. One of the local villagers who delivered fresh food on a regular basis told their cook there had been rumors of something in Manú National Park, but that was it. Peru was still more or less unscathed.

If he and Bea had something that was closer to a real relationship, maybe he would have confided in her. But they didn't really talk much, which was probably for the best, because she came from a pretty conservative family, which, come to think of it, might have explained why the sex was mediocre. Anyway, the more they talked the more awkward all of it was. So mostly they watched movies on one of the laptops or played Connect Four on the little travel set that Bea had brought with her. No, she wasn't the person for him to confess Julie's warning to, and finally, he'd gone to Dr. Botsford.

Dr. Botsford had done that thing he did where he tilted his head back slightly so that he could peer at you through the half-glasses perched at the end of his nose. There was a whole theatricality to the way he conveyed disappointment. He wasn't a yeller. But he'd look at you through his glasses, gently raise an eyebrow, and then exhale forcefully. He liked to wear an old bomber jacket and fedora, like he thought he was Harrison Ford playing Indiana Jones. To be fair, most women considered him handsome, and Pierre thought that if you squinted just right, Dr. Botsford really did kind of sort of look a bit like Indiana Jones. But old Indiana Jones. From the fourth movie. He must have been in his midfifties, already on his fourth marriage, all to former graduate students, and given what happened every night with him and Natalie, Pierre figured that Dr. Botsford would be moving on to wife number five soon enough. Not that it stopped him from acting like he had all the moral authority in the world.

"Oh, Pierre," he said. "I am so, so disappointed in you. How could you not tell us about this warning from your girlfriend?" Sure enough, his head was tilted back and he was peering through his glasses at Pierre. Dr. Botsford shook his head, and in his most solemn, fatherly voice, continued, "This feels like a great betrayal."

They were sitting around the campfire while they talked about it, and while the other graduate students were, ostensibly, trying not to listen, they were, of course, completely listening. Pierre stole a glance at Bea. Uh oh. That didn't look good. She'd definitely caught the word *girlfriend*.

"I think you're missing the point, Dr. Botsford," Pierre said as gently as he could.

"Oh, am I, Pierre? And what would the point be, if it's not that you have betrayed the trust of me, our whole team, and, yes, to some extent, the Peruvian people?"

Pierre had to resist rolling his eyes. "I think the point is that there might be more of those egg sacs full of spiders."

Dr. Botsford pushed his glasses up on his nose and considered Pierre. "Well. Yes. That seems like a reasonable concern. But if there were more of them, couldn't we have expected them to hatch by now?"

Pierre stared at Dr. Botsford. Like Pierre was supposed to know? "I'm just saying that, given the way the egg sac was placed in that box, like it was some sort of religious—"

"The whole spider line is likely of religious significance."

"Fine, yes, but maybe they're connected? Doesn't that seem likely? It was really clear that *somebody* put the egg sac there. It wasn't just, you know, randomly buried or whatever. It was arranged like a sacred object."

He hadn't noticed Bea moving closer. All the other graduate students had moved closer actually, but Bea was sitting on the rock next to him now. "Okay," she said, "let's assume there are more of those egg sacs, and the one you sent off to your girlfriend"— Pierre winced—"hatched, doesn't that mean the others would have hatched? And we would have been eaten. Ergo, no other egg sacs under the spider line. Probably. But that leaves the more important question. If the egg sac thing was buried there as some sort of ritualistic object, if it was put there because it had some sort of meaning, who buried it, and why?"

Pierre didn't have an answer. Dr. Botsford sucked air through his teeth and looked down his nose at all of them, playing the professor for all it was worth. "I think," he said, "tomorrow we'll try to find some answers."

Pierre was almost beside himself. Here he'd been panicked, worried that spiders were going to burst from the ground and eat them, and when he'd finally confided his fears, Dr. Botsford's response was that they needed to find some answers? How about they run the heck away?

If anything, Dr. Botsford looked thrilled, and Pierre realized that his advisor was already thinking about the papers he would write, the attention he could get, the new graduate students he would draw to him.

Dr. Botsford, Pierre realized, had profoundly different priorities than he did.

National Institutes of Health, Bethesda, Maryland

They'd taken the helicopters to Las Vegas, and to Kim's surprise, that wasn't the end of the road. All thirty-two of the Marines had been ordered to escort Shotgun and Fred and Amy and Gordo and their chocolate lab onto the waiting plane to accompany them to Maryland. "We're on orders the whole way," Staff Sergeant Rodriguez had told them. "Until further notice. Personal protection detail. Wherever these four go, uh, plus the dog, we go."

Usually, whatever the orders were, somebody in the platoon would bellyache, but there'd been no complaining about getting out of California. Standing guard over a few civilians sounded like an incredibly cushy job. Quickly, it became apparent that not only was this going to be a cushy detail, but it was also going to be sort of fun. Everybody loved Claymore, and Claymore thrived on the attention of an entire platoon. Shotgun and Gordo were nice enough guys, though only Honky Joe seemed nerdy enough to hold his own with them, but Amy and Fred liked the attention almost as much as the dog, and the truth was, Fred, in particular, was a hoot.

The trip was convoluted. With all the air operations and military traffic, they couldn't go direct. From Vegas, they'd been redirected to an air force base in one of the Carolinas—it was a bit of a blur—where they'd been billeted for two days. And then back in the air, to DC, all of them loaded up in five gunships. The helicopters had gone low and fast over Washington, cruising over readily identifiable landmarks and giving Kim a quick glance at her parents' house before heading out to Bethesda. Landing in one of the parking lots of the National Institutes of Health was rather anticlimactic. Shotgun and Gordo and the mysterious black box that was evidently the cause of all this fuss were whisked into the government building, and her fire team was tasked with keeping Fred and Amy out of trouble.

Easier said than done.

Amy insisted on taking Claymore for a walk. It was clear that if he spent much more time being guarded by thirty-plus doting Marines, he was going to become a fat-ass dog soon enough. So she and Elroy and Duran and Mitts walked with Fred and Amy while they walked Claymore. The dog was interested in sniffing and pissing on as many things as possible. Kim didn't mind pulling guard duty. Every time she tried to sleep she fell into an endless loop of images of firing on civilians, of the fast sweep of spiders moving toward them, of the bumpy, gritty flight across the desert to temporary safety. No, this wasn't too bad. It wasn't even like there was anything to guard Fred and Amy from. There was such a mix of army and Marines and navy and air force in the parking lot and general vicinity that the biggest threat to their safety was probably an accidental weapons discharge. Basically, it was just glorified babysitting.

After they'd done a lap around a few buildings and approached the outer edges of the security cordon—a pair of MPs had politely but firmly turned the party back toward the NIH building—Fred's attention had been drawn to the three M1 Abrams tanks that occupied the outer edges of the west side of the parking lot. He was delighted to find out, after a little conversation, that one of the tank drivers, a nineteen-year-old kid from Alabama who barely looked like he was sixteen, with close-cropped hair and not even the barest hint of stubble on his face, was also gay. Fred seemed fascinated by the contrast between what he termed the "hypermasculinity" of the soldier and his own more flamboyant self.

Kim thought Fred was making a little too much of the difference. Yeah, the kid had played football and liked to go hunting, and for all that, had been happily out as gay all through high school, but it wasn't such a big deal anymore. There were plenty of Marines who were openly gay, at least three that Kim knew of in their platoon. Sure, maybe there was a time when that could get you discharged, but that time had passed. Which was more or less what the kid was saying.

"Generational divide, sir. I was voted the prom king and my boyfriend at the time was voted prom queen."

"As a cruel joke? Like in *Carrie*? And then they dumped cow's blood on you?" Fred asked.

"I believe that was pig's blood, sir, but no, not like *Carrie*. Completely unironic. The student body actually organized a protest against the administration to force the vote. We shut the school down for three days. There was a nice article about it in the *New York Times*, and our principal apologized for not allowing the students to vote for two prom kings instead of forcing us to be king and queen."

Fred shook his head. "I was definitely born at the wrong time."

"Could have been worse, sir. I had a great-uncle who was gay and lived in San Francisco at the height of the AIDS epidemic."

Fred stared at the kid. "What the hell are you doing driving a tank?"

The soldier shrugged. He really did look young, Kim thought. "I like to blow shit up, sir. Tanks are good for that."

After a while, Fred and Amy wandered off, with Kim and her squad following, and then finally they ended up back at the gunships. By then, all of them were bored and a little cranky. Except for Claymore.

Chocolate labs, Kim thought. Those suckers are always happy.

National Institutes of Health, Bethesda, Maryland

The ST11 wasn't working like it was supposed to.

Shotgun had run through the basic concept with Melanie and the other scientists. Some of what he talked about was incomprehensible to Gordo, even though he'd worked on the project, but most of the scientists seemed to follow along. It wasn't, when you came right down to it, a particularly complicated idea: use subsonic sound waves to make the bugs, more or less, shake themselves to death. Thankfully, none of them asked why it was called the ST11, because as amusing as calling it the Spinal Tap 11 was to Gordo and Shotgun, Gordo figured they might lose some credibility if the scientists thought the name was just a joke. And they had a lot of credibility, at least when they first walked into the conference room. After all, they'd been delivered by military gunship at the behest of CIA director Gibbons. It didn't hurt either that Shotgun could hold his own with this group of PhDs. Gordo was no dullard himself, but Shotgun was smart enough to make Melanie stop fiddling around on her tablet and listen to him, and then for Melanie to get up and go get Julie, and then for Julie to go get the three other scientists.

Finally, they'd captured a single spider from the brood in the biohazard unit, which was actually a lot more complicated than it sounded, and involved a lot of false starts and patience and hitting the button on the air lock at just the right moment so they captured one, and only one, spider, and making absolutely sure there was one spider in the cage and no extra spiders inside the air lock just lurking and waiting to feast on human flesh. Once that was done, they'd taken the spider into another part of the building, hooked up the ST11, and . . .

Not much.

The spider had been scrabbling against the glass of its cage, in a display of fury and hunger that was, Gordo had to admit, pretty creepy. They'd rigged up a camera to record the results of the test, and then Shotgun had aimed the ST11 at the cage and turned it on. The field version would run off batteries, but the beta version needed to be plugged in. Standard 120-volt outlet was fine, thank you. Shotgun fired it up, and it was pretty darn anticlimactic.

Gordo knew the spider wasn't going to explode in some Technicolor rainbow of gore, but the idea was that the thing would, at the very least, keel over and die. Even though the frequencies were directed, they could all feel the table shaking from the low, rumbling growl of the ST11. But the spider didn't explode, and it didn't die. In fact, it didn't do much of anything other than scuttle over to the far side of the cage. After a few seconds it started scraping at the plastic liner on the bottom of the container, and then, after a few seconds of that, it settled down for what Gordo would have assumed was a nap if it weren't for the creepy way its many eyes stayed open and occasionally flicked around.

Nobody said anything. They didn't have to. Gordo could see Dr. Nieder's slumped shoulders, could see Dr. Guyer rocking back in her chair and looking at the ceiling, chewing on her lip, could see Dr. Haaf glowering at the table. He couldn't bear to look at his friend, because he knew that Shotgun would look bereft. He'd promised the director of the CIA a weapon to win this war; he'd been whisked across the country in helicopters and transport planes with a platoon of Marines as his guard. He'd taken the time of these scientists and brought them into this room to show them what he'd cooked up, and it didn't do anything other than make for a mellow-looking spider.

They were already through the lobby and out of the building, Shotgun carrying the ST11, neither of them saying a word, when a large, muscle-bound woman in uniform who Gordo recognized as Dr. Guyer's minder came running after them.

"Hold up," the woman said. She was out of breath. "Dr. Guyer has had a thought, and she'd like to talk to you again."

Gordo looked the woman up and down. SGT. FARIL was stitched on her nameplate, and she looked, frankly, kind of terrifying. He would have bet good money that she could have kicked his ass in any kind of fight.

"About what?" Shotgun asked.

The woman grinned and gestured at her uniform. "Do I look like I have a clue? I just do what the bug lady says."

Càidh Island, Loch Ròg, Isle of Lewis, Outer Hebrides

Aonghas put his hand on Thuy's shoulder. She was sitting in her favorite spot, in the Eames chair by the window in the library. He couldn't tell if she was reading her book or watching Padruig walk the rocks in front of her.

"How is he always so dapper looking?"

Well, that answered it. Watching his grandfather. "Don't know. He's always been a clotheshorse. Long as I can remember. He's like that about everything, really. That chair you're sitting on probably cost two thousand pounds."

Thuy looked down and then gently picked up her cup of tea from her thigh and moved it to the side table. Aonghas laughed. "The table probably cost just as much. He likes nice things, I guess, and there's no real reason he can't afford them. There was a time when that wasn't true, but since he started with the mysteries, money hasn't been an issue. He figures out exactly what he wants and then spends the money so he only has to buy it once. My theory is that he doesn't like people very much, so instead he surrounds himself with things he does like. And those things happen to be expensive and include handmade woolen trousers."

"And he doesn't care that you dress like—"

"Watch it," Aonghas said, giving her a kiss. He fell quiet, and they both watched Padruig pacing back and forth, a loop down the rocks to the water, risking the sea spray, then back up, and then down again. His grandfather had one hand tucked into the pocket of his overcoat and the other waving around as he talked to himself.

"How come he never remarried after your grandmother died?"

"I don't think he had it in him. My mom told me once that when my grandmother died, there wasn't much joy left in his life."

"Except for you."

"He was as good of a grandfather as he could have been," Aonghas said, "and while there were times I maybe wished it had been a little bit more of a regular childhood, it worked out pretty well." He kissed her again.

She smiled at him. "Do you think we'll hear back soon? About Peru?"

"Maybe."

"Do you think we're right?"

"Maybe. Maybe not. But I learned a long time ago," he said, "to give him the benefit of the doubt. Either way, there isn't a lot we can do about it. We've done what we can, and I think we're here for the long haul."

She leaned into him. "There are worse places to be."

She was quiet then, and he knew that she was thinking about her parents, about her brother. Padruig had told her that if they could get to the island, they'd be welcome, but all three of them knew it was an empty offer. News was scarce from Stornoway and the Isle of Lewis, but Aonghas and Thuy had seen that man split open at the airport, spiders swarming from his body. Edinburgh seemed untouched, but with flights grounded, there was no way for Thuy's parents and brother to get to them. Even if they could, it might be safer for them to stay where they were. And to pray. Nothing else was left to them.

At least the three of them were safe, Aonghas thought. At least he and Thuy and his grandfather were safe. He knew it was a self-ish thought, but he couldn't help himself. He'd lost his parents at such a young age, and he'd finally found a woman who made him understand what it could mean to love somebody for the rest of your life. It wouldn't have helped anybody for them to be in his flat in Stornoway, or for him to be visiting Thuy in Edinburgh. What could he have done? Written the spiders away?

No, much better for them to be here, on this ridiculous rock in his family's ridiculous castle. Padruig had made him and Thuy tour the building with him, room by room, cupboard by cupboard, in case, he said, "the old ticker goes." How to keep the generator in working order and how to service the spare. What to check on the deep freezer, how to make sure the seals in the dry storage area were intact. When to bleed the boiler once the winter came, and when to open and close windows to make sure the damp didn't invade the stone building. They did an inventory together, counting bins of flour and beans, canned fruit, chocolate in vacuum-sealed plastic. Padruig admitted he was less well stocked with sherry than he would have liked, "But with the little tadpole in your tummy," he had said, "we've only got me and Aonghas to worry about for the next while, and we can to stick to port if need be. We'll suffer through it together."

It was, in some ways, almost freeing. He and Aonghas had been talking about maybe starting a new series to go along with the Harry Thorton mysteries, and both men were excited about the idea of trying to write together again. Thuy seemed content to study her medical textbooks, to read, to cook, to spend her time playing cards and chess and talking with Padruig and Aonghas. There was no point worrying about what they couldn't control. They were safe as houses on Càidh Island, and there was nowhere they had to go. There was nowhere he *wanted* to go, he thought, except close to Thuy. He leaned over and kissed her gently on the mouth.

As long as the spiders didn't come to them, they'd be fine.

Boothton, South Dakota

Even if Jigger Spitz and his parents had still been alive, the house was too far from the highway for them to hear any explosions. They were too far from anything interesting to even see air force jets passing overhead. They were so far out in the middle of nowhere that it was a wonder Jigger Spitz had waited as long as he had to run away from the farm and head west, all the way to California, where he'd gone to university and then to law school and then settled in Los Angeles. He'd made a nice life for himself. Nothing too fancy, but certainly better than his parents could reasonably have hoped for him. Nope, he had no intention of moving back to South Dakota. Sure, he came home to visit twice a year, for Christmas and for a few days in the brutal heat of August, dutiful son that he was, and he called his mother every Sunday, usually exchanging a few words with his father about the weather and the crops and the new tractor. Once a year, in February, when things were at their gloomiest in South Dakota, and there wasn't a lot for his parents to do on the farm, they came out to visit him in Los Angeles. They were lovely people, his parents. Polite and thoughtful and, for farmers from South Dakota, good sports about trying new dishes when he took them out to sample the high end restaurants in Los Angeles. They were always a little disappointed that he couldn't introduce them to any movie stars. No matter how many times he tried to explain to them that just because he lived in Los Angeles didn't mean he was friends with anybody famous, they still had slightly pursed lips by the end of their vacations. Once, they'd seen Gwyneth Paltrow coming out of a restaurant as they were entering, and that seemed to make his mother happy for a while.

But when the spiders emerged, Jigger had made it out of Los Angeles—just barely—and he couldn't figure out where else to go but home. He'd been so scared, terrified. As soon as he'd heard what was happening he thought of the news out of Delhi. He made an immediate decision to jump in his Toyota hybrid and get the heck out of Dodge. Traffic was always a nightmare in Los Angeles, and of course it had been worse than normal, but he'd done it, he'd gotten out of the city. He thought he was going to make it without any problems until he hit the blockade. It was completely unfair. Five minutes earlier, even three minutes earlier, and he would have been through. There were only fifteen or twenty cars in front of him, but a whole line of Hummers with machine guns had shut down Highway 10, and he was stuck. He sure wasn't about to turn around and go back to Los Angeles, so he'd sat there in his car for hours and hours, wondering if they'd ever let him through, listening to the static-laced news on the radio and keeping his phone charged, even though the cell circuits were mostly overloaded. He'd been thankful that he had a hybrid; even with running the motor occasionally to make sure the radio and cell phone charger didn't drain the battery, he still had plenty of gas. At one point, some idiots had tried making a run for it, and one of the Hummers had opened fire. It was loud and scary and, Jigger thought, a miracle that the driver and his passenger had been able to get out of the vehicle with their hands up. But then, later, there were explosions and rockets and gunfire, cars smashing into other cars, a black flood of spiders sweeping up the road.

He'd been sleeping with the windows open to the slightly cool night air when everything went to hell. He hadn't known what else to do, with the bright flare of fire and the incredible noise behind him, so he'd laid on the horn, like everybody else had. He'd alternated between looking in front of him, desperate to see the cars moving but also scared of the machine guns, which were firing all over the place, and looking back at the flames and explosions and people running past his car screaming. A missile landed close enough that flames actually blew past his open window, which was the scariest thing that had ever happened to him, some of the hair on his arm getting singed off and a puff of black smoke coming through the open window, until the next second, when, even scarier, he looked in the rearview mirror and thought he saw some sort of black mass rising up and rolling toward him. A woman ran out of the mass, past him. She was shrieking, with five or six black balls rolling over her face and arms. That was the first moment Jigger realized the spiders were right there, on the highway with him.

And, hallelujah, just when he thought he didn't have a choice but to get out of his car and run for it, the military Hummers started driving off and the cars in front of him started moving, and he slammed on the gas.

He'd swatted at imaginary spiders for the next two hundred fifty miles, finally stopping for gas only when he was afraid he was going to piss himself. He went to the bathroom and washed up in the sink. He smelled like smoke and fire. Where the hair had been singed off his arm, the skin was an angry pink, and there was a smear of blood and a tender spot on the side of his neck that he wiped at with a paper towel. Once he finished cleaning himself, he heated up two convenience store frozen burritos in the microwave, grabbed a couple of sodas, a Snickers bar, a large bag of Peanut M&M's, and then kept driving as fast as he could, to South Dakota, stopping only for gas and to vomit once on the side of the road. By the time he hit the Colorado state line, his stomach was knotted up in pain.

The last six or seven hours of the drive were a blur of fever and sweating. When he got to the house, his dad had to help him from the car and up to his childhood bedroom. His mom treated his arm with some aloe and wrapped it with a bandage, and then wiped at the blood he'd missed on his neck, putting another bandage over the scab there that he hadn't even noticed. He was muttering and curled up in the fetal position by then, but his parents weren't the type to panic. They'd lived on that farm since 1971, and there'd been plenty of stiches and cuts and fevers, and Mrs. Spitz had told her son when he'd called her from the road that only a maniac would eat burritos you could buy at a gas station. They tucked him in and went down to eat their dinner of chicken and boiled potatoes, checking in on Jigger every now and then.

Mr. and Mrs. Spitz died the way they lived: early to bed. If they'd been accountants or teachers or people who had jobs that were nine to five instead of farmers, maybe they still would have been awake when Jigger spilled open, his insides almost mummified by spider silk. The spiders he'd carried from Los Angeles to South Dakota didn't have any trouble getting out of Jigger's bedroom, because his parents had left the door open as they had when he'd been sick as a child. Even if they had closed the door, the spiders could have squeezed through the inch-thick gap between the door and the wood floor, an artifact of the shag carpets that the Spitzes had installed in the third year of their marriage and then ripped out in the early 1990s, when Mrs. Spitz said she wanted the hardwood floors back. If they weren't farmers, maybe one of them would have been awake to see the spiders, black with a red stripe, spilling down the stairs and heading for their bedroom, where they'd slept since the day they were married in 1971, never a night apart. Maybe they would have been awake to see the spiders pouring through the open door, crawling over the floor, skittering across the ceiling, seeking out the hot, deep breath of the sleeping couple like there was some sort of flashing neon sign saying, GOOD EATS! GOOD EATS!

But they weren't awake. Mr. and Mrs. Spitz were sleeping when the first threads of silk began blooming in the air around them. They were sleeping when the spiders descended and bit them. The bites felt like the time Mr. Spitz crushed his fingers in the gears of the harvester, barely escaping the loss of his hand, like the time Mrs. Spitz spilled an entire cup of boiling water on her leg. But worse. Because whatever kind of venom the spiders were secreting kept the pain so vibrant that it made the paralysis an added torture: it would have been some relief, at least, to be able to scream.

But they couldn't scream, and they couldn't open their eyes. Mr. Spitz was the first of the two the spiders began to feed on, the first that the red-striped spiders started dipping into and carrying, mouthful by mouthful, to the glowing, pulsing cocoon growing in Jigger's room.

At least there was some small mercy: paralyzed, stuck with her eyes closed, Mrs. Spitz didn't have to watch.

She had to listen, though.

And she could hear the spiders moving over the surfaces of the bedroom, the soft brush and chitter of their eight legs, the sound they made feeding on her husband, the way, near the end, his breathing got ragged and wet sounding. And then she realized she was alone in the room. Her husband was no longer breathing. She didn't know that it had been a week since Jigger made it home. Time had stopped having meaning days ago. All she knew was the burning, pulsing pain of the spider bites, the original bites fading into something like warmth, but always, always, always, a new bite, a new source of agony, a new cup of boiling water poured on her.

She didn't know that at that moment Melanie and Shotgun were talking again inside the NIH, that President Pilgrim was back in the Situation Room, that Aonghas and Thuy were watching Padruig pace the rocks of Càidh Island. She didn't know that all over the globe, there were poor, unfortunate men and women suffering as she was. What she knew, without a doubt, was that she'd be next.

She prayed for it. She'd never been a religious woman. She'd gone to church most Sunday mornings, because that's what one did, but no, she couldn't have ever rightly said she was a believer. But she prayed. At first she prayed it would turn out to be just a bad nightmare, and then she prayed that the pain would stop. Then she prayed that she'd be able to open her eyes, so she could at least see what was happening. And then, she started praying that she'd just die from the pain, that her heart would stop, or that whatever it was that made it so she couldn't move would spread from her arms and shoulders and legs and feet, from the muscles of her face, to the muscles in her chest and into her heart, that she'd just stop breathing. And then she prayed that she wouldn't be able to hear anymore. And then, finally, she prayed for the spiders to just go ahead and finish what they'd started. She prayed for days and nights and days again.

And then she prayed most fervently that she would die before the thing upstairs came for her. She could hear it. The pain of the bites, the fear, the sound of her husband being eaten alive beside her, the soft, skittering movement of dozens, hundreds, even thousands of spiders around her while she was wrapped tightly in silk, so tightly that she couldn't have moved even if she hadn't been paralyzed, and the sound of her husband's last breath, none of it compared to the sound coming from her son's bedroom above her.

A thump. Tearing. Moist, shuffling, clacking. Oh god, she could hear the door open, could hear the movement on the wide plank floor, the first creak on the stairs . . . She prayed for it to be quick.

The White House

Manny didn't have to see a mirror to know that his face was giving away the news. He could tell how panicked he must look from the way Sharon took one glance at him and then suddenly looked panicked herself.

Three in the morning? Four in the morning? He'd been sleeping on the couch in his office when the phone rang. He'd been having a good dream, for once. Him and Melanie on a beach, in Florida, in those early years of their marriage. Nothing sexy or profound, just the warmth of the sun and the sand soft beneath him. Not wistful, not a dream about missing that marriage or wanting Melanie back, but just . . . peaceful.

The ringing phone jarred him awake, and by the time he figured out that he was talking to his counterpart in the prime minister of India's office, Sharon, who had been sleeping on the couch in the anteroom, had already come in and turned on his desk lamp.

It was a quick call. Manny put the phone down and just shook his head at Sharon. He couldn't even figure out what to say.

"For Christ's sake, Manny, just tell me, okay?" Sharon's voice was shaky. He wasn't sure he'd ever heard his aide sound scared, but he figured now was as good a time as any.

"News out of India," he said. "They're back."

What he didn't say, what he was afraid to say, was that from what he could tell by the panic in his Indian counterpart's voice on the other end of the line, it sounded like things were about to get much worse.

Los Angeles, California

The city was dead.

In Europe and South America, there are cities that only seem to come alive after midnight. In America, across the Midwest and in the small towns of the South and in New England, the lights go off and the roads roll up by nine. In larger cities that lack a cosmopolitan element, Wichita or Cleveland, Toledo, Tacoma, most things are buttoned up by eleven. On either side of the country, however, in New York City and Los Angeles, if you know where to look, things only begin to take off after the clock strikes twelve. In Los Angeles, even a month ago, that meant the Cobra Club, MacMac's Lobster Shack, back room poker at Disco City, the red taillights of traffic backed up in certain neighborhoods and outside certain bars and clubs and restaurants well past one in the morning, two in the morning, three.

But that was a month ago.

Now, it was midnight, and the city was a ghost town. The lonely sound of sirens still drifted through the night, but the cop cars weren't moving, and it was only a matter of time before the batteries ran down and the sirens slowed down like a record player growling and dying. Fires dotted the city, a different kind of flashing light from police cars and fire trucks. But there were no hopping dance clubs, no restaurants showing third-seating patrons to their tables. There were still close to a million people alive in the greater Los Angeles area, but they were hiding behind closed blinds, cowering in their bedrooms. They weren't lining up behind velvet ropes or cutting white lines on bathroom counters.

Anybody who had the means to leave had already fled Los Angeles. It wasn't a city of refuge, if it ever had been. Even with the air force destroying overpasses and cloverleafs, making the highways impassable, those who could get out had, taking pickup trucks through the sand around ruined stretches of highway, trading what cash and jewelry they had for a spot on an overloaded boat. In at least one case of delicious irony, a fervent anti-immigration activist had blown two tires while trying to drive over bombed-out blacktop and then decided to make a go of it on foot, ultimately dying of heat and thirst almost in sight of the border with Mexico nearly thirty hours later.

Those were the lucky ones. The ones who made it out.

The ones who couldn't flee? The old, the infirm, the poor? The ones who *wouldn't* flee? The stubborn, the hopeful, people who lived in a city built on monster movies and imagined heroes, but who couldn't believe in a terror as real as these spiders? Those were the unlucky ones. Of the list of more than five hundred confirmed infestation sites that Quincy and the military had been working from, more than three hundred had been destroyed by the army. But that wasn't enough. It wasn't even close to enough.

Not tonight.

Tonight was the night the spiders emerged again.

Midnight, and Los Angeles, the playground of the rich and famous, showed its true colors. No longer a playground. Los Angeles became a feeding ground. Black spiders with red stripes on their backs spilled out of basements and garages, out of parking garages and food trucks, from the pits of a fifteen-minute oil change shop. They marched across sidewalks and streets, across manicured lawns and alleyways choked with dirt and weeds. They crawled up the walls of office buildings and skittered through air vents and elevator shafts, squeezed through mail slots and windows that had been cracked open to let in the breeze.

Everywhere the spiders went, they left a trail of soft, whispering silk, sticking to trees and bushes, wrapped around men and women and children who found themselves unable to move, unable to even scream.

Soot Lake, Minnesota

They came before dawn.

    Mike and Leshaun were ready for them.

Mike had passed the afternoon reading in one of the red Adirondack chairs in the picnic area. He'd had to get out of the cottage. Fanny and Dawson kept the TV news on in the living room, the radio on in the kitchen, and there wasn't anywhere inside he could get away from the chattering buzz of doom and gloom. He could see it in the dark, hollowed circles under the anchor's eyes, the way that there wasn't enough makeup to stop him from looking pale and haunted under the studio lights. He could hear it in the voices of the broadcasters on National Public Radio. Panic.

He didn't blame them. He was scared himself. The military was turning the country into a patchwork quilt of islands, with bridges and roads already blown as far east as Chicago and St. Louis, heading rapidly toward Cleveland and Louisville. Over breakfast, Fanny had made a half-hearted joke about America as an archipelago. Nobody laughed, partly because the news was so unsettling, and partly because Fanny had to explain to Mike what an archipelago was. The video footage on the television was worse. He'd always liked disaster movies, liked watching Hollywood blow itself up, remembered how cool it had been the first time he'd seen the White House explode on-screen. Asteroids and aliens, tidal waves and earthquakes, even machines rising up to wipe the planet free of the human scourge. In a darkened cinema—Annie was perfectly content to watch movies on a tablet, but give him a big screen, comfy chairs, and a bucket of greasy popcorn any day of the week—it was a diversion. But watching it on the actual news? The videos were often shaky, hurried cell phone images or taken by cameramen running to catch the shot and played on an endless loop on CNN, FOX, MSNBC.

But it was almost peaceful out there, on the lawn. Leshaun was napping, and Fanny and Dawson were inside, prepping dinner or talking or just being married, and Mike was happy to stay out of their way. The living room had a bookcase stuffed with thick thrillers and horror novels, tomes about WWII and Vietnam and the invention of steel or gunpowder or the microprocessor, cooking magazines and home decorating magazines, and even a smattering of novels featuring the Oprah seal or stickers indicating they'd won something. Mike had already worked his way through the spy thrillers and now he was on the cop thrillers. They were more his speed. He liked reading about the good guys stopping the bad guys. The heroes were like him. Men with badges and guns. Except they were all taller, better looking, and more likely to get the woman. And they didn't have little girls lying on the grass beside them, giggling at a movie they were watching on a tablet.

He glanced down at Annie and smiled. She had covered herself with a towel and was hunched over the screen, headphones on her ears. He could see her feet sticking out and hear her laughing every few minutes. She'd burned through all the animated movies and kid-appropriate movies Fanny had brought, and the adults had more or less thrown up their hands and started letting her watch movies that were, perhaps, a bit much for a nine-year-old girl. At dinner the day before, she'd accidently dropped her chicken on the floor, yelled "Balls!" and then collapsed in a fit of laughter. The grown-ups, Mike included, were too startled—and amused—to offer anything approaching discipline.

So he'd been reading, listening to his daughter snickering every now and then, and glancing up occasionally over the lake when he'd heard the first buzz of the motor. He instinctively put his hand on his pistol, but he'd waited until the boat came closer before walking down to the dock. It was the grizzled-looking black dude with the white beard. He came in very slowly, holding his hands up to show Mike they were empty. He cut the motor but didn't make a move to get out of the boat, instead just reaching out and holding on to one of the pillars. Mike didn't draw his Glock, but he kept his hand on the butt of the gun.

"Just being neighborly," the old man said. "Not planning on getting out, and I don't need anything. Wife and I are fixed up fine. I know this isn't the time to be making new friends, though I've had a conversation or two in the past with that other fellow and his wife up there in the cottage, the ones who own the place."

"I appreciate that," Mike said. "But we aren't really set up for visitors at this time."

"I understand, I understand. I understand that well enough. Thought I'd make sure you and yours are all set. When I came by here the other day, you had a black fellow with you as well, and you didn't seem too shy about letting me know you weren't open for conversation."

"Interesting times we're living in," Mike said.

"Oh, yes. And I don't mean to say otherwise. I come in showing you my hands were empty because I didn't want you thinking anything else, but that's not to say I haven't been keeping my rifle close by. I wouldn't leave my wife alone in our little cottage if she wasn't a better shot than me."

"And are you a good shot?"

The man gave a slight grin. "Fair enough."

"Was that you I heard yesterday, taking target practice?"

The grin was gone. "Nope. And that's why I thought I'd stop by, have a word. I figured you and that other fellow for lawmen the way you held your pistols. You a cop?"

"Federal."

"So you know what it means to hear gunshots and then to see something burning up in the night. I was a sheriff until I retired a few years ago. Small town, but still. With the way drugs are, small town don't mean as much as it used to. I suppose you've seen some things, like I've seen some things. And last night I heard shots and then saw a good glow across the lake from us." He glanced past Mike and nodded. "Got myself a good pair of binoculars, and seen you had a kid with you, so I wanted to do right, wanted to make sure that I told you to keep that gun you got your hand on close to you, wanted to make sure you or that black fellow was keeping an eye on things. Not just during the day, but at night too."

Mike had said that, yes, he and Leshaun would be careful and thanked the man. The old guy had pushed off from the dock, started his motor, and went back down the lake, presumably to rejoin his sharpshooting wife.

Mike wasn't worried about the old man and his wife. He seemed plenty capable of taking care of himself. And he wasn't worried about intruders either. He and Leshaun would keep Annie safe.

The three shirtless, tattooed guys were utterly predictable and unsuited for the job. They came to the cottage close to four in the morning, which was smart. Dead of night, too early for anybody to be up making coffee, too late for night owls. And they approached through the woods, smart enough to know that the sound of a motor would have cut through the night like an alarm clock. But those were the *only* smart moves they made.

They all had camouflage pants and jackets and hunting rifles, making their intentions clear, which was dumb. And they came up the trail through the forest toward the cottage in a tight line, and that was dumb too. They had flashlights, each of them, and that was the dumbest thing they did. In the darkness before the dawn, they might as well have been holding flashing beacons instead. Mike supposed they had planned to turn off their flashlights when they got closer, would have quieted down and tried to spread out around the cottage as they got ready to commit whatever acts of malfeasance they had planned. But the three men never got close enough to enact whatever plan they had. They were dumb and he and Leshaun were smart. And the men may have been mean in their intentions, but he and Leshaun were meaner in their actions.

Mike had been clear with Dawson and Fanny about what he expected to happen. He'd told them to expect to hear some noises and to stay buttoned down, that he and Leshaun would be a while cleaning things up. Their job, he told Dawson and Fanny, was to tell Annie to go back to sleep in the event she woke up—the kid was an incredibly heavy sleeper and the cottage was well insulated, but still—and to hold on to the 12-gauge and the Glock 27 as a last resort, in case he and Leshaun had figured wrong.

But he and Leshaun hadn't figured wrong. The three white boys came traipsing down the path in the woods carrying their hunting rifles, one by one, showing no field discipline, so close together that if he'd had a high enough caliber rifle, Mike could have used a single bullet to string them together.

It wasn't sporting, but he and Leshaun had agreed ahead of time that, particularly given the friendly warning from the old man and the events of the days before, this was no time for sportsmanship. If those three men wanted to come in the light of day with their hands open and empty, why then Mike would be happy to talk with them, but if they came in the middle of the night with guns and bad intentions, Mike felt no need to play fair.

Dawson and Fanny had been quiet, hesitant, as Mike and Leshaun told them the plan, but Leshaun had put it plainly for them.

"Bad people do bad things," he'd said. "In normal times, Mike's job, my job, is to catch those kind of people, and we've both seen some things I'm not ever going to talk about. But these aren't normal times, and we're not going to wait for them to do whatever it is they want to do."

They waited for the three men to walk past them, and then Mike and Leshaun put them down. It was noisy, the flash of their service guns leaving them star-blinded, but it was quick and easy. Two of the men were just sacks of meat afterward, but the third was breathing in sloppy, ragged bubbles, so Mike used another bullet. They'd already dug the graves in the loamy dirt of the woods. All that was left to do was drag the bodies to the holes and cover them up.

It was pushing five in the morning by the time he and Leshaun flashed their lights at the cabin in the agreed-upon sequence, letting Fanny and Dawson know it was just them and that all was clear. They crept inside as quietly as they could, and by the time Annie woke up, he and Leshaun were both showered and cleaned up. If Annie noticed the extra rifles in the house, she didn't say anything.

National Institutes of Health, Bethesda, Maryland

I t was a motley group. Dichtel and Nieder, the kid from CNN, Julie Yoo and Melanie, Shotgun and Gordo. A single glass cage with a wire lid, holding two spiders, was centered on the conference table. Through the large window overlooking the parking lot, the early morning looked gorgeous again. No clouds, the sun slanting over the city, the glass and metal of low-slung office towers catching the light. It was Melanie's favorite kind of morning, the kind when she normally got out of bed and slipped on a pair of shorts and a jogging bra, laced up her shoes, grabbed her cell and some headphones, and pounded out three or four miles before showering and heading to her lab on campus. But she wasn't going to get to go for a run today. She wasn't going to get to do anything until Dr. Mike Haaf got back.

Finally, outside the glass door, Melanie saw Sergeant Faril step aside so that Haaf could come into the room. Before he even opened the door, however, they all knew what he was going to say.

"No dice. Still can't get a response."

Laura Nieder threw her pen on the table. "Crap. Why don't the goddamn Japanese understand—"

Melanie held up her hand. "Laura. Come on. They're dealing with their own problems right now. We'll keep trying, but in the meantime, let's work with what we've got. I know it's not much, but the truth is, we're running out of time."

They started at the beginning. Listing it out. The egg sac from Peru, calcified and old, pulled out of the ground in a box that pointed to it being at least ten thousand years old. China. India. How aggressive the spiders were. The way they used people as hosts, how their life cycles accelerated at a ridiculous rate, feeding and breeding and spawning even more quickly. They noted Teddie's point, that the die-out was too orderly, too consistent for a naturally condensed life cycle, that there should have been overlapping waves of spiders both being born and dying at the same time.

All the while, the two spiders in the cage crawled against the glass, pressing themselves first to one side and then the other, trying to get out. Not to escape, but to feed. In the moments when everyone was quiet, they could hear the tap of the spiders' legs against the glass. Midway through, Fred and Amy, trailed by the chocolate lab, came in bringing donuts and bagels, a carafe of coffee, a bowl of apples.

Claymore barked at the spiders until Gordo whistled him over and started scratching the dog's chest. The dog settled into an occasional low growl. Fred and Amy sat down and Melanie didn't bother to kick them out. It didn't seem worth the effort.

"And now we've got the Japanese video with what we think of as the 'normal' spiders and the new, red-striped spiders apparently feeding the giant egg sacs. But I think we need to start at the beginning. With the question of why these things are just coming out of the ground now," Melanie said.

Haaf spoke up. "We keep coming back to the same concept. Cicadas. Nobody really understands how they do it, either."

Melanie had to stop herself from shuddering. People always thought it was funny that she could work with spiders but be creeped out by cicadas, but there was something about them that just made her feel cold. Their blood-red eyes. The way their tymbals clicked and their discarded exoskeletons crunched underfoot. She loved living in Washington, DC, and working at American University most of the time, but the downside was the cicada swarms.

"So why would these spiders hide between cycles?" Dichtel asked.

"I don't know," Haaf said. "We think that it makes sense with cicadas, that by having the main swarms hatch on thirteen-year and seventeen-year cycles, it means that no predator can keep pace with them. They come out, breed, swarm, whatever, and there's no real natural predator. Sure, they're only out for a few weeks, but in that time, there's nothing that can stop them. There are plenty of things happy to feed on cicadas, but the numbers work in the cicadas' favor. There isn't a predator that has specifically evolved to feed on them, which means that things that eat cicadas are doing it just because they're there. They end up satiated."

Predator satiation, Melanie thought. One of those insane ways that evolution sidestepped problems. All the cicadas had to do was breed in large enough numbers so that no matter how many of them got eaten, whatever it was that was feeding on them eventually got full and gave up.

"Maybe these spiders originally had some sort of natural predator, then?" Nieder said. "So as a defense mechanism, the spiders evolved along the same lines as cicadas, developing hatching cycles with long enough gaps that whatever it was that had threatened them had died off?"

Teddie looked skeptical. "Like what? Giant spider-eating birds?

If you're telling me that the next plague that's going to happen is flocks of killer birds like in that Hitchcock film, I give up. I'll just go ahead and jump out the window right now."

"First of all," Haaf said, "that's safety glass so you'd probably just bounce off. Second of all, no, the point is that the hatching cycle means they can avoid specific predators."

Gordo opened his mouth to speak, thought better of it, and leaned back in his chair. But it was too late. Everybody was already looking at him. Screw it. "If they're like cicadas, can't we expect them to just sort of, you know, go back underground at some point?"

They all swung their attention back to Haaf.

"Maybe?" he said. "But the thing that worries me is, if we compare these to cicadas, well, cicadas use predator satiation as a defensive mechanism, but things are turned around here. The spiders are the ones feeding. Nothing is eating them. Unless the argument is that sooner or later the spiders are going to get sick of eating us, we've got a problem. And, well, I think we can all agree we probably don't want to wait until the spiders have had their fill of human flesh. Plus, it seems pretty clear we're on the verge of a new wave here. We've got the super-sized egg sacs—"

"That glow," Shotgun said mildly.

"—that glow," Haaf continued, gesturing to the cage, "and now we have spiders with red stripes mixed in with our good old black spiders, some of which have markings on their abdomens that seem to indicate they're breeders. And some sketchy reports that the spiders with red stripes may be either significantly less aggressive or significantly more aggressive, depending on the circumstances, plus we've got a mix of egg sacs that seem to be designed for the long haul and sacs that are, because we lack a better term, fresher."

Melanie stood up. All of a sudden she felt cooped up in the

conference room. She glanced at the two spiders. Caged. She felt
caged. "Thanks to Teddie's video editing, we know that the first
wave of spiders seems to let about one in five people live, and we
think about one in ten of those survivors are infected. Roughly
ten percent infection rates. Again, we aren't completely certain,
and I know those numbers have been moving around, but I think
we're comfortable with using those as our baseline. And we've all
seen the video of the way the spiders seem to move in patterns that
don't make a lot of sense. Or, rather, too much sense." Melanie
looked around the room at all the people nodding. "And we've got
the box from Shotgun that seems to turn our spiders into pacifists.
Again, I can only say these things with real confidence about the
first-wave spiders. Who knows what the red-backs are like or what
that giant thing is in Japan? But at least these ones seem to calm
down when Shotgun does his thing."

More nodding. They'd blasted the spiders in the biohazard
unit with the ST11 and dropped a goat in. The poor goat stood
there in the middle of the room bleating and shitting, its eyes rolling in the back of its head, but as long as the low thrum of the
ST11 washed over the room, the spiders left it alone. But, god, the
moment Shotgun powered the machine down? It was scary how
quickly they stripped it to the bone.

Melanie sat back down. She was out of steam. "Which leaves us
where, exactly?"

Silence.

"Completely screwed, still." It was Nieder. "And I say this
based only on what Teddie was able to pull together on the patterns. I've done most of my research on how we can apply insect
swarm behavior to the battlefield, and the truth of the matter is
that we mostly can't. There are applications for robotics in the battlefield, but swarm behavior is too complicated. It's like modeling

water flow in a dry riverbed filled with rocks. Once the water's in there, you can see the way the water splits and goes around the rocks, filling in behind them, but to try to model something like that for practical purposes? Imagine a dry riverbed where the rocks are always moving around, and then try to figure out what the water will do. So mostly, what we do is just program troops—and by troops, we're talking about mini-quad copters and autonomous vehicles—to maintain a specific distance from all other units and obstacles around them. It looks fancy, but it's static."

She pointed to the cage on the table. "But the way these spiders seem to interact and move is so scary because it's both more dynamic and more controlled than we'd expect. On the simplest level, ants swarm a picnic because one ant finds some crumbs and leaves a trail of pheromones, and then another ant reinforces that trail, and all of a sudden the trail is like a highway for the ants, and your picnic is ruined. With the spiders, however, it's different. They act and react in unison. Or, not in unison, exactly, but with a synchronicity that doesn't make sense. At some point, when enough spiders have swarmed somebody, the other spiders divert around the victim—like water around a rock in a river, actually—and seek out somebody new. And when somebody's been passed over, whether they are left for what we assume is a future meal, or whether they are infected with eggs, any spider that happens upon them seems to know it."

Dichtel leaned back and stared at the ceiling. "And we've got at least anecdotal evidence from Japan that the red-back spiders ate at least the first three people who tried to go in and get data unprotected, but they weren't aggressive toward the scientist in a hazmat suit. So, what? Scent? They couldn't smell him?"

"That would make sense," Nieder said. "Pheromones or something that would mark paths, more pheromones to indicate prey that should be left alone."

Fred took a donut and grinned. "Maybe it's brain waves. There's a giant queen controlling all of them. Spiders from Mars."

Shotgun sighed and patted his husband's thigh. "That's not funny, Fred. Sorry," he said. "Fred can only go so long without being the center of attention."

"No," Gordo said. He said it so loudly and emphatically that he startled himself. It was still only a half-formed thought, and he was trying to work it out as he talked. "Think about it for a second. We've been trying to figure out how exactly it is that the spiders started dying out at the same time. Not just in Los Angeles, but everywhere." He spun to point at Melanie. "You said it happened here in the hospital unit, too, after your grad student, uh . . . Anyway, it doesn't make sense that they all got exhausted at the same time. And then there's the way the spiders react to the ST11. I mean, just look at them. Shotgun, turn it on again."

They stared at the spiders, skittering up and down the cage, trying single-mindedly to get through the glass. And then came the hum and low thrum of Shotgun firing up the machine, and the spiders suddenly lost interest.

"That's not pheromones," Gordo said.

Fred looked delighted. "I was right? It's brain waves from an alien spider?"

"Oh my god." Shotgun had his fist balled up to his mouth. "Chicago. They weren't aggressive, right? We thought maybe it was bullshit reporting, but hadn't they hatched out of some guy's body, not a freestanding egg sac?"

"So?" Melanie asked, but she could feel it. They could all feel it: they were close to something. It was all just a puzzle. Research was simply gathering data and then figuring out where the pieces went. And for the first time, it felt like they might have the pieces.

"So, whoever that poor sap was, he wasn't from Chicago. There hasn't been an outbreak in Chicago. We've got to assume he came from Los Angeles or maybe somewhere else. He could have been infected in India and slipped through the cracks. Or Norway, or, heck, anywhere. And then if we've got spiders on a different cycle, if these red-backs come out slower, he's like a ticking time bomb. And maybe he knows it. He knows something's wrong, he's been hearing on the news about people splitting open, so he's scared, because what's going to happen if he tells people? He's afraid to tell people, but it's got to hurt. So what does he do?"

"He hides," Haaf said. They were all leaning in now.

"He hides," Shotgun agreed. "He's maybe a guest at the hotel or he sneaks in off the street, and he goes down to the subbasement maybe because he's scared and maybe because he thinks that might be safer for other people, or maybe just because of whatever that instinct is in our caveman brains that drives us to shelter. And when the spiders come out of him . . . Nothing. If we believe this was a real occurrence, that this, what was he, the guy who found him? A porter?"

"Night manager. Assistant manager. Something like that," Melanie said.

"If we believe he's not just making this up, which we need to believe because he described the red-backs accurately, before we'd seen the Japan video . . . Well, if we believe what he said, he sees the spiders come out of the guy's body and they don't do anything. They just sort of mill around like I'm giving them a shot with the ST11."

"So why wouldn't they have attacked him?" Nieder asked. "We can argue that in Japan it was because the scientist was fully suited up and they couldn't smell him or sense him for some reason. But why did they leave the guy in Chicago alone?"

Shotgun grinned and turned to Fred. "I can't believe I'm about to say this, but you are a genius, honey." He kissed Fred and then turned back to the room. "Because Teddie was right. We're thinking of this the wrong way. This isn't millions and millions of spiders. It's millions and millions of pieces of the same spider. And for some reason, down in the subbasement of that hotel, their signal was blocked. Like trying to make a phone call from the fourth level of an underground parking garage. Whatever it was that makes all those individual spiders a single unit couldn't get through, and the spiders were so disoriented that it was like the hotel manager *was* wearing a hazmat suit. Without the signal to guide them, to tell them to attack, he might as well not even have been there."

The room was still, and slowly Shotgun's smile faded from his face. He shook his head. "No. That doesn't work."

"Why not?" Haaf asked.

Shotgun looked frustrated. "It doesn't hold together. In Delhi and at least a few other places, these spiders came up from underground. And all over the world, they're coming out at the same time, dying off at the same time. They're communicating somehow. They have to be. So why couldn't they communicate in the subbasement of that Chicago hotel? What was it about that space that turned them quiet?" He reached out and tapped the ST11. "What is it about this device that seems to shut them off?"

He looked around the room and then sighed. "It's all pretty thin, isn't it?"

Melanie stood up and put her hand against the glass of the insectarium. "Thin? Well, I wouldn't skate on it, but it's a nice start. So if we don't know why your machine seems to turn off the spiders, we better figure it out."

Chicago, Illinois

It figured. Danny MacDowell had been a Cubs fan his whole life, despite being born and bred in St. Louis. It had caused him no end of grief, plus a few locker-stuffing incidents in high school, but he'd gone off to Columbia College Chicago and lived in Chicago his entire adult life. He only agreed to marry his wife when she said if they had kids he could name them Wrigley and Field, and he'd insisted on a December wedding because he sure wasn't going to take a honeymoon in the middle of baseball season.

There'd been some good years with the team, but there'd been more bad years. Such was the life of a Cubs fan. A few years back he'd gone to Vegas for a convention, and he'd met a salesman from Boston. They'd shared a couple of beers at a bar and talked baseball, and the fellow had complained how having the Red Sox turn into perennial winners had ruined things for the hard-core fan like him.

"You got these kids who are old enough to drive now who don't understand how big a deal it was for the Sox to win in 2004. They just sort of assume that of course the Red Sox are going to win the World Series every few years. No sense of the pain. No sense of the misery."

MacDowell told him he'd be happy to trade some of his misery if that would make things right. If having the Cubbies pile up
World Series wins was a cross to bear, well, he'd gladly suffer.

He constantly asked himself how it was that he could have
been born and raised in St. Louis and picked the Cubs over the
Cardinals. A question his father often asked. How much happier
would he have been with that scarlet bird on his hat, a fan of a team
that was a perennial winner? But no, there was nothing but the ivy
at Wrigley Field for him. Which meant, quite simply, that he had
to put up with a certain amount of misery, and he'd put up with it
for so long that he'd thought there wasn't enough winning in the
world to wash the taste out of his mouth.

And then, they'd done it! Oh, joyous day! And the best thing
was it wasn't a fluke. They were loaded! Arms like flamethrowers,
curveballs on a string. Contact hitters plus the big lumber. Opening day should have been a national holiday, and the day that
President Pilgrim grounded all flights, the Cubbies had lost only
one game in the young season.

So of course, now that the Cubbies were just lovable—losers no
more—here come the spiders. This is what it must have felt like to
be an Expos fan the year the strike wiped out the playoffs. What was
that old joke? Cubs up a run, top of the ninth at home, two outs,
two strikes, the pitcher winds up, delivers, and the world ends.

His condo was eight stories up, and he stood staring out the
window at the bumper-to-bumper traffic. Cars were up on the
sidewalks, smashed into each other, smashed into buildings
and fire hydrants. Complete gridlock. People were running and
screaming. Oh. And there. Here they come, he thought.

He wasn't going out there. There was nowhere to go. He finished his beer and went back in to check on his wife. They'd cried
and held each other and made love one last time, and then she'd

downed the whole bottle of sleeping pills. She was still breathing, but he didn't really know what that meant. Hadn't the pills been enough? They'd looked it up on the Internet, and it should have been more than enough. Maybe they just needed a little more time to work. He leaned over and kissed her on the forehead. There was another bottle, on the nightstand, waiting for him. He sighed, took off his shoes, and lay down next to his wife. It took him a couple of tries to choke down all the pills. He thought about taking off his Cubs cap, but in the end, he decided to leave it on.

The White House

I t wasn't like the White House was normally a quiet, relaxing place. Even in the best of times, there was always some sort of crisis that needed to be dealt with. But despite being deep into his first term as Steph's chief of staff, Manny had never seen it like this. Frantic didn't even begin to describe the scene.

He thought the phone call from India was going to be the worst of it. He was wrong.

Los Angeles. Chicago. Minneapolis. Denver and Phoenix and Seattle and Portland. Kansas frickin' City and Nashville. Towns he'd never heard of dotted across Nebraska and Idaho and New Mexico.

The Spanish Protocol had succeeded in breaking the country to pieces.

And now the country was falling apart in pieces.

Paris, France

Well, Brett McNeil thought, there were worse places to die. He'd waited his whole life for a romantic vacation in Paris. He'd waited through two marriages to women who wouldn't have recognized a romantic gesture if it was shot at them from a cannon, and he'd waited through five different affairs to women his age or younger, and two affairs with women older than him, and finally, now that he was seventy and on his third—and what looked like it was going to be his final—marriage, to a woman he actually liked, he'd made it to Paris.

The first day, he broke his ankle. Thank goodness he'd married Felicity. The woman was a superhero. She got him back from the hospital and then spent the rest of the day on the hotel computer and talking to the concierge, figuring the whole thing out: where they could rent a wheelchair, where they could actually use a wheelchair, and how to get around Paris with a grumpy, semi-crippled and newly retired insurance adjuster from North Carolina. A few hours out and about was all he could handle, but it was worth it. Paris had been everything he'd expected.

Then came the spiders. Fortunately, Paris seemed safe enough, and as soon as they realized they were going to have to extend the vacation at least an extra week because people were all in a tizzy and there was no air travel, Felicity responded like the champ she was. She'd rented a car and taken them out of the city for four days, stopping in little villages and towns where Brett imagined everything was filmed in black and white.

He'd been anxious, but Felicity had been clear that they could afford it, so he'd tried to relax. His ankle throbbed, and it made many places a challenge, but it was worth it. Why had he waited so long to come to France? Maybe, he thought, it was because he knew, deep in his soul, that he needed to experience it with Felicity. It had to be because Paris was meant to be a city discovered by couples in love, and he'd never really, truly been in love until Felicity. So what if he was seventy? Love didn't have an age limit. Though, to be honest, the broken ankle had put a damper on their sex life.

But today? Oh, today was the day. The Eiffel Tower.

They'd been saving it for a treat. He'd seen it, of course. How couldn't you see it riding around Paris in taxis? As far as he was concerned, the Eiffel Tower *was* Paris. But to actually go up, to stand up on the observation deck at night, to take in the lights of the city from the tower itself? They'd waited for that. They'd originally scheduled it for the last night of their trip, but they'd kept pushing it back as the trip kept getting extended, but with no clear resumption of flights to the USA in sight, Felicity had decided that there was no point in waiting any longer. They'd had dinner at a small bistro up a side alley, around the corner from their hotel, just close enough that he could hobble there on his crutches, and then they'd taken a taxi to the base of what had to be one of the modern wonders of the world.

They rode the elevator and went out onto the platform. Felicity was smiling, looking at him and looking around at the city, and Brett realized he was crying. It was absolutely, unquestionably . . .

Screaming. Horns honking. The sound of automobiles crashing. They moved to the edge, to look down, and could see people running in panic.

He was scared. They were both scared. But they were scared together. Brett leaned on his crutches so he could hold Felicity and the two of them could look out over the glow of Paris. There were fires now, the occasional explosion, and to the west, a great swath of the city suddenly went dark, but Brett realized he was okay with it. He'd come to Paris with the woman he loved and he'd stood on the Eiffel Tower and seen the city at night. So if this was where he had to die, there was nowhere else he'd rather be and nobody else he'd rather die with.

Berlin, Germany

They'd had to sacrifice the outer suburbs. The ring could only be made so big. But it was holding. The fire burning in a great ragged circle. Those working the barricades, the women and men tasked with making sure the fires spread outward, not in, who had to tend the flames with gasoline and diesel fuel, who were the only bulwark against the spiders, saw spiders throwing themselves into the blaze in a frenzied drive to break through. There were many reports of spiders trailing streamers of silk drifting through the sky and then being buffeted by the roiling waves of heat coming off the fires, their silk catching fire and leaving streaks in the night as the spiders fell into the flames.

But it was holding. It was holding.

The White House

Manny wasn't sure how much longer they could put off evacuating. The Secret Service was getting frantic, and there'd come a point when it didn't matter anymore what Steph wanted. They'd already flown the First Hubby off, and more than half the cabinet and senior members of the Senate and Congress had already been evacuated. Most of the politicians were going to the bunker in Tennessee, but the First Hubby and the cabinet had been taken to the USS *Elsie Downs*, fifty miles off the coast of Delaware, close enough to take a helicopter to instead of Air Force One.

As it was, he couldn't figure out what Steph's insistence that they stay in the White House as long as possible was really about. Penance? An act of contrition for the Spanish Protocol, a way of punishing herself for her decision to break the country into pieces, leaving so many Americans to fend for themselves? That wasn't the Stephanie he knew, however, and it wasn't until she asked him to come into the Oval Office to join her, Alex Harris, Billy Cannon, and Ben Broussard that he realized there was a strategy: she was clearing the room of the voices that didn't matter.

He sat in one of the chairs and stared over at Broussard with a grudging respect. He had to hand it to the man, he'd stepped up. And to Steph, for getting over her dislike of Broussard and taking his advice.

"The truth of it is," Steph said as Alex and Billy were still settling themselves, "the Spanish Protocol worked."

"Are you kidding me?" Alex said.

"No," Steph said to the national security advisor, "I'm not kidding. Look at how bad it is. How much worse would it have been if we'd allowed free movement, if we hadn't balkanized the country? You can see it on a map. There's a line dividing the country in half. If we hadn't done it, there wouldn't be a line. The whole map would be gone. Remember the analogy? Cut off the leg to save the patient?"

"It's like going into surgery to have your leg taken off and waking up with both of them gone and your arms to boot," Alex said.

Manny looked at Alex, Steph, and the two men. Broussard, the chairman of the Joint Chiefs of Staff, somehow still looking like his uniform was starched, and the secretary of defense, Billy Cannon, wore a grim, tight line where his mouth should have been.

Suddenly, Manny felt a laugh starting to bubble up. It was like he'd drunk a soda too quickly, and now the fizz was building and he had to let it out. It wasn't a loud laugh, but it was so out of place that everybody turned to look at him.

"Manny?" Steph did not seem amused.

"Sorry. I'm sorry," he said. "I was just thinking, you know, what I wouldn't give for something simple, like Vietnam or the invasion of Iraq, or to be figuring out the fallout of a sex scandal or Watergate." He shook his head. "There aren't any good choices here, are there?"

Billy put his boots up on the coffee table, never mind that it was a piece of furniture that dated to the Lincoln administration.

"Not with conventional weapons. Berlin seems to be holding, and we're going to try the same strategy in New York City, but our best estimate is that there's only a twenty percent chance there isn't already a brood of eggs ready to hatch somewhere in Manhattan. If we're lucky, and there aren't already spiders there, maybe it will work." He looked at his watch. "The Brooklyn Bridge and the Lincoln Tunnel are both already impassable, and all other ingress and egress points should be bombed in the next forty minutes. Once that's done, the air force is going to flatten everything from 125th through 150th to create a buffer zone, and then the hope is that they can keep fires burning long enough to keep the spiders out."

"How long is long enough?" Steph asked.

Nobody answered.

"Well, dammit, find out," she snapped at Manny. "Call your fucking wife again and get me an answer."

He didn't correct her, didn't remind her Melanie was his ex-wife, but he checked his phone again. He hadn't talked to her in, what, two days? He'd called and she hadn't called back, and he just hadn't had the chance to follow up. Which meant he hadn't had a chance to tell her about the conversation with the director of the CIA, the weird suggestion that they look to Peru.

Billy Cannon continued. "Isolating New York works either way. If there are spiders already in Manhattan, it will keep them hemmed in and prevent a spread to other parts of the East, and if there aren't already spiders in New York, maybe it will keep them out. We don't have any confirmed outbreaks east of Chicago yet, but they'll be coming. At this point, we are just hoping to carve out some safe havens. Ben?"

Broussard leaned forward. "Army Corps of Engineers is, if you'll pardon the phrase, blowing up shit as fast as they can, and the air force is burning fuel nonstop. Overpasses, cloverleafs, bridges, pretty much every highway or major road we can hit we are hitting. It's going to be a hell of a cleanup job." He coughed. "But I'm sorry, Madam President, I don't think we have a choice. Chicago is gone. Everything west of Chicago is compromised, and it doesn't matter how many highways or roads we destroy, some people will slip through. We need to reset the dividing line."

Steph stared at him. "Reset the line to where?"

"Make a rough line from Buffalo to Pittsburgh and then Charlotte, all the way through Jacksonville, cutting off the country north to south. Honestly, you need to ignore the border and go farther north, too, past Toronto. It's not like the spiders are going to respect international sovereignty. We know these spiders can move on their own, but not far and not that quick. They're dependent on human carriers. So anywhere that people can get through we have to also assume that at least some of them will be carriers. I know it sounds like a drastic expansion, but if there are still parts of the country that we can save, we don't have any time to waste, and this isn't the time to be conservative. No matter how quickly we work with conventional weapons, there's a limit to how much we can disrupt travel."

He didn't say the obvious. He left that to Steph.

"We have to turn everything west of Buffalo into a wasteland," she said. "We're back to the nukes."

Oxford, Mississippi

There wasn't much else Santiago could do. Even with wearing work gloves, his hands were blistered, and he knew both his wife and Oscar were exhausted. Oscar was a tough kid, but he was only eleven, and Santiago had worked him hard. Even their octogenarian neighbor, Mrs. Fine, had pitched in, painting the plywood signs he'd made with the words NO GAS.

Which was a lie. He'd boarded up the windows of the convenience store—Mrs. Fine had painted those with NO GAS and CLOSED, too—but he'd had the underground tanks filled only a couple of weeks before this disaster began. He had plenty of gas, and he'd been using it.

He'd dug a trench all the way around his properties, demolishing Mrs. Fine's house and putting as much space between the Garcia house and their gas station and store and the trench as he could. He'd dug past his property line, figuring that the police in Oxford had other things to worry about. When people passed by and asked him what he was doing, he told them he was building a moat. They'd laugh and usually make some smart-ass comment about how that wasn't going to stop the spiders.

But there was a reason he'd hoarded the gas.

He'd bought hundreds of bags of charcoal. All the charcoal he could find at grocery stores and hardware stores and the other gas stations in Oxford. And then when he couldn't find any more charcoal, he'd filled his pickup truck with lumber, taking more and more trips to the hardware store. Then, he'd bought what had felt like a ridiculous amount of insulation, and finally, garden pressure sprayers. The sprayers weren't ideal—he was able to find a dozen four-gallon backpack-style industrial sprayers, but the rest were only one- or two-gallon handhelds—but they'd have to do.

He'd finally finished preparing just that morning. His wife had constantly been running people off who were trying to buy gas. People who were trying to flee. They came by in sedans packed with college students or in minivans loaded up with kids, suitcases strapped to the top. He felt bad turning them away, but he had to protect his family, and there was nowhere for these people to go. By the time most people realized they needed to run, the government was already dropping bombs. He'd heard the explosions of Highways 6 and 7 being torn asunder.

It didn't matter to him, though. They couldn't run. Not with his daughter. His wife was inside with Juliet right now, handling her medications and getting ready to give her a bath. Normally, Santiago assisted with the baths, but he was on watch, and Oscar had volunteered to help get Juliet out of her wheelchair and into and out of the bathtub.

He was sitting on a folding chair outside the convenience store by the gas pumps, the shotgun across his lap. He'd never actually fired the gun, but after the first time he'd had a gun pointed in his face, barely a month after he and his wife bought the gas station and convenience store, he'd acquired the shotgun. It felt good to have right now, even if he knew it was useless against spiders.

The sun was warm on his face. He was tired, and there was a

part of him that thought it would be okay to close his eyes for a few seconds. But then he heard screaming.

He scrambled out of his seat, picked up his binoculars, and ran to the edge of the trench, which was pressed hard against the road. The road ran straight and true, and with the binoculars he could see nearly a mile out. It took him a second to get the binoculars in focus, and when he did he—

He dropped the binoculars and ran. There was no time to waste.

He screamed toward the house, first in Spanish, then in English, realizing that if his wife and Oscar were giving Juliet a bath, it might be up to Mrs. Fine to alert them. If he hurried, if they all hurried, they'd be okay. He'd spent every single dollar he could scrape together, maxed out their otherwise untouched emergency credit cards, and worked himself to exhaustion. He'd done absolutely everything he could think of.

Except get a lighter.

My god. He'd forgotten a lighter.

He yanked his keys out of his pocket and fumbled with them trying to get into his store. It took him three tries to stab the key into the lock. Inside, he knocked over the entire display of lighters. He and his wife had fought over whether or not to sell cigarettes and lighters, but ultimately, it had been too much money to say no, and in this moment he was glad. He grabbed two lighters that had spilled onto the counter, spun around, and ran back outside.

He could hear all kinds of screaming now, plus the honking of horns and even some gunshots. He rushed to the trench.

He'd spread an even layer of charcoal all around the ditch, then topped that with the lumber that he'd bought from the hardware stores. More than thirty thousand dollars' worth of charcoal and two-by-fours and every piece of wood he could buy and get home in his pickup. And then he'd hosed it all down with gasoline. He'd run his gas pumps nearly nonstop, soaking the charcoal and the wood and the dirt of the ditch. He'd been as surreptitious as possible, afraid that people would see him using the gasoline like this and insist that he allow them to fill their cars. But he needed it. He'd soaked the ditch and then filled half the tank sprayers. The yard reeked so badly of gasoline you could smell it a hundred feet away. Santiago's biggest fear, aside from the spiders, was that the gasoline might accidently go up too soon.

He looked up and saw a woman running down the street. She kept glancing back over her shoulder.

He'd wasted too much time getting the lighters.

He flicked the lighter and then crouched down and reached out to touch the flame to a piece of wood sticking up past the lip of the ditch.

At first, the flame was surprisingly gentle. A blue lick of fire the size of a paperback novel. But then, quickly, with a sound like a tornado, the flame gusted down into the ditch and spread both left and right and then burst upward.

Santiago was knocked onto his ass by the flare-up. He scrambled backward, swatting at his hair, thinking it was on fire, but it was just the heat from the trench, already uncomfortable. It wasn't quite the explosive fireball you'd see in the movies, but it *was* an almost instant inferno ringing his properties.

He saw a car go shooting past on the road, and then a young kid furiously pumping away at the pedals of a bike, but the fire in the trench was already surging heavenward, obscuring his vision of the street.

He saw Oscar come out of the house and run around to the side, where the hose was connected, just as he'd instructed the boy. Santiago had covered the outside of the house with boards of mineral wool insulation, which was fire rated beyond anything else he'd been able to find in town. Oscar immediately started spraying the walls and the roof. Mrs. Fine came out too, and picked up one of the smaller tank sprayers full of water.

Santiago turned back and looked at the fire. It was a magnificent beast. He had some of the tank sprayers filled with gasoline in reserve, but he was hesitant to use them. They had certainly not been designed for high heat, and he didn't want to turn himself into a human torch.

He squinted, looking more closely at the fire. He saw shapes on the other side. Bodies. People running and falling. Small things skittering and moving. But the fire kept them all at bay.

The question was, for how long?

Memphis, Tennessee

A week ago, she'd locked her studio apartment and then sealed the edges around the door with duct tape. She had some caulk, and she'd spent an hour or so sealing everything she could think of with either the caulk or the duct tape. At first, she'd been afraid she might asphyxiate, but even when her apartment got brutally hot, she could breathe just fine. And then it had been a waiting game.

Until today. Now.

The water had stopped running yesterday, but until only an hour ago, she'd still had power. When that went out, she was thankful it was still light out. It was bad enough looking out the second-story window and seeing people running in panic, and then . . .

The spiders.

She wanted to move away from the window, but it was like she was glued there, just watching. Even as the first spider skittered across the glass, and then more and more, blocking the light, turning her apartment into a dark cave, she couldn't make herself move away.

National Institutes of Health, Bethesda, Maryland

Honky Joe, Shotgun, and Gordo figured it out at the same time. Lance Corporal Kim Bock was only a heartbeat behind them: there was only one helicopter left in the parking lot.

"Well," Gordo said dryly, "last time I order a helicopter from my phone."

"This is bullshit," Melanie said. "We're supposed to be evacuating. How many passengers can one helicopter take?"

"On this one? Six," the pilot said. "I didn't get time to refuel before coming here. But if you ditch your bags and don't mind cramming, I can get a number on our weight and trim. We might be able to stretch it to seven." She looked at Claymore, who was lying on the parking lot tarmac, panting. "And the dog, too, maybe. We'll be burning fumes by the time we get to the aircraft carrier, but we can do it. I'll fuel up and come back for the rest of you right away. It's going to be a zoo, but I should probably be back in five, six hours. In the meantime, however, some of you are going to have to wait."

Haaf cleared his throat. "Women first, I guess," he said. "I'll stay."

The pilot shook her head. "Sexism aside, I'm under strict orders. Dr. Guyer and all scientific personnel first, and then ancillary civilians."

Staff Sergeant Rodriguez stepped forward. "Captain Ripps is being polite, sir. The actual orders are to make sure that you and your colleagues are on the helicopter. No choice in the matter. At gunpoint, if necessary. That's five seats for Doctors Guyer, Dichtel, Haaf, Nieder, and Yoo."

"Technically," Julie said, "I'm a PhD candidate and I don't—"

"Not the time, Julie," Melanie said.

Rodriguez turned to Fred, Amy, Gordo, Shotgun, and Teddie. "Which means one of you—two if Captain Ripps says the math works—can join. And as much as I'd like it to be different, I've been authorized to use lethal force to ensure that Dr. Guyer and her colleagues are the first ones out. Though, obviously, we'd prefer not to have to shoot you, because, well, I know this isn't very professional to say, but you all seem pretty cool."

Teddie shrugged. "I'll stay. Screw it. I'll shoot video and, assuming we don't all die, I'll win an Emmy for news reporting."

Shotgun turned to look at Fred, but Fred got there first. "I swear to God, if you so much as suggest that I go without you, I will skin you alive."

To Gordo's surprise, it was Amy who spoke next. "No, Fred. We're going. Me and you." She was trying not to cry. "It's got to be. You heard what the pilot said. She'll be right back, but if anything happens in the meantime, you know as well as I do that we'd both be in the way. Gordo and Shotgun can take care of themselves, but they can't take care of themselves if they're taking care of us, too. We'll be a distraction, and that's not going to keep them safe."

There was some hemming and hawing, but Amy had her way. Kim watched Amy say good-bye to Gordo, watched Fred cling to Shotgun, the couples kissing, hugging, crying, and then Gordo and Shotgun backing away as their spouses joined the scientists in the helicopter. The pilot started the engine and then gave the thumbs-up to Kim. She walked over, holding Claymore's leash. The dog was wagging his tail and panting. She'd been okay watching Amy get on the helicopter, watching Fred get on the helicopter, but there was something about this big, dumb galoot of a dog that turned her throat into a peach pit.

"Oh, for goodness' sake," Kim said. She leaned down and scooped up the chocolate lab. Claymore turned his head and licked her face, and she stumbled a little bit. Despite the awkward way she was holding him, he was still wagging his tail. She helped him get his front paws over the threshold, pushed him the rest of the way into the helicopter, and closed the door. They were packed in there, but she didn't want to look. She turned and walked over to where Sue and Duran and Elroy were leaning against a JLTV.

They heard the whine of the motors pitching up, the rotors starting to spin, and then the air sweeping grit and dirt toward them.

Kim watched it lift into the air, and not for the first time, she thought how buglike helicopters seemed. And then the chopper tilted forward and headed toward the sea. She glanced over at Shotgun, Gordo, and Teddie. All three of them stood watching the helicopter, and she figured they'd keep watching well after it was out of sight.

Duran took off his helmet. "Well," he said, "if that pilot doesn't come back, I guess we take the bus?"

"She'll come back," Kim said. "She said she'd come back, right?"

Duran started to say something and then cleared his throat. "Hope so. Hope so. Either way, we've got ourselves a few civilians to look after," he said, gesturing to Shotgun, Gordo, and Teddie.

Kim nodded. "Yeah, but the real question is, are we looking after them, or are they going to look after us?"

Shotgun, who had evidently been listening, turned to her. "No. That's not the question. The question is, how are we going to stop these sons-of-bitches?"

Denver, Colorado

She came out of the shadows.

The little ones, thousands of them, covered the walls and ceilings and skittered around her as she lumbered forward. There were several silk-wrapped shrouds on the floor, empty husks of prey that had once been close to her size. She moved slowly past them on her long, thick legs. But slow was fine. She had no need to hurry. She knew there were more of the little ones outside. Tens and tens of thousands of them close enough to serve as feeders for her, and farther away, there were more. So many more.

And, she knew, there were others like her, making their own way into the light.

EPILOGUE

Positano, Italy

Music played on speakers on restaurant patios over the sound of the surf breaking against the rocks. But if you listened closely, you could also hear the brush and skitter of spiders moving across stone and tile, crawling over cotton and linen.

There was nobody outside left to listen.

The screaming had been over for hours.

Which was not to say that there was nobody left alive in Positano. There were still many people, perhaps thousands, crouched behind shutters, huddled in locked bathrooms, and even an oblivious few who'd slept through the chaos and who sat on their balconies and wondered why their vacation paradise was so quiet.

Those were the lucky ones, because the others who were still alive had it much, much worse. Those would have cried out if they could have, would have shrieked at the pain and the terror of being wrapped alive in silk, of being completely paralyzed.

And waiting.

There were other living things besides tourists in Positano. So many things alive in Positano. Spiders crawling, breeding, constantly feeding. Tens of thousands of spiders, hundreds of thousands.

Cozad, Nebraska

The people of Cozad, Nebraska, were god-fearing folk. Which suited Bobby Higgs just fine. That's how far they'd made it before the bombs started falling and the highway became impassible. By the time they got to Cozad, the minivan that picked him up had been joined by twelve other vehicles that had been part of the original procession from LA. They'd started calling themselves the twelve disciples, and Bobby had let it ride.

With those twelve vehicles—nearly thirty adults and almost as many children stuffed into cars and pickups and minivans—as his base, Bobby had been an immediate sensation in Cozad. Within forty-eight hours, nearly a quarter of the population of Cozad, a thousand people, were ready to march with the Prophet Bobby Higgs.

They stayed off the rubble of the highways, taking side roads and marching across farmers' fields, only making ten, eleven miles a day, but by their third day of marching, their ranks had begun to swell.

Atlantic Ocean, off the coast of Delaware

Somehow, as the helicopter sped toward the aircraft carrier, the dog ended up on Melanie's lap. She could feel Claymore's hot breath in her face, and there was a part of her that wondered how the dog had managed to make his way from California to Washington, DC, and now to what was perhaps one of the only safe places left on earth. She held the dog tight and scratched his belly. She could see Amy leaning into Fred's embrace. They'd both been crying intermittently.

She couldn't blame them.

Nazca, Peru

If they hadn't been working in broad daylight, Pierre might have pissed himself. Dr. Botsford seemed fascinated, but Pierre found it terrifying. They'd gone back to the site where they'd found the original egg sac, looking to see if there was anything under where they'd stopped digging. They'd been careful, but they had barely dug another six inches when Beatrice came across a bone.

A femur, to be exact. A femur, which, according to Dr. Botsford, had been the subject of intense heat. When he pointed that out, it was easy to see where it had cracked open, the marrow bubbling and leaking from the middle of the bone.

And then they uncovered another egg sac.

An egg sac would have been bad enough, but he remembered how the one he sent Julie had been chalky and cold. How it had felt foreign but dead to him as he packed it up for FedEx. But this egg sac. Oh, this egg sac. He wanted to cry. He really wanted to piss his pants. This egg sac was warm. Perhaps it could simply have been the afternoon sun, but it was also sticky, and if you held your hand against it you could feel the slightest vibration. It was all Pierre could do not to scream at Dr. Botsford and the other graduate students as they debated what to do for more than twenty minutes, in the way that only academics can debate something that has a clear answer. The relief he felt when they finally agreed on a course of action was tempered by the fact that he was going to be the one to carry the sac back to their base camp. And then he had to sit and wait while Cynthia built a good, roaring fire, not sure the entire time if he was imagining it, or if the sac was really getting warmer, if the pulses were getting stronger. By the time they judged the fire hot enough, Pierre could barely get himself to pick up the egg sac.

He wanted to place it gently in the middle of the fire, but the flames were too hot. He couldn't stop himself from dropping it and springing back, his hands and arms stinging, his eyebrows singed.

For the first couple of seconds, nothing seemed to happen, but then, even among the glowing coals and the bright flames, they could see the sac catch fire. One side started to turn gold and then black, and Pierre was reminded of nothing so much as roasting marshmallows. He heard Beatrice gasp, and he realized it wasn't a shimmering mirage of heat and fire: the egg sac was shaking, vibrating. And then, with a loud cracking sound, a line splintered up the side of the shell.

He flinched. They all flinched. Even Dr. Botsford, who had never quite seemed to understand that there were real-world implications to these spiders, stepped back.

For perhaps the blink of an eye, Pierre thought the spiders in the egg sac would come bursting out, but the opening was too small. He saw a single, terrifying black leg probe out of the crack, but then the fire turned it into something worse, the leg twisting and shrinking in the heat. The sac cracked again, wider, and then split wide open, but the spiders inside—there were so many it made Pierre breathless—were still. As the angry fire licked over them, they burned and popped like sap in a log. They watched the fire until the egg sac and all the spiders were only ashes and embers.

None of them talked much as they ate dinner, and none of them suggested going back to the site with flashlights after they were done eating. The idea of being out there at night, the shadows that came from artificial lights, uncovering mysteries thousands of years old, perhaps stumbling across another egg sac—or something worse, some ancient warning—was too much to contemplate.

National Institutes of Health, Bethesda, Maryland

The group of them stood in front of the biocontainment air lock.

Teddie was running a video camera, though Kim was honestly not sure where it had come from. She was filming Shotgun tapping on the glass.

"Can you not do that?" Gordo said.

"What?" Shotgun looked so innocent.

Kim stared through the glass at the spiders. There were hundreds of them. But it was nothing, she knew, to what was coming.

"You're making them agitated," Honky Joe said.

Shotgun smiled. "I think they're naturally agitated."

"Fine," Gordo said, "but I don't see any reason to rile them even more."

Kim stepped forward and put her palm against the glass. Immediately, the closest spiders to where she was standing started pinging off the glass, trying to get to her. "Are you sure about this?"

"No," Shotgun said. "But it makes sense. We're all hoping that pilot is back here in a few hours, but if she's not, we might be on our own for a while. If we need a place to shelter, better in there than out here. If the spiders can't get out of the biocontainment area, I figure they won't be able to get in, either. All we have to do is kill all these spiders, bring in supplies, and we've got our own little panic room. Well, not little. I figure we can probably put, what, fifty people in there if we don't mind getting friendly?"

"Okay," Gordo said, "that makes sense. So, are you going to use the Spinal Tap on them?"

Honky Joe raised his eyebrows. "The Spinal Tap?"

Shotgun waved his hand. "Inside joke. But no. I don't think that would work. It seems to confuse them, but the effect isn't strong enough, and I don't want to risk it."

"So . . . How are we getting the spiders out so that we can get in there to hide?"

Shotgun bit his lip. "Good question."

Marine One, over Washington, DC

They rose hard and flew in a tight convoy over the city. Below them, Manny could see the streets choked with traffic. They were a thousand feet up and with the chop of the rotors and the headphones, there was no chance of him hearing the noise below. But he could imagine it. Cars honking at each other, people yelling, children crying. The spiders weren't here yet, but it might only be a matter of time.

He looked over at Steph. She stared out the windows and knotted her hands. He'd put it to her as plainly as he could: they'd lost at least half the country. There was no more room for restraint. They needed to hit every major metropolitan area they could, and they needed to carve away four-fifths of the country.

Finally, she looked over at him and nodded.

It was time to unleash the hounds of hell. There was nothing left to save.

Scorched earth.

Soot Lake, Minnesota

Annie's fingers kept slipping off the monofilament, but she wouldn't let Mike help her.

"I can do it, Daddy." The tip of her tongue was between her lips, and Mike loved every second of it. He loved that she watched him so closely as he tied the knot on his own hook, and that she wanted to learn how to do it herself. He loved that she could laugh at the Frankenstein bale of line she ended up with instead of a proper knot, and how she took one of the worms that she'd dug out of the loamy soil directly behind the house and bent the worm onto the hook herself. They were sitting on the edge of the dock, their feet skimming the cold water, and Annie threw a good cast, the bobber landing with a reassuring plunk, the worm and hook right behind.

Mike wasn't exactly relaxed. But he felt good. They had enough food, if they were careful, to last them a month. Longer if he and Annie could catch some fish. He had time to figure stuff out, he thought. They'd survive.

It was like a flashbulb from across the room. Bright even in the bright light of day. Bright even from as far away as Minneapolis. He knew immediately what it was.

"Inside now, beautiful," he said.

"But Daddy, I want to catch a fish."

"Right now. No arguing. Tell Rich and your mom I need them to get all the garbage bags and any duct tape we've got."

"Why?"

"I'll explain later, okay? But right now, just go."

He took her fishing pole and then reeled in her line. There was another flash of light. Would the sound carry from that far away? No. He didn't think so. But there'd be fallout coming. He figured they were far enough away to be spared the worst of it, and there weren't any cities close enough to Soot Lake to be worth the bother of a nuclear weapon. It didn't make sense to target the wilderness.

They'd close the windows and tape up garbage bags and seal as many cracks as they could, stay inside for a few days, and then he'd see where they were.

They'd be okay.

He looked at Annie slipping through the front door.

He'd make sure of it.

ACKNOWLEDGMENTS

Dear reader, thank you for braving these books. I apologize for any feeling of itchiness that may have accompanied your reading experience. I've included these acknowledgments because, while I spend a lot of time alone writing, getting a book from an author's desk into your hands takes a big group. So I hope you take a few seconds to read all these names. Thank you to:

At Emily Bestler Books/Atria: Emily Bestler, David Brown, Judith Curr, Suzanne Donahue, Lara Jones, Hillary Tisman, and Albert Tang. At Penguin Random House Canada: Anne Collins, Josh Glover, Jessica Scott, and Matthew Sibiga. At Gollancz, an imprint of the Orion Publishing Group: Marcus Gipps, Stevie Finegan, Craig Leyenaar, Jennifer McMenemy, Gillian Redfearn, and Mark Stay.

At the Clegg Agency: literary agent extraordinaire Bill Clegg, Chris Clemans, Marion Duvert, Henry Rabinowitz, and Simon Toop. At the Anna Jarota Agency: Anna Jarota and Dominika Bojanowska. At MB Agencia Literaria: Mònica Martín, Inés Planells, and Txell Torrent. At United Agents: Anna Webber.

At William Morris Endeavor Entertainment: stone cold killers Erin Conroy and Anna DeRoy.

The MacDowell Colony for the gift of time and space. And lunch.

Alex, Ken, Ken, Mike, Shawn, Will.

My family. Yeah. All of you.

Will humanity survive?

Turn the page for an excerpt from
thrilling conclusion to this story . . .

ZERO DAY

PROLOGUE

Mars Conquest Shuttle, Low Earth Orbit

Commander Reynard never used foul language, so pardon him, but this was some grade A bullpoop. Where the heck was his parade?

Reynard was born-and-bred a Saskatchewan wheat farmer. Canola and lentils and peas, too, but durum wheat most of all. His mom had managed the farm with an iron fist. She was quick with a kiss or a kind word, but she could squeeze a nickel hard enough to make it weep two quarters. Reynard's dad was in charge of the actual physical work of farming—sowing and reaping, disking fields and tasking the hired help, soil testing and fertilizing—but it was his mom who ran the show. And one of the things she'd always told Reynard and his sister was complaining about the weather neither makes it rain nor shine. If you can't change it, don't complain; and if you *can* change it, change it. And you still don't complain. For his entire childhood, he'd been taught that the worst accusation that could be leveled against another person was that they were a complainer. "A dog barking at the wind," his mother said. And if it held true when he was just a boy on a farm, his mother told him, it held doubly true now that he was an astronaut.

But still.

Bullpoop.

He'd left the farm for university at seventeen, and although he'd gone back for vacations and holidays, he'd never really looked back. Yes, in some ways he knew that the open skies of Saskatchewan and the red dirt roads of his childhood would always define him, but he'd spent his entire adult life working to trade that childhood in for the endless skies of space and the red dirt of an entire planet.

Commander Brian Reynard. The first man to set foot on Mars.

And *this* was what he was coming back to?

Forget the hours he'd spent studying—an engineering and biochemistry double major as an undergrad—or in flight simulators as part of the Royal Canadian Air Force. Forget the time he'd spent at Edwards Air Force Base during a joint program that allowed him to attend the US Air Force Test Pilot School, or the time he'd spent getting his masters in aeronautics. Forget the chunks of his life that were eaten by the basement offices at NASA and the meeting rooms of the Canadian Space Agency. Forget the time he'd spent running and working out at the gym, making sure that he was in better shape than the younger and more polished astronauts who were trying to bump him out of the spot he'd earned. Forget, even, all of the years he'd spent preparing specifically for this one single mission.

Just look at the mission itself: eight and a half months flying the *Mars Conquest* shuttle using a fuel efficient but relatively slow Hohmann Transfer Orbit to Mars; one and a half years establishing the first research station on Mars itself and waiting for the window to align for the trip back; another eight and a half months flying the return. How about that? Almost three years of his life. Sure, humanity had reached the point where simply going to space was no longer enough to make you famous—the Wikipedia list of people who've been in space was absurdly long—and even walking on the moon was a crowded field. But to be first person on Mars? The first man to set foot on the Red Planet? The first human to stride upon a giant, cold, dusty sphere floating among the stars? That had to count for something, didn't it?

As a kid, when it was already old news, the black-and-white echo of Neil Armstrong's one small step on the moon gave him the shivers. And even as Reynard stepped down the ladder and let the weak gravity of Mars pull him to the surface—even as he said the words that had been so carefully prepared for him by the committee that represented all six of the countries on the Mars Conquest Shuttle team—Armstrong's voice, static and all, ran through him like lightning. It felt electric.

So Commander Reynard thought it was reasonable to want a hero's welcome when he landed. He thought it was reasonable to believe that he'd take his place among the great explorers of human history. And, gosh darn it, he thought it was reasonable to expect a ticker-tape parade when he returned to Earth.

He knew he was being ridiculous. Even if he hadn't been raised by a mother who thought that complaining was a cardinal sin—followed closely by bragging and then using foul language— he would have recognized that it was crazy for him to be upset that there wasn't going to be a parade. There were bigger things to worry about.

Maybe that was why he was fixated on his disappointment about the lack of a parade. It gave him something to think about other than the unthinkable. He and the rest of the crew had fol-

lowed along when the first news of the spiders started making the
rounds—bandwidth was limited at times, but they did have Internet access—and they'd alternated between disbelief and horror. It
had seemed bad enough as they'd gotten closer and closer to earth:
a nuclear accident in China that turned out to be no accident and
was just a harbinger of things to come, followed by outbreaks of
spiders around the globe. And then, suddenly, it seemed like it
was over. The earth was reeling, but it still turned as it always
did. As they settled into low Earth orbit in preparation for landing
the shuttle, Commander Reynard thought how easy it would have
been for him and his crew to be oblivious to what had happened
below.

From two hundred kilometers up, Earth was luminous and
peaceful. So startling in its beauty that Reynard, who never tired of
gazing upon the planet of his birth, sometimes doubted that what
he was looking at was even real. If he hadn't been a man of science,
he might have entertained the idea that this was all some sort of
dream, or that Earth was the product of some great being beyond
his comprehension. Despite a childhood of being a good Protes-
tant, as an adult he'd become a member of the church of science.
He worshipped at the altar of math and engineering, so it was difficult to think of the hand of God. And yet, watching the sun rise
and set and rise and set over Earth as the shuttle sped around in
orbit at a speed of more than seven kilometers per second, it was
almost impossible for Reynard not to believe in a higher power. As
he'd said when he'd first stepped foot on Mars, "Mankind's place
is among the heavens."

And then there'd been the second round of outbreaks.

But first, in the days between the end of the first outbreak and
the beginning of the second, the crew spent a lot of time . . . Well,
no matter what kind of a spin he wanted to put on it, probably the

best way to say it was that they spent a lot of time freaking out. Science officers Ya Zhang and Vasily Sokolov had gotten extremely different information from the Chinese and Russian governments respectively, which made everybody nervous. They were all scientists, and they were used to working with data. Ya was being told not to worry despite the fact that China had basically nuked half of itself, and Vasily was told that there was a spider menace but it was being contained because of Russian ingenuity.

Reynard had called a meeting to talk about it, and after hours and hours of comparing information, of going back and forth, they'd decided that there wasn't anything to do but wait for orders. So they'd done everything they could to prepare for landing the shuttle, which under normal conditions would have kept them busy and anxious enough as is.

But it quickly became clear that these were not normal conditions, and when the second round of outbreaks began, it was almost a relief; Reynard realized he'd been expecting it from the moment the first outbreak died out, and to have it finally happen felt like a release.

They watched President Pilgrim's address to America, listened to her explain her plan to try to break the country apart in order to save it. Out of respect, Reynard and the rest of the crew acted like they didn't see the flight engineer, Shimmie, crying. And then, as near as they could tell, all hell broke loose.